They searched for gold and glory . . .  **W9-AXK-312**

JOHN SUTTER, an entrepreneur, and **JAMES MARSHALL**, a carpenter . . . They were partners in the building of a sawmill on the banks of the American River in the Sierra Nevadas. When Marshall found gold in the river's gravel bed, the discovery lured hundreds of thousands to the California mountains in search of a fortune—and sparked the infamous Gold Rush of 1849.

BOONE BLAKELY . . . Fleeing a murder charge, the Texan came to California and was hired by John Sutter to help build the sawmill. Certain that none of his fellow workers know he's a wanted man, he feels far away from his troubled past. But when gold fever hits, he finishes his job and digs for the big strike—hoping he'll discover gold before he's found out . . .

NATHAN JONES . . . The young, college-educated man was searching for his niche in life—and most of his schemes and endeavors ended in failure. When his Aunt Emily proposes to outfit him for a trip to the gold mines in exchange for a share of his profits, he jumps at the chance. Maybe he's found the one thing that will make him a success—and he puts all his hopes in his search for gold . . .

EMILY WOODWARD . . . A shrewd businesswoman and owner of a San Francisco mercantile store, she wouldn't dream of missing out on the biggest opportunity of her lifetime—and she's unwilling to accept failure. To make the most of the Gold Rush, she comes up with an ingenious plan that has nothing to do with finding gold, but a much more valuable commodity: selling supplies to the miners.

CASSANDRA WOODWARD . . . Emily's strong-willed daughter, she hears the call of gold as clear as any man—and dresses like one to sneak her way into the mining camps. It's Boone Blakely who discovers her secret when he sets out to rob her—and finds himself overwhelmed with the desire to protect her from harm. But was their unexpected attraction the greatest danger of all?

DAN LOGAN . . . The Texas Ranger came west in search of Boone Blakely, to bring him back home to face justice. Then Logan unexpectedly strikes gold—and the fates of both men change: the lawman settles in California, and the outlaw is given a reprieve. Now Boone's destiny rests on the hope that Logan doesn't change his mind . . .

RIVERS
OF
GOLD

J.L.
REASONER

JOVE BOOKS, NEW YORK

RIVERS OF GOLD

A Jove Book / published by arrangement with
the author

PRINTING HISTORY
Jove edition / June 1995

ISBN: 0-515-11524-X

A JOVE BOOK®
Jove Books are published by The Berkley Publishing Group,
200 Madison Avenue, New York, New York 10016.
JOVE and the "J" design are trademarks
belonging to Jove Publications, Inc.

PRINTED IN THE UNITED STATES OF AMERICA

10 9 8 7 6 5 4 3 2 1

For Gary Goldstein

And they came to Ophir, and fetched from thence gold, four hundred and twenty talents, and brought it to King Solomon.

—I Kings 9:28

RIVERS
OF
GOLD

One

Boone Blakely stirred restlessly on his cot, murmuring incoherently in his sleep as dreams of the past raced through his brain. He turned over and burrowed his head deeper into the thin pillow, finding little if any comfort in it. The nights were the worst, had been ever since he had left Texas.

Rolling over again, Boone blinked his eyes open and stared blearily up at the canvas roof of the tent only a couple of feet above him. He shared the tent with three other workmen. Snores came from a couple of them, but one man was already up and moving around, even though only a faint gray light filtered around the flap of canvas over the tent's entrance. Boone figured it was still a while until dawn.

So what was Harbison up to?

Adam Harbison was an Englishman, and God knew how he had wound up out here in California. Harbison was tight-lipped about his past. But that was nothing unusual. Most of the men building this sawmill on the American River were closemouthed about who they were and where they came from. Backgrounds didn't matter. All the boss, James Marshall, cared about was whether or not a man could do the work.

But Boone didn't like Harbison anyway, didn't trust the man. From what he saw now out of slitted eyes, his mistrust seemed to have some basis in fact. Harbison was squatting on the dirt floor, a couple of feet from Boone's cot, and reaching out carefully toward the war bag stowed under the cot.

The damned Englishman was after his goods, Boone thought. Harbison was nothing but a sneak thief.

Boone opened his eyes all the way and said softly, "What the hell do you think you're doing, Harbison?"

Jerking back in surprise, Harbison opened his mouth and started to say, "Don't be alarmed, Blakely—"

That was as far as he got before Boone came up off the cot with a smooth uncoiling of muscles hardened by months of labor. Boone's fist shot out and cracked against the Englishman's jaw, sending Harbison sprawling back on his rump. Boone landed on top of him and drove a knee into Harbison's stomach.

Harbison gasped as the wind was knocked out of him, but like Boone he had been toughened by the work on the sawmill. He sent a punch up into Boone's face and heaved up with his back at the same time, with the result that Boone was knocked off to the side. Boone rolled into the legs of one of the other cots, almost upsetting it and drawing a startled yell from its occupant.

Both of the other men in the tent started shouting curses and demanding to know what was going on. Boone ignored them as he came to his knees and lunged at Harbison again. This time he managed to get his arms around the man as Harbison tried to get up, and they both fell heavily to the ground. Boone got the fingers of one hand halfway around Harbison's neck and locked them there, while he used the other hand to pummel the Englishman with savage blows to the body.

Even in the dim predawn light, Boone could see Harbison's eyes bulging from their sockets as the man fought for breath that would not come. Boone smashed punch after punch into Harbison's midsection, grunting with the effort he put into each blow. Harbison tried to knee him in the groin, but Boone twisted aside and made him miss. His fingers dug cruelly into the flesh of Harbison's throat.

Suddenly, strong hands grasped Boone's shoulders and wrenched him aside, pulling him away from Harbison. One man couldn't have budged him, but both of the other workers who shared this tent managed to haul him to one side. Harbison rolled the other direction and came up against the side of the tent, huddling there and holding both hands to his bruised, raw throat as he desperately sucked air back into lungs starved for the stuff. He made a pathetic whimpering noise.

"Damn, Boone, you like to have killed him!" exclaimed one of the men. "What got into you?"

Boone jerked away from their grip and pushed himself to his feet. "That Englisher tried to rob me!" he accused as he leveled a finger at Harbison's still-shuddering form. "I woke up and found him going after my goods."

"I . . . I just wanted some tobacco," Harbison choked out in a hoarse voice.

"You expect us to believe that?" Boone said angrily.

The entrance flap was thrust aside abruptly, and a tall man with a closely trimmed dark beard stalked into the tent. "What's going on here?" he demanded. "You've disturbed the entire camp with your yelling and commotion."

"Sorry, Mr. Marshall," said one of the other men. "There was some trouble between Boone here and the Englishman."

James Marshall, the carpenter who was heading up this sawmill project for John Sutter, glared at Boone and said, "I hope you've got a good reason for this ruckus, Blakely."

"Damn right I do," the Texan nodded. "Harbison tried to rob me."

"It . . . it's not true," Harbison said as he got shakily to his feet. "I was merely looking for some tobacco, and Blakely went insane and tried to kill me."

Marshall looked at the other two men. "You boys see how the fight started?"

"Sorry, boss, we were both asleep," one of them replied. "I reckon it's Boone's word against the Englishman's."

"All right. In the absence of any proof, I'm going to have to take action based on what I think is right. Harbison, find yourself another place to sleep tonight. I'm not going to fire you, but if there's any more trouble, I will. You're not such a good worker that we can't get along without you." Marshall swung around to face Boone. "And neither are you, Blakely. Next time make certain you know what's going on before you jump a man."

"I know what was going on," Boone growled. "I saw his type often enough back in Texas. Goddamn scavengers."

"That's enough," Marshall said sharply. "You men might as well stay awake. I'd've been rousting you out in another ten minutes or so anyway. We've plenty of work to do today." He turned and started out of the tent, adding over his shoulder, "I'm going to check the millrace."

When Marshall was gone, Boone rolled his shoulders to get some of the stiffness out of them. His jaw ached a little where Harbison had hit him, but the Englishman had gotten the worst of the fight. He moved gingerly and moaned as he gathered his gear and shuffled out of the tent.

Boone reached for his shirt. He was wearing canvas pants and long red underwear, and after he had shrugged into the woolen shirt and buttoned it, he reached for his work boots. As he stamped into them, he scrubbed his face with his hands, getting the last of the sleep out of his eyes. Then he went to the entrance, pushed back the flap, and stepped outside.

It was going to be a fine day here in the western foothills of California's Sierra Nevada range. The sky was clear overhead except for a few streaks of high white clouds. The sun was not up yet, but the eastern horizon was growing lighter by the minute with its approach. Boone dragged in a deep breath of the crisp, cool air. Winters could be harsh in the Sierra Nevadas, he had heard, but so far this one had been pretty mild. He'd seen worse weather back on the rolling plains of central Texas.

Boone was a good-sized man, an inch or two over medium height, with the long arms and broad shoulders of a man accustomed to hard work. He had a strong jaw, a thick shock of sandy hair, and pale blue eyes in a deeply tanned face. He could swing an ax all day long, carry more than his weight in logs, handle mules, use a hammer and an adze, and even read and cipher some. He was a good worker, even though he had a temper, and he didn't think Marshall would run him off over something like a fight. Boone hoped not, anyway. He had been drifting ever since leaving Texas a couple of years earlier, and this was the first good, steady job he'd held since coming to California.

Not that he wanted to settle down and work as a carpenter for the rest of his life, no sir. Boone Blakely was cut out for better than that. He had known that ever since he was a youngster. He'd had his eye on some land in Texas, a place that would have made a fine ranch, and it would have been his one day . . . if it hadn't been for a girl named Samantha and a no-good bastard called Jason Stoneham.

Boone shook his head and forced those bitter memories out of his thoughts. Like Marshall had said, there was work to do, and before that, some breakfast. Boone could smell the aroma of frying bacon coming from the cook tent.

The tents where the workers slept were scattered haphazardly around the large wooden structure that had taken shape over the past few months. The sawmill was a joint enterprise of Marshall and John Augustus Sutter, the Swiss entrepreneur who owned vast tracts of land in the Sierra Nevadas, including this place on the American River called Coloma. There was no settlement here, only the still-unfinished sawmill, but it was Sutter's hope that once the mill was operating, more people might move into the area. More settlers meant more potential customers for Sutter, who had built a large trading post forty miles downriver called Sutter's Fort, near the spot where the American and Sacramento Rivers came together. A village known as New Helvetia had developed around the fort—a feudal fiefdom, for all intents and purposes, since Sutter owned everything—and Sutter hoped that history would repeat itself. But if not, at least he and Marshall would profit from the lumber produced by the sawmill. With American settlements in California growing by leaps and bounds since the end of the war with Mexico the year before, lumber for building was always in demand.

Boone Blakely had been at Sutter's Fort looking for work when Marshall put out the word that he needed experienced carpenters to build the mill at Coloma. Like any good Texan, Boone had never been one to let the truth hold him back, so he had told Marshall he'd worked as a carpenter back home, and Marshall had believed him. It wasn't a complete lie; Boone had been at a few barn raisings, so he knew a little about such work. And he had caught on fast once he and Marshall and the other workmen arrived up here.

The sawmill was going to be finished soon, and Boone hoped he could stay on, at least for a while, and help Marshall with the operation.

The millrace, the big ditch where the water from the river would be diverted to power the mill, had just been completed, and Marshall had turned the water into it the night before, so that any loose dirt and rocks remaining in the channel would be carried away. As Boone ambled toward the cook tent, he saw his boss at the far end of the race, making his way slowly along it, peering down into the clear water of the river.

Boone glanced up at the mill as he passed. The building itself sat on thick, stiltlike beams that lifted it higher than a man's head. The millrace passed beneath it, turning the huge wheel that powered the saws. Steps led up onto a porch that ran along the front of the building. The mill was sturdy, constructed of heavy timbers hewn from the abundance of trees in the foothills. A fairly steep bluff dotted with scrubby brush rose behind the mill, and beyond that bluff were the snow-mantled peaks of the Sierra Nevadas themselves. The sun was about to come into view above those mountains.

In the cook tent, Boone filled a tin plate with bacon, some watery grits, and a couple of hard biscuits; a cup of what passed for coffee completed his breakfast. Taking the food outside, he went to sit on a big rock with some of the other workmen as he ate. One of the men said around a mouthful of biscuit, "Heard you had some trouble with that Englisher, Blakely. Tried robbin' you, did he?"

Boone nodded. "He won't try it again. I'd've kicked him out of camp, was it up to me."

"If he does try it again, I reckon we ought to put a rope around his neck and string him up from one o' them trees," another man commented. "We can't have no thieves in this camp."

"Marshall and Sutter wouldn't like it if we was to do that," Boone pointed out. "They're trying to civilize this part of the country, to hear them tell it."

A third man snorted in derision. "Tryin' to make money, that's all they're doin'. They don't care about law an' order, long as the profits keep comin' in."

"Folks got to have some sort of law," Boone said mildly. His rage at Harbison had faded now, although he still felt a smoldering resentment. Maybe the Englishman *had* just wanted some tobacco, he thought. Maybe he'd let his temper get away from him too quickly. Wouldn't be the first time, after all.

Boone wondered what these men sitting and eating breakfast with him would think if they knew that back in Texas, he was wanted for murder . . .

Suddenly, James Marshall caught Boone's attention again. The boss of the sawmill operation had made his way along the millrace, past the mill itself, and was now down near the other end of the ditch. Marshall was standing stiffly beside the race, staring down into the water, and something about the way he was acting struck Boone as odd. As Boone watched, Marshall got down on his knees and bent forward, leaning even closer to the water and looking down into it like he'd seen something that had shaken him. Boone started to point out Marshall's behavior to the other men, who were paying no attention to the foreman. But then he caught himself and decided not to say anything. Marshall was a pretty strange cuss to start with, and given to moody periods of bleak despair. Best not to get on the man's bad side by pointing out any oddities about him, because word of it could always get back to Marshall.

Marshall was certainly acting a little crazy, though, because as Boone chewed his bacon and biscuits and watched out of the corner of his eye, Marshall suddenly leaned over even more and plunged his arm into the water of the millrace. After a moment, he pulled something out, shook off his dripping arm, and brought the thing up close to this face to study it. Marshall was too far away for Boone to be able to tell what he was holding. Whatever it was, Marshall put it down on the ground after looking at it for a couple of minutes, then picked up a fist-sized chunk of ground and started pounding on the thing. Marshall did that a couple of times, then tossed the rock away, picked up whatever he had been pounding, and wrapped it carefully in his handkerchief.

If it had been hotter, Boone would have said that the sun had gotten to the man. But the sun was barely up now, and the air was still cool. Boone shook his head and then drained the rest of his coffee. At the same moment Marshall stood up and hurried off toward the mill.

No point in worrying about it, Boone told himself. There was work to do, and in that respect this day—January 24, 1848—was no different than the day before or the day after. Boone took his plate and cup back to the cook tent and went to get his ax. The mill wasn't finished yet, and there were still trees to cut.

Two

James Marshall was trembling as he sat down behind the table in the makeshift office inside the sawmill. Even though the mill was not yet operational, this small area had already been partitioned off so that the manager—Marshall—would have a place to conduct business once things got started.

He reached into his pocket and took out his handkerchief, through which he could feel the hard lump of metal. The handkerchief was slightly damp in spots, because despite the pounding he had administered, a few drops of water had clung to the yellow nugget he had taken from the millrace.

With shaking hands, Marshall unwrapped the lump and placed it on the table. He used the handkerchief to wipe away the beads of sweat that had sprung out on his forehead despite the fact that the weather was cool. The nugget sat there in front of him, and to Marshall's fevered brain it seemed almost to be calling to him, singing a siren's song of desires fulfilled. Its shape was different now than when he had taken it from the water: the pounding had flattened it somewhat and spread it out.

That was the simplest test Marshall knew of for gold. Due to its brittle nature, fool's gold, which was so easily mistaken for the genuine element, would shatter under such pounding. The real thing was much softer, much more malleable.

Marshall reached out and picked up the nugget carefully, handling it as if it was scalding hot. He turned it over and over in his fingers. Although its color appeared rather dull and lackluster here inside the sawmill, it had sparkled brightly when he spotted it on the bottom of the millrace, shining through the crystal-clear waters of the diverted river like a miniature sun. There had been other bits of brilliance scattered around the bed of the man-made ditch, but this one had been the brightest and most tempting.

James Marshall's fingers closed around the nugget, and his lips moved as he whispered the word that was blazing through his brain.

"Gold!"

Meanwhile, John Augustus Sutter—born Johann August Suter in Germany forty-five years ago of Swiss parents—was leaning back in his comfortable chair and looked out the window of his office in Sutter's Fort. He liked to sit here and survey his domain, as it were. For a man who had known more than his share of failures in life, it was quite enjoyable to bask in such a thriving success as New Helvetia.

The fort, a sprawling adobe stronghold with stockade walls eighteen feet high and three feet thick, was the center of the settlement that had grown up around it. The three cannons mounted on the walls were reminders of the days when Sutter's bold enterprise had faced danger from both the Spanish and the local Indians, but these days New Helvetia was a peaceful place for the most part. Although the Spanish had not yet officially ceded California to the United States, the Americans were firmly in control of the area, and the Indians were no longer a problem, the hostile tribes having migrated north and west, away from the spread of civilization. The settlement was bustling with growth, and in the seven years since Sutter had founded the fort, he had established a blacksmith shop, a gristmill, a tannery, and even a distillery. Other merchants had moved in, although ownership of the land on which their shops were built was retained by Sutter. Mexican *vaqueros* tended to the large herd of cattle that grazed on acreage outside the walls of the fort, and Indian laborers tilled fields that would be planted in wheat and barley. In the summer, a nearby orchard—also owned by Sutter—produced an ample supply of apples and peaches. New Helvetia was a beautiful place, and when its master looked out over it, he was well pleased with what he had done.

A stocky, balding man with an impressive sweep of moustache, Sutter clasped his hands over his belly and smiled as he gazed out the window of the office. His eyes swept his holdings and then fastened on a man approaching the fort on horseback, riding along the bank of the American River. Sutter frowned slightly. The rider was in a hurry, wherever he was going, and he looked to Sutter something like James Marshall, the carpenter hired to build the sawmill upriver at Coloma. As the man came closer, Sutter saw that he was indeed Marshall.

Perhaps there was trouble at the mill, Sutter thought as he turned his chair away from the window and sat up straighter. He would know soon enough, the way Marshall was practically flogging his horse into a gallop.

A few minutes later, Marshall flung the door open and strode wide-eyed into the room. Sweat coated his bearded face. Sutter knew that Marshall was not the most stable of individuals, having endured more than his own share of failure in his life, like Sutter himself. But where Sutter had never given up hope of succeeding once again as grandly as he once had, Marshall had become prone to fits of depression and black moodiness.

That wasn't the case today. Marshall looked extremely agitated, true, but not in a despairing way. He came across the room and leaned over Sutter's desk, resting his palms on it. Sutter could see that he was shaking slightly.

"I have to talk to you, Mr. Sutter," Marshall said without

preamble. "I've something of the utmost importance to tell you. But in private, it has to be in private."

Sutter gestured to indicate the room, empty except for the two of them. "There is no one here but us," he said.

Marshall shook his head vehemently. "Someone might overhear," he insisted. "Isn't there anywhere else?"

Sutter sighed. He wanted to find out why Marshall had such a bur in his tail, as the Americans would say, and the quickest way to do that would be to go along with his wishes. Sutter pushed himself to his feet and said, "Come along. We will go to my rooms upstairs."

He led the way out of the office and up a flight of stairs to the second floor, where his living quarters were located. He and Marshall were alone. That wasn't enough to satisfy the carpenter, however.

"Is anyone else in the house?" Marshall demanded. "Anyone at all?"

"Only my bookkeeper," replied Sutter, growing more impatient with the man.

"Lock the door," Marshall snapped, giving orders as if *he* rather than Sutter were the master of New Helvetia.

The entrepreneur's frown deepened, but he complied with Marshall's command, throwing the latch on the door so that no one could enter. "Now, what is it you have to tell me that is so important?" Sutter asked.

Instead of answering, Marshall slumped into a chair, still quivering. "I wouldn't have believed it if I hadn't seen it with my own eyes," he muttered. "I still didn't believe it, even after I knew it was true. I waited a day before I started down here, just to make sure I hadn't imagined the whole thing."

Sutter was rapidly running out of patience, and the worry was also growing that Marshall might have lost his mind. The man had fought in the so-called Bear Flag Revolt a couple of years earlier, when the American settlers in California had first risen against Spanish rule, and perhaps even after so much time, he was having a reaction to the fighting in which he had taken part.

"Excuse me for a moment," Sutter said, suddenly feeling uneasy about being in here alone with Marshall. He unbolted the door and stepped outside, then walked down the corridor and drew several deep breaths to steady himself. It was quite possible that Marshall had something important to tell him, and Sutter knew he had to go back in there. But he also hoped that this slight delay might serve to calm his partner somewhat.

Indeed, when Sutter stepped inside the room again, he saw that Marshall was not breathing quite as hard. Sutter left the door unlocked this time, and Marshall didn't seem to notice. That was a good sign, Sutter thought.

"All right," Sutter said, keeping his voice level and friendly, "tell me what brings you down here from the mill. What is it that has agitated you?"

"I'll show you," Marshall said. He reached inside his coat and took out a piece of cloth that was folded around something. He stood up as he began to carefully unwrap the object. Sutter felt a little tremor of apprehension as he leaned forward to see what Marshall had. Marshall was acting as if his discovery was something horrifying.

At that moment, the door swung open behind Sutter, and the man he employed as his bookkeeper strolled into the room. "There you are, Mr. Sutter," the man said. "I thought you might be up here when I didn't find you in the office. I have a question—"

Marshall recoiled as if he had been struck, and he tightly clutched the cloth around the object he had been about to expose. "My God!" he shouted at Sutter. "Didn't I tell you to lock that door?" Marshall's eyes were wide and staring, and he was looking at the bookkeeper as if he might attack the man at any second.

Sutter moved quickly between them and held up his hands, palms out toward Marshall. "Don't worry," he said. "I apologize for the interruption. Please don't be upset, James." He swung sharply toward the bookkeeper and hissed, "Whatever it is that brings you up here, it can wait!"

"But, sir—" protested the man, who held an open ledger in his hands.

"Leave now," Sutter ordered, and with a grimace and a muttered comment under his breath, the bookkeeper did so. As soon as the door was shut behind him, Sutter turned to Marshall again and said sincerely, "I assure you, James, that was an accident. I meant to lock the door when I came back in."

"He . . . he was spying on us!" Marshall's fingers were clenched tightly around the cloth-wrapped object.

Sutter shook his head. "I swear to you, the man was here on his own business, not to eavesdrop on our conversation or see whatever it is you have there. Please, James, can we continue?"

"Not until I'm sure we won't be disturbed again," Marshall said. He looked around the room, then pointed to a heavy wardrobe. "Help me shove that up against the door."

"Really, you can't be serious—"

"I won't show you what I found until you help me!"

Nodding quickly, Sutter said, "All right, all right. It will be as you say." He went to the wardrobe and put his shoulder against the bulky piece of furniture. Marshall positioned himself alongside Sutter, and together the two men shoved the wardrobe in front of the door. Unaccustomed to such hard physical labor, Sutter was breathing heavily by the time they were finished.

Marshall stepped back and began unwrapping his find

again. "Here," he said, his voice little more than a whisper. "I'll show you. I took this out of the new millrace four days ago."

He held out the cloth, and nestled in the center of it was a small, misshapen lump of yellowish metal.

Despite its unlovely appearance, something about the nugget made Sutter catch his breath. He peered closely at it for a long moment, then straightened and looked at Marshall, who was blinking rapidly.

"Well? What do you think?" demanded the carpenter.

"It looks like gold," admitted Sutter. "Let us test it."

"I already pounded it with a rock," Marshall said. "Flattened right out, it did."

"There are other tests." Sutter turned toward a set of shelves against one wall where several leather-bound volumes rested. "I have an encyclopedia here. Let us see what it says about the identification of gold."

Sutter's heart was thudding heavily in his chest as he took down one of the books and leafed through it until he found the appropriate section. He studied the book for a moment and mused, "You say that you pounded it . . ."

"Look!" Marshall placed the cloth containing the nugget on a table and took a chunk of rock from another pocket. Before Sutter could say anything, Marshall slammed the rock down on the yellowish nugget. When he lifted the rock, the nugget was noticeably flatter.

Sutter felt his pulse increase even more. "We will immerse it in water," he decided, putting down the encyclopedia and reaching for a glass and a pitcher of water that stood on a side table.

He filled the glass, then held out his hand for the nugget. Instead of giving it to Sutter, Marshall himself dropped the chunk of yellow rock into the water. It sunk rapidly.

"Obviously quite dense," Sutter said, feeling his excitement grow and along with it a certain amount of trepidation. He picked up the encyclopedia again, studied it, then went on, "Gold resists corrosion. There is nitric acid in the fort's store. I'll get some and bring it back up here."

Marshall nodded. He wrapped the nugget in the handkerchief again and stowed it away inside his coat. "Here, I'll help you move that wardrobe so you can get out," he said. Now that one more test had indicated the genuineness of his find, he seemed to have calmed down slightly.

Working together, Sutter and Marshall shoved the wardrobe aside so that Sutter could leave the room. He went downstairs and out of the house, hurrying across the large enclosed yard of the fort to the general store on the other side of the compound.

Within ten minutes, he was back with a small glass vial of colorless liquid. He handled the nitric acid carefully, taking pains not to drop the vial. Marshall produced the nugget again, and at Sutter's command, he placed it in a small tin saucer that Sutter had also brought from the fort's trading post.

Marshall set the saucer on the table while Sutter unstoppered the vial. Both men winced at the strong, unpleasant odor of the acid. Slowly, Sutter tilted the vial over the nugget until a couple of drops of the colorless liquid splashed down onto the gold.

The acid had no effect, rolling off the nugget and landing on the tin saucer, where the drops immediately began eating away at the metal, producing tiny tendrils of smoke. Sutter replaced the stopper in the vial of acid and set it aside, staring at the nugget as he did so. "There is no doubt," he said softly. "You have found gold, James."

"I knew it," Marshall said in a hushed voice. "I knew it as soon as I saw it."

"You said there were more nuggets in the millrace?"

"I saw other things shining on the bottom, but I don't know how big they were. They could have been actual nuggets like this, only smaller, or maybe just little flecks of the stuff."

Sutter crossed distractedly to a chair and sat down. His pulse was hammering in his head, and he was not sure what he ought to do next. He was certain of only one thing, and that was that this discovery did not bode well for him.

Sutter glanced out the window at the fort and New Helvetia. Finally, after years of struggle, he had achieved what he wanted out of life. He was surrounded by land that he loved and businesses that were profitable. Soon he would be an old man, and he wanted nothing more than to continue as he had for the last few years, watching his holdings increase and enjoying his hard-won success. But that nugget Marshall had taken out of the millrace had the power to change everything.

"Have you told anyone at the mill about this?" Sutter asked abruptly.

Marshall started to shake his head, then said, "Well . . . I mentioned it to a couple of the men. I shouldn't have, I know that, but a few of them had noticed me acting rather oddly, they said, and they were curious . . . and, well, I just didn't think, I reckon. Since then I've kept it quiet, though. You saw how careful I was."

Careful was an understatement, Sutter thought. Marshall had been practically obsessed with secrecy upon his arrival. And now Sutter could understand why. Men would drop everything to answer the call of gold. He could close his eyes and practically see what would happen if word of this discovery got out to the general public. The foothills would be covered with wealth seekers swarming over the land like flies on a carcass.

And that carcass would represent Sutter's dreams of a

peaceful, profitable old age. Because nothing would be the same, nothing . . .

The entrepreneur took a deep breath. "Tell no one else," he instructed Marshall sternly. "All the men at the mill doubtless are aware of this by now. No one can keep such a secret in close quarters. But tell them they have strict orders not to mention the discovery to any outsiders until after the mill is finished and running. I want some time to get my spring crops in the ground, too, before my workers hear of this."

"You think they'd run off to the hills if they found out?"

Sutter laughed. "I know they would, my friend. I know they would."

Because no one could resist the lure of gold, not even— God help him—John Augustus Sutter . . .

Three

Nathan Jones was whistling as he made his way down one of the narrow aisles toward the back of the big general mercantile store owned by his aunt. That didn't necessarily mean he was happy, though. Nathan was cheerful by nature, at least on the surface, but there was something inside him—an uneasiness, a gnawing dissatisfaction—that had nothing to do with the face he presented to the world.

"Damn it, Nathan, I told you to take this keg of nails with you when you went back to the storeroom," Matthew Havins called from the front of the store.

Nathan stopped in his tracks and grimaced. He was a young man, not much past twenty, with dark brown hair and a medium build, wearing a clerk's apron over corduroy pants and a cotton shirt. During his days at Harvard a few years earlier, he had anchored the rowing team, and the muscles he had developed then were still put to good use and kept in trim by loading and unloading goods here in the store.

Harvard was thousands of miles away now, clear across the continent, in fact. At the request of his aunt, Nathan had made the long sea voyage around South America and Cape Horn, coming here to the burgeoning settlement called San Francisco to help with the running of the store Emily Woodward had established in absentia last year. He had been under the impression that he would be in charge, but upon arriving, Nathan had found that Woodward's Emporium already had a manager—Matthew Havins. Since then he had been little better than a flunky, jumping every time Havins issued a command, which was often.

When Nathan returned to the front of the store, Havins pointed at a large keg sitting on the counter. Nathan wrapped his arms around the keg and grunted as he lifted it, then started toward the rear of the building. It was true that Havins had told him earlier to put the nails in the storeroom, but Nathan had forgotten.

Woodward's Emporium was huge, occupying an entire city block in this settlement that until a year earlier had been under Mexican rule and had been known as Yerba Buena. The sleepy little seacoast village had experienced brisk growth since the Americans had taken over, and even merchants like Emily Woodward, who still resided back in Boston, were enjoying healthy profits.

More than once, Nathan had thought that he ought to leave the store and try to establish some sort of business on his own, but he believed that would have been disloyal to his Aunt Emily. After all, she *had* given him a job, even if it hadn't worked out quite as he had expected. Nathan's parents were both dead, and he was alone in the world now except for his aunt and his cousin, Emily's daughter Cassandra. He ought to feel grateful for Emily's assistance, he thought.

"Excuse me, do you have any calico fabric?"

The question broke into Nathan's thoughts, and he paused in carrying the keg to the back to look over at the young woman who had asked it. There were three young ladies standing at a large table piled high with bolts of cloth, and Nathan was unsure which one had spoken to him. He gave all three of them a friendly smile and said, "I'm sure there's some calico in there somewhere. Let me help you look."

He set the keg of nails on top of a cracker barrel and went over to the table. The young women were giggling and talking to each other in low whispers, and Nathan flushed in embarrassment. He wasn't sure what they were talking about, but as long as there was a chance that he was the subject of the low-voiced conversation, he was going to feel self-conscious.

"Did you used to be a sailor?" one of the young women asked as Nathan pawed through the bolts of cloth looking for the calico he knew was there somewhere.

He shook his head. "I came around Cape Horn from Massachusetts, but it was strictly as a passenger, not a sailor."

"Oh. You look like you should have been a sailor."

"I was on Harvard's rowing team," Nathan offered.

That information drew another round of giggles for some unfathomable reason. Nathan's features grew even warmer, and he gave one of the bolts of cloth a particularly firm yank as he tried to look at it. Some of the bolts on top began to slide, and Nathan looked up in horror as fully half of the bolts stacked on the table moved inexorably toward the edge. He lunged forward and tried to hold them in place, but his arms weren't long enough. The rolls of fabric began to spill onto the sawdust-covered floor.

"Nathan, what the devil are you—Oh, excuse me, ladies," Havins said as he came around a display of hats to see the bolts of cloth falling despite Nathan's best efforts to stop them. The store manager went on, "I didn't see you there. Is this young man annoying you?"

"Oh, no, he was just trying to help us," one of the young women said quickly. "This isn't his fault, it really isn't."

Havins snorted. He was bald except for a fringe of hair around his ears, and Nathan had often thought somewhat disrespectfully that Havins looked like an egg with a thin mustache. Now wasn't the time for such thoughts, though, because Havins was plainly angry.

"Just get the cloth picked up if it ever stops falling, Nathan," he said. "And I see that keg of nails *still* isn't in the storeroom."

"I was taking it there, sir, when I stopped to help these ladies," Nathan explained as he began shoving the fallen bolts of cloth back into place.

"Help them what?" Havins demanded sarcastically. "Throw fabric on the floor?"

Nathan's jaw tightened as the young women laughed again and moved on, evidently no longer interested in buying any calico; but he did not make any reply. Havins was something of a bully, but Nathan couldn't really blame the man for becoming frustrated with him. In the months that he had been working here at the store, he had made more than his share of mistakes and caused more than one minor catastrophe. Things had a habit of falling over when Nathan was around, whether he actually did anything to cause the mishaps or not.

"You'd better not ever go up into the mountains," Havins said dryly when they were alone again. "I reckon you could cause an avalanche without even trying."

Nathan just grinned and swallowed his anger. Havins was right, he told himself. If there was such a thing as a jinx, he deserved that description.

But at least he didn't have to worry about the prediction Havins had just made. The Sierra Nevadas were visible in the distance from San Francisco, but Nathan had no reason on earth to travel into them. He didn't even like mountains, and he intended to stay as far away from them as possible.

Boone Blakely watched the two men walking slowly along the millrace, both of them peering into the water. One of the men was James Marshall, who had come back from Sutter's Fort just about as agitated as he'd been when he left, and the other was John Sutter himself, the big boss of this whole area. Boone inclined his head toward Marshall and Sutter and asked the man on the other end of the crosscut saw, "What do you reckon they're looking for? More gold?"

"That'd be my guess," the man replied. He and Boone were sawing their way through one of the big logs that had been rolled down a nearby hill to the camp. The mill would soon be operational, and when it was, logs like this one, cut down into manageable lengths, would be sawn into planks by the big water-powered saw inside the building.

Boone shifted his stance a little, and as he did so, he felt the nugget in his pocket press against his leg. It was about a quarter of the size of a man's fist, and he had found it downstream from the millrace a couple of days ago, just lying there in plain sight on the bottom of the river, near the bank. Boone had reached into the water and scooped it up. As far as he could tell, it was pure gold.

He wasn't sure yet how much the nugget was worth or what he was going to do with it. Finding gold was all well and good, but it didn't pay as steady as a real job. At least that was what Marshall had told all the men on his return from Sutter's Fort. He'd said that partially to keep the men from abandoning their work and running off to become prospectors, Boone thought, but there was some truth to it. Hunting gold was a risky business, and a man might leave his job and wind up with nothing to show for it.

Still, Boone mused as he and the other man paused in their sawing, the appeal was undeniably there. Boone reached down and let his fingers brush against the hard shape of the nugget. If a man could find enough of those lumps of yellowish metal, he'd be rich in a hurry and never have to worry about a job again.

Finding a fortune in gold would make even leaving Texas worthwhile.

Marshall had meant to keep the discovery a secret when he found the first nugget a couple of weeks ago, but he'd blurted it out and the word had spread quickly through the camp. Boone knew that Marshall had been uneasy about leaving to go downriver to the fort after that. Marshall had been worried that nobody would be in the camp when he got back.

The men had kept working, however, although a few of them had started spending their spare time tramping through the hills or along the banks of the river, looking for that telltale flash of color. Boone was among them, and that was how he had come to find the nugget now in his pocket.

Some of the men were saying that all the rivers in this part of the country were full of gold and that the hills were made of the precious stuff. They were talking about leaving the mill once it was finished and looking for gold full-time.

Boone liked that idea, liked it a lot. He had never intended to spend the rest of his life as a sawmill hand.

Besides, if he could make a strike and put together enough money, he could move on and put Texas even farther behind him. He didn't think about it often—he had taught himself not to brood about the past, since it couldn't be changed anyway—but there was no telling how long the reach of the law really was. The more miles he put between himself and that old trouble, the better.

There was a sawmill to finish first, though.

By mid-March, the mill was completed. Despite the efforts of John Sutter and James Marshall, word of Marshall's discovery spread rapidly from the mill downriver to Sutter's Fort and beyond. Some of the men who had helped build the mill returned to San Francisco and carried the news with them.

April found most of the workers from the mill deserting

their jobs, and many of the men employed by Sutter at the fort also turned their backs on their work and headed for the hills, intent on finding gold. It seemed to be pretty much a local phenomenon, however. Sutter began to breathe a little easier; maybe the dreaded boom that was bound to completely disrupt his enterprises wouldn't materialize after all. Perhaps the gold wasn't as widespread as he had feared, and once the men had realized they were not going to get rich, they would come back to work.

The goldseekers were stubborn, though. Maybe even damned fools, Boone thought as he knelt with his tin pan beside one of the numerous creeks that fed into the American River. He scooped the pan into the sandy creek bed and brought it back up, bringing with it several handfuls of dirt, sand, and gravel. With a twisting motion of his wrists, Boone tilted the pan back and forth, swirling the water that remained in it. With each twist, a little of the water spilled over the sides of the pan.

Boone kept up the routine for several minutes, until all the dirt and sand had been washed out of the pan, leaving a scattering of pebbles on the bottom of it. He poked among the pebbles, grunting in satisfaction as he saw several flecks of gold among them. Being much heavier than the sand and dirt, the gold naturally sank to the bottom of the pan as the water was swirled around. Boone took a small leather poke from inside his shirt and opened it, then carefully picked out the gold dust—that was what the miners had started to call the little flecks of color—and added it to the dust already in the pouch. Boone smiled as he hefted the poke. The work was slow but steady, and he had quite a bit of dust already.

Days passed in a mind-numbing routine, and more than his mind was going numb, Boone thought frequently. Squatting in cold creeks and rivers—made even more frigid by the snow melt as spring began—left a man's legs and rear end half-frozen. Gold had a heat of its own that could warm up just about anything, though, and make a man forget the discomforts he was enduring to get his hands on the stuff.

By mid-May, Boone had several pokes full of dust tucked away in his shirt as he walked into the settlement of Sutterville, on the Sacramento River a few miles downstream from the fort. A lot of the men had laughed at him for spending his time panning dust from the creeks when there were nuggets lying on the ground, but finding gold like that was chancy. Some men got rich in a hurry, true, but more never found anything and wound up just as poor as when they had started. The supply of gold dust in the streambeds seemed to be endless, even though it was harder to procure.

It was time to see just how much of a stake he had built up, Boone had decided a few days earlier, and he had caught a ride on a boat from the mill down to Sutter's Fort and then on here to Sutterville. As he strolled down the street, he spotted a sign in the front window of a store announcing GOLD DUST WEIGHED AND BOUGHT HERE. Boone grinned and stepped out of the muddy street onto the boardwalk made of rough planks. He opened the door and went into the dim, musty store.

"Help you with something, mister?" a man called from a counter in the back.

Boone strode up to the counter and took out one of his pokes. As he thumped it down, he said, "Tell me how much that's worth."

The storekeeper grinned. He was a lean man with muttonchop whiskers, a small goatee, and piercing eyes under heavy brows. "Be glad to," he said as he reached for a set of scales and drew them in front of him. Carefully, he opened the pouch Boone had given him and he poured the gold dust onto one of the small pans attached to the scales.

It took only a moment to determine that Boone had seven

ounces of gold on the scales. The storekeeper looked up at him and said, "Seven ounces. That's a hundred and twelve dollars worth of dust, son."

Boone blinked in astonishment. "A hundred dollars?"

"A hundred and *twelve*." The storekeeper's grin widened. "Don't let anybody cheat you. Gold's worth sixteen dollars an ounce." He stuck a hand across the counter. "Sam Brannan, and I'm pleased to meet you."

"Boone Blakely," Boone introduced himself as he shook hands with Brannan.

"I'll be glad to take this gold off your hands, Mr. Blakely," Brannan said as he gestured at the dust on the scales. "I'll pay you in hard money that you can spend anywhere. Not all the stores and saloons accept dust and nuggets yet, you know."

"Yet?" repeated Boone.

"They'd better get used to it, to my way of thinking, because there's going to be plenty of gold coming out of these hills soon enough. Folks'll be coming all the way from San Francisco to look for it."

"You sound pretty sure of that."

"I intend to *make* sure of it," Brannan said with a wink. "Now, how about it? Do you want to sell your gold?"

Boone frowned in thought. If Brannan was right about some of the saloons in town not accepting payment in gold, maybe it would be better to sell the dust. Boone intended to have himself a high old time now that he had come out of the hills for a while, and that included getting good and drunk.

"All right," he said with an abrupt nod. He reached into his shirt and started pulling out the other pokes. "I want to sell all of it, though."

"I'll be glad to buy it. You'll find that hard money spends a lot easier."

Half an hour later, Boone left Brannan's Mercantile with a little over three hundred dollars in his pockets. Those pockets were in new pants, because he'd worn out the ones he'd been wearing when he got to town. He had on a new shirt, too, and boots that didn't have holes in the soles. There was even a new broad-brimmed hat on his head. He'd bought all the new clothes from Brannan and still had a small fortune left over. The storekeeper had charged him a pretty penny for the goods, of course, and Boone figured Brannan had turned a substantial profit on the deal, even buying the gold dust straight up like he had. Brannan had probably figured on as much when he offered to buy the gold. The man struck Boone as a pretty shrewd individual.

But that was all right. For now, anyway, Boone Blakely was a rich man, and this was his night to howl.

A week later, Sam Brannan strode up and down the streets of San Francisco carrying a large glass bottle full of gold dust, some of which he had gotten from Boone. Brannan showed the bottle of gold dust to everyone he met, and when there weren't enough people paying attention, he threw back his head and shouted, "Gold! Gold from the American River! Just take a look, folks! Gold from the American River!"

Naturally, men flocked around him, and in their excited questions Brannan could almost hear the sound of coins ringing into the till of his store in Sutterville. Panning for gold or digging it out of the side of a mountain was hard work, and Sam Brannan intended to make his fortune another way. People looking for gold would need supplies, and they had to pass right through Sutterville on their way to the hills. The miners would spend their gold with him once they'd found it. There was more than one method of getting rich, and the rush of gold hunters was the key to Brannan's method.

The boom was coming. Sam Brannan was going to make sure of that.

''Gold! Gold from the American River!''

Four

Nathan leaned against the jamb of the emporium's front door and looked out into the street, which was almost deserted. One wagon rolled along a couple of blocks away, and a pair of pedestrians crossed the street in the other direction. And here it was, Nathan thought, the middle of the day—normally one of the busiest times for traffic. San Francisco had become something of a ghost town in the past few months, ever since Sam Brannan had come down from Sutterville and brought the news of the gold strike.

For weeks after that, Woodward's Emporium had been packed with customers. Would-be miners had bought every pick and shovel, every tin pan and washbowl, every packsaddle and bit of harness. Sturdy pants and shirts and work boots were in demand, and Nathan and the other clerks trooped back and forth almost continuously, carrying sacks of flour, sugar, and salt out of the store and loading the provisions on wagons and mules bound for the Sierra Nevadas. Eventually the demand had outstripped the supply, and now the shelves and counters of the store had been picked almost clean.

Nathan's gaze traveled up and down the street, resting briefly on all the closed and boarded-up businesses. Drawn by the lure of gold, men had abandoned thriving shops to head for the hills. A glance the other way showed the tops of the masts of ships anchored in the harbor, ships that had been deserted by their crews almost as soon as they were docked. Everyone was going to the Sierra Nevadas.

Even Matthew Havins had proven unable to resist the
temptation. Once the rush of business was over and the
store's supplies were exhausted, Havins had taken off his
apron and tossed it on the counter one morning.

"You're in charge, Nathan," Havins had told his startled
assistant. "I hear there's been a big strike on the Yuba River,
and I think I'll take a look."

"But . . . I can't run the store!" Nathan protested, forget-
ting for the moment that he had been disappointed when he
arrived in San Francisco and discovered that he was not going to be in charge of the emporium.

Havins looked around at the almost empty aisles and the
deserted street and smirked at Nathan. "I think you can manage," he said dryly.

The prediction had proven correct. All the other clerks had
left to search for gold, too, so Nathan was alone, but since
only a bare handful of customers came in each day, he had
no trouble. Actually, he thought with a sigh, he might as
well walk out, lock the doors, and never come back. He
doubted if he would be missed.

His gaze turned across the bay and toward the mountains,
shrouded by clouds and barely visible as a thin blue line on
the horizon. He could become a goldseeker like practically
everyone else in San Francisco. Despite his dislike of the
mountains and Havins' sarcastic comment about his starting
avalanches wherever he went, Nathan's thoughts were turning more and more toward the Sierra Nevadas. He had always wanted to do something on his own, and this might be
his chance. The problem was that he didn't have enough
money to buy an outfit; stores in San Francisco that still had
mining equipment and supplies in stock were charging exorbitant prices for them. And like a fool, Nathan had stood
by and sold gear to countless other would-be miners without

giving any thought to the possibility that he might want to try his luck, too.

No, he was just going to have to stay here, he thought with a sigh. There were still a few people left in San Francisco, and maybe more would be arriving in the future.

Movement caught Nathan's eye, and he looked toward the harbor again. A ship was coming in. He could see the tops of the white sails as they moved with stately grace among the forest of bare masts. Within a matter of moments, the vessel would be docked, the sails struck, and the crew could abandon ship as all the other ship's crews had done lately. Nathan turned and wandered back into the store. Some of the sailors might stop at the emporium for supplies, although there was little enough here to sell them now.

Nathan went behind the counter, and sure enough a few minutes later a couple of figures appeared on the porch in front of the store. They weren't what he was expecting, however. Instead of the duck trousers and striped jerseys of the sailors off the newly arrived boat, these newcomers wore starched petticoats and heavy gowns, as well as matching bonnets tied on their heads. Nathan had been leaning on the counter, but as the women came into the store he straightened quickly and said, "Good day, ladies. Can I help—Aunt Emily!"

The exclamation was startled out of him by the sight of the familiar face of his aunt. He could make out the features of the women as they came closer, and he had no trouble recognizing Emily Woodward and her daughter Cassandra. Emily was a quite handsome woman of middle years, with a surprisingly unlined face and wispy brown hair that was touched only lightly with gray. Cassandra was about the same age as Nathan, with fair skin, a dusting of freckles across her nose, and thick blond hair that framed strong but attractive features. Cassandra took more after her late father than her mother, but she and Emily had always been close, Nathan recalled.

"Hello, Nathan," Emily said with a faint smile. "I didn't expect to find you here alone." She glanced around at the empty shelves. "Nor did I expect to find my store looking like the bare bones of a corpse after the vultures are through with it."

Nathan blinked. Emily had always been plainspoken, as far back as he could remember, and obviously she hadn't changed. He said, "I'm sorry, Aunt Emily. We sold out of most things, and we haven't been able to get any more supplies."

Emily nodded briskly. "Well, you must have done a booming business for a while, at least. Where is Mr. Havins?"

"Gone to look for gold," Nathan replied. "He left a few weeks ago. The other clerks have gone to the mountains, too."

"But you're still here, I see."

Nathan shrugged his shoulders and said, "I thought it was my duty to make sure the store was taken care of. You trusted me, Aunt Emily, and I didn't want to let you down."

Emily walked slowly up and down the largely barren aisles. "You've done well, Nathan. As well as you could under the circumstances. The gold rush has practically emptied the town, hasn't it?"

"Just about," admitted Nathan. "You've heard about the gold rush back in Boston?"

"Why do you think Mother is here?" Cassandra asked. She held out a hand to him. "By the way, hello, Nathan. It's good to see you again."

He took Cassandra's hand, embarrassed by the fact that he had failed to greet her. He supposed he was just so surprised by their unexpected arrival that he wasn't thinking straight. "Hello, Cassandra. You look lovely." The compliment felt a little strange coming from his lips. Growing up with Cassandra, he had always regarded her almost as another boy. She had been able to climb trees better, throw rocks farther, and run faster than he.

She had grown into quite a young lady, though, Nathan thought as he looked at her now. And he was not quite sure that he was comfortable with that idea.

Nathan turned back to the older woman and asked, "What *are* you doing here, Aunt Emily? Not that I'm not glad to see you, of course. It's just that I had no idea you were coming."

"I wasn't trying to surprise you, if that's what you're worried about, Nathan. I was sure you were doing fine out here. It's just that I wanted to take a look for myself at this boom we've been hearing about back east. It's been in all the papers, you know. Gold in California is all one reads about anymore."

"It probably doesn't look like much of a boom right now," Nathan said ruefully. "The town is practically deserted. It wasn't always like this, Aunt Emily. San Francisco was thriving, and I'm sure it will thrive again."

Emily nodded. "I think you're right. It may take a while, though." She smiled at him. "I appreciate you staying here to look after my interests, Nathan. Haven't you thought about going to the gold fields, though?"

Nathan hesitated, then admitted, "The idea *has* crossed my mind. I heard about a man who was walking along and tripped over a rock, only the rock turned out to be a giant gold nugget. He made a fortune just by falling down." Nathan grinned. "I ought to be able to manage that. Mr. Havins always said I could trip over my own feet."

"How would you like to go?" Emily looked squarely at him as she asked the question.

"To the mountains, you mean?" Nathan blinked in confusion. "To look for gold?"

"Of course."

"Well, I . . . I suppose I could give it a try."

"Good," Emily said firmly. "Cassandra and I will stay here and run the store while you look for gold." She looked around again at the nearly empty store and added dryly, "I think we can manage."

Nathan was flabbergasted by the suggestion. "But . . . but I don't have any supplies."

"We can take care of that. Take what you need from the store here."

"We sold all our picks and shovels and most of our provisions," Nathan pointed out.

"Surely other stores in town still have what you need," Emily said with a frown.

"Well, yes, but they charge so much—"

"Don't worry about that," she said. "I'll stand good for the cost of your supplies in return for a share of whatever you find up there. Don't you think that's fair enough?"

"More than fair," agreed Nathan. "But are you sure—"

Cassandra interrupted him by saying, "Mother is *always* sure of her plans, Nathan. You ought to know that by now."

Emily shot her a sharp look. "You could have stayed in Boston, dear. No one forced you to come."

"Stay in Boston and miss out on this grand adventure? I don't think so, Mother."

Nathan sensed the tension between mother and daughter and hoped fervently that they would leave him out of whatever hostilities were going on. He said quickly, "I'll need a pack mule, too."

"Buy whatever you need, and I'll give you bank drafts to cover the bills," Emily said. "The living quarters are upstairs, I take it?"

"That's right. I have a room up there, and all the other rooms are empty now."

"Cassandra and I will go up and settle in. Our bags are still on board the ship. Can you get them and bring them here, Nathan?"

He nodded quickly. "Sure, I can do that. There are always a few loafers around the docks who'll give me a hand with them. Not everybody's gone off hunting for gold. Just most of them."

"Very well. Come along, Cassandra."

Cassandra gave Nathan a quick smile before she followed Emily to the stairs at the rear of the store and began climbing them to the second floor. Nathan waited until his aunt and cousin had disappeared before taking off his apron and reaching for his hat, which lay on a shelf below the counter. He left the store and headed for the harbor.

Had he made a mistake by agreeing to go to the Sierra Nevadas and search for gold? Emily had swept in and barely given him a chance to think, making changes and taking over just like the headstrong woman he remembered from his youth. The mountains were a dangerous place, full of wild animals and wilder men now that miners were swarming all over the wooded slopes. San Francisco had become rather dull, but there was little chance of being bored to death here.

On the other hand, Nathan reflected, he had never taken many chances in his life. Coming here in the first place had been about the most daring thing he had ever done. He could barely imagine how exciting it would be to discover a fortune in gold. Just once in his life, he thought, he deserved to experience the heady feeling of a rip-roaring success.

He would do it, he decided. He would take Aunt Emily up on her offer and let her provide an outfit for him, then he would head for the hills and claim some of that golden bounty for his own. Today was the start of a new life for

Nathan Jones, he told himself, a life of adventure and triumph.

Nathan began whistling a tune as he strode toward the docks, and this time it was genuine.

It took a little over an hour to get all the trunks unloaded from the ship that had brought Emily and Cassandra Woodward to San Francisco, put them on a wagon with the help of several men recruited from stragglers who had nothing better to do, and transport them back to the emporium. Nathan lugged the trunks upstairs by himself to the rooms his aunt and cousin had claimed, and he was tired and drenched in sweat by the time he was finished with the task. Emily had already changed her traveling outfit for a sensible gray dress and was downstairs behind the counter, just in case any customers came in, which so far had not occurred.

Cassandra brought Nathan a cup of water when he had finished wrestling the last trunk into one of the rooms. "I thought you might like this," she said.

"Thanks," Nathan said, taking the cup from her and sipping the water. "You and Aunt Emily must have brought half of Boston with you, judging from the number of trunks you have."

Cassandra laughed. "It only seems that way. A lady requires a great deal of baggage to maintain a proper image, don't you know."

"You didn't use to feel that way," Nathan said with a grin. "All you needed was a slingshot and a pocketful of rocks. Then if anybody said you weren't a lady, you could bounce a stone off his head."

"Your memory is too good, Nathan Jones," she said with a warm smile.

Nathan sat down on one of the heavy trunks. "How was your trip around the Horn?"

"Terrible. It was cold and damp the entire trip. I thought it would be warmer when we got here to San Francisco, since it's almost summer."

Nathan shook his head and said, "It's nearly always chilly here, from what I've been told, and the fog comes in almost every night. The clear days are worth waiting for, though. Then you can see all the way to the mountains."

"I wish I was going with you," Cassandra said with a wistful sigh.

Nathan's eyes widened in surprise. "To the gold fields? I've never heard of women going to the gold fields. There aren't even that many of them here in San Francisco."

"Like I said earlier, I came for the adventure." Cassandra laughed, but there was little humor in the sound. "Mother wants me to find a nice, respectable young man and marry him."

"That's not going to be easy in San Francisco," Nathan said with another shake of his head. "This is still a frontier town, Cassandra. Most of the men are pretty rough."

"You're not. You're a gentleman, Nathan."

He stared down at the cup on his hand, unwilling to meet her eyes. "I've always been an exception, I guess," he said, not knowing what else to say.

"Yes, you have."

Nathan felt a flush creeping over his features. Cassandra sounded almost like she was smitten with him. He had never had any romantic feelings toward her; she was his cousin, after all, and although a marriage between them would have been legal enough, such a possibility had never entered his head.

"Well, maybe you can come visit me in the goldfields one of these days," he said, "after I make my strike."

"I'll do that," Cassandra promised. "Thank you for bringing our things from the ship, Nathan."

"Oh, I was glad to." He drank the rest of the water, stood up, and handed the empty cup to her. "I'd better get started gathering my gear for the trip. I'm sure Aunt Emily wants me to leave as soon as possible. She's never been one to waste time."

"No, she hasn't," Cassandra agreed. "Be careful up there, Nathan."

He grinned at her. "Don't worry. I don't intend to let a mountain fall on me."

He wasn't going to give Matthew Havins the satisfaction of being proved right.

Five

Dr. Thaddeus Palmer hefted the carpetbag and swung it into the back of the buggy parked in front of his house. This was the last bag, and there was no need to delay any longer. Palmer turned toward the house and called, "Come along, Anne. It's time to go."

A woman stepped onto the porch of the neatly kept little house and rested one hand on the railing beside the steps. She hesitated, lifting her other hand to brush back a lock of blond hair that had escaped from under her bonnet. Anne Palmer was thirty-three years old, and though this made her a dozen years younger than her physician-husband, to her way of thinking it was too old for her to be uprooted like this. Especially since this move came less than a year after the one that had brought them from Virginia to San Francisco.

"I'm coming, Thaddeus," she told her husband, who was waiting rather impatiently beside the buggy, but she didn't step down from the porch. Instead she let her eyes drift over the scene in front of her. Their house was built on a hillside, affording a spectacular view of the city spread out below them, the harbor and the bay, the rounded tops of the Coast Ranges on the other side of the water, and far in the distance the more rugged peaks of the Sierra Nevadas. Anne had thought she would never become accustomed to living in San Francisco, and now that the strangeness was finally beginning to wear off, Thaddeus had them moving again.

"Please, Anne—" he began, then broke off abruptly and

went into a spasm of coughing. He bent over slightly, holding one fist to his mouth, as his body shook with deep, wracking coughs.

Concern for her husband made Anne forget about her bitterness over this departure. She hurried down the steps and went to him, putting one hand on his arm and the other on his back. "There, there, Thaddeus," she said. "It'll be all right." As always, she felt the same helpless frustration she experienced every time he had one of these fits. There was really nothing she could do for him except comfort him as they both waited for the spasm to pass.

After a few agonizing minutes, the coughing eased, and Palmer was able to stand up straight again. He drew a couple of deep breaths and pounded a fist against his chest. Then he turned a weary smile toward his wife and said, "That was a bad one, wasn't it?"

"I'm sorry I kept you waiting, Thaddeus. I'm ready now. Let's go."

Palmer nodded and took her arm, helping her to step up into the buggy. As she settled herself on the hard seat, he went around to the other side and climbed in. Anne cast a last glance at the house as Palmer picked up the reins. It was just a simple frame house, nothing special about it at all, she told herself. True, she had gone to quite a bit of trouble to make it into a home for them, and she had hoped that it would remain home to them for the rest of their lives. But a wife's place was with her husband, and she loved Thaddeus dearly, no matter how stubborn and irritating he could be at times. If he wanted to go to the gold fields, Anne had no real choice but to go with him.

Palmer flicked the reins against the backs of the pair of horses hitched to the buggy. The horses started forward, and the buggy rolled toward the harbor. The road down the hillside was rather steep, and Palmer handled the reins carefully, not wanting the vehicle to get away from him. Once they reached the docks, they would board a ferry with the buggy, and the ferry would take them across the bay where their real journey would begin.

Anne looked over at her husband as he concentrated on handling the team. His features were pale and drawn from the recent coughing episode, and there were more lines on his face now, more gray in his neatly trimmed beard, telltale signs of his failing health. More than once, Anne had heard him mutter bitterly under his breath, "Physician, heal thyself," but both of them knew there was no real cure for what ailed him. Moving to San Francisco had been a mistake; the cold, damp climate was bad for him.

That was one of the things that had led him to come up with the idea of going to the gold fields. Palmer had followed the story of the discovery of gold in the newspapers, and he had seen how men had flocked by the hundreds, perhaps even thousands, out of San Francisco and to the mountains in search of wealth. He was too old and frail to dig for gold himself, but the miners would need medical attention. There would be accidents, exposure to the elements, attacks by wild animals. Establishing a practice in the gold fields would not only be highly lucrative, he had explained to Anne, but he would also be doing some good, probably even saving some lives. And the thinner, drier air of the mountains might well be good for his condition, which had worsened since they had left Virginia.

Of course, Thaddeus had also been optimistic about the move to San Francisco. A new territory and a burgeoning new settlement would have need of doctors, he'd said, and eventually he had brought her around to his way of thinking. They had no children, no close family, nothing to keep them in Virginia. The move to California had been exciting. An adventure, Thaddeus had called it.

That was what had prompted Anne to agree. She had been married to Palmer for fifteen years, ever since she was eighteen. Prior to that she had lived on her father's plantation all her life, and after the wedding she and her new husband had settled down to a life together in Richmond. Palmer's practice was successful enough that they were quite comfortable, and at first Anne had enjoyed the security of being married to a doctor. For years everything had gone along smoothly, although they were somewhat disappointed when there were no children and evidently few prospects of any in the future. There were worse things than being barren, Anne told herself, and for the most part she believed it.

"This is going to work out just fine, Anne," Palmer said, breaking into her memories. "You'll see."

"I hope so, Thaddeus," she said. "I'm a little worried about living up there in the mining camps, though. Will we have to sleep in tents?"

Palmer laughed. "I don't think so. I've heard that some permanent settlements are being built. It won't all be rough-and-tumble, my dear."

"What about other women? Will there be any around?"

"I should certainly think so."

He didn't say anything else on that subject, and Anne knew what he was probably thinking. There would be women around the gold fields and the mining camps, that was true, but they would hardly be the respectable kind. Anne wasn't worried about being molested or harassed, however. Even the most hard-bitten ruffians knew enough to leave a decent woman alone. There was no quicker way to find yourself in bad trouble west of the Mississippi than to harm a respectable woman.

They reached the bay and the landing for the ferry, which was already loading. There was a line of wagons and buggies and men on horseback waiting for transport across the water.

Palmer maneuvered the buggy into line and the wait began. It took over a quarter of an hour, but finally they were on board. More time passed, and then the ferry moved out into the choppy waters of the bay.

"We're on our way at last," Palmer said as he reached over to grasp his wife's hand.

"Yes," Anne said. "We're on our way . . ."

Boone swung the pick, driving the head of it into the rocky hillside. He hauled up on the handle and pried loose another chunk of earth that tumbled down the slope past his feet. Boone bent closer to the hill and peered intently into the shallow depression he had just made.

Nothing but dirt. There wasn't even any gravel mixed in with the soil right here. He moved a couple of steps to his right and lifted the pick again, brought it down and felt the impact shiver up his arms as the point of the blade smacked into rock. That was more like it.

The sun shone down brightly in the narrow gully where Boone worked. The walls of the declivity seemed to trap the heat and hold it there, so that it felt like Boone was standing in a furnace as he swung the pick again and again. He had taken his shirt off earlier, and his long red underwear was dark with sweat. The floppy-brimmed hat he wore kept the sun off his head, but the back of his neck and his forearms were burned a dark reddish brown by weeks of exposure.

Boone paused, leaned on the pick for a few moments, and drew in deep breaths of the hot, dry air. When he looked around, he could see about a dozen other men working up and down the gully. He could hear their harsh breathing and the near-constant chinking of picks and shovels against the rocks, punctuated by the occasional heartfelt curse and the even less frequent cry of excitement whenever one of the miners spotted some color.

It was at times like this that Boone wished he were still panning for gold, instead of trying to dig it out of the ground. His belief that panning was the more profitable method of goldseeking had lasted a little over a month, during which time he had found only a fraction as much dust as what he had taken into Sutterville on his first trip to the settlement. The money he had gotten from Sam Brannan represented Boone's most substantial payoff from months of work. Beginner's luck, he supposed bitterly. And most of the luck he'd had since then had been bad.

Switching over to hard-rock mining hadn't made things any better in the long run. He found a few nuggets and once had uncovered what seemed to be a vein of gold, only to have it play out within ten inches. The vein, if such could be honored with that name, had been shallow as well as short, and Boone had gotten less than two hundred dollars' worth of gold out of that find. All in all, he doubted if he had taken even a thousand dollars out of these hills, and although that was more money than he'd made in years, it was nothing compared to the fortunes that other men were discovering every day.

Not only that, but prices were so high—forty dollars for a pound of flour, and a like amount for sugar—that small profits such as the ones Boone was making disappeared almost immediately. This was getting damned frustrating, he thought as he sleeved sweat off his forehead. He almost wished that James Marshall had never found that nugget in the millrace. Then Boone never would have known what he'd missed.

"Hey, Blakely!" The shout came from one of the other men working in the gully about fifty yards away from Boone. "Finding anything over there?"

Boone shook his head. "Not a damned thing," he called back.

The other miner shouldered his pick and strolled over, obviously tired and searching for an excuse to stop digging for a while. His name was Carson, Boone recalled.

"Nothing over there, either," Carson said with a weary grin. "Where do you reckon all them giant nuggets are that we keep hearin' about?"

"The ones worth thousands of dollars by themselves?" Boone replied with a tired grin of his own. "The ones that some bastard trips over while he's not even looking for gold?"

"Them's the ones." Carson chuckled. "I'm ready to stumble over one of 'em myself."

"Me, too," Boone agreed. He lifted the pick and swung it down again. "Reckon the only way gents like you and me will ever have anything, though, is if we work ourselves half to death for it."

"Yeah." Carson changed the subject by saying, "I went down to Missouri Flats the other day."

"That so?" Boone asked disinterestedly. Missouri Flats was one of the many mining camps springing up all over the foothills, but Boone had never been there.

"Felt the need of a drink," Carson went on, "and a woman, too. Heard tell that a fella brought some *Chilenos* out from San Francisco, and I thought I might have me a tumble with one of 'em."

Boone grunted. He had heard other miners talking about the Spanish prostitutes, some of them from Chile, who were so common in San Francisco these days. He didn't like to think about such things too much, though, because it had been a long time since he'd had a woman. Too damned long, in fact.

"Turned out it wasn't true," Carson said glumly. "There's barrels and barrels of homemade whiskey in Missouri Flats, but no women. I was right disappointed, let me tell you.''

"I can imagine.''

"Funny thing happened while I was havin' a drink in one of the tent saloons, though. Fella came in and started askin' questions, lookin' for somebody. He didn't name no names, but the description he gave out sounded a lot like you, Blakely.''

Boone lowered his pick and looked sharply at Carson. "What?''

"I said, this fella came into the saloon and was lookin' for somebody who sounded a lot like—''

Boone dropped the pick. His hands shot out and grasped the front of Carson's shirt, twisting in the woolen material and jerking the man toward him. Boone's lips drew back from his teeth in a grimace as he asked, "This stranger, what'd he look like?''

Carson licked his lips. Fear danced around in his eyes as he said, "He was tall, sort of slender but not skinny. Wore a big hat and had a moustache.'' The miner swallowed hard. "Talked a little like you, he did. Sort of slow and deliberate-like.''

A Texan, Boone thought. A pulse was pounding in his head as he asked, "Did he give his name?''

"Logan,'' Carson replied nervously. "Said his name was Dan Logan.''

Boone frowned. The name didn't mean anything to him, but the other things Carson had said did. There was only one reason somebody from Texas would have come all the way out here to California looking for him. The law had gotten on his trail somehow and sent somebody after him. This man Logan might be a deputy, or even a ranger.

Carson looked too damned scared for this to be simple gossip that he was passing on. Something else had happened in Missouri Flats, and Boone had a good idea what it was.

"Did you talk to this fella Logan?" he asked in a low, dangerous voice.

Carson licked his lips again. "Well, hell, Blakely, he was buyin' drinks for folks—"

"You did talk to him, didn't you?"

"I'm a friendly sort," Carson protested. "I didn't see nothin' wrong with havin' a drink with the man!"

"And when he asked if you'd ever seen anybody who looked like me around the diggin's?" grated Boone.

"I . . . I said I wasn't sure, that I might've—"

Boone turned, hauling Carson around with him, and thrust the man hard against the side of the gully. "You son of a bitch," Bonne said between clenched teeth. "You told him where to find me, didn't you? As soon as he bought you a drink, you sold me out!"

"I don't know nothin' about this!" Carson wailed. He was a large, powerful man, but whatever courage he possessed had evaporated in the face of Boone's anger. "I just told him I might've seen a gent who looked like the one he was talkin' about. But I didn't tell him you were up here, Blakely! I told him I seen you down on the Calaveras!"

Boone dragged a deep breath into his lungs and relaxed slightly. The Calaveras River was a good thirty or forty miles to the south. There had been some gold strikes there, too, or so he'd heard. "Are you saying you sent Logan in the wrong direction?"

Carson managed to nod. "I wouldn't sell you out, Blakely. Honest, I wouldn't."

Boone let go of the man's shirt and stepped back, taking another deep breath to calm himself some more. "All right," he said. "Sorry I jumped you, Carson. I've got some trouble behind me, and I don't want it catching up."

Holding his hands palms out toward Boone, Carson said,

"I don't want to know about it. That's your business." A sly look appeared on his heavy, beard-stubbled face. "But if you was to be a mite grateful to me for sendin' that gent off on the wrong trail, well . . ."

Boone understood now, and he had to suppress the urge to smash a fist into the middle of Carson's face. Carson had made it plain enough—Boone was going to have to pay him or risk Carson getting word to that man called Logan and telling him where the fugitive could be found. Carson had Boone in a corner, all right.

Or so he thought. Boone didn't like the idea of being forced into anything. He growled, "I'll show my gratitude by not killing you, Carson. I reckon you'd better go find yourself another claim, though, because if I see you again I'm liable to forget what I just said."

Carson's features hardened. "You got no call to talk to me like that," he began.

"I've got every right, you sneaking bastard." Boone stooped quickly and retrieved his pick, and his fingers curled tightly around the handle. "Get out of here now, or I'll put this pick through your skull. And don't even think about hunting up Logan and telling him where I am, because by then I won't be there anymore." Boone paused meaningfully and added, "By then *I'll* be looking for *you*."

Carson paled and swallowed hard again, then muttered, "No need to get so damned mad. I wouldn't cross you, Blakely. Folks like us got to stick together."

"I'm nothing like you," Boone said coldly. "Now git!"

Carson turned and picked up his shovel, casting a few worried looks over his shoulder as he hurried away. Boone watched him, well aware that some of the other men in the gully had paused in their work to watch the confrontation. He cursed silently. He had lost his temper and drawn attention to himself again, and one of these days that was going

to be his downfall. It would have been better if he had controlled his anger and maybe even paid off Carson for that
bit of misdirection in Missouri Flats. Then he could have
slipped away and headed in the opposite direction from that
Texan who was looking for him, maybe find a claim up on
the north fork of the American. There was gold up there,
too . . .

Boone cast a disdainful glance at the hillside where he
had been working, then shouldered his pick and turned his
back on the place. Either way, it was time for him to be
moving on.

He walked quickly out of the gully, following it until it
flattened out into a broad bench at the base of one of the
foothills. The creek formed a pool there, and a camp had
sprung up, one of hundreds of temporary settlements that
hadn't been in existence long enough to even have a name.
The camp would probably be gone before anyone got around
to naming it. To Boone it was just a place to pitch his tent.
The camp was all but deserted at this time of day, since there
were still a few hours of daylight left and the other inhabitants were out searching for gold. Boone headed for his tent,
which was pitched beside a thick-trunked pine.

He was only a few feet away from the tent when a man
stepped out from behind the pine, leveled a Walker Colt at
him, and said, "Elevate, Blakely! In the name of the state
of Texas, you're under arrest!"

Six

Boone froze where he was, staring at the man with the gun. The big revolver never wavered, and Boone knew it took a strong man to hold such a massive weapon steady.

His pulse hammered inside his skull as he met the stranger's cold stare. The man was tall and lean, just as Carson had said, and he sported a big white hat and a dark mustache that drooped over his wide mouth. He wore a faded blue bib-front shirt and buckskin pants tucked into high black boots. The gun belt looped around his waist was well cared for, as was the gun that had come from its holster.

Boone's lips had gone dry, but he managed not to lick them. He didn't want the man knowing that he was spooked. He put a faint smile on his face and managed to say, "I wish you'd point that hogleg somewhere else, mister. You've got the wrong man, and I don't want it going off by accident."

"If this Walker goes off, it won't be by accident," the stranger said. "And you're not the wrong man. Your name's Boone Blakely, and you're wanted for murder back in Texas."

Boone shook his head. "I never heard of anybody named Boone Blakely. My name's Smith, Tom Smith." He knew it sounded feeble, but it was difficult to think while staring down the big bore of the Colt.

"Don't waste our time by lying. I know damn well you're Blakely. I'm a Texas Ranger, name of Dan Logan, sent out here from San Antone to fetch you back, boy. You might've knowed you couldn't kill Judge Stoneham's son and get away with it."

Boone's tongue felt like a husk in his mouth. He said thickly, "You're wrong, mister. I didn't murder anybody."

"The law says different. Now put down that pick and lift your hands. My cap'n said to bring you back alive if I could, but I don't reckon too many folks'd shed any tears if I had to kill you."

That was too damned true, Boone thought bitterly. He had no family in Texas anymore. That was one reason it had been so easy to ram through that murder charge against him. With Samantha dead, there was no one to speak up for him. It had been a foregone conclusion that once the bodies were found, the law would come looking for him. That was why he had run, hard though it had been to leave Samantha behind like that.

Even now, on the bad nights, he sometimes woke up drenched in cold sweat, the horrible image of her once beautiful features battered into a bloody mess haunting his dreams . . .

He had to try again, even though it wouldn't do any good. "You've got the wrong man, I tell you—" he began.

"No, you don't, mister," someone said from behind Boone. "That's him, that's Boone Blakely."

Boone recognized Carson's voice. His jaw tightened, and he realized he had made a bad mistake by threatening the other miner and sending him back here to the camp to pack up and leave. Of course, there had been no way of knowing that the ranger would be here, too. Logan should have been down on the Calaveras, looking for him there.

Logan's gaze flicked toward Carson, but only for an instant, not long enough for Boone to jump him. Then, without looking at Carson, Logan said, "You look a lot like a gent I talked to over at Missouri Flats the other day. That fella told me the man I was looking for was a long ways south of here.''

"I—I was wrong," Carson said quickly. "Sorry, Mr. Logan. I thought I'd seen Blakely down there, but then he turned up here."

"And you didn't try to warn him that somebody was looking for him, did you?" Logan's tone was cold and mocking.

"No, sir, I wouldn't do that!" Carson said. "I wouldn't never interfere with the workin's of the law."

"Well, then, it's a good thing I decided to follow you, ain't it? Accident or not, you led me straight to the right spot. The state of Texas owes you some thanks."

Boone heard rapid footsteps as Carson came forward. "You mean there's some sort o' reward for Blakely?" Carson asked eagerly.

In his haste to step up and claim any bounty that might be on Boone's head, Carson got careless. His route took him within arm's length of Boone. Logan said sharply, "Look out, you damned fool—"

The warning came too late. Boone lunged to the side, toward Carson. His left hand grabbed Carson's arm, while his right whipped the pick off his shoulder and flung it toward Logan. The ranger ducked instinctively as the pick spun wickedly over his head.

At the same time, Boone shoved Carson toward Logan as hard as he could. Carson couldn't catch his balance in time, and he crashed into the man from Texas. Both of them went down. Boone was charging ahead right on the heels of Carson, and as he reached the fallen men, he lashed out with a foot. The toe of his work boot cracked against Carson's skull. The miner, who was sprawled on top of Logan, went limp as the blow knocked him out.

With Carson's dead weight holding him down, Logan couldn't bring his revolver to bear on Boone. Boone leaned over, straddling Carson and Logan, and smashed a fist against the side of the ranger's head. That punch stunned Logan, and Boone leaped past them to scoop up the pick he had thrown at Logan a few seconds earlier. He whirled, lifting the pick in both hands. A couple of fast blows would shatter the skulls of both Logan and Carson. Boone was filled with enough red rage to strike those blows, too.

But he stopped, the pick handle clutched tightly in his hands. If he killed Carson, the miner's friends would come after him, and if he killed Logan, the rangers would hear of it sooner or later and send someone else to find him. Next time, there would probably be more than one lawman after him, and they wouldn't have orders to bring him back for trial. They would gun him down wherever they found him.

Boone pulled in a deep, shuddery breath. Reason had triumphed over rage, and he was glad of it. The Sierra Nevadas were a big place, with lots of holes in which a man could hide. He had run before, and he could do it again.

He dropped the pick and stepped closer to the men. He wouldn't smash Logan's skull, but a good hard kick to the head would keep the ranger unconscious long enough for Boone to get a good lead on him. Boone drew back his foot.

Logan moved then, his arm shooting out with the speed of a striking snake, and Boone realized with a sick feeling in his stomach that the ranger had been at least partially playing possum. Logan grabbed Boone's ankle and yanked on it as hard as he could. Boone felt himself going over backward and pinwheeled his arms, trying to right himself, but Logan's unexpected move was too much for him to counter. He landed hard on his back as he fell.

Logan shoved the still-unconscious Carson aside and scrambled up on hands and knees. The big white hat had been knocked off his head during the ruckus, revealing a rumpled thatch of dark hair. He lunged toward Boone, lashing out with the revolver he still held in his right hand.

Boone rolled, avoiding the ranger's attack. He caught Logan's wrist and held on tightly, forcing the barrel of the Colt away from him. With his other hand, he sent a punch at Logan's face, but Logan ducked his head so that Boone's fist scraped almost harmlessly along the top of his skull. While his head was down, Logan lowered it even more and drove it into Boone's face.

As the two men struggled on the hard ground, Boone hammered a couple of blows into Logan's midsection, but it was like hitting a washboard. Boone felt his strength slipping away. Unlike the ranger, who was relatively fresh, Boone had been working in the gold fields all day, swinging the pick until he was halfway exhausted. He sensed that in a contest of endurance, he was going to give out before Logan did.

Which meant that he had to end this fight in a hurry. Instead of launching more blows at Logan with his bare hand, Boone reached out and scrabbled over the ground, searching for something he could use as a weapon. Logan was slowly but surely bringing the gun closer to Boone's head. If the ranger ever got the barrel lined up, Boone knew he was a dead man. At this range, a .44-caliber ball from a Walker Colt wouldn't leave much of his head behind.

Boone's fingers closed over a rock that was a little bigger than his fist. With a grimace of triumph, he closed his hand over the rock and brought it up in a sweeping blow aimed at Logan's head. The rock might crush Logan's skull and kill him, but at this point Boone had no choice. It was his life or Logan's.

The ranger must have sensed the rock coming, however, because again he frustrated Boone's desperate move. Logan hunched his shoulders and ducked his head once more, and the rock slammed into his left shoulder instead of the side of his head. Logan cried out in pain, and his finger jerked instinctively on the trigger of the Colt.

The gun blast sounded to Boone like a thousand crashes of thunder rolled into one as the Colt went off beside his head. The ball didn't hit him, though. It smashed into the ground a few inches from his ear, sending rock splinters slicing into that side of his face. Flecks of burning powder from the muzzle seared his skin. He screamed in pain, both from the rocks peppering him and the echoes of the blast that surged through his head like an ocean wave, seeming to grow ever louder and louder. From the corner of his eye as he instinctively jerked his head away, he saw the ranger's gun lifting again, then starting down toward him.

The last thing he thought before the Colt slammed into his head and sent him spiralling away into a well of blackness was that he should have killed Dan Logan while he had the chance.

Consciousness came back to Boone in bits and pieces. First there was a hideous slamming noise that echoed each time it struck. Then he became aware of a faint light that grew brighter until it was a red glare like flames in the bowels of hell. As the light grew stronger, it brought with it pain: sharp, intense bursts of pain that came in rhythm with the crashing noises.

Gradually, Boone became aware that the crashes were nothing but the sound of his pulse inside his skull, and the pain came with each beat of his heart. The light wasn't really connected. The noises faded somewhat, but the jolts were consistently agonizing.

Boone pried his eyelids open. They seemed to weigh as much as the mountains themselves. He winced as the glare from the campfire struck his eyes, making the clamor in his

head worse again. He could feel the heat of the flames
against his face now.

"Comin' around, are you?"

The question came from somewhere nearby, but Boone
was so disoriented that he couldn't locate the source. The
voice was familiar, and after a few seconds he remembered
where he had heard it before. It belonged to Dan Logan, the
Texas Ranger who had captured him, the man who intended
to take him back to Texas and see him hanged for murder.

Boone gasped as he tried to move his head so he could
see Logan. The ranger chuckled and said, "I expect you've
got one hell of a headache, Blakely. Sorry I had to hit you
so hard. Better'n gettin' your brains blowed out, though."

With his eyes watering from the heat and the glare of the
flames, Boone finally managed to lift his head and peer
across the fire at Logan, who sat on a log with his elbows
propped on his knees and a cup in his hands. He'd knocked
the big white hat back into shape, and it was settled on the
back of his head.

Boone felt a surge of hate for the Texas Ranger, but it
was wiped away in the next instant by a wave of sickness
that went through him. He shuddered and closed his eyes for
a long moment. When he opened them, the world seemed to
have righted itself a little and he wasn't quite so dizzy.

He was still helpless, though. Slowly, he was coming to
realize that the only thing he could move was his head. His
arms and legs wouldn't respond to any of the commands his
brain sent them, and in fact he could barely feel them. For
a few seconds, he was afraid that he was crippled, that the
blow to the head from Logan's .44 had done something to
him besides knocking him out. Then he looked down and
saw the rope looped and tied around his ankles. From the
feel of it, the same rope ran up to and around his wrists,

which were pulled uncomfortably behind his back. Logan had him trussed up like a pig.

Boone swallowed hard a couple of times, trying to work up some spit to moisten his mouth. The effort wasn't very successful, but he was able to say, "Is . . . is that coffee?" He croaked like a goddamned frog, he thought.

Logan nodded, an amiable enough expression on his face considering that the two of them had been doing their best to kill each other earlier. He sipped from the cup, then put it aside and stood up. "I'll set you up so's you can drink," he said as he came around the fire.

The ranger's Walker Colt was back in its holster, Boone noted. He wished he could get his hands free and get them on that gun for a few seconds. That was all it would take.

Logan wasn't the sort to be easily tricked, however. Boone could see that in the way he moved and carried himself— the watchfulness seemed ingrained in him. If Logan had been a ranger for very long, chances were he had fought Comanches and Mexican renegades and white outlaws by the dozen, and a man who survived such as that couldn't be taken lightly.

Logan gripped Boone's shoulders and pulled him upright. The motion made Boone sick again and he bent forward as the spasms hit him. He might have fallen over again if Logan hadn't held on to him.

"There you go," Logan said. "Are you sure your stomach's up to havin' some coffee?"

"I can handle it." Boone's voice was stronger now as the sickness in his gut subsided a little.

"Suit yourself," Logan said. He went back around the fire, took another tin cup from a pair of saddlebags that were draped over the log he had been sitting on, and filled the cup from a battered coffeepot that had been resting in the ashes at the edge of the fire. He used a rawhide glove from the saddlebags to protect his fingers from the hot metal handle of the coffeepot.

The ranger brought the cup over to Boone and knelt in front of him, holding the cup so that Boone could sip some of the steaming black liquid from it. Boone gasped at both the heat and the bitter taste of the coffee. "That stuff's so strong it could've walked around the fire by itself," he told Logan.

The comment drew a chuckle from Boone's captor. "You're right about that. It'll brace you up a mite if you give it a chance. Sorry I don't have any whiskey, or I'd put a dollop in the cup for you."

"Yeah, I'm sorry, too," muttered Boone. His stomach clenched as the coffee hit it, and he realized he was hungry. "Got any grub?"

"Some biscuits and jerky left over from my supper. You're welcome to 'em."

"Can't have a prisoner starving to death before you get him back to Texas, is that it?"

"Something like that," Logan said. "Have some more coffee, and then I'll get you that food."

For the next few minutes, they were both preoccupied with the meal. Boone had never realized how difficult it was to eat when you couldn't use your hands. Even with Logan feeding him bites of the jerky and biscuits, the experience was disorienting and uncomfortable. And he didn't want to even think about what would happen if the ranger wouldn't untie him so that he could relieve himself.

When Boone was finished with the food and had swallowed the rest of the cup of coffee, he leaned back against the rock by which he had been lying when he woke up. His head still ached like the devil, but he was feeling distinctly more human than when he had first regained consciousness. He watched as Logan perched on the log again and took out a pouch of tobacco and a pipe. Logan asked, "Want a smoke?" Boone shook his head.

While the ranger continued packing the pipe, Boone said, "I don't reckon it'd do any good to tell you again that you've got the wrong man."

"Nope." Logan took a burning twig from the fire and puffed the tobacco in the pipe into life. He blew out a cloud of smoke and said, "You're Boone Blakely, all right. You wouldn't have fought like a wildcat if you weren't."

"Yeah, I'm him. But I didn't murder anybody."

"Law says different. Says you murdered Jason Stoneham."

"I killed him," Boone said flatly. "But it wasn't murder. I was defending myself . . . and avenging Samantha McCarter."

Logan looked up sharply. "What are you sayin', Blakely? After you lit out the way you did, everybody figured you killed the McCarter girl, too, since you knew she was messin' around with Stoneham. It was just that there wasn't any way of provin' it. But half the folks in Indian Rock heard you talkin' about how you were goin' to kill Jason Stoneham, and they saw you ride out to his daddy's ranch. Wasn't an hour later that some of Judge Stoneham's hands found the boy, shot dead in the barn."

"What about the pitchfork?" Boone demanded.

Logan frowned and asked, "What pitchfork? I don't recollect hearin' anything about a pitchfork."

"He tried to run me through with it," Boone said in a quiet voice, a tremor running through him as his memory went back to that sunny, blood-drenched afternoon so long ago. "I found him in the barn and told him what a no-good bastard he was. I'd been out to the McCarter farm and found Samantha. He . . . he killed her because she'd told him not to bother her anymore. She told him she was going to marry me, and he couldn't stand the thought of losing to some no-account drifter without any family. So he beat her to death right then and there, while her pa and her brothers were working out in the fields.'' Boone's voice shook, just like his insides, as he went on, ''That was why I went after Jason Stoneham, why I had to find him. He acted like he didn't know what the hell I was talking about when I told him Samantha was dead, but he knew, all right. And when I made the mistake of turning my back on him, he tried to put that pitchfork right through me. I got out of the way just in time, and then . . . well, hell, yes, I shot him, Logan. What man wouldn't have?''

Logan had sat quietly through Boone's story, the frown on his face deepening as the words tumbled out from the prisoner. Now the ranger asked, ''If all that's true, you could've stood trial and told what happened. Why didn't you?''

Boone laughed bitterly. ''Stood trial in the court of the man whose son I'd killed?'' He shook his head. ''What chance would I have had, Logan? Who would've listened to me, whether I told the truth or not? Nobody around Indian Rock has more money or more power than Judge Stoneham. I'd've been dangling from a tree limb less than an hour after any trial started, and you know it.''

''So you ran.''

''Damn right I ran. Jason Stoneham deserved to die.''

Logan puffed reflectively on the pipe for a few moments without saying anything, then he took it from his mouth and pointed the stem at Boone. ''I got no way of knowin' if you're tellin' the truth about this or not, and anyway, that's for somebody else to decide. All I know is that there's a warrant out for your arrest on the charge of murder, and I intend to take you back to Texas to face that charge. If it all happened like you said, then I'm sorry as hell, boy, but there's not a damned thing I can do about it. For what it's worth, though, I reckon they'll bring in another judge from somewhere else to hear the trial. You won't go before Judge Stoneham.''

Boone grimaced. ''If you think that'll really make a difference, Logan, you're dumber than I thought you were.''

''You'd best shut up talk like that. We got a long ways to go, Blakely, and the trip can be a hard one or an easy one. It's up to you, mister.'' Logan stood up and slipped a bowie knife from a sheath on his left hip. He started around the fire toward Boone, firelight glittering on the long, heavy blade of the knife. He stooped, and a slash of the bowie parted the rope between Boone's ankles and wrists. Logan shoved the prisoner forward so that Boone was lying face down in the dirt next to the fire. As Logan began to cut the bonds around Boone's wrists, he said, ''I'm goin' to tie your hands in front of you so you can get around a little better and tend to your business. You try anything now and I'll put this bowie right through you. Any tricks later on and I'll shoot you down. You understand what I'm tellin' you, Blakely?''

''I understand,'' Boone replied, his voice muffled by his position.

''Good. Because like I said, I'd hate to have to kill you before I got you back to Texas.''

Boone's wrists came free, and as Logan stepped back, Boone followed the ranger's commands and rolled over to sit up again. His arms and shoulders were numb, and sharp pains began to shoot through them as the blood flow returned to normal. He looked up at Logan, who had palmed out the Colt and was covering him. With a grim smile, Boone said, ''Even after I told you what happened back in Texas, you'd shoot me down if I tried to escape, wouldn't you?''

''Damn right I would,'' Logan said. ''Might not like it, but I'd do it.''

"Don't worry, Logan. I won't give you any trouble."

At least not yet, Boone added to himself. Not until Logan had had more time to think about what Boone had told him. He had seen the suspicion in the ranger's eyes when he started talking, and he had seen the doubt begin to creep into Logan's expression by the time he was finished. The injustice of the whole thing was already starting to eat on the lawman from Texas, at least a little bit.

For now, Boone was counting on that. It was a slim hope, but better than none. He was still going to need a miracle to come out of this mess with a whole skin.

But the Sierra Nevadas were full of miracles these days, weren't they? Just ask any miner who'd tripped over a gold nugget and made his fortune by falling down . . .

Seven

As he tried to stay in the saddle of the mule that was carrying him down the side of the mountain, Nathan Jones hung on desperately to the reins and the saddle horn. The mule's gait wasn't particularly rough, but even after several months in the gold fields, Nathan was still not accustomed to riding the animal. He would have preferred to walk, and much of the time he was forced to do just that, due to the narrowness of the trails in the Sierra Nevadas. But the path he was on today was nice and wide, and Nathan was tired. He hadn't thought it would hurt anything to ride for a while.

He let out a frightened yelp as the mule went around a bend in the trail. That made Nathan's weight shift, and he slipped in the saddle again. Clamping down tighter with his legs, he hung on and caught his balance, straightening up again.

This was ridiculous, Nathan thought. He already had to lead the pack mule, which was loaded with provisions brought from San Francisco and paid for by his Aunt Emily, so he might as well lead the other animal, too. He hauled back on the reins, but it was several seconds before he could manage to bring the mule to a halt.

Taking a deep breath to steady himself, Nathan slid down from the saddle and stood beside the mule. He patted the stolid animal on the flank and then turned around to look at the scene presenting itself to him.

The view from this mountainside trail was magnificent, Nathan had to admit that. The Middle Fork of the American

River, along with several other smaller tributary streams, meandered through narrow valleys spread out below him. The
hills forming the valleys were covered with pine and spruce
and juniper, the thick stands of trees occasionally interrupted
by rocky clearings that stood out from this height. The
streams themselves were like blue ribbons among the green
and brown of the wilderness. Arching over everything was
a deep blue sky dotted with a few fluffy white clouds.

The landscape was lovely, Nathan thought. At least it was
appealing from a distance. It was less attractive close up,
especially when you were trying to chip a fortune out of it
with a pick and shovel.

The trail he was on began in a fairly new settlement called
Murderer's Bar. The name of the place had made him nervous while he was there, but there was little to distinguish the
settlement from dozens of other mining camps that had
sprung up like weeds in the months since the news of the
gold strike had first become common knowledge in San
Francisco. A scattering of tents, a few rough buildings made
of timber and oilcloth and tin, a couple of more substantial
log cabins—that was Murderer's Bar. Nathan had no idea
how the camp had gotten its name. Some of the inhabitants
looked rugged enough to be killers, but so did some of the
men in every settlement he'd visited since coming up here.

All the land around Murderer's Bar already had claims
staked on it, so Nathan had stayed there only long enough
to buy a few supplies and rest his mules. Emily had given
him some money to purchase the things he ran out of, but
neither of them had counted on the incredibly high prices of
goods in the mining camps, nor on the scarcity of provisions,
which led to a sort of rationing system. He bought his flour
and salt a few pinches at a time, rather than by the pound,
and as for sugar, he had almost forgotten what it tasted like.

After leaving Murderer's Bar, he had struck out for a place

with an equally unlovely name: Tar Ridge. Word was that quite a few nuggets had been found in the vicinity, and Nathan was only one of dozens of men streaming toward Tar Ridge. He had seen probably a score of miners during the day, all of them pushing on deeper into the mountains.

The trail followed a ledge about twenty feet wide around the shoulder of this peak. The drop to Nathan's left—probably a couple of hundred feet—was fairly steep, although not sheer. The slope could have been negotiated carefully, but if a man ever made one misstep, he wouldn't stop tumbling for a long time.

Nathan took a deep breath and looked up at the sun. There were still a few hours of daylight left, but he needed to push on if he was going to be able to reach Tar Ridge by nightfall. He didn't want to have to make camp out here on the trail.

Bunching the lines of both mules in his right hand, he began trudging down the path. He wore high black boots, canvas pants, a red woolen shirt, suspenders, and a black hat that had sported an elegant crease in its crown when he left San Francisco. Now the hat had been rained on, stomped by the mules, and generally battered enough to make it nearly shapeless. Nathan had come to hate the hat almost as much as he hated the mules.

"Come on, you damned jackasses," he muttered as he tugged on the lines. Most of the time the mules allowed him to lead them, only occasionally balking and refusing to move at all, but even when they appeared to be cooperating, they had a way of hanging back just slightly that made him work all the harder. He felt as if he had dragged them halfway over the Sierra Nevadas and back.

He *had* covered quite a bit of ground since beginning this expedition. After Emily Woodward had made the rounds of the stores in San Francisco and outfitted him, he and the mules had ridden the ferry across the bay and then skirted

the low, rounded peaks of the Coast Ranges into the great
central valley of the Sacramento and the San Joaquin. That
broad valley with its rich soil and thick grasslands had struck
Nathan as perfect farming country, although he was hardly
an expert on farming. Indeed, some of the *Californios*, the
Mexican settlers who had managed to hang on to their land
despite the American takeover, had vast *ranchos* in this area,
and Nathan had passed more than one impressive *hacienda*
on his journey. He steered well clear of the sprawling adobe
houses, though, since the *vaqueros* who rode for the Mexican
ranchers were notoriously unfriendly to Americans. And
there were plenty of Americans to spark their ire, a constant
stream of them, in fact, going back and forth between the
coast and the gold fields inland.

Following the American River past Sutterville, Sutter's
Fort, and finally Sutter's Mill, Nathan thought that the man
certainly knew how to get his name on a lot of places. Nathan wondered briefly if anyone would ever name anything
after him, but the thought was too ludicrous for him to take
it seriously.

All along the way he had seen men panning for gold in
the river, standing hip-deep in the stream or kneeling beside
it, swirling their tin pans and peering anxiously to see if there
was any color in the bottoms of them. That seemed too difficult to Nathan, especially when in every camp there were
stories of men digging giant nuggets out of the hillsides or
uncovering actual veins of gold in the earth. That approach
appealed more to Nathan, so he used the pick and shovel he
had brought along, found what looked like a suitable spot,
at least to his untrained eyes, and started digging. He realized
he was an amateur at this, but so were most of the other
men swarming over the hills. Only a few of them had ever
done any mining in the past.

He had stayed a week at the first place he'd stopped, upriver a few miles from Coloma, the village that had grown up around Sutter's Mill, site of the first discovery. In that time he had found only a few small nuggets, enough to excite him at first. That initial excitement had quickly worn off, however, when several days passed with no more signs of gold at all. Growing impatient, Nathan had moved on, stopping again after he had traveled another mile.

This time he was less tolerant of failure and quicker to move on when it became obvious to him that he wasn't going to strike it rich in this particular spot. That pattern was repeated several more times as he wandered north and west, leaving the river to follow some of the smaller creeks in hopes that the more isolated areas wouldn't have so many men already scouring them for the precious metal.

There didn't seem to be a square yard of ground anywhere Nathan went that didn't have men gouging it up with picks and shovels. He knew that was an exaggeration, of course; these foothills and mountains were a vast area, and thousands of men could only barely begin to cover them.

Sooner or later, though, at the rate fortune-seekers were pouring into the Sierra Nevadas, such a fate might be true. Nathan had already heard it said that a man couldn't piss without the stream landing on somebody else's claim.

His feet began to ache as he led the mules along the trail. The path continued to twist and inexplicably turned upward again, just when Nathan thought it was about to finish its descent back into the river valley. From the crest of the slope, he caught his first glimpse of the settlement at Tar Ridge. It was still several miles ahead of him, but he could make out several light-colored dots against the backdrop of a bluff and knew they were tents.

He lost sight of the camp as the trail rounded another bend and suddenly dropped sharply. Nathan came to an abrupt stop and put out a hand to stop the mules. A dozen feet in front of him, the trail narrowed down until it was about a yard wide. Nathan swallowed hard. There was room for him to walk down the trail and lead the mules single file, and again, the drop-off to the left wasn't sheer. But it was still steep enough to make him slightly dizzy when he looked down. He just wasn't cut out for picking his way along these trails like some sort of mountain goat, he thought.

But maybe Tar Ridge was where his luck would change, he told himself. The reports from there were very good. Men were taking thousands of dollars worth of gold out of their claims, it was said. He couldn't turn back.

"Come on, now," he said aloud to the mules, knowing the beasts were too brainless to understand him. The sound of his own voice was a little reassuring to him, though, and maybe it would be to the mules, too. He started forward, getting the mules going again with a series of sharp tugs on the reins, and placed his feet carefully as the trail narrowed and slanted down.

About a hundred yards ahead of him, the path curved again, disappearing around an outcropping of rock. Nathan couldn't see beyond it, had no way of knowing how much farther this stretch continued. He hoped it was short. The day was warm, but not all the sweat he felt trickling down his body under his shirt came from the heat.

A sudden rumble made him look up. His breath caught in his throat. Was that the sound of an avalanche? Anxiously, his eyes scanned the slopes above him and saw nothing unusual. The noise came again, low and menacing, and he looked off to the south, where the sound seemed to be coming from. His view in that direction was largely blocked by the mountain, but he saw the fringes of some dark clouds gathering beyond the peak. A storm was coming up.

"Oh, no," Nathan breathed. A downpour was all he needed to complicate his trip down this treacherous path.

Rain would make it difficult to see, as well as causing the rocky trail to become dangerously slippery. He and the mules could slide right off the path and go plummeting down the side of the mountain, even if they were careful.

Take it easy, he told himself. Panicking wasn't going to help his situation. The thunder was quite a distance away, and it would take some time before the storm reached him. It might even miss him completely. With any luck, he would be at the bottom of this difficult stretch of trail before the rain started.

He didn't let the mules stop, because it would just take more time to get them started again. The bend up ahead drew nearer, and after several long minutes, Nathan reached it. He stepped around the rocky outcropping, anxious to see how much farther the trail continued like this.

Nathan froze in his tracks again. Plodding up the trail toward him from the other direction was another man, leading a single mule.

The man spotted Nathan at about the same time and came to a stop. He was short and thick-bodied, with a bushy salt-and-pepper beard that covered most of his leathery face. He was dressed in filthy buckskins and the felt hat crammed over his dark hair was as battered and shapeless as Nathan's. Something was wrong with one of his eyes; it wandered aimlessly, independent of the other eye, and the pupil was milky. A thick, ropy red scar slanted across the man's face above and below that eye, and it was easy to see that he had suffered some sort of hideous injury in the past. His good eye narrowed suspiciously as he peered up the trail at Nathan.

"What you doin' up there, boy?" he demanded in a harsh voice.

"I . . . I'm on my way to Tar Ridge," Nathan replied.

"This is the right trail, isn't it? They said back in Murderer's Bar for me to follow it."

The bearded man nodded. "They told you a-right. Tar Ridge is back yonder a ways." He inclined his head in the direction from which he'd come. "You can't get there from here, though."

Nathan frowned. "Why not?" He could see past the bearded man and could tell that the narrow section of the trail ended some fifty yards farther on, widening out into a much safer path that led all the way down into the valley to run alongside the stream until it reached Tar Ridge.

The man snorted in disgust at Nathan's question. "Why not?" he repeated. "Any damn fool can see why not. 'Cause you're in my way, that's why not. This trail ain't wide 'nough for both of us to pass."

"But . . . the narrow part ends right there behind you," Nathan pointed out, his confusion growing. "It won't take long for you to back up and let me by, then you can have the trail to yourself."

"Back up?" The man spat out the words like they had a bitter taste. "Jack LeCarde don't back up for nobody, sonny. You know what they call me 'round here?"

Nathan shook his head wordlessly.

"Cougar Jack," the man growled as he squinted his good eye even more. " 'Cause I'm as mean as a cougar and I eat pilgrims like you for breakfast. I trapped all over the Rockies with Bridger and Hugh Glass and them boys. I seen Colter's Hell and the Grand Canyon of the Yellowstone and the Great Falls of the Missouri. I'm Cougar Jack, and I sure as hell don't back up for *nobody*!"

"But . . . but surely you don't expect me to . . . it's more than twice as far back up to the other end!"

Cougar Jack folded his arms across his broad chest and glared at Nathan. "If you reckon you're man enough to budge me, you just come on and try it. But I warn you, better men than you have tried before and wound up slit from gizzard to gullet for their trouble!''

Nathan looked at the big hunting knife sheathed on the man's hip. There was a pistol tucked behind Cougar Jack's belt, too. As Nathan weighed his chances of forcing the old mountain man to move—which were pretty slim, he figured—a low-pitched rumble of thunder sounded once again.

"All right," Nathan said, his shoulders slumping in defeat. "I'll see if I can get these mules to back up. It may not be easy, though."

"Smack 'em a few times 'tween the eyes with a gun butt," advised Cougar Jack. "That'll get their attention."

Cursing to himself, Nathan began struggling with the mules. They were as recalcitrant as usual. If the path had been a little wider, he would have tried to make them turn around, but there wasn't enough room for that. He had to force them to back up, and they wouldn't go more than a few feet at a time without balking. The thunder continued to grow louder, and Nathan realized in dismay that he would never reach the camp at Tar Ridge before the storm hit.

"Keep a-goin'," Cougar Jack called up to him. "And let this be a lesson to you, boy."

"What lesson?" Nathan asked bitterly.

Cougar Jack frowned at that, and his bad eye jerked back and forth agitatedly. "Don't rightly know," he finally mumbled, "but there's got to be one. Don't get in the way, and respect your elders. One o' them'll do, I reckon."

There was another lesson Nathan could think of, one that had been impressing itself on him ever since he had left San Francisco and ventured into this rugged wilderness.

Don't try to be something you're not.

•   •   •

Rain slanted down from the sky in coarse silver sheets as Nathan trudged into the camp a couple of hours later, leading the mules. He was soaked to the skin and shivering with cold. Black clouds had rolled in and covered the sun, taking away the warmth and bringing a dank chill in advance of the rain itself. Now night was closing in earlier than usual due to the overcast.

Even under these miserable conditions, Nathan counted himself lucky. He had lost over half an hour in backing up his mules so that Cougar Jack LeCarde could ascend the narrow trail, but the storm had held off long enough for Nathan to reach the bottom without any mishaps. He had been taking a chance to start down the second time with a storm looming nearby, but he didn't want to try to wait out the rain on the side of the mountain. He had heard too much about mudslides and avalanches to feel safe doing that.

Cougar Jack and his mule had disappeared down the trail to Murderer's Bar, and Nathan felt fortunate that the man hadn't tried to gut him with that hunting knife. The light of insanity had been shining in the man's good eye; Nathan felt sure of that.

The rain had begun soon after Nathan reached the bottom of the trail, first as large, heavy, widely spaced drops, then as a sluicing downpour. Nathan had an oilcloth slicker he'd dug out of one of his packs, but so much rain dripped down the collar of the garment that he might as well not even be wearing it. The dusty trail seemed to turn instantly to thick, clinging muck as soon as the rain hit it, and with each step he had to make an effort to pull his boots free of the mud's grip. The mules didn't like the rain, either, and they were more stubborn than ever. Nathan put the reins over his shoulder and leaned forward, pulling the beasts along.

He had finally reached the settlement, and through the rain he could see the yellow glow of lanternlight up ahead, shin-

ing through the canvas of a large tent. It was probably a
saloon, Nathan knew, and although he wasn't much of a
drinking man, at least he could get out of the rain for a while.
The place might even have a stove where he could warm up
a little.

A large piece of canvas had been tied between some tree
trunks to form a crude shelter next to the saloon, and several
horses and mules stood under it, their heads drooping dis-
piritedly. Rain blew into the makeshift stable despite the canvas covering over the heads of the animals, but it was better
than nothing, Nathan supposed. He led his own mules into
the shelter and tied their reins to a thick post that had been
driven into the ground for that purpose.

Over the pounding of the rain, Nathan could hear laughter
and the sound of a fiddle being scraped inside the big tent.
He left the mules in the shelter and went around to the front
of the tent, thrusting aside the flap over the entrance and
stepping inside.

The place was packed with men, the air hazy with smoke
from more than a dozen pipes. Tobacco wasn't the only thing
in the air; the smell of unwashed men, wet wool, and stale
beer also assaulted Nathan's senses. He stood there in the
entrance and looked around, seeing that a bar of sorts had
been set up in the back of the tent by laying planks across
the tops of several barrels. Those big kegs no doubt con-
tained homemade beer and whiskey, which was being dispensed by three burly men behind the bar. They were kept
busy filling tin cups and wooden buckets from the kegs, in
exchange for nuggets or small pouches of gold dust being
passed across to them by the clamoring customers. An old
man with white whiskers danced a jig in one corner while
playing a fiddle, and some of the men standing around
watching him clapped their hands in time with the music.
Nathan didn't recognize the tune, but it was loud and rau-

cous, and he supposed that was all that was required in a
place like this.

A man standing near the entrance turned and glowered at
Nathan. "You gonna stand there all night with the door
open, boy?" he demanded.

Nathan stepped into the tent saloon and let the canvas flap
fall shut behind him. There were a couple of lanterns sitting
on the bar and another hung from the ridge pole of the tent,
all three giving off harsh yellow light and smoke and fumes
from their burning oil. The acrid tang of the oil was no worse
than the other odors in the air, however. Nathan muttered,
"Sorry," to the man who had complained about his holding
the entrance flap open, then moved toward the bar at the rear
of the tent. Several men bumped into him heavily along the
way, but he didn't complain. After the day he'd had, getting
into a fight was the last thing he wanted.

When he finally reached the bar, one of the men on the
other side of the planks asked curtly, "What'll it be?"

Nathan shivered in his wet clothes. "You don't have a
stove in here where I could dry off, do you?"

The bartender laughed. " 'Round here, folks tend to warm
up by drinkin'. We got beer and some fine rye whiskey.
What'll you have?"

Nathan knew the "fine rye whiskey" had probably been
mixed in a tub out back of the tent saloon, a blend of alcohol,
gunpowder, strychnine, and God knew what else. He had
heard tales of men going blind or having fits after drinking
such concoctions, so it would be safer to stick to something
milder. "A bucket of beer," he told the bartender.

The man filled one of the small buckets that sat on a
rough-hewn shelf behind the bar, but before passing it over
he said, "It'll cost you a pinch of dust, lad."

Nathan shook his head. "I don't have any dust, but I've
a few nuggets."

"Let's see 'em," the bartender said coldly.

Nathan put his hand in his pocket and brought out practically all he had to show for the miserable months he'd spent up here in the hills. Half a dozen nuggets rested on his palm, ranging in size from a little bigger than a pea to one almost as large as a man's eye. The bartender grunted and took the smallest one. "That'll buy you this bucket and a couple more," he told Nathan.

Nathan wasn't interested in drinking that much, but evidently the saloonkeeper didn't make change, which was understandable considering that nearly everyone in the camps paid in gold, either nuggets or dust. Arguing wouldn't do any good, so Nathan just nodded and picked up the bucket. He took a long swallow of the beer, which, as he has expected, managed to be both bitter and watery. It did warm his belly a bit, though.

Water dripping from the clothes of the customers and seeping in under the edges of the tent had turned the normally hard-packed earthen floor into mud, although it was not as thick as what was underfoot outside. There were a few crude tables scattered around the room, with smaller kegs serving as chairs, and by being patient and moving quickly when one of the miners left the tent, Nathan finally managed to sit down and rest his legs. He ached all over, but as he finished his second bucket of beer, the stuff began to have a sort of numbing effect. He was getting drunk, he realized, but pleasantly so. Someone handed him another bucket, and he tilted it to his mouth, spilling some of the beer down the front of his shirt, which was already so wet that the spill made no difference.

He didn't remember buying more beer after that, but he must have, he realized later. Never one to drink very much, the beer affected him more than he would have thought possible. But at least he didn't hurt so much anymore, and the soaked clothes no longer bothered him. He had no idea how many of the buckets he drained before he finally passed out.

Nathan woke up with his cheek pressed against the table. Splinters from the roughly sawn wood dug painfully into his skin. He groaned as a ball of sickness expanded to fill his belly and then welled up his throat. When he tried to lift his head, the world spun crazily around him and he slipped off the keg he had been sitting on. He landed on the muddy ground with a soggy thud.

Most of the miners had left the saloon. A few men were still sitting around another table, gambling, and the lantern that had been placed on that table was the only light still burning in the place. Hours had gone by, Nathan realized as he lay there on the ground and tried to keep his head as still as possible. Exhaustion, tension, and the buckets of beer had taken a toll on him, stealing away his senses for an uncounted time.

He looked up and saw that the bartenders were among the men playing cards at the other table. The saloon must be closed for the night. He let out a groan, and the man who had served him earlier looked over his shoulder.

"You can't sleep here, boy," the man said. "Since you're awake again, get up and get out. This ain't no damned hotel."

"I . . . I'm sick," Nathan gasped.

"That don't make no nevermind to me. Get your ass outta here, or we'll throw it out."

Nathan got his hands against the ground and heaved himself upward. "I'm going," he muttered, trying to fight off the waves of nausea that battered him every time he moved. He got to his feet somehow and stumbled toward the entrance.

As he pushed past the flap he saw that the rain had stopped. The air was clear and cold, with stars sparkling brightly in the black sky over his head and a newly risen half-moon glowing in the east. The fresh air had a bit of a bracing effect, and he felt a little stronger as he forced his unsteady steps toward the shelter where he had left the mules. He shuddered at the thought of having to pitch his tent somewhere before he could crawl into it and go back to sleep, but he couldn't spend the night in the open.

There was enough light from the moon and stars for him to make out the dark bulks of the animals under the canvas shelter. Nathan hoped none of the mules would kick him as he moved among them, searching for the pair he had left there earlier. His senses were still so dulled that it took him several moments to realize they weren't there.

Panic replaced the sickness inside him. His pulse hammered frantically. The mules were gone, and with them all his gear. Had they pulled their reins loose from the hitching post and wandered off? Nathan was certain he tied them securely, and since he had been sober when he left them there, he was sure they could not have gotten loose on their own.

That left only one answer. Somebody had stolen them.

The realization hit Nathan's brain like a physical blow. Here he was, alone and friendless in a rough-and-tumble mining camp, and all of his supplies were gone. He was lost, helpless, devastated. At the moment, his brain was so fuzzy from the beer and the despair washing through him that he couldn't see any way out of this dilemma. He turned and started to stumble out of the makeshift stable, but his feet would no longer carry him. He fell to his knees, and his mud-spattered hands came up to cover his face.

Silently, his shoulders shaking from the depth of his misery, Nathan Jones began to cry.

Eight

Emily Woodward strode determinedly along the street that lined the harbor. The place was a beehive of activity, and Cassandra was hard put to keep up with her mother and not be separated from her by some of the dozens of men and wagons and horses and carts that filled the street. As usual, Emily seldom looked back to see that her daughter was still with her. Where Emily was concerned, one either kept up or was left behind.

Months had passed since their arrival in San Francisco, and Cassandra found herself surprised almost daily that they were still here. She had expected that they would return to Boston before now, especially since the store was such a disaster, but Emily was stubbornly hanging on to the idea that she could turn the enterprise into a success.

Her mother had a right to that belief, Cassandra thought. After all, in the years since her husband's death Emily had turned one emporium in Boston into a chain of successful stores in cities across New England. Before that, while Cassandra's father was still alive, Emily had been content to be a wife and mother, but after she was widowed, everything had changed. True, she could have married again; she was still relatively young and attractive, and there was no shortage of respectable gentlemen callers at the Woodward house on Beacon Street. But Emily had discovered that she enjoyed the business world, despite the fact that so few females were allowed into it, and she found as well that she had a knack for turning a profit. The idea of opening a store in San Francisco had occurred naturally to her when the Americans had taken over the city the previous year and word of its rapid growth reached Boston.

"Come along, Cassandra. Don't dawdle."

The words weren't spoken in a particularly sharp tone, but Cassandra flinched a little anyway. Her mother was not possessed of an abundance of patience, either for herself or anyone else. Cassandra hurried along behind Emily, unsure why her mother had insisted that she come along today on this errand.

In the harbor to their right, scores of ships lay idly at anchor, most of them deserted. San Francisco was a busy port, but ever since the news of the gold strikes had spread, the crews of ships that docked there often deserted as soon as the vessels were tied up. Ships' captains had started dropping anchor far out in the harbor and unloading their cargo slowly, in small boats, to make it more difficult for crewmen to abandon their tasks and head for the hills in search of gold. But for the most part, the captains' effort had come too late. When Cassandra glanced at the harbor, she could barely see the waters of the bay for all the ships docked there.

Some of the ships had not even been brought to the piers but merely run aground before ever reaching the docks. A few enterprising men had found a use for the beached, deserted vessels, and as Emily and Cassandra made their way down the street, they saw several teams of mules hauling one of the abandoned ships into an open space between two buildings. The ship was called the *Niantic*, and Cassandra had heard that there were plans to turn it into a hotel. Up and down the street, other vessels had been dragged onto solid ground and turned into hotels, restaurants, and stores. It made for a bizarre sight as the prows of ships protruded abruptly from between more normal structures.

San Francisco was thriving again. When the Woodward women had arrived in the settlement, it was only sparsely populated, most of the citizens having scurried off to the gold fields. Now, though, with the constant influx of miners into the city, hundreds of them arriving daily from all over the country, businesses were opening again and some of the newcomers were electing to stay behind and try to make their fortunes by catering to the needs of the goldseekers. A "boom town," people had begun to call it, and that was exactly what it was becoming.

There was still the problem of supplies. Emily had managed to secure a small amount of inventory for the store, but she and Cassandra sold almost all of the goods as soon as the items were placed on the shelves. They could have done ten times as much business if only the necessary merchandise had been readily available.

This trip today had something to do with that, Cassandra knew. Emily was going to see a man called Sam Brannan, who had recently opened a large store near the harbor. Brannan had come to San Francisco from a place known as Sutterville, as Cassandra recalled being told. According to her mother, that settlement had grown and merged with another new village into a good-sized town named Sacramento City, after the river on which the rapidly growing community was located. Brannan still had his store in Sutterville, or rather Sacramento City, but he was expanding his enterprises to San Francisco.

Cassandra came up alongside her mother and asked, "Do you really think this Mr. Brannan will help you find some merchandise? After all, the two of you are competitors."

"From what I've heard of Sam Brannan," replied Emily, "he wants San Francisco to grow by leaps and bounds. That growth will require more than one successful emporium. Mr.

Brannan can help himself in the long run by lending us some assistance.''

''Well, if you say so, Mother,'' Cassandra said dubiously.

Both women wore plain, tasteful dresses, Emily's of dark brown material, Cassandra's a simple gray. There were other women on the streets now, respectable women with husbands and families. San Francisco was still a rather wild place most of the time, but the new inhabitants were having something of a civilizing effect on it. The city had a long way to go before it was as genteel as Boston, however, and it might not ever achieve that level.

Cassandra was not sure she wanted San Francisco to become like Boston. The brawling, sprawling settlement by the bay had its own personality, she thought, a mixture of brazen hussy and rugged goldseeker and jaded traveler. A part of Cassandra thrilled to the colorful, somewhat dangerous air that San Francisco seemed to cultivate. Living in Boston had never been like this. Aware that she had been rather sheltered as a child and a young woman, she appreciated the fact that out here she was exposed to a great deal more of life, its pleasant aspects and its ugly sides as well.

Surprised as she might have been that she and her mother had not yet returned to Boston, Cassandra was happy about that turn of events, too.

A few minutes later, she and her mother reached Sam Brannan's store, which was a large, two-story frame building across the street from the harbor. When they went inside, Cassandra saw that the shelves were better stocked than the ones in Woodward's Emporium, but even here there were quite a few empty spaces where goods had been sold and not yet replaced.

A tall man with bushy muttonchop whiskers and a small goatee came forward to greet them. He wore a well-cut suit and carried himself with an air of prosperity. ''Good morning, ladies," he said. "I'm Sam Brannan. What can I do to help you?"

"I am Mrs. Emily Woodward. I sent you a note, Mr. Brannan, requesting that you and I meet regarding business."

Brannan's face split in a grin as he said, "Of course. I'm very glad to meet you, Mrs. Woodward." He took Emily's hand, and for a second Cassandra thought he was going to kiss it like some sort of European nobleman. He just gave Emily's fingers a brief shake, though, as he went on, "I've heard that you're quite the canny businesswoman. Will I be cutting my own throat by talking to you?"

"Only if you've no interest in seeing San Francisco become a large, vital, successful city," Emily told him.

"I wouldn't have done all the things I've done if that was not my aim, Mrs. Woodward." Brannan gestured toward the rear of the store. "Come back to my office, and we'll discuss whatever you'd like." He looked at Cassandra and lifted his heavy eyebrows. "And this is?"

"My daughter Cassandra," Emily said briskly.

"Hello, young lady," murmured Brannan as he nodded to her, but Cassandra could tell that he had already largely lost interest in her.

Emily and Cassandra followed Brannan into a small office at the rear of the store, where they sat in leather-upholstered chairs while Brannan took a seat behind the paper-cluttered desk. He leaned back in his chair and asked, "How can I be of assistance to you, Mrs. Woodward?"

Emily didn't waste any time on preliminaries. She said bluntly, "You have the best supply of goods in California, Mr. Brannan, and I want to know where you get them."

The merchant chuckled. "There's no secret to it. I pay well for my goods, and the captains of the ships that bring them in keep an iron hand on their crews. My goods are unloaded and delivered, whatever it takes to accomplish that.''

Emily nodded, her expression calm and controlled, but Cassandra knew that inside her mother was upset. Emily had contracted for more than one shipload of goods, only to see the vessels abandoned with the cargoes still in their holds, where they couldn't do anyone any good.

"Would it be possible for me to buy some of your inventory, Mr. Brannan?" she asked. "I realize I would have to cut my own profits by dealing with you, but a store with empty shelves is no store at all."

Brannan leaned forward and laced his fingers together, resting his clasped hands on the desk. He regarded Emily solemnly as he said, "I agree with you, Mrs. Woodward, and I sympathize with your problem. But why should I sell any of my stock to you when I can sell everything I get my hands on to the public at better prices?"

"A growing town needs more than one mercantile," Emily pointed out, using the same argument she had mentioned to Cassandra on the way over here.

"True. But I'm having my own problems securing enough inventory, and if I sell any of those goods to you I'm only weakening my enterprise without enabling yours to succeed. Surely you can see that." Brannan looked genuinely distressed that he had disappointed Emily by turning down her proposal.

"You're certain that you can't see your way clear to—"

Brannan shook his head firmly, causing Emily to break off her question and take a deep breath. Cassandra felt a pang of sympathy for her mother. To Emily, being forced to ask for a competitor's help must have seemed like begging, and Cassandra knew how proud her mother was.

Emily smiled thinly as she stood up and motioned for Cassandra to do the same. "Thank you for your time, Mr.

Brannan,'' she said crisply. "We'll be going now. Good day."

He hurried out from behind the desk. "I'm sorry, Mrs. Woodward, I truly am. If there was a way to benefit us both, I assure you I'd jump at the chance to work with you. Please, feel free to stop by here any time you please. I'll always be glad to see you."

"Yes, well, I'm afraid I shall be too busy with my own store for any . . . social visits." Emily's voice was chilly now, and Brannan frowned.

"Whatever you wish, madam. Let me escort you out—"

"Cassandra and I can find our own way, thank you." Emily turned to her daughter. "Come along, Cassandra."

Cassandra looked back at the merchant. "Good-bye, Mr. Brannan," she said.

He smiled ruefully and nodded a farewell to her.

When they were outside again, Cassandra gathered up her courage and said, "You were rather rude to Mr. Brannan, Mother."

"Perhaps I was," Emily said slowly. "It was just that I had such hopes for this meeting . . ." She let her voice trail off and sighed.

After a moment, Cassandra ventured, "I think he liked you."

"Nonsense. Mr. Brannan is a Mormon, and I have no intention of becoming a member of such a man's stable of wives."

"He has more than one wife?" Cassandra gasped.

"Well . . . I don't know that. I don't even know if he is married at all. But the purpose of this meeting was business, Cassandra, not social. You know that. I've no time for anything else."

"Of course not, Mother," Cassandra murmured, keeping

her eyes downcast so that if Emily gave her a stern look, she wouldn't see it.

They walked along toward the emporium, which was several blocks away, and Cassandra thought about what her mother had said. Emily's romantic feelings seemed to have died with her husband. That was none of Cassandra's concern, of course, but she hoped she would not end up like that herself. She'd had a few suitors back in Boston but none of them serious. Still, she hoped that sooner or later the right man would come along and sweep her off her feet, just the way it happened in the romantic poems she sometimes read. She didn't want to spend her life with nothing but business— cold, impersonal business—to fill her days. No, she wanted adventure and passion and excitement and—

"Oh!" Cassandra ran into her mother, who had stopped at the head of one of the piers while Cassandra was daydreaming. Emily was staring out at the deserted ships with their forest of bare masts, and she was frowning in thought. Cassandra could tell that her mother had had an idea, although what it might have been, Cassandra couldn't have said.

Emily didn't seem to notice that Cassandra had bumped into her. She turned away from the harbor and said briskly, "Come along, dear. There are plans to be made."

"Plans?" repeated Cassandra. "What sort of plans?"

Emily glanced at her, and for the first time in quite a while, Cassandra saw a smile appear on her mother's face. "Plans that will show Mr. Sam Brannan he made a mistake by not dealing with me when he had the chance," Emily said. "If he wants competition, then by heaven, he's got it!"

"What is it they call this place again?" Anne Palmer nervously asked her husband as they sat in the buggy looking at the mining camp spread out before them.

"Bloody Gulch," Thaddeus replied. "I wouldn't worry, my dear. I'm certain the name doesn't really mean anything. These miners just like to be colorful."

Anne frowned dubiously, unsure that her husband was correct in his assessment. From the looks of it, the place might be bloody indeed.

Thickly wooded hills rose steeply to the north and south, forming a valley perhaps three-quarters of a mile wide. A creek—clear and cold and bubbling—ran through the center of the valley and meandered away to join the Mokelumne River a few miles downstream. A settlement had sprung up on both sides of the creek as goldseekers flocked to the area following word of a strike. Many of the dwellings were tents, but several more permanent buildings were going up, too, and the air rang with the sound of axes as trees were cut down on the hillsides, dragged to the settlement by mules, and then hewn into planks for building. Men shouted curses and mules gave out loud brays that sounded almost as obscene as the words their masters bellowed at them. Saw blades bit deeply into wood. Hammers pounded home pegs, and picks and shovels thudded and chinked into the earth as miners dug for gold. Most of the men were bearded and roughly dressed and didn't look like gentlemen at all, at least not to the eyes of Anne Palmer. A tiny shudder ran through her body.

"And this is where you want to establish your practice, Thaddeus?" she asked, hoping he would hear the discomfort in her voice at the idea.

"Yes, it is," Palmer replied firmly. "You heard what the men said in Volcano and Dogtown. This area is rich in ore, and it's going to be the center of the gold fields before much longer."

"That's been said about other places in the past, surely."

Palmer ignored the point Anne was making and went on,

"There's no doctor within fifty miles, perhaps more. This is perfect, Anne. My practice will thrive here, you'll see. And smell this air!" He drew in a deep breath and patted his chest. "My God, how invigorating!"

Anne had to admit that the autumn air was crisp and clear and bracing. But how would it be when winter arrived in a couple of months? she wondered. She and Thaddeus certainly couldn't spend the winter in a tent.

"We'll have to have some place to stay," she said, hoping to bring him back to practicality.

"Of course. We'll find a place. I'll see that we have a cabin built—a nice snug cabin that'll see us through this winter and all the winters to come. How would that be?"

"All right," Anne agreed. With a good cabin, she might be able to stand the conditions here in this rugged wilderness.

Palmer flicked the reins and clucked to the horses to get them moving again. The buggy rolled down what someday might become an actual street but was now only a path between some of the tents. No one paid much attention to the couple at first, but then one of the miners they drove past glanced up, saw Anne's blond hair peeking out from under her bonnet, and shouted, "Goddamn! A woman!"

That exclamation brought other men on the run, and Palmer frowned in disapproval as they began stepping in front of the buggy to get a better look at its occupants. As for Anne, she felt a tingle of fear race through her. It would have been all right with her if these rough-looking miners hadn't even noticed her. Thaddeus had said that there were respectable women in the mining camps now, but so far Anne hadn't seen very many. She hadn't seen very many women, period, respectable or otherwise. As the miners flocked around the buggy, she felt almost like a scrap of meat thrown into a pack of starving dogs.

"Here, you men, get out of the way!" Palmer commanded sharply as he was forced to bring the buggy to a halt again. "Let us pass!"

"Don't get upset, mister," one of the miners advised him. "We just want to look at your lady. Been a long time since most of us seen one. We won't bother her none."

"You're bothering her already," snapped Palmer. "I insist you let us pass."

"Where are you goin'?" asked another man. "You don't look like any miner I ever saw, mister. You look more like some sort o' dandy."

Admittedly, both Palmer and Anne were much better dressed than these men, who for the most part wore red-checked wool shirts, canvas breeches, and muddy boots. The trip from San Francisco into the foothills of the Sierra Nevadas had not been an easy one, but Palmer always prided himself on his appearance. His beaver hat was recently brushed, and his gray suit still held a few vestiges of creases. A silk cravat was tied neatly at his throat.

"I'm a doctor," Palmer told the men who barred their way. "I've come to this community to establish a practice."

"A sawbones, eh?" one of the men said as he rubbed an unshaven jaw. "Reckon we could use one around here. Know why the place is called Bloody Gulch?"

Anne didn't want to hear the answer to that question, whatever it was, but Palmer said, "No, we don't. But I assume it's for some physical reason, such as reddish soil or the color of the sky when the sun sets."

The miner shook his head and grinned. "Nope. It's because a fella named Jake Greevey accidentally chopped off his hand with an ax, and it bled all over the place 'fore Jake finally died. Spurted up in the air like one o' them fancy fountains down in N'Orleans. We never saw the like, so we figured we'd call the place Bloody Gulch, in honor of ol'

Jake." Several of the miners slapped their thighs in appreciation of the grisly humor.

Palmer stared at them in a mixture of horror and anger as Anne clutched his arm tightly and tried to fight down the feeling of nausea in her stomach. "My God, man," demanded Palmer, "didn't any of you try to help the poor wretch? What did you do, just stand by and watch him bleed to death?"

The man who had told the story shrugged his shoulders and said, "Jake was cuttin' timber up on one of the hills when it happened, and there wasn't nobody close enough to help him. We heard him screamin' and went to see what was wrong, but by the time we got there, he had passed out. Never woke up, the unlucky bastard. Pardon my French, ma'am." He tugged the stained brim of his hat in apology as he nodded toward Anne.

"If I'd been here then and you had brought Mr. Greevey directly to me, I might have been able to save his life," Palmer said. "I've come here to help you men, and I hope you'll remember that."

"Oh, you've helped us already, just by bringin' that little lady with you. Sure has brightened things up around here, just havin' her around. Ain't that right, boys?"

There was a chorus of agreement from the other miners, and Anne didn't know whether to feel flattered or embarrassed. These rough-looking men stared brazenly at her, that was true, but they seemed to be keeping their distance. Perhaps they would all respect the fact that she was married. She put that to the test by saying, "Dr. Palmer and I are going to need a place to stay. Could some of you gentlemen help us?"

Thaddeus cast a quick glance at her out of the corner of his eye, as if he wished she hadn't spoken, but he said to the miners, "That's right. I'd like a good solid cabin for my wife and myself. I'd be happy to pay any man who wanted to work on such a project—''

The man who had been doing most of the talking for the miners waved a hand, cutting short Palmer's offer of payment. "No need for that," he said magnanimously. "We'll be glad to pitch in, won't we, boys?"

Again the other miners echoed his statement, several with calls of "Damn right!" The spokesman went on, "Like you said, Doc, we need a sawbones around here, and we'll do what we can to keep you in Bloody Gulch. Welcome to you an' yer lady both." He came closer to the buggy and extended a grimy hand. "Name's Barney Cumberland."

Palmer hesitated only an instant, then took the hand offered to him. "Pleased to meet you, Mr. Cumberland. Now, if you could show me a suitable spot where Mrs. Palmer and I can pitch our tent until construction begins on our house . . . ?"

"Sure thing. Clear off, gents, and let Doc Palmer through. Come on, Doc, follow me."

Anne smiled weakly at her husband. She knew that Thaddeus hated being called Doc, but under these circumstances he wasn't likely to complain. So far things had worked out better than they had any right to expect, given the rough appearance of their welcoming committee. The miners of Bloody Gulch seemed to be friendly enough, and they called out their farewells as Palmer drove the buggy past them and followed the long-striding Barney Cumberland toward an open grassy spot near the creek.

This might work out all right after all, Anne told herself. There was at least reason for hope now, hope that she and Thaddeus had found a new home.

Now, if they could just do something about the *name* of the place . . . !

Nine

Dan Logan rode a big golden sorrel that was probably the most magnificent horse Boone had ever seen. The animal had brought Logan all the way from Texas, and the long, grueling journey appeared to have had no effect on it. It stepped along lightly and proudly, and at times there almost seemed to be an unspoken communication between horse and rider. A man on a horse like that could outrun almost any pursuit, Boone had thought more than once during the two days since he had been captured by the Texas Ranger.

As for Boone himself, he had to make do with a mule for a saddle mount: an ugly, rawboned animal with a temperament to match its appearance. Boone knew without being told that if he made a break for freedom on the mule, Logan wouldn't have any trouble chasing him down.

The ranger explained that he had bought the mule in one of the mining camps during his search for Boone.

"I knew I might not find you," Logan said as they rode through the foothills, "even though that letter we got made it sound pretty certain you were out here in California. Wasn't much point in getting a mount for you until I was sure I'd be bringing you back, though. Once I'd talked to that fella Carson, I was sure enough."

"He wanted me to pay him so that he wouldn't go to the law and tell where I was," Boone said. "That son of a bitch."

"Pretty damned underhanded, all right," agreed Logan. "Like lyin' to me in the first place. Luckily he wasn't very good at it, and I figured he was up to something."

"Lucky for one of us," Boone muttered. "So it was a letter that put you on my trail, huh?"

"Yep. Don't know who it was from; there wasn't no signature on it. Just said that if we were still lookin' for you, we might could find you out here in California. I reckon somebody else from Indian Rock must've come out here lookin' for gold and spotted you, maybe a relative of Jason Stoneham or the McCarter girl. They didn't want to brace you themselves, so they figured tippin' off the rangers was the next best thing."

Boone blew out his breath in a long sigh. "I don't suppose you've given any more thought to what I told you about what really happened."

"I've thought on it," Logan replied curtly. "Still got a job to do."

Boone looked down at the back of the mule to hide the faint smile that played briefly over his lips. Logan's doubts were still working on him, Boone thought. The ranger was stubborn, though. He wasn't going to just take the word of a fugitive.

That was all Boone had: his word. It would have to be enough. Maybe . . . if deep down Logan believed him . . . the ranger would relax his vigilance just enough to allow Boone to make a move. If he could just manage to fork the saddle on that big sorrel, Logan would never catch him, not on the mule or any other mount. Boone was sure of it.

In the meantime, all he could do was wait and watch for his opportunity.

After all, it was a long way back to Texas.

Logan kept Boone's hands tied to the saddle horn most of the time when they were riding, and although they passed dozens of miners during the first few days of the trip, no one offered to help Boone. He was a stranger, and nobody was going to neglect his own diggings to help a stranger who'd been arrested. Logan wore his ranger badge pinned to his shirt, so that folks would know he was a lawman. Boone had gotten a good look at the badge, a five-pointed star surrounded by a silver circle. Logan noticed him studying it and explained that he had carved it himself out of a Mexican ten-peso silver piece.

"It's worth a lot more than ten pesos to me, though," Logan said as he lightly touched the badge.

"Set a lot of store by it, do you?"

"Damn right," Logan replied fervently. "I've been a ranger almost since the first. Rode with Jack Hays and the Lewis boys and ol' Bigfoot Wallace, fought the Comanch' at Bandera Pass, scouted against the Mexes in '42, and been ridin' border patrol most of the time since. Damn right it means a lot. Texas wouldn't be much of a place if it wasn't for the rangers."

Boone managed not to snort in disgust. He knew good and well that the rangers weren't the paragons of virtue and law enforcement that Logan made them out to be, but it wouldn't serve his purpose to argue with the man. Instead Boone kept silent and let Logan talk. Once he got started, Logan had plenty of stories to tell about the various battles and adventures in which he'd been involved as a ranger.

That night they made camp on a narrow shelf of ground overlooking a deep gully. There were trees at the back of the shelf, where the land sloped up again into a rocky bluff. Most of the bench was covered with short grass that would provide graze for Logan's sorrel and Boone's mule. There was no water, but the ranger's canteens were still mostly full after being topped off earlier in the day at a creek the two men had forded.

After Boone had dismounted awkwardly, his hands still

tied together but freed from the saddle horn, he walked over to the edge of the shelf and looked down into the gully. The slope falling away from him was fairly steep and dotted with scrubby brush. The bottom, which was only a few feet wide, was covered with a layer of gravel. The gully twisted and turned and bent out of sight in both directions. Something about it struck Boone as familiar, and he frowned as he tried to figure out what it was.

After a moment it came to him. The gully was actually a creek bed. At some time in the past, a stream had run through here and carved the gully out of the earth. Something had happened to the creek; either the springs that fed it had gone dry, or the flow had been diverted by man or nature.

"What are you starin' at?" Logan asked from behind him.

Boone shook his head. "Nothing." He turned back to the ranger. The discovery was faintly interesting but didn't really mean a thing, at least not to him.

Or did it? Boone's eyes suddenly narrowed as an idea occurred to him. The gully was forty or fifty feet deep, and while a fall into it probably wouldn't kill a man, it would bang him up enough so that it would be a while before he could clamber out.

It was a chance Boone had to take. He might not get another.

He paused and glanced over his shoulder at the gully again. "You really ought to take a look at this," he said to Logan.

The ranger was at the edge of the trees, gathering some fallen branches for their campfire. The sun would be setting soon, and the nights were quite cool at this time of year. The two men would need a good fire to warm them.

Logan carried the armload of branches over to the spot he had selected for the fire and dumped them there, then walked toward Boone, brushing his palms together as he came.

"What've you found down in that gully, Blakely?" He grinned. "Gold?"

"No, not gold, but I think you should see it," Boone said. He had to make an effort to keep his voice calm. Logan didn't act suspicious at all. Boone's cooperation ever since Logan had captured him had lulled the ranger into thinking that he was no longer a threat. If Logan heard any nervousness in Boone's voice, he probably ascribed it to the nonexistent thing Boone claimed to have seen in the gully.

Logan stepped up beside him, thumbs hooked in his gun belt, and peered down into the gully. "Now, what the hell is it you saw?" he asked.

"This," Boone grunted as he swung his clubbed hands at Logan's head with blinding speed.

The ranger saw the blow coming and tried to get out of the way, twisting away from Boone and reaching for his Colt at the same time. The gun was only halfway out of its holster when Boone's hands smashed into Logan's right shoulder. The blow didn't land with the power behind it that Boone wanted, but the impact was enough to send Logan lurching toward the edge of the slope. Logan cursed and tried to catch his balance as he drew the gun.

Desperately, Boone reached for the Colt and closed the fingers of one hand around the barrel, holding it down so that Logan couldn't bring it to bear on him. At the same time, Boone drove forward, lowering his shoulder and ramming it into Logan. The ranger went over backward, his feet going from under him.

Boone fell, too, but he landed on the edge of the gully. Logan hit a couple of feet down and kept rolling, tumbling over and over down the slope. He yelled harshly in pain and outrage, and Boone had a bad moment as Logan managed to grab hold of one of the straggly bushes about ten feet down the side of the gully. The roots of the bush were not embedded deeply enough to hold the ranger's weight, however, and they ripped free of the earth, sending Logan plummeting on down. He latched on to another bush, but again it pulled loose.

Logan had managed to slow his momentum, though, and he came to rest spraddled against the side of the slope before reaching the gravel bottom. He didn't move, but Boone heard him groan.

The ranger was just stunned, Boone realized. He wasn't going to have as much time to get away as he had hoped. But it was still going to be enough, he told himself. He pushed to his feet and looked down in surprise at the gun heheld in his hand, his fingers still wrapped tightly around the barrel. Logan must have lost his grip on the Walker Colt when he fell, Boone thought. That was another break. He tucked the revolver behind his belt and turned to run toward the spot where the sorrel and the mule were tethered to a pair of saplings.

He jerked the reins of the mule loose first and slammed the flat of his hand against the animal's rump as he let out a loud yell. It took a couple of swats to get the mule moving, but once it did it galloped off down the trail in an ungainly gait. As soon as the mule took off, Boone swung toward the sorrel, which was eyeing him suspiciously. Boone cast a glance over his shoulder at the gully. There was no sign of Logan yet. Soothingly, Boone said to the sorrel, ''Take it easy, boy, just take it easy. It'll be all right.''

The big horse seemed to settle down a little at the sound of Boone's voice. Boone stooped, picked up Logan's saddle blanket, and threw it over the sorrel's back. Then he lifted the saddle itself and settled it in place. The routine of being saddled seemed to calm the sorrel even more. It was used to what was being done to it, even though a stranger was buckling the cinches on the saddle instead of the tall Texas ranger who usually handled that chore.

Boone looked at the gully again and was relieved to see that Logan hadn't appeared yet. He wanted to run over there and see how much progress the ranger was making, if any, but he couldn't waste that much time. Instead, he grasped the sorrel's reins, took hold of the saddle horn, and swung up onto the animal's back.

He might as well have dropped his leg over a whirlwind.

The sorrel had tolerated someone other than Logan putting on the saddle, but it was outraged that somebody else was actually trying to ride him. The horse leaped into the air, arching its back, switching ends, and generally launching into a frenzy of bucking that had Boone howling in terror and hanging on for dear life. Boone held on to the horn with one hand while hauling back brutally on the reins with the other, and he tried frantically to find the stirrups with his feet. The sorrel screamed in fury and contorted wildly as it tried to dislodge the man on its back.

Boone felt his grip on the horn slipping. He let go of the reins and used both hands to hold on. The jolts that ran through him as the sorrel bucked felt as though they were going to break his back. The horse gave a particularly vicious twist, and Boone's fingers slid off the saddle horn.

Suddenly he was flying through the air with the sorrel no longer underneath him. Boone yelled, a shout that was cut off as he slammed into the ground. The thick grass cushioned his landing a little, but not enough to prevent every bit of air from being knocked out of his lungs. Gasping for breath, Boone rolled over and managed to climb onto his hands and knees. He lifted his head, his hair hanging in front of his eyes, and saw exactly what he didn't want to see.

Dan Logan was clambering over the edge of the gully, and the ranger's face was dark with rage.

Boone reached for the butt of the Colt as Logan started

running toward him. He didn't want to shoot Logan, but he might not have any choice. Not when the alternative was going back to a lynch rope in Texas.

Fumbling, Boone closed his fingers around the smooth walnut grips of the gun and tried to pull it free. The front sight hung on his belt, delaying him for a moment as he tugged on it. The gun came loose, and he lifted it toward Logan.

He was too late. The onrushing Texas Ranger was almost on top of him. Logan's foot lashed out, and the toe of his boot cracked against Boone's wrist. Boone cried out in pain as the Colt spun out of his hand. Logan still had plenty of momentum, and he put it all behind a punch he threw at Boone's head. Logan's knobby fist cracked against Boone's jaw, driving him backward.

Bright lights exploded in Boone's brain as Logan landed on top of him and started pummeling him. His head was jerked back and forth by the blows. Boone heaved his body upward, trying to throw off Logan, but the ranger had the upper hand and wasn't going to let it go. Two more punches slammed into Boone's face, and the back of his head bounced on the hard ground. He moaned as consciousness tried to slip away from him.

He was aware that Logan was no longer on top of him, and then a few seconds later a strong hand took hold of his shirt and hauled him to his feet. Logan had retrieved his gun. He jammed the barrel underneath Boone's jaw and pressed painfully on it.

"I ought to blow your damned head off, Blakely," Logan gritted. "I didn't figure you to be low-down enough to try a trick like that." He gave Boone a hard shove toward the gully. Boone stumbled, and Logan caught his collar again, forcing him to the edge of the slope. "Maybe I ought to just put a bullet in you and dump your body in the gully, like you tried to do to me," Logan went on harshly. "How about it, Blakely? Reckon that gully's a good enough grave for the likes of you?"

Boone was still light-headed from the beating Logan had handed him, but he was thinking clearly enough to be angry. In a hoarse voice, he demanded, "What the hell did you expect me to do? Go back to Texas and let 'em hang me for something I didn't do? Damn it, Logan, I didn't murder Jason Stoneham, and I never touched a hair on Samantha McCarter's head!"

"Shut up!" Logan told him. "Shut up and look down there, you son of a bitch. I could've busted my head open fallin' down that slope—"

The ranger stopped abruptly, and even without turning around, Boone knew that Logan was staring into the gully in shock, because Boone was doing the same thing. This side of the gully faced west, and the sun was about to slide behind the peaks in that direction. Its last rays of light were slanting down into the gully, shining on the small bushes that Logan had uprooted during his tumble. Clumps of dirt still clung to the roots of the plants, and more dirt was scattered along the slope.

There were a dozen or more gleaming nuggets embedded in that dirt.

"Good Lord," Boone breathed, "that's color!"

"You mean gold?" Logan asked in a hushed voice.

"That's right. Let me go down there and I can tell you for sure."

Logan hesitated, then released Boone's collar. "All right. But I'll be holdin' this gun on you all the time, and if you try anything, I'll shoot you down. I mean it, Blakely."

"I know you do," muttered Boone. Carefully, he stepped over the edge of the gully and let himself down into a sitting position. With his hands and feet to brace him, he slid down slowly to the spot where Logan had pulled up the first bush.

He reached out to pull one of the dirt clumps off the roots and began brushing at it. When the dirt was gone, what was left was a small nugget of metal that was a dull yellow. Boone held it to his mouth and bit gently into it, then looked at the impressions his teeth had made. There were more scientific tests, of course, but even to a relatively inexperienced miner, no other confirmation was needed. The nugget was gold, all right.

Boone looked up at Logan with a grin. "That's what it is," he said. "And there's a bunch of 'em down here. Shoot, Logan, the whole side of this gully may be mostly gold for all we know. Have you got a shovel?" The excitement of the discovery had driven all thoughts of the botched escape from Boone's mind. Here was the strike he had spent months looking for.

Logan brought him back to earth with a crash by cocking the big Colt. "Gather up them nuggets and bring 'em up here if you want, but don't get any ideas, Blakely. You're my prisoner, remember?" The ranger smiled grimly. "Besides, I'm the one who ripped up that bush. If anybody owns the rights to this gully, it's me."

Boone stared at him. "That's not fair. Hell, Logan, you'd never know this gold was here if I hadn't knocked you down the slope."

"Tried to kill me, that's what you mean. That ain't much of an argument for ownership, Blakely. Come on, quit stallin'. Get up out of there."

"You mean you're not going to see how much gold is really here?" Boone's tone was one of astonishment.

"I'm a lawman, not some damned prospector." Logan gestured with the Colt. "And you're still on your way back to Texas."

Boone sighed. His luck was running true to form. He was

sitting on maybe the richest strike these mountains had seen
yet, and he had to get up and walk away from it. Even worse,
he had to leave the gold behind and go back to face a gallows. Fate had played one hell of a trick on him.

"Well?" demanded Logan. "What's it goin' to be?"

"I'm coming," Boone said. "But you're a fool, Logan,
you know that?"

"How do you figure?"

"You could have all this"—Boone gestured at the side
of the gully and the nuggets gleaming there in the last light
of day— "and you turn it down because of some damned
star on your shirt."

"Well, Blakely, I reckon that's the difference between you
and me."

But as Boone looked into Logan's eyes, he saw the un-
certainty there, and he knew that maybe the two of them
weren't so different after all.

Ten

San Francisco had changed a great deal in the months that Nathan had been gone. Streets that half a year earlier had been all but deserted were now thronged with people and horses and wagons. Stores that had been boarded up were open for business again and thriving. New buildings were being constructed, covering the hills of the peninsula where the city was located. San Francisco, which had been nearly dead, was now alive and booming.

Of course, he himself had changed considerably, Nathan thought glumly. He was thinner, his features more drawn. Beard stubble covered his cheeks. His clothes were threadbare in places, worn completely through in others, and his boots had holes in them. After the theft of his outfit, he had used what little gold he had left to buy a few supplies and he had started walking back out of the mountains toward the coast. The provisions had run out, and for the past few weeks he had been subsisting on what little bit of wild game he could catch, along with whatever he could beg from more prosperous travelers heading into the Sierra Nevadas. Finally he had hitched a ride on a boat that was returning downriver to the city, and it had carried him all the way to the harbor. Now he was trudging toward his aunt's store, fearful of what Emily would say when she saw what an utter failure he had turned out to be as a miner.

People were making their fortunes all over California, he thought bitterly, but not Nathan Jones. No, sir, not him!

Nathan saw the emporium up ahead. Despite the cold,

damp weather that had him shivering in his coat, the doors of the store were open at the moment, and a man was carrying out boxes from inside and loading them in the back of a wagon parked beside the porch. Nathan frowned. That looked almost like crates full of supplies that the man was loading. The store had been practically bare of merchandise when Nathan left for the foothills. What was going on?

Weary and footsore, Nathan stumbled up to the wagon as the man emerged from the store again and placed another box in the back of the vehicle. He gave Nathan a cold stare, as if afraid that the ragged-looking young man might try to steal something. "Move along, tramp," the man snapped as he straightened up from placing the box in the wagon.

Nathan ignored the warning. He gestured at the storefront and asked, "Is this still Woodward's Emporium?"

"That's what the sign says, ain't it?" The man's answer came in a harsh voice.

"Are . . . are those supplies?"

"What business is it of yours?"

Nathan shook his head. "None, I guess. I was just wondering . . ."

"Yes, they're supplies. What else would they be? Man's got to be outfitted properly before he goes off looking for gold."

"You're a miner?" muttered Nathan.

"Going to be." The man did not sound quite so hostile now, evidently having decided that Nathan was no threat. "Came all the way out here from Connecticut to try my luck. Made it across that steaming hellhole of a jungle down yonder in Panama, so I don't intend to let anything stop me now. I'm coming back from the Sierra Nevadas a rich man."

"I hope you do, friend," Nathan said. "I really hope you do." He turned away and started toward the steps leading up to the store's porch.

Other men and women were going in and out of the emporium. Nathan gave his head a shake as he paused in the
doorway, not sure he believed what his eyes were showing
him. The shelves and counters, which had been almost completely empty when he left, now held merchandise again.
True, the shelves still weren't full, but there were many more
goods than had been there before. He saw bolts of cloth,
racks full of picks and shovels, kegs of nails, barrels of pickles and crackers, bags of flour and sugar and salt and coffee
and tobacco. Big circles of cheese sat on one counter, and
ham hocks and sides of bacon and salt pork hung behind
another. A glass-fronted case held needles and thread and
other sewing notions, and some ready-made clothing for both
men and women hung from hooks on the wall. There was
even a large glass jar full of sweets on the long main counter
at the rear of the store.

Nathan stood there blinking in astonishment for a moment,
then slowly started forward. The customers paid little attention to him, with the exception of several ladies shopping
together who made a point of moving quickly to another
aisle when they saw the haggard, bearded stranger coming
toward them.

The attractive, middle-aged woman behind the rear
counter glanced up at Nathan and began automatically, "Can
I help y—" before clapping her hands to her mouth and
exclaiming, "Nathan! My God, is that *you*?"

"It's me, Aunt Emily," Nathan told her, managing a weak
smile as he did so.

Emily Woodward hurried along the counter and around
the end of it. She came up to Nathan and put a hand on his
arm, peering into his gaunt face. "What happened to you?"
she demanded, her tone a mixture of concern and impatience.

"Well, I sure didn't make a gold strike, I can tell you that
much," Nathan answered ruefully. "In fact, I lost the whole

outfit you gave me, mules and all.''

"Oh, Nathan . . .''

He couldn't decide if she was angry at him or felt sorry for him. With Emily it was hard to tell. But he felt the need to apologize anyway, casting his eyes toward the sawdust-littered plank floor and saying, "I'm sorry, Aunt Emily. I tried to find gold, I really did, but—''

"No, Nathan, you don't have to apologize," Emily said quickly. "I'm sure you did your best. Not everyone can strike it rich, though.''

Nathan glanced around at the activity inside the store. "Looks like you did," he commented. "Where did all these goods come from?''

"The same place they were supposed to all along: the ships in the harbor.''

Nathan frowned in bewilderment. "But . . . those ships were abandoned . . .''

"I know." Emily turned her head and called, "Cassandra! Come out here!''

A door behind the counter that led into the storerooms and offices at the back of the building opened, and Nathan's cousin emerged. Her blond hair was slightly disheveled as if she had been running her fingers through it, and there was a small smudge of ink on her cheek. She asked, "What is it, Mother? I'm trying to figure out those ledgers, so I need to concentrate—Nathan? Is that you?" She came out from behind the counter and almost flew into his arms. "Nathan!''

He summoned up a grin as he hugged her. "Hello, Cassandra. It's good to see you again.''

"It's been so long since we've heard from you," Cassandra said as she smiled up at him. "Mother and I didn't even know if you were still alive.''

"Just barely," Nathan said dryly. "And considering how

my trip to the mountains turned out, I'm not sure if that's good news or not.''

"Don't be ridiculous,'' Emily crisply told him. "We're certainly glad you came back safely, Nathan.'' She turned to her daughter. "Cassandra, keep an eye on things out here while I talk to Nathan.''

Cassandra nodded, although she looked as though she too wanted to hear what Nathan had to say about his travels. Nathan had noticed that there were a couple of clerks working in the store, but it was like Emily to want someone keeping an eye on them if she couldn't do that herself.

Emily took his arm and led him around the counter. "Come into the office and sit down,'' she said. "You look exhausted.''

"It was a hard trip back,'' Nathan admitted as he went with her into the office. Several large ledgers were opened and spread out on the desk, and a pen stood in a pot of ink. Obviously, Cassandra had been doing the bookkeeping for her mother. Nathan knew Emily had made sure Cassandra was well educated enough to handle something like that. Because of Emily's own business background, she had not been content to send her daughter to some finishing school that would have taught Cassandra nothing except how to find a husband and run a proper household.

Emily sat down behind the desk and motioned for Nathan to take one of the chairs opposite her. As he sank down gratefully, wincing a little at the pains in his legs, Emily asked, "How did you get back here if you lost the mules?''

"I walked most of the way.''

"Walked!''

Nathan nodded. "I got a ride on a boat about halfway between here and Sacramento City, and that helped.''

"What happened up there in the mountains?''

Awkwardly, Nathan explained to her about his lack of

success as a miner. "I . . . I'm afraid I don't have anything
to show for all the time I was up there. I used what little
gold I had left to buy supplies after my gear and the mules
were stolen."

"And you don't have any idea who took the mules?"

He shook his head. "It could have been any one of hundreds of men. The hills are swarming with them."

"Did you try to find out?"

Nathan hesitated, then shook his head again. "I knew it
wouldn't do any good," he said lamely. "And a lot of those
miners are pretty rough characters. They'll fight at the drop
of a hat. I knew if I went around accusing any of them, I
might wind up with a knife in my back."

Emily looked at him for a long moment without saying
anything, but he thought he could detect a hint of scorn in
her expression. *She* wouldn't have let somebody waltz off
with her mules and her gear if she had been there, Nathan
thought. No matter what the circumstances, she would have
stood up to anyone who tried to take something that was
hers.

Finally, she sighed and said, "Well, I'm sorry it turned
out like that, Nathan. I'm sure you did your best. At any
rate, I'm glad you're back. I have something important for
you to do here, if you're interested."

For a second, Nathan considered telling her that he was
going back east, that he had had his fill of California. But
he supposed it wouldn't hurt to at least listen to whatever
she had in mind, so he said, "I'm interested."

Emily leaned back in the chair, a rather mannish pose that
still seemed natural for her. "You asked me how I got hold
of the merchandise out there in the store."

"And you said it came from the boats in the harbor,"
Nathan said with a frown.

"That's right. Many of them were abandoned by officers

and crew alike with their cargoes intact. Crates full of goods were left in the holds to rot, because no one could be bothered to unload them. But I remembered how you found some loafers on the docks who were willing to unload the trunks that Cassandra and I brought with us, and I went down there to look for more men like that.''

Nathan's eyes widened slightly. "The docks can be a rough area," he commented.

"So they can, but I needed those goods."

That answer was typical of Emily, too, Nathan mused. She wasn't one to let problems stand in her way when she wanted something. He wished he could be more like her in that regard.

"What about the owners of those cargoes?" The instant Nathan asked the question, Emily's eyes flashed, and he wished he had kept his curiosity to himself.

"I paid the captains of the ships a fair price, when I could find them," replied Emily. "In some cases, though, the captain was long gone with the rest of the crew. Those abandoned cargoes were fair game for anyone who could salvage them, so that's what I did."

"The plan certainly seems to have worked," Nathan said. "The store is doing well."

"The whole city is doing well. Folks are coming in from all over the world to look for gold in the Sierra Nevadas, and each and every one of them passes through here first. This gold rush has saved the town."

"For a while there, it looked like it was going to kill San Francisco," Nathan pointed out. "I'm glad things have changed." His weariness was growing, and by now all he really wanted to do was go upstairs to his room—assuming it was still his—and lie down for about a week. He went on, "Now, what was this about you having something for me to do?"

"I've been talking about it," Emily stated bluntly. "The store is so busy that it takes up most of my time now. I want you to take over the job of salvaging the goods from those ships in the harbor."

"Me? But I don't know anything about—"

"What is there to know about it?" Emily cut in. "You hire men to take the crates out of the holds, you have them put on wagons, and you bring them here. It's simple. You just need a firm hand with those idlers down at the docks."

Nathan grimaced. Displaying a firm hand with anyone had never been his strong suit. However, he had let Emily down in the mining venture; he supposed the least he could do was give this task a try for her.

"All right," he said. "I can't start today, though. I've got to have some rest."

"Of course," Emily agreed, her expression softening slightly. "You've been through a rough time, Nathan, and it's my fault. I hope you'll forgive your old aunt for being so stubborn."

That was as close to an apology as anyone was going to get from Emily, and Nathan only half-believed in its sincerity. But he nodded and said, "I'll do a good job for you this time, Aunt Emily."

"I know you will. Go on upstairs and get some rest, and we'll talk more about the job at dinner. I imagine you'll have quite an appetite after all those weeks in the mountains."

"Yes, ma'am." To tell the truth, Nathan didn't know if he could sleep or not, despite his exhaustion, because his stomach was so empty. He hadn't eaten anything since a hard, stale biscuit on the boat that morning, and very little the day before.

But he plodded up the stairs anyway, his legs feeling like each one weighed a hundred pounds, and he found his old room. The narrow bunk with its thin mattress felt incredibly soft as he stretched out on it, and his hunger was forgotten as he closed his eyes and let out a little moan.

He was asleep almost before the sound left his mouth.

"Be careful there!" Nathan called as one of the men in his work crew let a full crate crash heavily to the bed of the big wagon. "You'll bust those things open letting them drop like that."

The man gave him a cold glare and stepped down from the wagon, then went back up the gangplank from the pier onto the ship without saying anything. Nathan let him go.

It didn't pay to argue too much with these men. They could always quit and head for the gold fields themselves, although to a certain extent they must have lacked that much ambition or they would have been there already. Still, Nathan needed them, and he didn't want to anger them too much.

Several weeks had passed since his return to San Francisco, and he was looking and feeling more like himself again. He had gained weight eating Cassandra's cooking—Emily was an adequate cook, but just barely, while Cassandra was as skilled in the kitchen as she was with the ledger books—and his lean features had filled out a little. The muscular aches that had almost made him weep had eased as well. He wasn't going soft, by any means; it was more a matter of adequate rest and good food restoring his natural strength and vitality.

He would have felt pretty good, in fact, if he hadn't gotten roped into bossing this job for his aunt. The work was not very difficult, because the men he recruited from the streets around the docks were the ones who actually took care of the heavy labor of unloading the cargoes, but he had to deal with their arrogant attitudes and keep track of everything that was taken off the ships, just in case the previous owner of the goods showed up to claim them. That had happened a few times, and in each case, the ship's captain had been happy to receive fair payment for the cargo from Emily. After all, most of these men had deserted their vessels to go off looking for gold, and they hadn't really expected to find anything waiting for them when they got back. Nathan had to admit that it had been quite smart of Emily to set her sights on these abandoned ships.

But then, that was typical of Emily Woodward, always shrewdly looking for a new source of profits.

When the wagons were fully loaded, Nathan picked several men from his crew to drive all of them except one, and he climbed onto the seat of that vehicle himself and took up the reins. He flapped the reins and called out to the mules to get them started. The stubborn animals hesitated, then pulled against their harness and sent the wagon rolling forward. The other wagons followed along behind.

Negotiating the crowded streets took some time, but a little while later the heavily loaded wagons came to a halt in front of the Woodward Emporium. Emily's clerks were waiting for them and emerged from the store to begin unloading the crates. As usual Nathan and the other drivers pitched in, too, and it didn't take long to get the cargo into the building.

Emily came out of the double doors behind the clerks and called to her nephew. "Leave the lads to handle that, Nathan," she said to him. "Come with me. I want to talk to you in the office."

Nathan tried not to frown. Emily looked solemn, as if something might be wrong. He hoped not; things were settling down into a routine again, tedious though it might be at times, and he wasn't anxious to have his life disrupted.

A little shiver went through Nathan as he crossed the porch to follow his aunt into the store, and he couldn't be sure that it was prompted by the cold winter wind blowing through the streets of San Francisco.

They made their way past the customers crowding the aisles of the emporium and went behind the main counter to enter Emily's office. Cassandra was waiting there for them, and that increased Nathan's feeling of unease. If the whole family was involved in this, it had to be something important.

"Sit down," Emily told him as she went behind the desk. "How are your efforts at the docks going, Nathan?"

He settled himself in a chair beside the one Cassandra occupied, and she gave him a quick smile as he sat down. Looking across the desk at Emily, he replied, "It's going well, Aunt Emily. All you have to do is look in the store to see that."

"Yes, I know. You've recovered more cargo from those abandoned ships in a few weeks than I did in several months, Nathan. You're doing a fine job. I want you to know that, so that you won't think I'm displeased with your work."

Now that didn't sound promising at all, Nathan thought. In fact, it sounded as if Emily had a change in mind.

Nathan didn't say anything, just sat quietly and waited for Emily to go on. After a moment, she continued, "I have something else I want you to do. Not right away, but as soon as the weather improves some and the passes in the mountains start to clear."

Nathan swallowed hard. "You're sending me back to the mountains?"

"That's right. *If* you're willing to go, after what happened last time."

Emily was nothing if not blunt. Nathan licked his lips and tried to think of something to say, and Cassandra reached over and laid a hand on his arm.

"I'm sure Mother didn't mean anything bad about your

first trip, Nathan,'' the young woman said gently. ''We both know you did your best.''

''Sure,'' Nathan answered. ''I did my best, all right. But it wasn't very good.''

''So you weren't cut out to be a miner,'' snapped Emily. ''There's no shame in that, Nathan. I've seen you working around the store and down at the docks, though, and no one could complain about the job you've done here.''

''Then why do I have to go back to the mountains? There's enough business here to keep us all busy—''

Emily leaned forward and rested her palms on the desk. ''There's more business in the mountains,'' she said briskly. ''You told me yourself about how precious supplies were in the gold fields. Men who have goods to sell can ask a price double or triple or even four times higher in the Sierra Nevadas than they can here in San Francisco.''

Nathan saw what she was getting at, felt her scheme burst into realization in his brain. He said thickly, ''You want me to . . . to take supplies up to the gold fields and sell them.'' He didn't bother making it a question; he knew Emily Woodward too well for that. Once she had smelled a profit, there was no getting her off the scent.

''That's exactly right,'' his aunt confirmed. ''Like I said, when the weather improves you can take one wagonload to start with, just to see how it goes. I think we'll clear a healthy profit, though, healthy enough to justify sending you back up there.''

''The goods will fetch a much higher price in the gold fields, Nathan,'' Cassandra put in, reinforcing her mother's argument. ''And besides, you've done so well at recovering those cargoes from the ships that the store is getting too crowded with supplies. This idea of Mother's is the perfect solution.''

''Well, I suppose I could give it a try . . .''

"Of course you can," Emily said. "We'll begin planning immediately, so that when the worst of the winter weather is over, you can get an early start. I don't want somebody like Sam Brannan having the same idea and getting a jump on me."

"And when you're ready to go, I'll go with you," Cassandra said to him.

Nathan looked at her sharply, and so did Emily. Frowns appeared on both of their faces. "What did you say?" asked Nathan.

"I said I'll go with you," Cassandra declared forthrightly. "Mother always likes to have family taking care of anything that's very important—"

"That's why I'm sending Nathan," Emily interrupted. "I'm certain he can handle this without your assistance, dear, although we appreciate the offer. Don't we, Nathan?"

"Sure," Nathan mumbled, still surprised by Cassandra's suggestion. The very idea of a young, innocent girl like her going off to the gold fields . . . a place that was full of rough, unprincipled, sometimes savage men . . . well, it was almost incomprehensible to him.

Cassandra's features tightened as she glanced back and forth between her mother and her cousin. "You both think I'm insane," she accused. "You don't want me to go along."

"It's not that," Nathan began quickly.

Emily forestalled his protest. "It most certainly is," she said. "You're a young woman, Cassandra. You've no business up there in a place like that. No young woman does."

"I'm sure there are women in the gold fields." Cassandra swung toward Nathan. "Aren't there?"

Nathan hesitated, not sure how to reply. True, there *were* women in the gold fields, just as Cassandra said. But they were hardly respectable. The few females Nathan had seen during his months in the foothills had all been heavily painted, gaudily dressed trollops, their faces ravaged by time and dissipation and hardship; all of them were older than their years and full of despair.

Gently, he said to his cousin, "I just don't think it would be a good idea, Cassandra. The gold fields are too rough for someone like you."

Angrily, Cassandra turned back to Emily. "What about you, Mother?" she demanded. "If Nathan wasn't here to take the supplies and sell them, what would you do?"

"I suppose I'd take them myself."

"Of course you would! That's the way you are. But you won't let *me* be part of this!"

"You're different," Emily insisted. "The entire situation is different. And I won't hear any more about it. You're not going, Cassandra, no matter how much you may desire what you consider to be an adventure. Your place is here, helping me with the store."

For a moment, Nathan thought Cassandra was going to continue to argue, but then she settled back in her chair, crossed her arms, and sighed. "I suppose I can't fight with both of you," she said. "But I warn you, Mother, I didn't come out here to do the same things I was doing back in Boston."

"We'll talk about this later," Emily said firmly. She turned her attention back to Nathan. "We're agreed, then? You'll take a wagonload of supplies to the gold fields when the time comes?"

He nodded. "I'll do it. I just hope this turns out better than the last time I went up there."

"It will." Emily's voice was full of confidence, as usual. "You'll see. This will be our biggest success so far."

Nathan hoped she was right.

Because if she wasn't, he might not even come back from the mountains this time.

Eleven

Arrows thudded into the thick log walls of the cabin, and the bloodthirsty shrieks of Comanche warriors filled the night. Dan Logan crouched at the loophole, the butt of the long-barrelled flintlock rifle socketed firmly under his shoulder blade. Sweat trickled down his forehead and into his eyes. He blinked it away as he peered through the tiny opening and tried to draw a bead on one of the shapes flitting past in the darkness outside. Some Indians wouldn't attack at night, but lack of daylight had never seemed to bother the Comanches. In fact, they loved to raid on a night like this, when a big yellow moon was floating in the Texas sky.

Logan squeezed the trigger, and the rifle bucked against him as it blasted, flame spurting like a geyser from the barrel. He couldn't tell if he'd hit anything or not, but he thought he heard a yelp of pain from one of the red devils. He grimaced. The rifle had a powerful kick, and it had made a twinge go through his left side where a Comanche arrow had already ripped out a hunk of hide earlier in the evening. The raiders had hit at dusk, just as Logan was getting the milk cows back in the corral, and he'd barely made it inside the cabin. He had been lucky that the lone arrow that hit him had struck only a grazing blow.

He turned away from the loophole and shoved the empty rifle into the waiting right hand of his wife. With her left hand, Jessie gave him the spare rifle she had just finished loading. Her face was pale and drawn in the light from the candle that sat on the table, but she was holding up as well as could be expected. Some nineteen-year-old girls would have hidden in a corner and wailed and whimpered when the Comanches came raiding. Not Jessie Logan. Not Dan Logan's wife.

She started reloading the empty rifle while Logan crouched at the loophole with the loaded one, waiting for another target.

That was when they both smelled the smoke.

"Damn it!" Logan exploded, although he knew that Jessie didn't like for him to curse. Her daddy was a Baptist preacher, and she was a good Bible-believing girl. She prayed every night, and she had even gotten her rough cob of a husband to pray every now and then, too.

Logan wished Jessie could pray up a miracle for them right about now. He was a mite too busy, himself.

He pressed the trigger, felt the buck of the rifle against his shoulder, heard the roar of exploding powder. When the echoes died away, he could hear the crackle of flames. And it was getting hotter in here.

The damned Indians had set the cabin on fire . . .

Boone woke up to a howl of rage and looked over to see the Texas Ranger thrashing around on the ground. The man was having one hell of a nightmare, Boone thought. For a moment, he considered trying to wake up Logan, then decided to let him sleep.

As far as Boone was concerned, Logan could suffer through a nightmare or two. After all, *he* could wake up sooner or later. Boone didn't have that luxury.

He was living his nightmare.

Awkwardly because of the hands tied behind his back, Boone pulled himself into a sitting position. He had to kick his feet back and forth and get himself rocking a little, then thrust out with his legs to lever himself upright. His ankles were bound as securely as his wrists, but at least his feet were only a little numb. His arms and shoulders and hands were almost completely dead, the feeling in them shut off by the bonds and the uncomfortable position in which he had been forced to spend the night. Boone tried to wiggle his fingers, but he couldn't feel them responding.

He glared toward the horizon to the east. The sky there was bright pink and orange from the approaching sunrise. Most mornings, Logan was up and around by this time, getting the coffee and breakfast ready so that he and his prisoner could get an early start on the trail. Boone reflected bitterly that the man was sure anxious to get back to Texas and see him hanged.

This morning was different, though. Logan was still asleep, although judging from his muttering and yelling and restless rolling, his slumber at the moment was anything but restful.

Boone glanced at the other side of the bench where they were camped. He couldn't see the slope of the gully, but he could see where it dropped off and knew that just on the other side was likely a fortune in gold. The nuggets they'd already found were in Logan's saddlebags, but Logan hadn't explored the gully to see how much more of the wonderful yellow metal might be there. Boone couldn't understand a man like that, couldn't figure out how anybody could sit around with a damned treasure right under his nose and not do anything about it. Logan was either dedicated or crazy— or both.

Or maybe neither. Boone remembered how the day before, he had seen a glimmer of *something* in the ranger's eyes, something that seemed to surprise Logan himself as much as it did Boone.

Greed, maybe? A hunger for some of that gold?

Boone hoped so, but at the moment he had more pressing

worries. His bladder was full, and there was nothing he could do about it as long as he was tied up like this. He was going to have to wake up Logan after all.

"Hey!" Boone called softly. "Hey, Logan!"

The ranger muttered something under his breath, but Boone couldn't make out the words.

"Wake up, Logan." Boone's voice was more urgent now. "We got a problem over here, damn it. My back teeth are floating. Logan! Wake up!"

Logan heard the crashing against the shutters of the window and spun around in time to see Comanche war axes chopping through the shutters. A hideous red face loomed in the opening and Jessie let out a scream. Logan fired the rifle in his hands and saw the face duck back.

Jessie's cry had trailed away into a series of choking coughs. Smoke filled the little cabin now, and the heat was like an oven. The roof was ablaze, Logan was sure of that. It would fall in soon, trapping them. They could stay here and burn to death, or they could try to flee the cabin and be cut down by Comanche arrows. If they were lucky they would be killed quickly. Otherwise, he would face hours or even days of the most excruciating torture those fiends could imagine. And Jessie . . . it would be even worse for Jessie.

Logan bit back another curse as he reached for one of the loaded pistols lying on the floor beside him. He had been saving the pistols for the time when the Indians broke into the cabin. Now it looked like the Comanches wouldn't even bother. They would wait and let the flames get the young couple who had been foolish enough to think they could settle here on the edge of the hill country, far away from settlements like San Antonio and Austin where they would have been safe.

If he could just go back and change things, Logan thought.

If he could forget about his dreams of having a ranch of his own, a place he and his wife could call home, a place where they could raise horses and cattle and a fine mess of kids . . .

One of the beams in the roof, weakened by the fire, cracked loudly and sagged but did not give way. Jessie shrank against Logan's side, looking up at the roof.

"Dan," she said quietly, "I don't want to burn to death."

"We can try to make it out the back," he began.

She shook her head. "No. They'd kill us, and you know it. At least they'd kill you."

"You might have a chance to get away. I'll take the pistols and keep 'em busy—"

She lifted her face to his and silenced him with a quick kiss, pressing her lips hard against his. "You have to do it," she whispered. "You have to."

He swallowed hard, licked dry and cracked lips, and sleeved sweat off his forehead. "I . . . I can't," he rasped, the words full of pain.

Jessie put a hand on one of the other pistols. "Then I'll have to do it myself." Her voice shook, and Logan knew that no matter how brave she was, she wouldn't be able to do it.

"No," he said. "I'll take care of it."

She kissed him again and managed a tired smile. "God bless you," she breathed. "I love you, Dan."

"I love you, too, Jessie," he told her as he lifted the pistol and put the muzzle against her head, right behind her ear where she wouldn't be able to see anything. All he had to do was press the trigger, and she wouldn't have to worry anymore about burning to death or being captured by the Comanches. She wouldn't be tortured or used over and over by those filthy bucks until she died, nothing but a mindless husk. He had to do it. He just had to.

Another beam cracked, and the roof began to come down.

Logan cried, "Jessie!" and pulled the trigger at the same time, his shout lost in the roar of sound that washed up from the pistol and crashed over both of them.

Boone saw Logan roll over, and then the ranger bellowed something incoherent as he surged to his feet and threw himself across the ashes of the campfire. His left hand swept down to his waist and came up with the bowie knife sheathed there. The thick, heavy blade gleamed dully in the early morning light.

There was just enough time for Boone to shout, "Logan!" before the ranger crashed into him. Boone went over backward, driven hard against the ground by Logan's weight. The knife came up toward his throat. Boone croaked, "For God's sake, Logan, *don't*!"

Logan froze, the sharp point of the knife barely pricking the skin of Boone's throat just under the chin. He stared at Boone with glazed eyes, their faces only inches apart. Then, slowly—much too slowly to suit Boone, who could feel a tiny thread of blood trickling down his throat from the spot where the bowie was pressed against his neck—he saw reason begin to ease back into the ranger's eyes.

A shudder wracked Logan, but luckily he took the knife away from Boone's throat an instant before he began to shake. After a moment, Logan rolled off of Boone and lay on his back, drawing in great, heaving breaths. "Oh, Lord," he said hoarsely. "Oh, Lord . . ."

Boone echoed those sentiments. That was as close to dying as he ever wanted to come. He didn't say anything, just waited for Logan to get over whatever kind of fit had gripped him. He didn't want to set the ranger off on a tear again.

Finally, Logan pushed himself up on an elbow and peered over at his prisoner. "You all right, Blakely?" he asked.

"I . . . I think so. Reckon this place on my neck is just a scratch."

Logan grimaced and pushed himself into a sitting position. He slid the bowie knife back into its sheath and reached over to take hold of Boone's shoulders. As he lifted Boone upright, he said, "I'm sorry as all hell, Blakely. I didn't mean for that to happen. I . . . I reckon I was dreamin', and for a few seconds I didn't realize I was awake."

"That's all right," Boone told him. The pounding in Boone's chest and head was beginning to ease a little. His heart had been going a mile a minute for a while there, when he'd been convinced he was about to die.

He wondered fleetingly if Jason Stoneham had experienced the same thing in those last few seconds of life.

Then, shaking that thought out of his head, he asked Logan, "Are you all right now?"

"I reckon I will be. Were you callin' me, tryin' to wake me up?"

"Yeah, I had a problem." Boone glanced down at the front of his breeches and saw the dark stain spreading there. He shook his head wryly. "Don't have it anymore, though."

"Sorry," Logan grunted. The ranger got to his feet. "I got some spare trousers. I'll loan 'em to you." He started toward his saddlebags, which lay on the ground beside his bedroll.

A little later, after Logan had untied Boone's ankles and helped him into the dry pair of pants, the ranger built up the fire again and set the coffeepot in the low flames. Looking at the fire seemed to bother him for some reason, and he stood up quickly and strode away, going over to the edge of the gully to peer into its still-shadowy depths. Boone wondered what was going on in the man's head, but he wasn't going to ask. Not after Logan had already gone crazy once this morning.

As he stood by the gully, images filled Logan's head. The nightmare was etched into his brain, but the worst of it was that the dream had been real, not some twisted distortion of what had really happened. The events of the dream had occurred just as he had relived them in his troubled slumber, and even now the pull of the memories was too strong to resist. In his mind, he was back there in that burning cabin in Texas, his wife's dead body sagging against him, blood from her shattered skull soaking his shirt as sobs wracked him. That was when he'd heard the shots from outside the cabin, the blasts sounding like a long roll of thunder.

The reports came too close together to be from single-shot weapons like the rifles and pistols Logan had inside the cabin. And the Comanches didn't have any guns at all, as far as he knew. That meant the shooting had to come from some of those newfangled Paterson Colt repeating pistols.

The kind of pistols carried by the ranging companies.

Men on horseback were sweeping around the cabin as Logan stumbled out into the night, Jessie's limp form cradled in his arms. By the light of the blazing structure, which grew brighter as the roof finally fell in, he saw that the riders were fellow Texans, the men who had ridden by here a few days ago on one of their patrols. He recognized the one called Cap'n Jack, and those wild Lewis boys from over on the Brazos, and a tall man wearing a pair of fancy silver spurs whose name Logan didn't know. They were rangers, all right, and as the firing quickly died away, Logan knew they had either killed or routed the whole Comanche war party, even though they'd been outnumbered considerably.

Cap'n Jack and the man with the silver spurs turned their horses and trotted back to the cabin while the other men continued giving chase to the fleeing Indians. The captain's face was grim as he swung down from his saddle. He looked at Jessie and said fervently, "Damn! I'm sorry, Logan. We heard you shooting and got here as quick as we could. Looks like we weren't soon enough.''

"I . . . Jessie was afraid . . . There was nothing I could . . .'' Logan could barely get the words out. "She didn't want the Comanches to get her . . .''

Cap'n Jack said to the other man, "Adam, lend a hand here.'' The second ranger quickly dismounted and gently took Jessie's body out of Logan's arms. Logan wanted to resist, but he just didn't have the strength.

"I'll take care of her, Mr. Logan,'' the ranger promised solemnly. "You don't have to worry about a thing.''

Cap'n Jack took Logan's arm and led the stunned settler away from the still-burning cabin. "Those savages won't ever raid anybody else again,'' Cap'n Jack said. "And once the fire's out, we'll give you a hand clearing off and rebuilding.''

"No,'' Logan said abruptly. He jerked his arm out of the ranger's grasp. "No need to rebuild.''

Cap'n Jack looked at him intently. "What do you mean, Logan?''

"I never should've come out here, never should've brought Jessie. Not when it was so dangerous. I . . . I won't be stayin'.''

"Texans aren't much for running,'' Cap'n Jack said with a frown. "I know you're hurting right now, Logan, but—''

"I'm not running,'' Logan cut in, not sure where he was finding the strength or where the words were coming from. "I just can't stay here anymore and go back to the kind of life Jessie and me had. Not without her.'' He took a deep breath. "You got room in your patrol for another rider, Cap'n?''

Slowly, a smile touched with sorrow and sympathy appeared on the other man's face. He clapped a hand on Logan's shoulder. "Damn right,'' Cap'n Jack said. "If you want to ride with the rangers, Dan, you'll be more'n welcome.''

And ever since, that was exactly what he had been doing.
Until now.

Logan drew a deep breath and swung away from the gully. He strode toward Boone, drawing his bowie knife as he came. Boone's eyes widened as he watched the ranger approaching. Logan had that crazy look in his eyes again. As Logan bent toward him, the blade flashing now in the light of the newly risen sun, Boone exclaimed urgently, "Wait a minute, Logan! Don't—''

The razor-sharp blade cut expertly through the ropes around Boone's wrists, severing them without even nicking him. Another slash of the bowie, and the ropes binding Boone's ankles fell away.

Logan straightened and rammed the knife back in its sheath. He gestured at the pot and said, "Help yourself to some coffee, and you can have some of my jerky and hardtack. Then get the hell out of here.''

Boone practically gulped as he said in amazement, "What?''

"You heard me," grated Logan. "I'm lettin' you go, Blakely.''

"You . . . you believe what I told you about what happened back there in Texas?''

"I ain't sure whether I do or not, but that don't matter no more. I realize now I don't want to go back to Texas. I've had my fill of the place.''

Boone glanced at the gully. "Finding that gold wouldn't have anything to do with your decision, now would it, Logan?''

The ranger's jaw tightened, and he growled, "Shut up. What I decide is my business, not yours, Blakely. I'm warnin' you: soon as you've ate, get gone from here, and don't come back. If I ever see your face again, I'm liable to change my mind and figure I made a mistake. Go somewhere else and look for gold.''

Boone nodded. ''All right. You don't have to worry about me, Logan. You won't ever see hide nor hair of me again.''

''Good,'' grunted the Ranger.

Boone didn't know what had come over the ranger. That must have been *some* nightmare Logan had had, he thought. But he wasn't going to waste this opportunity. He had hoped that his story would arouse the ranger's sympathy and make Logan doubtful of his guilt, but Boone had never dreamed that Logan would set him free. If he'd been the praying kind, he would have thought this was some sort of miracle.

He didn't waste the chance, nor any time. Less than half an hour after Logan's unexpected decision, Boone was mounted on the mule and riding away down the canyon, heading west again. Logan had given him some supplies but no gun. The ranger might have had a change of heart, but he was no fool. He wasn't going to tempt his former prisoner to come back and bushwhack him.

Boone didn't intend to try anything like that. He wanted to put as much distance as possible between himself and Dan Logan. If Logan didn't return to Texas, the rangers might send somebody else after him, but that would take some time. By then, Boone thought, maybe he would be lucky and find a fortune of his own. Maybe he'd buy a berth on some sailing ship and sail off to an island somewhere, a place where the Texas rangers could never find him. For now, though, he just wanted to put Logan well behind him.

There was just one worry nagging at Boone's mind as he sent the mule along the winding trails through the foothills.

Logan had changed his mind once. He could change it again. And if he did, he could still come after Boone, intending to take him back to Texas and the gallows.

That wasn't going to happen, Boone told himself. He had let himself get caught once, but never again. If he ever crossed paths with the ranger again, he wouldn't hesitate.

He'd just kill Logan and be done with it.

Twelve

Some might have thought it impossible, but as 1848 turned into 1849, the flow of goldseekers to California increased. Spurred on by newspaper reports of fabulous fortunes there for the taking, as well as editorials by Horace Greeley and others extolling the wealth to be found in the Sierra Nevadas, men came from not only the United States but practically every country on earth, all of them bound for their own private El Dorado. They came to be known as Argonauts, taking the name from the mythical sailors who sought the legendary Golden Fleece. If '48 had been a boom year, then '49 was a veritable explosion.

On an overcast morning in the spring of '49, Anne Palmer stepped out of the cabin she shared with her husband Thaddeus and paused to look at the settlement that had been called Bloody Gulch when the two of them first arrived. It had grown tremendously in the months since then, and now it had a new name, too: the camp had been christened Ophir, after the famous lost city in the Bible.

There were still quite a few tents serving as homes for the miners, but now there were almost as many permanent structures. The biggest, most impressive building was a saloon and gambling den called the Alhambra, which was owned by a man named Trent, but Ophir also boasted a town hall, a general mercantile, a blacksmith shop, and an assay office. There had been talk of putting up a church, but none of the miners had gotten around to it yet.

The cabin where Anne and Thaddeus lived also served as

the doctor's office and a crude hospital when necessary. When the camp was called Bloody Gulch, it had more than lived up to its name: shootings and stabbings and violent fistfights had been all too common, and it was a rare week when Palmer wasn't summoned to attend to three or four men who were dying from some sort of angry confrontation. Even with the high death toll, however, the settlement continued to grow. More Argonauts came in upright than went out feetfirst. Now that the name of the village had been changed to Ophir—by vote of the inhabitants when some Bible-thumping miner had stirred them up—the violence had abated, though only slightly.

But at least there was reason to hope that someday Ophir might be a civilized place, Anne thought as she looked at the camp spreading out in front of her. She wasn't the only woman around any longer. There were the painted trollops from Trent's saloon, of course, but there were also several respectable women—the wives and daughters of some of the miners. There were enough ladies to form a quilting circle, in fact, and that was where Anne was headed now, for that weekly get-together.

"Would you like for me to walk you over to Irene's, dear?" Palmer called from inside the cabin, where he was pouring over one of his medical books.

Anne smiled as she looked back at him and shook her head. "No, that's all right, Thaddeus. I'm sure I'll be fine."

She hadn't felt like that when they first got here. Then she had been afraid to leave their tent unescorted, for fear that some bushy-bearded, filthy miner might throw her over his shoulder and carry her off like a beast. Such a thing had never happened, and although Anne suspected some of the men still made lewd comments about her behind her back, she had come to realize that they treated her with complete courtesy most of the time. She liked to think they were gentlemen under their rough exteriors.

Of course, the fact that they wanted to keep her husband around to tend to their sicknesses and injuries probably helped matters, too.

Palmer grunted his acceptance of Anne's decision and said, "I'm going over to Jaston Gruber's shortly. He's fallen ill, and I'm afraid it may be cholera."

Anne repressed a shudder and hoped Thaddeus was wrong, although she had every faith in his diagnostic abilities. She had heard about the waves of cholera that had swept through other mining camps, but so far Ophir had been spared. "Be careful," she told her husband. "You don't want to catch whatever Mr. Gruber has."

Palmer chuckled. "You've been a physician's wife for many years, my dear. You know that can't be a consideration. I'm honor bound to do my duty and treat the sick."

She bit back a sharp retort. More than once, she had spoken to him about the dangers and diseases he exposed himself to by going among the Argonauts, and it never did any good. He was right; it was time she stopped worrying.

"I'll be back later, dear," she told him, then started toward the small, recently completed town hall where the quilting circle met. She was carrying her bag and the piece of quilt on which she was currently working.

The cabin was on a small hill, little more than a knoll, really, at the end of Ophir's only real street. The avenue, if such it could be called, was a broad stretch of mud at the moment, chopped and stirred by the hooves of mules and horses and the wheels of wagons until it was a nearly impassable swamp. If a wagon stopped moving or even slowed down too much, it would likely get stuck, so drivers usually whipped their teams mercilessly, and the air was full of shouted oaths. Anne and the other women had learned to ignore the profanity, no matter how blue the air turned. As for the mud, the ladies avoided it by staying on the board-walks of roughly hewn planks that had been laid down along both sides of the street, in front of the tents and buildings of the settlement.

The town hall was made of logs, a sturdy-looking building with the name *Ophir* burned into a plank and hung over the door. As Anne approached, she saw several other women coming along the boardwalk. She nodded greetings to Mrs. Alice Morrison and Mrs. Gertrude McDermott and Mrs. Mary Eula Finnegan. They were the founding members of the Ophir quilting society.

"Good day, ladies," Anne said to them as they all met at the door of the town hall. She was glad to see them. They were like anchors for each other in this world full of crude, unwashed miners. For the next couple of hours, Anne could sit with them and work on her quilting and enjoy a polite conversation, much as if she was back in San Francisco or Boston or some other civilized city.

Mary Eula looked worried about something, and she didn't waste any time in sharing her concern. "I saw that horrible creature called Red Sally coming this way, ladies, and she was carrying something that looked like a quilting bag!"

Anne frowned and looked down the boardwalk toward the Alhambra. Sure enough, Red Sally was marching deter-minedly along the planks. She was dressed fairly decorously, at least for a woman in her profession, in a high-necked gray dress that was still tight enough to brazenly display her op-ulent figure. And even in that dress, there was no mistaking her calling, not with the garishly colored hair that had prompted her name and the heavy paint on her features. Anne wasn't sure how old Red Sally was, but probably no more than twenty-five. That was no longer young for a pros-titute, though.

"Hey, girls," Red Sally called out as she came down the boardwalk toward them. "Got room for another in that sewing circle of yours?"

"This is a quilting society," Alice replied coldly, keeping her gaze carefully fixed on a point somewhere beyond Red Sally's shoulder so that she wouldn't have to look such a creature in the eye. That much was painfully obvious from the expression on her face and the disdainful tone of her voice.

If Red Sally took any offense, she didn't show it. She just grinned and said, "That's all right. I can quilt. My mama taught me."

"It's a shame she didn't teach you some other things," Gertrude said, "such as how to act like a lady."

Red Sally's jaw tightened a little at that gibe. But she went on determinedly, "I'd really like to join you ladies for a little while. It's not often a gal like me gets to sit down and gab with some other girls."

Anne felt a touch of sympathy for the soiled dove, but it was overwhelmed by her outrage at the fact that Red Sally would try to intrude herself on a group of respectable ladies. "I'm sorry," she told the woman with forced politeness. "We don't have any chairs open right now. Perhaps another time."

"But . . ." Red Sally began, then looked from face to face among them and saw nothing but stony contempt. Her lips thinned as she pressed them together, and for a second Anne thought she saw something shining in the prostitute's eyes. Surely not, though, because it was common knowledge that her kind never cried.

"All right," Red Sally went on heavily. "Another time." She turned and walked back toward the saloon, her shoulders drooping now.

"Imagine the nerve of that harlot," Gertrude sniffed, not

caring if Red Sally was still within hearing distance or not.

Anne sighed. She had been as angry and uncomfortable as the others at the very idea of even talking to such a woman, but she still felt a little sorry for Red Sally. The soiled doves led a drab, pathetic existence, and Anne couldn't blame Red Sally for wanting a respite from it, even for a little while.

"Come along, ladies," she said, reaching for the door. "Let's go inside."

For the next hour, the members of the quilting circle sat in the town hall and worked on their projects, talking in low voices of the things they had left behind back in Boston and Philadelphia and Charleston and Baltimore. Anne was rather distracted and took only a small part in the conversation, instead of leading it as she often did. Her mind was still on the encounter with Red Sally. Her friends would be shocked if they had heard some of the things that Thaddeus had said to her in the past about how women like Red Sally actually served a very valuable purpose in the mining camps.

"Morally, they're an outrage, of course," Thaddeus had proclaimed on more than one occasion. "But unfortunately, given the base nature of man and the rough conditions around here, without the whores there would be even more killings. That's a fact, sad but true."

Anne supposed he was right. It was difficult for her to be sure because Thaddeus was the only man she had known intimately, and passion was not a large part of his makeup, unless it was his passion for medicine and healing. It was incomprehensible to Anne how a woman like Red Sally could bear the touch of so many different men and not just die of sheer embarrassment. Why, she didn't even undress in front of Thaddeus after all these years. What must it be like to have so many different men? Even the mere thought . . .

"Are you all right, Anne?" Mary Eula asked anxiously. "Why, you're positively flushed, my dear, and you're breathing so hard!"

"I . . . I'm not feeling very well," Anne replied hurriedly, turning an even deeper shade of red. "Perhaps I'm coming down with a touch of the grippe."

"I wouldn't be surprised," Gertrude said. "With all the rain and cold weather during the winter, it's a wonder we didn't all die. I'm glad it's spring now, and we'll have some warmer weather."

That comment set them off on a round of speculation about what sort of weather the spring and summer would bring, since none of them had spent those seasons in the Sierra Nevadas yet, and Anne was glad for the change of subject.

The ladies were still discussing the weather when the hoarse yells suddenly began in the street outside.

Anne looked up. The man who had shouted was obviously in pain. A glance around at the other women told Anne that they were busily ignoring the cries, although she could tell from the set of their jaws that they heard them.

"Oh, God, somebody help me!"

The plea carried clearly inside the town hall. Anne caught her lower lip between her teeth. She didn't want to leave the building, but she was not like Alice or Gertrude or Mary Eula. She was a doctor's wife.

Acting before she lost her nerve, Anne leaned over and placed her section of quilt in her bag, then stood up quickly. The others gaped at her, and Gertrude said, "For goodness' sake, Anne, you're not going out there, are you?"

The shouts had died away to a series of loud whimpers. Steeling herself, Anne nodded and said, "I have to see if I can help that poor man until Thaddeus arrives. After all, I've assisted my husband for years. It's not like I've never seen the results of trouble before.''

She walked quickly to the door, and none of the others tried to stop her. None of them followed her, either. Anne grasped the latch, twisted it, and opened the door, stepping out onto the boardwalk.

The man had collapsed about ten yards down the walk, the upper half of his body lying on the planks and the lower half stretched out in the mud. A small crowd of miners had gathered around him, standing and talking but doing nothing to help him. To make herself heard above their chatter, Anne called loudly, ''Step aside, please! Let me through!''

One of the men turned and looked at her, and she recognized Barney Cumberland, the miner who had been so helpful when she and Thaddeus came to Bloody Gulch. He had done most of the work when their cabin was built, too, and was probably Thaddeus's best friend in the settlement. He nodded to Anne and then said to the others, ''Out of the way, boys. The doc's wife is comin' through.''

Anne paused and asked Barney, ''Has anyone gone to summon Thaddeus? He's either at our cabin or at Jaston Gruber's.''

''No, but that's a right fine idea. Somebody go fetch the doc!''

Anne swallowed her impatience. Had they intended to stand around watching until the poor man died of whatever ailed him? That was how it appeared. Sometimes the callousness of these men still shocked her.

The miners stepped aside and made a path for her, and she knelt beside the man who lay on the boardwalk. She paled and swallowed hard at the sight of the blood pooling underneath his body. He was lying on his side, and she could see blood welling between the arms he had crossed over his stomach. He had been either knifed or shot in the belly, and since Anne hadn't heard any gunshots, she suspected the injury came from a blade. As she gently pried his arms loose and moved them back so that she could inspect the wound, she saw that she was right. The long, thin, ragged gash had been made by a knife.

"Did anyone see what happened?" she asked, trying not to let her voice shake too much.

"Nope," Barney replied. "Rusterman come staggerin' out from behind his tent like that and made it this far 'fore he collapsed. I reckon somebody jumped him and knifed him for his poke."

Anne didn't doubt it for a moment. Many of the men in the camps were capable of murder over something as small as a pouch of gold dust. Rusterman's assailant would probably never be found.

That was a matter for someone else to deal with. At the moment, all she was worried about was stopping the bleeding. Rusterman had finally fallen silent, but only because he had passed out. A deathly pallor covered his stubbled face, but he was still breathing, the air rasping in his throat as he drew it in.

Anne didn't stop to think. She reached into her bag, pulled out the section of quilt, and pressed it to the gaping wound in Rusterman's stomach. That was all she could do.

Suddenly a hand reached out from beside her and held the quilt against Rusterman's body. "I'll do that," a familiar voice said.

Anne looked over to see Red Sally kneeling at the edge of the boardwalk. The soiled dove grinned at her and went on. "I've patched up more than one poor son of a bitch who got his belly opened up with a knife. I'll take care of him until your husband gets here, Mrs. Palmer."

"I . . . I . . ." Anne searched for the words she needed. "Thank you, Sally. But I'm all right. I can do this."

"Reckon you can, but there ain't no need."

The ludicrous thought struck Anne that she might have to fight this prostitute for the right to tend to the injured man. She could just see the two of them, rolling around in the mud of the street, biting and spitting and pulling each other's hair . . .

Even in these grim circumstances, Anne found herself smiling slightly at that image. She relinquished the piece of quilt, which was rapidly becoming sodden with blood anyway, and stood up. "Thank you," she said quietly to the painted woman.

Red Sally didn't have a chance to reply, because the crowd around the wounded man parted again and Dr. Thaddeus Palmer came bustling through. "What's all this?" he asked. "Someone's been knifed?"

" 'Fraid you're too late, Doc," Red Sally said with a sigh. "Ol' Rusterman's dead."

Palmer knelt beside the body and quickly checked for a pulse, then nodded solemnly. "I'm afraid you're correct. There's nothing I can do. If some of you gentlemen will take charge of the body . . . ?"

"Oh, sure," Barney Cumberland said. "We'll bury 'im, Doc. The ground's thawed out some now. Don't you worry."

Palmer straightened and turned to his wife. "I'm sorry you had to see this, Anne," he said quietly as he took her arm. "Come along."

Anne exchanged a quick look with Red Sally as Thaddeus led her away, and she frowned as she turned her attention to her husband. Had there been some sort of connection between her and the prostitute, no matter how fleeting and shallow? For a few seconds there, had it been almost as if they were . . . friends?

That was as ridiculous as the thought of the two of them

wrestling in the muddy street. Anne shook her head and
thrust such ideas out of her mind. She looked at Thaddeus,
and her frown deepened. Beads of sweat stood out on his
forehead, and the day was not warm enough to warrant that.
He seemed a little pale underneath his normally ruddy com-
plexion, too.

"Are you feeling ill, Thaddeus?" she asked. Earlier, her
flush in the town hall had prompted the same question from
Mary Eula, but Anne had lied about a touch of grippe. Thaddeus actually looked sick.

"I'm fine, just a bit tired," he told her. "It's nothing for
you to worry about, Anne."

"I'm glad. You should rest more."

Palmer smiled. "That's difficult for a doctor to do in a
place like this. Remember, I promised you that my practice
would thrive if we came to the gold fields, and I like to keep
my promises."

"Well, you won't do your patients any good if you're too
worn out to treat them properly. Not that I would ever doubt
you, Thaddeus." She hurried on, "How was Jaston
Gruber?"

The smile on Palmer's face was replaced by a worried
frown. "I'm afraid that Mr. Gruber is a very sick man."

"Is it cholera?" Anne asked in a half-whisper.

Palmer nodded wearily. "That's certainly what it looks
like. He has all the symptoms—the fever, the vomiting, the
loose bowels . . . Well, I needn't go into all the indelicate
details. The worst of it, though, is that this isn't the first case
I've seen recently."

Anne looked at him sharply. "You didn't say anything to
me about it."

"I didn't want to worry or frighten you unnecessarily.
Gruber's case is the fourth one I've seen in the past two
weeks, though, and the situation is becoming quite serious."

"What can we do about it?"

Palmer sighed heavily. "I don't know. No one knows what causes cholera or how it's spread. All we can do is warn everyone in the settlement about the possibility of an epidemic and caution them to take as good care of themselves as they can. A person stands a much better chance of surviving the disease if he's relatively healthy to start with. Unfortunately, so many of these miners are malnourished or suffering from an assortment of other maladies. It could get bad, Anne, quite bad."

She reached over and took his hand as they walked toward the cabin. "I'll do anything I can to help, Thaddeus. We'll get through this, just like we always have in times of trouble."

"Dear Anne!" Palmer smiled at her and squeezed her hand. "I would have thought that I would be saying such things to *you* once I told you about what was happening. I'm a lucky man to have married such a woman."

"Of course you are," Anne said, returning his smile.

Inside, though, she was worried. More than worried, actually. She was frightened. If a cholera epidemic swept through Ophir, it might spare no one. The entire settlement could be wiped out.

They would just have to pray and work hard and hope for the best, she told herself. And she remembered at that moment that she had left the piece of her quilt pressed to the body of the miner called Rusterman. It was probably being buried with the man right now, because graves were dug quickly and funeral services conducted with dispatch in the gold fields. Every minute spent on the ceremony was another minute when no gold was being found.

With the possibility of a deadly epidemic looming over the camp, though, a piece of quilt was much too trivial a thing to worry about. All she really wanted, Anne thought, was for her and Thaddeus to come through this all right.

Thirteen

Nathan hauled back hard on the reins of the mule team, shouting, "Whoa! Whoa, blast it!" Why was it, he wondered distractedly, that mules were so damned difficult to get moving and then so hard to stop once they got started?

The wagon lurched to a halt alongside a creek that bubbled through a meadow between some rugged hills. The rocky slopes of those hills were covered with the tents of miners who had come here with wash pans and picks and shovels to seek their fortunes. Nathan knew what frustrating, backbreaking work that was, since it was only last year that he had been one of them. Even though he hadn't been enthusiastic about coming back to the mountains, he had to admit that what he was doing now was much better than mining.

He swung down from the high seat of the wagon, and as he did so the weight of the heavy pistol holstered on his right hip bumped against his leg. Nathan still felt awkward about carrying the gun. Emily had insisted, though. There was more at stake than the outfit of one man; in the wagon were enough supplies for dozens of men, and they represented a sizable investment for Emily. Nathan couldn't blame her for wanting him to be armed so that he could guard the goods.

Back in San Francisco, Nathan had practiced for several weeks with the Walker revolver that Emily had had shipped out from the factory of a man called Samuel Colt. Colt manufactured most of his guns for the army and the Texas Rangers, Emily had told Nathan, but some of these so-called civilian models were available. It was the most dependable, most powerful handgun to be had, she went on, but that claim didn't do much to ease Nathan's mind. He had never carried a gun in his life.

During his target practice, he had gotten accustomed to the deafening roar of the black powder exploding when he pulled the trigger, and his hand and arm and shoulder had finally stopped aching from the powerful recoil of the weapon. But he was still a miserable shot, able to hit only a fraction of the targets at which he aimed—and they weren't even shooting back at him! Still, Emily hoped that the simple fact he carried a gun would deter any trouble.

So far, it had. Nathan had made four trips to the gold fields, and this was his fifth. Every time, he had sold all of the goods he carried within a matter of hours, even at the exorbitant prices Emily insisted upon. The enterprise had been so successful, in fact, that she was talking about adding more wagons and drivers. Of course, that would just add to Nathan's headaches, because she would expect him to supervise the other men as well as go on handling his own wagon.

But she was paying him a generous share of the profits, and Nathan couldn't complain about that. He'd been saving the money, so that eventually he might be able to start some sort of business of his own.

A few miles downstream, the creek beside which Nathan had parked the wagon ran into the north branch of the Yuba River. He had been working his way northward along the fringes of the Sierra Nevadas during these trips, although it was rumored that other lucrative gold fields were opening up to the south. He would get around to those sooner or later, he thought. If Emily had her way, Nathan would eventually visit every gold camp in California with a wagonload of supplies.

Now, as he untied the cords that held down the canvas cover over the wagon bed, he glanced at the hills around the creek and saw curious miners already heading his way. When they saw the goods he carried, many of them would return to their cabins or tents and fetch their nuggets and dust, then come back ready to buy. Nathan finished untying the last cord and threw back the canvas with a practiced flip of his wrist to expose his cargo.

Inside the wagon bed were large sacks of flour and salt and sugar and beans, crates full of crackers and salt pork, tools, bolts of canvas for repairing tents, small barrels of pickles and dried apples, scales for weighing gold dust, two boxes full of assorted books, and a stack of old newspapers tied together with string. Any sort of reading material was precious in these hills, no matter how out-of-date it was. The other provisions and supplies would sell even more quickly.

The miners who were approaching on foot were close enough now for one of them, a bearded man, to hail him. "Howdy, mister!" he called. "What you got there?"

"Anything you might need, my friend," Nathan replied with a grin as he waved a hand at the supplies in the back of the wagon. "Step right up and take a look. You'll find the prices are quite reasonable, too."

The men crowded around the wagon, their obscenity-laced conversation reminding Nathan of the clucking of a bunch of chickens swarming around a bug in a barnyard. They picked up the goods in work-roughened fingers and examined them intently, then replaced them and moved on to the next item. Nathan glanced at the hills and saw more men moving toward the creek. He cleared his throat and said, "It's first come, first served, gents. Just thought I should warn you, since it looks like there are more customers on the way.''

"Salt pork!" one of the men said excitedly. "And beans! Mister, I got to have some of this. How much?"

"The meat is ten dollars a pound, the beans four." Nathan always expected someone to balk and become angry at the prices Emily set for him to quote, but no one ever did. In fact, the miners were so glad to get the provisions that there usually wasn't even much grumbling. This time was no different.

"I'll be right back, soon as I get my poke from my tent," said the man who wanted to buy salt pork and beans. "Don't sell all of this stuff before then, you hear?"

"Then you'd better hurry, friend," Nathan told him. "This is going to be a mighty popular spot for the next few minutes."

Most of the miners took his advice and rushed off to their tents and cabins to get their nuggets and dust. Nathan took advantage of the lull to set up his own scale, so that he could weigh the gold when the miners returned with it. It looked like this trip was going to be as profitable as all the others he had made.

An hour later, the wagon bed was bare of supplies, and Nathan had over six thousand dollars in nuggets and dust and a few odd coins. The dust was bagged in small pouches and then those were stored in a larger oilcloth sack. That sack, along with the nuggets, went into a special compartment under the seat of the wagon which could be locked. Nathan twisted the key in the lock and put it in his pocket, then glanced up at the sky, which was a breathtaking mixture of purple and orange and red and deep blue from the sunset. He would camp here for the night and then start back to San Francisco in the morning. It would take him several days to reach the city, perhaps as long as a week, depending on the weather. Heavy spring rains could slow him down.

He had already unhitched and hobbled the team of mules so that they could graze in the new grass along the creek. They were in good shape for the night. Nathan's bedroll was stored under the seat, in front of the compartment where the gold was kept. His own supplies were there, too. He had to be careful to keep them out of sight while he was doing business, or else some of the miners would have wanted to buy his own food, leaving him with nothing to eat on the return trip.

Nathan ventured briefly into a grove of trees further along the creek, staying just long enough to gather an armload of dry branches for his campfire. Soon after returning to the wagon, he had a cheerful blaze going with the help of one of the crumbly sulphur matches called lucifers that he always carried with him. He would need the warmth of the embers before morning; already the temperature was starting to drop now that the sun was down. At these high elevations the nights were cool even during the summer.

Nathan brewed some tea, then cooked a few slices of bacon and warmed a pot of beans that he had cooked several days earlier. Along with some hard biscuits and a handful of dried apples, these made a filling, if not fancy, meal. By the time he was finished eating, full darkness had fallen. The hills around him were dotted with other fires from the camps of the miners, and in some places he saw squares of yellow lanternlight that shone through the windows of cabins. To a man standing on a height and looking out over this country in the daylight, it might well appear to be the same pristine wilderness it had been only a few years earlier. At night, though, with campfires covering the hills, it was easy to see just how widespread man's incursion had been.

As he spread his blankets on the ground underneath the wagon and crawled into them, Nathan thought about that.

From what he had heard, the whole country was gripped with gold fever, and people were pouring into California at an incredible rate, some of them sailing around South America, others making their way across the jungles of Panama and then up the west coast of the continent, others daring what was called the Great American Desert, the vast, uncharted region west of the Mississippi. All the commotion was going to make a difference, Nathan mused. Even if the gold rush ended eventually—and it showed no signs of doing so now—the country was going to be affected forever. There would be no turning back from what had gone before.

And as he went to sleep, Nathan could not decide if that was a good thing or not.

He woke up to the sound of angry shouting.

"Hang the bastard!" "String 'im up!" "Goddamn thief!"

Nathan rolled over and lifted his head, blinking against the bright morning sunlight that slanted under the wagon. The outraged yelling was still going on. Using his elbows, Nathan pulled himself from under the wagon and looked toward the nearby hills, which seemed to be the source of the commotion.

He saw a group of men clustered around a spruce tree. One of them waved a coiled rope in the air and cried, "Got my dust, he did! He's been sneakin' around the camp lookin' for something to steal for days now! I say we get rid of him!"

One of the other men lifted a single-shot rifle. "I can shoot him," he offered.

The first man, the one who had evidently lost his poke to the thief, shook his head and said loudly, "Shootin's too good for him. I say we string 'im up!"

Nathan felt a shiver of apprehension go through him. Dur-

ing his days as an Argonaut, he had seen a few examples of
the rough justice that was dispensed in the mining camps
and heard stories of other times when miners' courts had
been convened. Such proceedings didn't really follow any
rules, and they were usually more concerned with vengeance
than justice. From what he had seen and heard so far, some
poor fellow was about to be hanged, and Nathan wasn't sure
he wanted to wait around to witness the gruesome spectacle
of a man strangling and kicking away his life at the end of
a rope. He stood up quickly and began gathering his gear.
The shouting from the mob grew louder and angrier as Nathan pitched his blankets into the back of the wagon. He
could roll them up later, after he was away from here; and
he could stop when he was well out of earshot to fix himself
some breakfast.

As he reached for his gun belt and buckled it around his
waist, it struck him as a little strange that he hadn't heard
the accused man trying to defend himself. Of course, if the
thief had said anything, the other men likely would have just
shouted him down. Still, Nathan thought it odd that a man
would go to his death, would allow himself to be lynched,
without even trying to speak up in his own behalf.

At that moment, there was a burst of loud snarling and
growling, and one of the men yelled, "Look out, he's bustin'
loose!"

Involuntarily, Nathan jerked his head toward the mob. He
never would have expected the sight that met his eyes. A
dog had broken free of the circle of men and was running
toward him with a loping, ungainly stride that still managed
somehow to cover ground in a hurry. The animal was a huge,
ugly brute, with shaggy brown fur and a blocky head almost
as large as a horse's. Its tongue lolled from its mouth and it
trailed slobber from its muzzle as it raced toward the creek
and the wagon.

Nathan's eyes widened. Was the dog attacking him? He tensed, ready to vault up into the wagon bed, then he realized that wouldn't do him any good if the dog meant to maul him. A beast that large would have no trouble leaping into the wagon after him. Nathan's hand went to the butt of the gun on his hip. He might have to pull the Colt and try to shoot the dog. That thought made him so nervous he completely forgot about the things the miners had been saying only moments earlier.

Before Nathan could slide the revolver from its holster, the dog veered away from him and darted underneath the wagon instead. Nathan stepped away from the vehicle, worried that the dog meant to go under it and attack his legs. The animal stayed where it was, though, whirling around to face the men rushing after it. It bared its fangs and growled harshly at them.

The furious miners pounded up but stopped about a dozen feet short of the wagon. The dog was snarling at them now, and Nathan thought the sound was almost like a dare for them to come on and try to force the dog out from under the wagon. Nathan had backed away a good distance himself, and he still had his hand on the butt of his gun.

One of the miners threw an angry glance at Nathan. "That your dog, mister?" he demanded.

Nathan shook his head. "I've never seen the beast before," he replied.

"It came a-runnin' toward you like it knowed you," the miner pointed out.

Before Nathan could again deny owning the animal, one of the other men said, "Don't be a fool, Brody. That damned dog's been around nigh onto a week, a long time 'fore this fella got here."

"I don't care," the man called Brody said hotly. He was the one carrying the rope, and Nathan realized that he was the one claiming to have been robbed of his gold dust.

But how could he have been robbed by a *dog*?

Brody shook the coiled rope at the dog and went on, "Look at the way he's hidin' under that wagon! I still say it's mighty suspicious."

"Look, mister," Nathan began, "I'm mighty sorry about whatever happened, but I don't know that dog, and he doesn't know me. He's just looking for a place to hide because he's so scared."

One of the other men laughed and said, "He ain't scared, he's just found hisself a place where he can fort up and chew our arms off if we try to get him out."

Brody slapped the rope impatiently against his thigh. "I'll get him out. He's got to hang, I tell you!"

"You're going to hang a dog?" Nathan asked incredulously.

Brody glared at him. "He ain't a dog no more. He's just a thief, and he'll hang like any other thief. He snuck into my tent this mornin' and got hold of my poke. Chewed a hole in it, he did, and scattered my dust all over the camp! I'll never find all of it. Two weeks' worth of work, gone because of some goddamn mutt!"

Nathan suddenly felt a laugh welling up his throat. A grin tugged at his mouth. He could imagine the dog getting hold of Brody's poke and playing with it, slinging it back and forth until all the dust had sifted out through the holes the dog's teeth had made. He imagined that if the dog's mouth was to be examined, flecks of gold would still be clinging to its muzzle.

From the look on Brody's face, however, the miner was in no mood to appreciate the humor of the situation. All he cared about at the moment was revenge. Nathan ducked his head for a moment to hide the grin and managed to swallow the laugh before it escaped. When he looked up again, his face was appropriately solemn.

"I'm sorry about your gold dust," he told Brody, "but I don't see what I can do about it."

"You can move that dad-blasted wagon!" snapped the miner. "I'm a pretty good hand with a lasso. I'll dab a loop on that mangy son of a bitch and drag him out, then throw the rope over a limb and haul him up. That'll shut him up and teach him to scrounge around in things that ain't his."

It seemed to Nathan that scrounging around was a dog's natural calling. He'd had several dogs when he was a boy, and all of them had been alike in that respect. This one must have sensed his sympathy, because it turned its great head toward him and stopped growling as its dark eyes fixed on his face. To Nathan's astonishment, a tiny whine came from the dog's throat.

"Look at that!" one of the miners burst out. "He's asking this fella Jones for help!"

Brody fixed Nathan with a cold stare. "Well? You movin' that wagon or not?"

Nathan took a deep breath, trying to understand the impulse that had just gripped him. It made no sense, he decided, but hell, a man couldn't be practical *all* the time, could he?

"How much gold dust did you lose?" he heard himself asking.

Instantly, Brody's eyes narrowed shrewdly. "Why you askin'?" he wanted to know.

"I'm just curious," Nathan replied, knowing that none of them believed that. "How much was in your poke?"

"Close to a pound," Brody declared. "Call it a pound, for good measure."

He might have gotten away with it—Nathan had no way of challenging the man's claim—if one of the other miners hadn't guffawed and said, "Shoot, Brody, that pouch weren't more'n half full, and you know it. Don't go tryin' to take advantage of Jones here. After all, he brung us some mighty good supplies."

"And charged us a pretty penny for 'em, too," grumbled Brody. He crossed his arms, the coiled rope still hanging from one hand, and went on, "Just what've you got in mind, mister?"

"I'll replace the gold dust you lost," Nathan said, "and in return you won't hang that dog or hurt it in any other way."

"You're crazy as a damn loon! What's that dog to you? You sure it don't belong to you?"

"I swear I've never seen it before today," Nathan said. "I just don't want to see some dumb animal coming to any harm for something it didn't know was wrong."

The dog looked at him again, and he could have sworn it almost frowned when he said the words "dumb animal." That was a ridiculous idea, Nathan told himself, and he forced it out of his thoughts.

Brody rubbed a lean, undershot, heavily stubbled jaw. "Well, I don't know . . ." he said slowly. "I don't trust that dog, and I don't want it around here no more."

"I'll take it with me and turn it loose back down the trail a ways," Nathan suggested. "Think about it, Brody. You hang that dog, and all you've got to show for it is a dead dog. Take my offer, and at least you get your dust back."

For a few seconds, Brody hesitated, then nodded abruptly. "All right. But I had a good ten ounces in that poke."

No one was willing to dispute that version of Brody's claim, so Nathan broke out his scale again and got one of the pouches of dust from under the seat of the wagon. He measured out ten ounces, making sure that Brody could see the scale so there would be no argument about the weight. Nathan tipped the dust into an empty pouch.

The dog was still snarling and growling occasionally under the wagon; it didn't venture out. As Nathan handed over the gold dust to Brody, he said, "All right, you've been paid. You and the others should back away now, and I'll see what I can do with that dog."

"Watch out you don't get your balls bit off," one of the miners advised with a chuckle. The other Argonauts joined in the laughter, all except for Brody, who looked only slightly mollified by the bargain he had struck with Nathan. He was still glaring at the dog and twitching the rope against his leg.

The miners all withdrew from around the wagon, even Brody, and Nathan began trying to coax the dog out. It stopped growling when the other men were a good distance away, but it lifted its lips and showed its teeth again when Nathan came closer and leaned toward it, extending his hand.

Nathan took a quick step back, then caught himself. It wouldn't do to show fear to a dog, even a massive brute like this one. He said firmly, "Here now, is that any way to act? You asked me to help you, and I did. I saved your life, you know."

The dog cocked its head to the side as it looked at Nathan, who thought its dark eyes shone with intelligence. But that was probably too much to hope for. He snapped his fingers and pointed to the back of the wagon.

"Get up there."

The dog came out from under the vehicle and leaped agilely into the wagonbed.

Nathan blinked in surprise, and some of the miners watching from a distance hooted. One of them cupped his hands around his mouth and yelled, "Looks like you got yourself a dog, mister!"

Nathan frowned and took a step toward the wagon. The dog let out a bark that made him jump back again. He couldn't tell if the bark was an angry one or not, but it had certainly been loud. Holding his hands up toward the dog, he said, "Now just take it easy. I have to get on the wagon to drive it."

The dog glared at him.

Nathan sighed in exasperation. He should have known that something would happen. These trips to the gold fields on behalf of his aunt had been going entirely too smoothly. It was certainly past time that his usual bad luck cropped up again.

This story would make the rounds of the foothills. Within a few weeks, hundreds of miners would have heard about how he'd rescued the dog from a lynching only to have it refuse to allow him on his own wagon. They would get a good laugh out of the yarn, too. Enough was enough, Nathan thought. He took a deep breath and strode up to the wagon. The hair on the dog's back bristled as it growled at him.

"Sit down and be quiet!" Nathan said sharply. "I'm tired of this, and we're leaving. Now, I'm going to hitch up the mules, and you're going to sit there and behave yourself."

Once again, the dog turned its head to the side and stared at him quizzically, but it seemed to relax slightly.

Aware that the miners were still watching, Nathan briskly rounded up the mules and led them over to the wagon, hitching them into their harness. By the time he was finished, the dog was sitting down in the back of the vehicle, watching him noncommittally.

Hoping that the animal couldn't sense how nervous he was, Nathan swung up onto the seat and took up the reins. The knowledge that the great beast was behind him made the skin on the back of his neck crawl. Determinedly, he kept his gaze to the front. The wagon had to be turned around before he could leave, and as he got the mule team moving, the cluster of miners came into view again. Nathan called out to them, "Does this beast have a name?"

One of the men shouted back, "We been callin' him Hard-rock!"

Nathan glanced over his shoulder. The dog had lain down and was resting its head on its outstretched front paws. The motion of the wagon didn't seem to bother it, and Nathan wondered if it had come out here to California on the wagon of some goldseeker. If that was the case, what had happened to the animal's former owner? There was no way of knowing, Nathan realized. The miner could have died, or given up and gone home, or struck it rich and headed for San Francisco, leaving the dog behind. It didn't really matter now.

"Don't get too comfortable back there, Hardrock," Nathan told the dog. "You're only going to be traveling with me for a short while, and then you're on your own again."

He flapped the reins and called out to the mules and got the wagon rolling again, heading toward home this time.

Fourteen

Nathan covered quite a bit of ground that day, following the creek back down to the Yuba River where there was a decent trail leading toward the coast. The dog stayed in the back of the wagon during the morning, jumping down only when Nathan paused for a brief midday meal. As Nathan got the sack of biscuits from under the seat, Hardrock sat on the ground next to the wagon and waited patiently.

"You don't think I'm going to feed you, do you?" Nathan asked as he glanced at the dog. "This is my food, not yours. Besides, you're a hunter, remember? You can go out and catch a rabbit or something."

Hardrock whined.

"No," Nathan said firmly. He bit a piece off a biscuit he took from the sack, chewed and swallowed, then went on, "I'm not going to feed you, and that's final."

The dog bared his teeth again but made no sound, and Nathan discovered that the silent snarl was even more unnerving than the growling and barking.

"Oh, all right," he said. He tore off half of the biscuit and tossed it in the direction of Hardrock. There was a blur of motion from the dog and a loud snap as his jaws came together. The piece of biscuit was gone, and Nathan hadn't seen him chew or even swallow. It almost seemed as though Hardrock had sucked down the biscuit whole. The dog licked his lips and looked expectantly at Nathan.

"No, that was all you're going to get from me," Nathan said. "You might as well go on about your business. We're far enough away from that mining camp now for me to turn you loose. I don't think you'll find your way back there any time soon. You'd better hope not, because if you show up there, Brody's liable to try to hang you again.''

Hardrock stood up and padded toward Nathan, who swallowed hard but stood his ground as the dog approached. With a snuffling sound, Hardrock pushed his head against Nathan's hand. The long red tongue darted out and swiped across Nathan's wrist.

"This is ridiculous!" Nathan's voice was a mixture of frustration and nervousness. "I'm not going to feed you anymore, and I'm not going to take you with me. You're on your own, don't you understand that! Now, go on! Go away!''

Hardrock gave him that inquisitive look again, then turned and with a lithe bound leaped into the back of the wagon.

Nathan closed his eyes and grimaced. "No, not in the wagon! It's over! You can leave now. Come on, Hardrock, don't make me be mean to you.''

As if he could force the dog to leave if Hardrock didn't want to go, Nathan thought bleakly. Hardrock probably weighed almost as much as he did, and there were those long, sharp teeth to consider, too . . .

With a sigh of resignation, Nathan said, "I suppose it wouldn't hurt to take you a little farther away from the camp before I let you go. That way I'll be sure you don't run into Brody again.''

Hardrock gave a bark, then suddenly leaned over the wagon seat. His head darted toward the sack of biscuits Nathan had left on the seat, and before Nathan could stop him, the dog had plunged his muzzle into the bag of provisions. As Nathan shouted, "Hardrock, no!'' the animal's big head emerged, the massive jaws busily chewing, the dark brown eyes daring Nathan to try to take the food away from him.

It was going to be an even longer trip back to San Francisco than usual, Nathan thought.

Hardrock showed no signs of wanting to split up. Nathan had thought that sooner or later the dog would go bounding off into the woods in search of some wild game and that when he did, Nathan could get the wagon moving and leave Hardrock behind. The big brute seemed perfectly content to ride in the back of the wagon, though, and as the sun set and shadows began to gather that evening, Nathan still had his unwanted companion.

"I may be stuck with you now," Nathan told Hardrock as he went about setting up camp for the night, "but when we get back to San Francisco things will be different. You'll have to find a new home."

Hardrock just sat beside the wagon, tongue lolling out of his mouth, and Nathan would have sworn that the dog was laughing at him.

After supper—which was something of an adventure once Hardrock got a whiff of the salt pork sizzling in the frying pan over the flames of the campfire—Nathan spread his bedroll under the wagon and stretched out gratefully. A day of driving the wagon always made him tired, and the tension caused by the big dog's presence had only increased his weariness. They were camped alongside the river, in a clearing in the woods that bordered the stream, and as Nathan rolled onto his side, he saw Hardrock wandering toward the trees. A surge of hope went through him. Maybe the dog would wander off, and when morning came Nathan could break camp and get back on the trail before Hardrock returned. He had no qualms about leaving the dog up here; although the arrival of the miners had sent some of the animals who normally populated these hills retreating into deeper forests, there was still plenty of game around. And the miners themselves would probably take pity on the dog if it showed up at another camp. Hardrock wouldn't have any trouble finding a new home, Nathan told himself.

In the light from the moon and stars, Hardrock was nothing but a moving patch of vague darkness, and the dog had disappeared into the woods by the time Nathan dozed off. Nathan's tiredness took its toll, and he was soon sleeping soundly, an occasional snore issuing from him.

He had no idea how long he had been asleep when he awakened suddenly. Blinking rapidly in confusion, Nathan started to lift his head. Something must have disturbed him, and he wanted to find out what it was. There were still some grizzly bears in these hills, and one of the monsters might be after the mules. Or there could be some other kind of predator out there in the darkness . . .

A hand clamped itself over Nathan's mouth, shoving downward so that his head slammed into the ground. What felt like a bony knee drove into his belly. He curled up around the pain of the blow. Acting out of instinct, he threw a weak punch at his attacker and tried to heave himself upward, hoping to force the man against the underside of the wagon. The assailant was too strong and had too much of the advantage of surprise on his side. Nathan's head banged against the ground again, and a wave of dizziness and nausea washed over him.

Something cold and hard and round pressed against his flesh just under his chin. Even in his stunned state, Nathan realized that the thing was the barrel of a pistol. He smelled raw whiskey and knew it came from the breath of the man on top of him. The man hissed in an ugly voice, "Thought you'd make a fool of me, didn't you? You and that damned dog!"

Nathan recognized Brody's voice. The miner dug the pistol barrel into Nathan's neck, obviously relishing the cruelty of his actions.

"I saw where you put all that dust and those nuggets," Brody went on. "I reckon that'll be a fair payment for what you done to me. Where's that goddamned key?" The man pawed at Nathan's shirt, trying to find the pocket where Nathan kept the key to the locked compartment.

Nathan wanted to struggle. Brody was nothing but the common thief he had accused Hardrock of being. Nathan couldn't let himself lose the gold to such a man. But his muscles refused to work, and his brain was still swimming in a sea of pain. There was nothing he could do.

Now that his eyes were adjusted better to the dim light, Nathan could see Brody's lean face hovering over him, the features twisted into a grimace of hate and avarice. Brody wouldn't stop with stealing the gold, Nathan suddenly sensed. The man would kill him, too.

Abruptly, out of the corner of his eye, Nathan spotted movement on the other side of the clearing. Something was coming, a dark bulk at first that quickly resolved itself into a huge, furry shape bounding across the clearing with the unexpected silence of a striking wolf. It was Hardrock, and Nathan's eyes widened as he saw the dog's slavering jaws open hungrily.

Brody was kneeling half under the wagon, with his backside out and tilted in the air toward the charging Hardrock. If the dog bit him, the man's trigger finger would no doubt jerk instintinctively.

And the barrel of the pistol was still planted firmly under Nathan's chin.

Nathan tried to scream a warning, to call off the dog, but Brody still had his free hand pressed over Nathan's mouth. All that came out was some frantic, muffled grunting. Hardrock was still a few yards away, but he launched himself into the air in an ungainly leap toward the tempting target looming before him.

Finding strength he didn't know he had, Nathan wrenched his head to the side, away from Brody's hand and the barrel of the gun. He heard a loud chomping sound, and then Brody screamed and was driven forward by a hard impact. Just as Nathan had feared, the gun went off with a deafening blast, but the bullet whipped past Nathan's ear and slammed harmlessly into the ground. Nathan drove an elbow into Brody's ribs as hard as he could, shoving the man aside so that he could roll away.

Nathan wound up on his belly on the far side of the wagon, panting heavily as he tried to catch his breath. The space underneath the vehicle was a tangled melee of arms and legs and paws. Brody was still screaming, and his shrieks were counterpointed by fierce growls and snaps from Hardrock.

Nathan pushed himself up onto hands and knees. He knew he had to get to his own gun. Brody might get a chance to shoot Hardrock, and then Nathan would have to face the man again. Before turning in for the night, Nathan had taken off his gunbelt as usual and placed the coiled belt and holster on the ground just inside one of the front wheels of the wagon, where it would be within easy reach if he needed it during the night.

Now he crawled toward the wheel and tried to hook an arm around it in search of the Colt revolver, but he had to jerk back when Hardrock and Brody rolled in the same direction and slammed up against the inside of the wheel. Their struggling bodies were on top of the gun. Nathan grimaced and waited for his chance, and when the man and the dog rolled away again, he dove forward, reaching out. His head was still unsteady, but luck guided his hand. His fingers closed over the smooth walnut butt of the weapon.

Jerking it free of the holster, Nathan scuttled away from the wagon and forced himself to his feet, staggering a little from the aftereffects of the blows to his head. The gun seemed heavier than usual in his hand, but he managed to lift it. At that moment, Brody broke free of Hardrock's attack and plunged out from under the wagon with the angry dog right behind him. Brody twisted, and Nathan saw moonlight reflect off the pistol the man had somehow managed to hang on to. For an instant, Nathan was afraid that Brody was going to fire at Hardrock, but the thief lashed out with the weapon instead, slamming the barrel against Hardrock's head as the dog leaped out into the open. The blow was a savage one, knocking Hardrock off his feet and sending him rolling on the ground on the other side of the wagon.

Brody's face was marked by dark streaks of blood, and so was his body through the tatters of his coat and shirt. The seat of his pants was in shreds. He paid no attention to Nathan as he aimed the gun at the dog. At the moment, all of his rage was directed toward Hardrock, and in a matter of seconds, the hammer of his pistol would fall.

''Brody!'' shouted Nathan.

The man turned and brought the gun with him, the muzzle swinging toward Nathan and looking like an enormous black hole in the moonlight. Nathan was still deaf in one ear from the gun blast, and his pulse was throbbing so loudly in his head that he couldn't hear anything anyway. Brody's mouth moved, but Nathan had no way of knowing if the man was shouting something at him or not. There was no mistaking the gout of flame that burst from the barrel of Brody's pistol, though.

Nathan fired and felt the Colt buck against his palm. Brody had gotten off the first shot, but he had been an instant too quick on the trigger. Nathan felt the wind of the bullet going past his cheek, then saw Brody jerk backward and go sailing through the air like a puppet whose strings had just been yanked hard. The man's arms and legs splayed out, and they stayed that way as he landed on his back, spread-eagled on the ground. His pistol spun away in the darkness after slipping from his nerveless fingers.

For a long moment, Nathan just stood there, his arm still extended. The Colt began to waver violently, and he lowered it. Then, realizing that he couldn't see Brody that well, he hurried around the wagon for a better look.

The man was lying there motionless, his eyes open, their glassy surfaces reflecting the moonlight. Nathan approached him cautiously, holding the cocked pistol where he could use it quickly if he needed to. He knelt beside Brody and laid his hand on the man's chest, above where the dark stain was spreading on the ruined shirt. Brody wasn't breathing, Nathan realized after a moment. He was dead.

And Nathan had killed him.

But only after Brody had tried to kill him first, Nathan reminded himself. He stood up, letting the hand holding the gun dangle loosely at his side. He felt even sicker than he had before, and the ache in his head was worse. But when he heard a low whining, he realized that his hearing was beginning to come back.

The sound also reminded him of Hardrock, and he ran over to kneel beside the dog. Hardrock was moving all four legs and trying to get up, but he seemed to be having trouble. Nathan put the pistol on the ground and took hold of the dog's shoulders, feeling the strength and power still there. He shoved against the heavy body, helping Hardrock get his feet under him again.

Hardrock stood up, holding his head low to the ground and shaking it slowly, looking for all the world like a man trying to get the cobwebs out of his brain. Then Hardrock lifted his gaze to the sprawled figure of Brody, and a fierce snarl came from deep in his throat.

"You don't have to worry about him anymore, boy," Nathan told the dog, his voice sounding strange to his ears. "He almost did for both of us, but he won't bother us or anybody else ever again."

With only a slight unsteadiness to his gait, Hardrock padded over to Brody and nosed around the body for a moment, his growls gradually dying away. Then he turned around to face Nathan again, lifted a hind leg, and relieved himself on the corpse. There was a look of satisfaction on the dog's face as he trotted back to Nathan.

Sick, dizzy, not knowing whether to laugh or cry, Nathan wrapped his arms around Hardrock's thick neck and hung on, the coarse fur pricking his face, the musky smell of the dog filling his nostrils. The two of them sat that way for a long time as the moon and the stars wheeled through the black night sky overhead.

Cassandra put the bolt of cloth on the counter with a little more force than was necessary, thumping it down pretty hard, in fact. If Emily noticed the gesture, she showed no sign of it. Instead, the older woman turned her back and went through the door leading to the office, closing it behind her.

"Mother," Cassandra muttered under her breath, "you're just *impossible*!"

The argument was nothing new. Sometimes the subject of the disagreement changed, but that was all. At the base of the problem was the fact that Emily didn't trust her daughter. She wanted to keep Cassandra on a tight leash, just like some sort of pampered pet.

At least that was the way Cassandra saw it. It had seemed such a simple thing. Once again, Cassandra had mentioned that she wanted to go to the gold fields with Nathan on one of his trips up there, and Emily had replied brusquely, "That's out of the question. Not only are conditions much too rugged for you, dear, but a young lady does *not* travel alone with a gentleman.''

''For goodness' sake, Mother, Nathan's my cousin!'' Cassandra had exclaimed.

''That doesn't matter. Cousins have done foolish things before.''

''You can't be serious. I don't have any sort of romantic feelings for Nathan. Heavens, he does well not to trip over his own feet, and he's certainly not going to sweep me off mine!''

''I'll hear no more about it,'' Emily had declared, then she went into the office and left Cassandra to stand there fuming by the store's main counter.

It simply wasn't fair, Cassandra thought. She had endured the weeks-long trip on the boat around South America, suffering incredibly from seasickness in the process, and since arriving in San Francisco, all she had been allowed to do was work in the store. She could have stayed in Boston and done that, she mused bitterly. When she went down to the harbor—on one of the few occasions when her mother allowed her to do *that*—and looked out across the bay at the mountains in the Coast Range and the dimmer heights of the Sierra Nevadas beyond, she knew that a great adventure was going on out there, an adventure she could almost see but was not permitted to be a part of.

She had come to California to see new things, to live life to a fuller extent than she ever could have back in Massachusetts. And instead, what was she doing? Working for her mother as a clerk and a bookkeeper. It was too depressing for words.

There were no customers in the store at the moment. It was early evening, and most people were having supper about now. Later, though, business would pick up again. Emily regularly kept the store open late, sometimes not closing until almost ten o'clock. Longer hours made for higher profits, in Emily's estimation.

Cassandra continued with what she had been doing before the argument broke out, which was sorting the bolts of cloth stacked on the counter. During the day they tended to get rather disarranged, and Emily liked things neat. As Cassandra picked up another bolt, the front door of the store opened and a man strode in, followed by a huge dog.

Cassandra glanced toward them, then looked again, her eyes widening as she recognized her cousin and saw what a dangerous-looking beast was right behind him. "Nathan!" she cried. "Look out!"

Nathan tensed and crouched, looking around nervously. "What is it?" he demanded.

"That . . . that dog!"

"Oh." Relief was evident in Nathan's voice. He straightened and grinned at Cassandra, then glanced back at the brute. "Don't worry. This is just Hardrock."

And then, to Cassandra's amazement, he reached back and patted the dog, ruffling the fur on top of its massive head. The dog's mouth was slightly open, a thread of drool hanging from it, and those jaws looked like they could snap Nathan's entire arm off without any effort.

"He . . . he's friendly?" Cassandra asked, her voice still shaking a little.

"Most of the time," Nathan told her. "As long as he gets enough to eat."

"But where did he come from?"

"Now, that's a pretty strange story. Where's Aunt Emily?"

"She's in the back." Cassandra moved behind the counter, glad to place its bulk between her and the dog, no matter what Nathan said about the animal being friendly. Then she realized that a dog of that size would have no trouble vaulting right over the counter: it wouldn't be any protection if the beast decided to come after her.

The dog seemed to be quite fond of Nathan, though, and stayed at his heels as he walked toward the rear of the store. Cassandra opened the door to the hallway and stepped through to the office.

"You'd better come out here, Mother," she told Emily, who was sitting behind the desk going over some bills of sale. "Nathan's back."

"He is?" Emily said, barely looking up from what she was doing. "That's fine. Ask him to come in here, and he can tell us how he did on this trip."

Cassandra hesitated, thinking about how crowded the office would be with three people and that . . . that dog in it, and she said, "I think you should come out front, Mother. Nathan's not alone."

"Not alone?" repeated Emily. This time Cassandra had caught her attention. She looked up with a frown and asked, "Who does he have with him?"

Cassandra was losing her patience. "Just come with me, Mother, please."

"Oh, all right," Emily said as she got to her feet. She followed Cassandra out of the office and into the area behind the counter.

Then stopped short as she got her first good look at the beast sitting there on the floor beside Nathan.

"Hello, Aunt Emily," he greeted her with a smile as he tossed his broad-brimmed black hat on the counter.

Cassandra felt a smile of her own tugging at her lips. With her mouth open a little, Emily was staring, taken totally by surprise and speechless for once in her life. Seeing her mother that way was a new experience for Cassandra, but she found that she liked the feeling. For once, she'd had the advantage over Emily. She had known there was a monster waiting on the other side of the counter.

"What . . . is . . . *that*?" Emily finally managed to ask, the question drawn out of her slowly.

"It's a dog," Nathan said mildly. "He seems to have adopted me. His name's Hardrock."

Emily swallowed. "You should take him back outside."

"He seems to want to go where I go," Nathan said with a shrug. "And he's too big to argue with."

"Well, why don't you take him out back and tie him up? There's some sturdy rope on that shelf over there."

Nathan looked dubious, but he nodded. "I'll try, but I can't say for sure he'll cooperate." He went over to the shelf, picked up one of the coils of heavy rope lying there, and said to the dog, "Come on, Hardrock."

Emily and Cassandra moved to the far end of the counter as Nathan and the dog came around it and went through the door. Emily put a hand to her breast and said in a low voice, "My God, did you ever see such a beast?"

"He seems to like Nathan, thank goodness," Cassandra replied. Her argument with her mother was forgotten for the moment, swept away by the impressive sight of the dog.

Nathan returned a few minutes later and said, "I tied him to the carriage post back there. I don't think he can pull it up if a team of horses can't."

"Was he . . . upset? asked Emily.

"Well, he didn't seem very happy about the arrangement, but he allowed me to put the rope around his neck and tie it. We'll see."

"At least he's outside," Cassandra said.

"Come into the office, Nathan," Emily told him, sounding more like herself again. "You look tired. Did you have any trouble?"

"A little," Nathan replied. "Nothing for you to worry

about, though. I sold all the goods and got back safely with the gold."

Emily nodded. "Excellent."

Cassandra followed them into the office, halfway expecting her mother to send her back out into the store. Emily still seemed a little shaken by the encounter with Hardrock, though, and she neglected to shoo Cassandra out of the room. Cassandra stood behind Nathan's chair as he gave Emily his report on the trip, glossing over whatever problems he'd had and sticking to what interested Emily the most—the profits involved.

Nathan started to get up when he was finished, saying, "I'll fetch the dust and nuggets from the wagon."

Emily stopped him. "They're locked up securely, aren't they?"

Nathan nodded.

"Then that can wait," Emily went on. "I have something else to discuss with you, Nathan, an idea I've had."

Nathan sank down into his chair again and glanced back at Cassandra, a worried expression on his face. Cassandra gave a tiny shrug. She had no idea what her mother was talking about; her mother rarely confided in her about business matters, especially speculation concerning future endeavors. But both Nathan and Cassandra had learned by now that Emily's ideas usually meant some new sort of trouble for Nathan.

Emily clasped her hands together, the simple wedding band she still wore shining in the lamplight. "I've heard that certain individuals in this town are offering to provide supplies and mining equipment to men who want to go to the gold fields, in exchange for a share in whatever the men find there. They're functioning as sponsors, I suppose you could say."

Nathan nodded hesitantly and said, "I've heard a little

gossip in the camps about such things. The miners have a name for the practice. It's called grubstaking.''

''Whatever it's called, I want to be part of it,'' Emily declared. ''The risks are higher than simply selling our goods to the miners, but the potential rewards are much greater. Those Argonauts will be eager to sign over a substantial share of their earnings in order to continue their digging and panning, especially once the gold fever has them firmly in its grip.''

Cassandra stepped around to the side so that she could see Nathan's face better, and she was not surprised to discover that he was frowning in concern. ''Are you talking about grubstaking men who are already in the gold fields?'' he asked Emily.

''Exactly. You've told me before about men who have given up on mining because they ran out of money and supplies. I can provide both.''

''You'll lose out on many of them,'' Nathan told her bluntly.

''Perhaps. But think about it, Nathan. Suppose one of the miners is just a week away from a huge find, only he doesn't know it. He gives up and goes back to his home, a broken, defeated man. What I intend to do is give him that extra week, or however long it takes, within reason, of course.''

''And if he *does* make a strike, you get the lion's share of it.''

Emily smiled. ''It seems equitable, doesn't it?''

Nathan leaned back in his chair and thought over the proposal. After a moment, he said, ''You'd have plenty of takers on an offer like that, all right. Like you said, once the gold fever has hold of a man, he'll do almost anything to keep looking for the stuff. But it seems sort of . . .''

''Unfair?'' Cassandra finished for him.

Emily shot an angry glance at her. ''There's nothing unfair about it,'' she insisted. ''My supplies will be at risk, and as Nathan pointed out, the men may* fail more often than they succeed, even with my help. But the successes will make it all worthwhile.''

Nathan said, ''So you want me to go to the gold fields, find men who have run out of supplies, and grubstake them so they won't have to abandon their efforts?''

''That's right,'' Emily nodded.

''I can do that,'' Nathan decided grudgingly. ''We can give it a try, anyway.''

''I'm glad you're being reasonable about this,'' Emily began, then broke off as a frightened shout came from the store.

The three of them hurried out of the office and through the door behind the counter to see that several customers had entered the store during their discussion. Those customers, three men and two women, were cowering in a corner, and sitting a few feet in front of them, fastening them with a cold stare, was Hardrock. A couple of feet of rope, ending in a frazzled break, dangled from his neck.

''Oh, no!'' exclaimed Nathan. ''He didn't come past the office. We would have seen him.''

''He must have broken loose and gone back around to the front,'' Cassandra speculated.

One of the male customers leveled a shaking finger at the dog and said, ''That . . . that thing came in the front door and herded us back here!''

''Get a gun and shoot it!'' one of the women cried. ''None of these gentlemen are armed!''

Nathan hurried around the counter. ''There's nothing to be afraid of, folks,'' he assured the terrified customers, but to Cassandra's ears he didn't sound completely sure of that. He went up to Hardrock and took hold of the rope. ''Come on, Hardrock. Come on, boy.''

''Nathan,'' Emily said shakily, ''get that beast out of my store.''

''I'm trying, Aunt Emily, I'm trying.''

''And when you go back to the gold fields, take it with you!''

Nathan looked up and nodded, then resumed tugging futilely on the rope attached to the big dog. ''Please cooperate, Hardrock,'' he pleaded.

Cassandra giggled, drawing glances from her mother and her cousin. Having a huge beast come into the store and frighten the customers wasn't funny, of course, but it seemed somehow right that it was Nathan who had gotten saddled with the brute. His luck was running true to form.

Now, Cassandra thought as she remembered the earlier disagreement with her mother, if only her luck would change a little . . .

Fifteen

Dr. Thaddeus Palmer thrust the soiled, reeking blankets into a large wooden bucket and snapped, "Take them out and burn them. They'll never be fit to use again."

Anne nodded. She took hold of the bucket's handle, and she tried not to breathe too deeply as she carried it out of the cabin. The stench wafted up to her anyway, impossible to ignore. She fought down the gagging sensation it caused.

There was already a fire burning outside the cabin, watched by several men who stood around looking miserable and helpless. Some of them had friends or relatives inside the building, the makeshift hospital that Palmer had set up at the beginning of the cholera outbreak in Ophir. Others had already lost someone to the disease and were mourning.

"More blankets that need to be burned," Anne called to Barney Cumberland, who was one of the men standing around the fire. He nodded, took the bucket from her, and upended it so that the soiled blankets fell into the flames. They caught fire, and the smell of burning wool and human waste filled the air.

"Does the doc need any help in there?" Barney asked as he handed the bucket back to Anne.

She shook her head. "There's nothing more any of you can do. We're giving them tea and calomel to try to settle their stomachs and making them as comfortable as possible."

Indeed, that was all that could be done for the cholera patients. Once the terrible cramps hit them, twisting their arms and legs and making their fingers hook into claws, and they began the uncontrollable voiding of their stomachs and bowels, it was almost impossible to save them. More than a dozen men had died of the disease already, and there were that many more lying in the cramped quarters of the cabin, suffering the tortures of the damned.

One of the other miners spoke up, saying to Anne, "I heard tell that if you mix red pepper in some whiskey and give it to them that has the cholera, it'll cure 'em."

"Stick their bare feet in hot ashes," another man said. "That'll do the trick. My ol' granny always said that, and she was a witch woman."

Anne didn't doubt it, but she kept that comment to herself. "Dr. Palmer prefers more scientific methods, gentlemen," she told the assembled miners. "Although I'll be happy to pass along the ideas you mentioned."

"Them scientific methods ain't done a lick of good so far," grumbled one of the men. Anne recalled that he was one of three brothers who had come to California from Mississippi. The other two were dead now, among the first victims of the epidemic.

"I promise you, we're doing everything we can," Anne told him, directing the pledge at the other men as well.

One of them waved a hand in front of his face as some smoke from the fire billowed up toward him. "Don't see what good it does to burn up all these blankets," he complained. "We could wash 'em out in the stream."

Anne shook her head. "We don't know what causes cholera or how it spreads, but Dr. Palmer feels that the safest thing to do is to burn the blankets once they've been soiled. It's just a precaution."

She might have tried to explain more, but at that moment, Thaddeus appeared in the doorway of the cabin and called her name. She sensed the urgency in his voice and turned quickly toward him.

Any vestiges of Palmer's once dapper appearance were gone. Several days ago, when the outbreak had begun in earnest, he had discarded his coat and tie, and the collar of his shirt hung open. Large sweat stains circled under the sleeves of his shirt and the armholes of his vest. He was perspiring heavily now, and his bearded face was drawn and haggard. Large dark bags from lack of sleep had appeared under his bloodshot eyes.

Anne knew that she herself must look almost as bad, although she had gotten more sleep than Thaddeus. He had insisted upon that, though she doubted if he himself had slept more than ten minutes at a time in the last five days. Her blond hair was lank and greasy, and it fell in her face often, making her push it back roughly. The gray dress she wore was stained in places from her handling of the soiled blankets, and she knew it ought to be burned, as well. So far, though, she hadn't taken the time to change into one of her other dresses.

Besides, what she was doing was no more risky than her husband's tasks. He dealt even more closely with the sick men.

She hurried toward him, asking, "What is it, Thaddeus?"

"Tully Gage just died," he said wearily, wiping a trembling hand across his brow.

"What? Goddamn it!"

The angry exclamation came from behind Anne, and she looked over her shoulder to see one of the men who had been standing by the fire stalking toward the cabin. His face was contorted by grief and rage and fear. She recognized him as Tully Gage's partner and remembered his name was Maguire. Other than that she knew nothing about him.

Except that he was furious, and that his rage seemed to

be directed toward Dr. Thaddeus Palmer.

"You killed him, you son of a bitch!" Maguire shouted. His hands balled into fists, and his stalking stride became a run. "You killed him! And I'll kill you!"

Barney Cumberland and the other miners came running after him as he charged toward Palmer. The doctor cried, "Look out, Anne!"

She ducked aside as Maguire dashed past her. She wanted to stop him, but he obviously didn't even see her. His gaze was fixed on Thaddeus, and nothing was going to stop him from reaching the physician. He would have trampled right over Anne if she had gotten in his way.

Cumberland and the others caught up to Maguire, grabbing his arms and shoulders and jerking him to a halt, before he reached the cabin. "Hold on there, you blamed fool!" Barney shouted. "You want to hurt the only man who can maybe help us?"

"He ain't helpin' nothin'!" Maguire yelled as he struggled futilely against their grip. "Ever'body's dyin'! *Ever'-body!*"

Palmer had not budged from the doorway, nor had he made any preparations to defend himself if Maguire had reached him. His eyes were dull, as if he no longer cared what happened to him. That was because of his exhaustion, Anne knew. If he didn't get some real rest soon, he would collapse.

"I'm sorry about Gage," he said heavily. "Some of you men had better take him out and bury him."

"We'll take care of it, Doc," Cumberland promised. "Some of you boys take Maguire back to his tent, and the rest of you come with me."

Maguire didn't want to go, but he quieted down a little under threat of being hit over the head with a shovel, and he allowed three of the men to lead him away from the cabin and back toward his tent, half a mile away on one of the hillsides surrounding the small valley where Ophir was located. Some of the other miners went into the cabin to collect Tully Gage's body, while the rest of the group got their shovels and headed for the camp's graveyard at the far end of the settlement. The graveyard was growing faster these days than anything else in Ophir, although most of the saloons and stores were still operating. Some of the businesses whose owners had died had been taken over by others, and no one objected.

Gage's body was wrapped in canvas and carried out of the cabin and down the hill into the camp. Anne watched the grim procession for a moment, then frowned as she saw a figure hurrying in the opposite direction, toward the cabin. There was no mistaking the brightly colored hair of the woman.

"Howdy, Missus Palmer," Red Sally said as she drew nearer, lifting a hand in greeting. She wore her saloon outfit, which was spangled and brazenly low-cut and shockingly short. But she had at least had the decency to wrap a shawl around herself, Anne noted.

"What can I do for you?" she asked the prostitute. "You're not sick, I hope?"

"Nope, not me, not since I got that last mess o' crawlies out o' my knickers, I just thought I'd come up here and see if I could lend a hand. I know there's a lot of sick folks around here, too many for you and the doc to tend by yourselves."

"We have all the help we need," Anne replied stiffly, blushing at the indelicate nature of the woman's bold comments.

"Yeah? Like who?"

"The other ladies of the quilting circle—"

"Ain't been up here even once since they got a good look

at what the cholera does to a man. And a good whiff o' the stink, too. Those high-toned bitches ain't goin' to subject their fragile little eyes and noses to that, now are they?''

Anne had to admit that Gertrude and Alice and Mary Eula had not been back to the cabin since their initial visit following the outbreak of the sickness. But the thought of working side by side with a creature like Red Sally . . .

"Was it your idea to come up here?" she asked softly.

Red Sally shrugged. "I did think about it some. But then Mr. Trent said it'd probably be a good idea if we pitched in to help however we could, so I thought I'd come up and lend a hand."

"Mr. Trent said that, did he?" Anne had only seen the gambler and saloon owner from a distance and had never spoken to him, but she had a difficult time believing that such a man could be motivated by any charitable purposes. "What's wrong, is he losing too many customers to cholera for his saloon to keep making money?"

Red Sally frowned darkly. "You ain't got no call to talk about Mr. Trent like that. You don't know him. He's a good man. He just wants us to help."

"Well, we don't need your help," Anne said crisply, being careful not to let the woman see just how tired she really was. "Thank you anyway."

For a moment, Red Sally glared coldly at her, then nodded abruptly. "If that's the way you want it," she said, then turned her back and started down the path toward the settlement.

Anne turned and went quickly into the cabin, just in case Sally looked back at her. She didn't want to have to meet the woman's eyes again. Inside, in what had once been her sitting room, she found her husband standing over one of the crude cots where the patients lay. The man on the cot was moaning and thrashing feebly, and Anne could tell from the smell that his bowels had emptied themselves recently.

"Havins isn't going to make it," Palmer said in a low voice, but not so quietly that the man on the cot couldn't have heard him. The patient must be very close to death indeed, Anne thought, for Thaddeus to make such a pronouncement in his presence.

Anne took a step toward him. "You've done all you could for him, Thaddeus," she said softly. "You've done everything humanly possible for all of them."

"Everything humanly possible," Palmer repeated, then he muttered, "Not enough, not enough . . ."

Then his eyes rolled up in his head and he collapsed on the floor at Anne's feet.

"Thaddeus!" Anne screamed. She clapped her hands to her mouth and stared down at him, saw the twitching in his arms and legs as the cramps hit his muscles. The words, "Oh, my God . . ." came out of her mouth in a muffled whisper.

Palmer writhed, and his mouth opened to let a gout of foul-smelling liquid spew out. He had the cholera, there was no doubt about that. And Anne was here alone with him and the other patients.

She spun around suddenly, hating to leave him lying there on the floor like that but knowing she could not deal with this alone. She ran to the doorway and outside, into the fresh air, gulping it down gratefully after breathing the fetid atmosphere inside the cabin. Down the hill, at the head of Ophir's main street, Red Sally was striding along determinedly, the shawl held tightly around her shoulders.

"Sally!" Anne cried as loud as she could, scarcely aware of what she was doing. "Sally, help me!" Her voice dropped. "For God's sake, help me . . ."

It would serve her right, she thought suddenly, if Red Sally just kept on walking and ignored her cries. After all,

Anne had practically spat in the woman's face, and all Sally had been doing was offering to help. Well, Anne needed that help now, needed it desperately. She was almost afraid to watch as Sally slowed down and looked back up the hill at the doctor's cabin. Anne stood there, shivering, her hands held out imploringly.

After a couple of seconds, Red Sally turned and started back up the hill.

Anne could not have asked for a better assistant than Red Sally. The saloon woman was a tireless worker and didn't flinch from any of the chores Anne gave her, no matter how disgusting they were. She took over the care of the other patients, leaving Anne free to devote all of her time and energy to nursing Thaddeus back to health.

At lease, that was what Anne tried to do. But after three sleepless, nerve-wracking days and nights, Dr. Thaddeus Palmer died.

Anne refused to believe it at first. She was sitting beside his cot, bathing his forehead with cool water and from time to time trying to ease some of the liquid down his throat. She saw the great shudder that went through him, and she heard the gasping rattle of air in his throat as his last breath left his body. That was a sound she had heard too many times before not to recognize it, but at this moment she refused to believe her ears. She leaned over him frantically, seeing the way his gaunt features, so contorted by pain and suffering over the past three days, had smoothed out, as if a great burden had been lifted from him at last. She saw the way his narrow chest lay utterly still, never to rise and fall again.

"Thaddeus," she said urgently. "You've got to wake up, Thaddeus. There are patients here, and you have to take care of them. We need you, Thaddeus. *I* need you . . . *Thaddeus!*"

She collapsed on her knees beside the cot, resting her head on her husband's unmoving chest. Great sobs shook her. She clutched at him, moving her hands over his body, searching desperately for any sort of response, any sign of life.

Gradually, she became aware of Red Sally's voice and the woman's strong hands on her shoulders. "Come away from there," Sally urged. "Come on, Mrs. Palmer, you can't do this. He's gone, and it won't do nobody any good if you catch this goddamned contagion yourself."

Anne refused to be budged. Grief had her in a grip even stronger than Red Sally's. After a few moments, the prostitute turned her head and shouted out the open door of the cabin, "Barney! Get in here, I need a hand!"

Anne was beyond coherent thought, but Sally wasn't. One thought burned through her brain as she looked down at the grieving woman.

With Doc Palmer dead, God help us all!

None of them knew it, but the worst was over before Thaddeus Palmer was even in the ground the next day. One other man in the cabin died that night, but he was the last victim claimed by Ophir's great cholera epidemic of '49. More men may have died up in the hills later, their deaths either unknown or marked only by a partner or two, but by and large the sweeping wave of sickness departed as mysteriously as it had arrived.

Anne had little memory of the funeral service itself. Barney Cumberland stood on one side of her with a hand under her elbow to help hold her up, and Red Sally was on the other side, also with a hand on Anne's arm. Without their support she might have fallen. At Sally's suggestion, she had drunk a little laudanum from Thaddeus's medical bag the night before, just enough to make her fall asleep, and she was still feeling some of the effects of the drug the next day.

There were quite a few mourners at the service. Palmer
had been well liked in the community, and as the only doctor
he had been an important person. The Bible-thumping miner
who had been responsible for Bloody Gulch changing its
name to Ophir read some passages from the Scriptures over
the grave, then lifted his face to heaven and launched into a
seemingly endless prayer. Anne later recalled glancing
around at the others while the makeshift preacher was dron-
ing on, but the bearded faces of the miners all seemed to
blur before her eyes. The only man she recalled seeing af-
terward was a tall, lean individual in a dark suit, with
smoothly brushed brown hair and a moustache that drooped
slightly over the corners of his wide mouth.

When the funeral was finally over, Sally and Cumberland
led Anne away from the graveyard and back to the cabin.
There were still patients there to be cared for as they recu-
perated from the disease that had laid waste to the community. Sally stayed at the cabin, since Anne was in no shape
to tend to the sick men.

Days passed and turned into a week. The stricken miners
were growing stronger, and it became evident that the crisis
had passed. At least everyone in Ophir hoped so. As for
Anne, she spent her days in a haze of grief. More laudanum
would have brought her some blessed relief from the suffering, but she avoided the drug, having seen too many times
how it could get a person in its grip and never let go. Thaddeus had always prescribed it sparingly, knowing how dangerous it could be.

Finally, ten days after the funeral, the last of the miners
who had been patients in the crude hospital went back to
their claims, strong enough to work again. The call of gold
was a powerful drug by itself. The men were anxious to get
back to the diggings, fearful that someone else would stumble over a strike that might have been theirs otherwise.

Later that same day, Red Sally came into the small room Anne had shared with Thaddeus and found Anne sitting in a rocking chair, looking out the single small window.

"Reckon I'll be goin' now," Sally said. "You ain't got no more patients, so I 'spose I ain't needed anymore."

Anne turned her face quickly from the window. Her features were more pale and drawn than they had been before this ordeal began, but she was still an attractive woman. "You don't have to go," she said to Sally. "You can stay as long as you like."

"And what the hell would I do?" Sally laughed to take any sting out of the words. "Honey, I've had my hands full with those sick men, but now they're all gone. I got to go back to the only other thing I know, and that's gettin' miners to buy me drinks and dance with me and take me to the cribs out back o' the saloon. Ain't no point in tryin' to be something I'm not."

"But . . . but you wouldn't have to live that kind of life—"

"It's what I know, Anne," Sally said softly. "Don't you fret none, I'll be fine."

Anne stood up, hesitated only a second, then threw her arms around Sally. "I don't know what I would have done without your help," she whispered.

"Glad to lend a hand," Sally said gruffly. She pushed away from Anne, and for an instant Anne thought she had insulted the other woman somehow. But then she saw that Sally was embarrassed by this show of genuine affection. It was something she probably hadn't had much experience with in her life.

"As far as I'm concerned, you'll be welcome at the quilting circle any time, as soon as we begin meeting again," Anne declared.

"Well, that's sweet of you, honey, but I ain't really the

quiltin' sort after all, I reckon. But maybe you and me could get together at Mr. Trent's place sometime and have us a drink . . . No, I reckon not. You're not *that* sort and never will be. So long, Anne.''

With that, Sally turned and strode out before Anne could say anything else, and when the redheaded woman was gone, Anne realized that the cabin felt utterly empty. She missed Sally, but most of all she missed Thaddeus . . .

A couple of days later, she had a visitor. Anne left the rocking chair where she was spending most of her time now and went to answer the knock on the door. Barney Cumberland stood there, his beefy features set in an uncomfortable expression, his thick, blunt fingers twisting the black hat he held in his hands.

''Hello, Barney,'' Anne greeted him. ''What brings you here?''

He swallowed hard and said, ''Howdy, ma'am. Some of the boys and me, we was just wonderin' . . . are you doin' all right? Is there anything you need?''

Short of a miracle that could restore her husband to her, Anne couldn't think of anything. But was she all right? No, and she doubted if she ever would be again.

But she couldn't bring herself to say that to Barney, so she forced a wan smile onto her face and said, ''I'm fine. At least some of the time I am. There are bad times, but . . .'' She shrugged and left the sentence unfinished.

''Well, if there's anything you need, you be sure and just let me know. We're all mighty obliged to you, ma'am, for what you did during the sick spell.''

''Red Sally did more than me. You might thank her.''

''Yes, ma'am, I will,'' Barney promised.

Anne waited a moment, and when he didn't say any more, she asked, ''Was there anything else?''

''Well, yeah, I reckon . . . What are you going to do now

that . . . now that you're alone?''

That was a strange question to be coming from Barney Cumberland, Anne thought, and it was also a question she had been avoiding in her mind as much as possible. She was still too stunned to be making any rational decisions.

"I don't know, Barney," she answered honestly. "Do you have any suggestions?"

He looked nervous as a cat, which was strange in such a large, competent man, but he managed to say, "Yes, ma'am, I do. You could do me the honor of becomin' my wife."

Anne's eyes widened in surprise. "Your . . . wife," she repeated slowly. "I . . . I wasn't expecting a marriage proposal, Barney."

"I know it's mighty soon, too soon to be proper, but a lady like you don't need to be livin' up here by yourself without no man to take care of you. It's a hard life here in the gold fields. But you know that already." He hurried on as Anne tried to say something. "Now I know I ain't nearly as handsome as the doc, God rest his soul, but I'm strong and I don't mind workin', and I don't even beat my mules. I'd treat you right kind, ma'am . . . Anne."

Anne hesitated while she tried to gather her thoughts, then said, "I'm very flattered, Barney, but—"

His face fell. "But you don't want to be married to no ugly ol' jackass like me."

"I haven't given any thought to being married to *anyone*! I . . . I'm sorry, Barney, but it's just out of the question right now."

He nodded ruefully. "I was afraid that's what you'd say, but I wanted to be the first one to ask you, just in case you might've said yes."

"The *first* one?" Anne repeated.

"Yes, ma'am. You know as well as anybody that there ain't too many respectable women in these hills, and . . .

well, there's plenty of miners who'd be more'n happy to take
you to wife.''

Anne stared at him, stunned by the prospect of dozens of
miners trooping up to her door to ask for her hand in mat-
rimony. Thaddeus was barely cold in the ground, and already
these men had their eyes set on her.

"Tell them that I'm not interested in having another husband, Barney," she said, keeping her anger under control.
After all, Barney Cumberland was her friend, one of the few
real friends she had in Ophir. "Can you do that for me?"

He scratched his jaw. "Well, yeah, I reckon I can tell 'em.
But I don't know if it'll do any good. If anybody bothers
you too much, though, you let me know and I'll have another
talk with 'em." One of his hands clenched into a fist.

"I'm sure it won't come to that," Anne said quickly.

Over the next few days, she found out just how wrong
she was.

Sixteen

If anything, it was worse than what Barney had warned her about.

The news that she was a widow had evidently reached every miner in a ten-mile-wide circle around Ophir, and it seemed as if each and every one of them appeared on her doorstep over the next week, hat in hand and marriage in mind. Anne turned down all the offers as politely as she could, but her patience began to wear thin. Some of the men didn't take rejection well, either, and she was frightened a few times when they looked like they wanted to pick her up and carry her off to their claims, whether she wanted to go or not.

She couldn't live like this. So for the first time since Thaddeus's death, she was able to shake herself out of her lethargy and give some hard thought to the future.

There was only one answer, Anne realized. She had to leave the mining camps and go back to San Francisco. Whether or not she would return to the East after that, she didn't know yet, but the first step was definitely to leave these rugged foothills of the Sierra Nevadas.

But that was going to take money.

Once she had reached her decision, she went quickly to the trunk where Thaddeus had stored the nuggets and gold dust that he had received as payment for treating the miners' illnesses and injuries. It was in the bedroom of the cabin, shoved under the bed itself. Anne knelt, lifting the coverlet, and peered underneath the bed. The trunk was there, a brass handle set into the end facing her. She reached for the handle, grasped it, and began to pull.

The trunk was small but heavy, thick wood with brass on the corners and leather straps around it. The brass had acquired a greenish tinge due to the damp air back in San Francisco, and Thaddeus had never polished it, being more concerned with the trunk's utility than its appearance. Anne slid it around on the floor of the bedroom until she could see the lock on the front of it. She frowned as she tried to remember where Thaddeus had kept the key.

My God! she thought suddenly. What if the key had been in Thaddeus's pocket and gotten buried with him?

She took a deep breath. Thoughts like that weren't going to help anything, she told herself sternly. Standing up, she went to the bureau one of the miners had made for them and began pawing through the personal effects that had been piled there after her husband's death. She had not been able to bring herself to go through them until now.

"It must be here somewhere," she muttered under her breath. If it wasn't, there was still his medical bag to try. Thaddeus could have kept the key in the bag, Anne supposed.

She didn't have to go that far. After only a moment, she found what she was looking for, a small key, lying on the bureau.

Turning, she hurried back to the trunk, knelt in front of it, and thrust the key into the lock. It turned easily, and the lock sprang open. Anne felt a wave of relief wash through her. The biggest obstacle was behind her. She lifted the lid of the trunk.

And stared into the emptiness within.

The trunk wasn't completely barren, she saw after a stunned moment. There were several empty pouches of the type that miners kept their gold dust in, as well as a couple of medical books and a small Bible. There was also a leather case in one corner of the trunk. Anne reached for it with trembling fingers and lifted the lid. Inside was a tiny pistol. The case had "Allen & Thurber" engraved on the inside of the lid, and the same names were etched on the hammer of the weapon. Anne knew that Thaddeus had owned a pistol, but she hadn't seen it in a long time. He was a man of peace, a healer, not a taker of lives.

None of that was important now, however. All that mattered was that the money Anne would need to go back to San Francisco and reestablish some sort of life there seemed to be gone, utterly vanished.

Her first thought was that someone had stolen the nuggets and dust. But to do that, it would have been necessary to sneak into the cabin, find the key, pull the trunk from under the bed, and unlock it. The trunk itself showed no signs of tampering. But that theory was impossible. In any case only Anne and Thaddeus himself had known where he kept the gold, and it was beyond credibility that anyone could have slipped into the cabin and accomplished the theft without one of them being aware of it.

Thaddeus must have done something with the gold, Anne thought. Perhaps he had hidden it somewhere else, even though she had no idea why he would do such a thing, especially without telling her.

For the next hour she searched the cabin, practically ransacking it as she grew more desperate. She wanted to leave this place of tragedy and hardship forever, and the gold represented her way out. She had to find it. She simply *had* to.

But when Red Sally knocked tentatively on the open door of the cabin, she found Anne sitting on the floor, her face in her hands, her body shaking with sobs.

"What is it, Anne?" Sally asked anxiously as she came

into the room. "One o' them miners been botherin' you? I'll take a knife to him—"

"No," Anne said with a shake of her head. She lifted her tear-streaked face to the prostitute. "I . . . I've been looking for the gold dust and nuggets Thaddeus was paid for his services. I can't find the gold anywhere."

Sally frowned, hesitated for a moment, then said, "Maybe I ought to keep my big mouth shut and not be tellin' you this, honey, but . . . I got some idea where that gold went. I didn't have no idea the doc had used up all of it, though."

Anne looked at her uncomprehendingly, but slowly an unbelievable image began to form in her mind. Thaddeus had never been an ardent lover, had never been the type to make excessive demands of the flesh on her. Anne had always assumed that was just the sort of man he was, but what if he had actually been satisfying most of his needs with someone else, someone like . . .

"Oh, my God, Sally," breathed Anne. "He . . . he wasn't paying *you* . . ."

Sally let out a braying laugh before she could stop it. "The doc was a real gentleman, and he wouldn't have ever been interested in a broken-down old whore like me. Not when he had a lady like you at home. But he *did* stop by the saloon a couple of times a week."

Anne frowned. "You mean he was drinking?" That idea was almost as difficult to comprehend as Thaddeus pleasuring himself with Sally. He had not been opposed to a glass of wine every now and then, but he had never been a heavy drinker. And if he was drinking in secret, Anne was sure she would have found out about it sooner or later.

With a shake of her head, Sally replied, "He wasn't no boozer. But he did like to play poker."

"He . . . gambled the gold away?"

Sally shrugged. "He had a run of bad luck, that last month

or so 'fore the cholera hit. Just couldn't seem to draw the right cards.''

Anne pushed herself to her feet, struggling to cope with what Sally was telling her. She said, "So Thaddeus lost all our money at poker. He was probably cheated!''

"No!" Sally exclaimed. "He always played with Mr. Trent himself. They was friends. Mr. Trent wouldn't cheat nobody.''

From the sound of it, Red Sally was infatuated with the saloon owner. She was obviously unwilling to believe anything bad about him. But Anne was equally unwilling to believe that Thaddeus would have squandered away their savings in such a fashion, unless he was being taken advantage of in some way.

She turned toward the door of the cabin. "I'm going to see your Mr. Trent and find out about this," she declared. "If he was Thaddeus's friend, as you claim, he wouldn't have taken all his gold.''

"Not if he'd known," Sally said as she hurried after Anne. "But Mr. Trent's a gambler. Cards is his business. He's not in the habit of askin' a man if he's in any position to lose.''

"Perhaps that is a habit Mr. Trent should develop," Anne said coldly.

For the first time since Thaddeus's death, she felt some of the sorrowful lassitude releasing its grip on her. She had a purpose again now, something she had been lacking these past days. That purpose was to find out how Patrick Trent had wound up with all of Thaddeus's hard-earned gold.

Sally trotted along beside her. The prostitute's legs were a little shorter than Anne's, so she had to step quickly to keep up. Anne was in no mood to waste time.

The two women went down the hill and along the main street of the settlement, staying on the boardwalk. Quite a few people nodded greetings to Anne along the way, greetings she didn't take the time to return. She was too angry to worry about politeness. Red Sally didn't try to stop her, but the saloon woman said several times, "You're wrong about Mr. Trent. I know you're wrong."

Anne ignored her. She was going to have an explanation for what had happened to the gold, and if Trent's explanation wasn't good enough, she was going to demand the money be returned to her as Thaddeus Palmer's rightful heir.

Curious about what was going on, some of the miners and storekeepers began to trail after Anne and Sally. Nothing excited people in these boom towns quicker than the prospect of trouble.

Trouble was what Ophir got, but not in the way that Anne or Sally or any of the others expected. When the two women were still a block away from Trent's saloon, gunfire suddenly erupted, the loud explosions filling the warm afternoon air.

Anne stopped in her tracks so quickly that Sally bumped into her shoulder. Screams followed the shots, and like the blasts they came from inside Trent's saloon. Sally said in a low voice, "Oh, Lordy . . ."

A man burst through the doors of the saloon, slamming them open with his shoulder, then staggering out of the building. He crossed the boardwalk and half-fell into the muddy street, but he was able to catch his balance and keep himself from sprawling full-length in the muck. He had a pistol in one hand, an ugly thing with an incredibly long barrel. As bystanders on the boardwalk near the saloon and directly across the street began to scatter, the man with the gun began to turn slowly back toward the building.

Another man stepped through the still-open doors, and like the first one, he held a gun in his hand. The resemblance ended there, however. The first man was roughly dressed and had the bushy-bearded countenance of a miner, while the man who now stood calmly on the boardwalk in front of the saloon's entrance wore a long, cutaway coat, a linen shirt, and neatly pressed trousers. At the sight of him, Sally exclaimed, "Mr. Trent!"

Trent didn't even glance in her direction. All of his attention was focused on the man in the street. "Put the gun down, Masters," Trent called to the man. "Show some sense for a change. You're already wounded."

It was true; there was a spreading stain of blood on the man's shirt, low on the belly. Anne saw it and knew he was virtually doomed. A man shot in the stomach could bleed to death internally in a matter of minutes, or he could linger for agonizing hours before death claimed him. Either way, gutshot men rarely survived. That was one of the hard lessons Anne had learned from being the wife of a frontier physician.

"You . . . you had no call to shoot me, Trent," shouted the man in the street. His voice was hoarse and cracked with strain.

"You were trying to rob my place," Trent returned coolly. "I couldn't stand for that, now could I?"

"You son of a bitch!" The words rang out from the man in the street, and he jerked the pistol in his hand toward Trent.

Both weapons cracked, Trent's first. The gun in the other man's hand didn't go off until Trent's bullet had bored into his chest and thrown him backwards. The shot went harmlessly into the mud at the feet of Masters as the man fell.

Without taking his eyes off Masters, Trent said loudly, "You all saw it. I gave him a chance to throw down his gun and surrender."

Calls of agreement came from some of the bystanders, who were already beginning to emerge from their hiding places, as soon as they sensed that the violence was over.

Satisfied that he wouldn't be wrongly blamed for the man's death, Trent pulled his coat aside to put away his gun. As he did so, even from a block away, Anne saw the crimson flower blooming on his shirt.

"Mr. Trent!" she called to him as she started along the boardwalk again.

He had been turning toward the saloon, but he stopped and put out a hand against the railing on the edge of the boardwalk where horses were tied. It was a seemingly casual pose, but Anne knew he was using the rail for support. She had recognized him by now and knew he was the man with the brown hair and moustache who had been at her husband's funeral.

"Mrs. Palmer," he said in a surprised voice. "What can I do for you?"

Anne came up to him. She had intended to give him a thorough dressing-down for the way he had taken Thaddeus's money away in those card games, but now that she was closer to the man, she could see the pallor under his tan and the fine beads of sweat that had appeared on his forehead. Instincts honed by years of experience took over.

"You're injured," she said softly to him. "Can I help you?"

He made a negligent gesture with his free hand. "Just a scratch," he said. "A bullet graze, that's all. Nothing for you to worry about."

Sally came up beside Anne and said anxiously, "If you're hurt, Mr. Trent, you ought to let Anne look at it. I reckon she knows more about doctorin' than anybody else in town, now that her husband's gone."

"I was very sorry to hear about Dr. Palmer's passing," Trent said solemnly. "He was a good man. But of course, *you* know that."

"He was," Anne agreed. "And if he was here, he'd be

insisting that you go inside and lie down on a table so that he could take a look at the bullet wound. I can do no less.''

Trent frowned. ''You're not a physician—''

''The closest thing to it in Ophir,'' Anne cut in sharply.

''See here, I said I was all right.'' Trent sounded angry and impatient now.

Anne was angry, too, however. She didn't want this man dying before she could settle the matter of the gold he had won from Thaddeus. She was on the verge of saying something about that when Trent suddenly swayed and would have fallen if Sally hadn't leaped forward and caught his arm. ''He's hurt bad, Anne!'' the prostitute said as she held up Trent. ''You've got to help him!''

''Get him inside,'' Anne replied briskly.

Some of the bartenders and customers from the saloon had come outside, and it was no problem finding men to help Trent back into the building and lift him onto a poker table that had been quickly swept clean for that purpose. The men stood aside to let Anne through, and she pulled back Trent's coat and shirt to examine the wound.

It was more than a scratch, contrary to his claim. The bullet had entered on his left side. Anne couldn't tell if it had penetrated his stomach or not, but when she got a couple of the bartenders to roll him onto his right side, she could see plainly that the bullet hadn't emerged from his back. The chunk of lead was still inside the gambler somewhere.

''Someone give me a knife,'' Anne said, holding out her hand.

Trent reached up and caught her wrist. ''Wh-what are you . . . going to . . . do, Mrs. Palmer?'' he asked in a husky, pain-filled voice.

''That bullet must be extracted,'' Anne said. Her anger had retreated to a far corner of her mind now, and she was surprisingly calm.

"Get . . . get one of my boys . . . to do it. You can't—"

"I've seen my husband extract countless bullets these past months, Mr. Trent. I can do this."

She wished she felt as confident as she sounded. She had assisted Thaddeus in dozens of surgeries and helped him patch up countless bullet wounds, as she had just said. But helping Thaddeus and removing a bullet from a living man's body herself were two entirely different things.

But if she allowed any doubts to creep into her mind, she would not be able to go through with this. And there was a good chance Trent would die, even if the injury itself was not that serious. At least she knew how to keep such a wound clean.

"Well?" she snapped. "Is anyone going to give me a knife?"

"Give her a knife, goddamnit!" Red Sally ordered. "Can't you muleheads see she knows what she's doing?"

Anne smiled faintly at the words. She hoped Sally was right.

One of the miners pulled a short-bladed knife from a sheath on his belt and extended it to Anne. "It ain't very clean," he began apologetically.

"That doesn't matter now," Anne told him with a nod of thanks. "But someone else who has a longer knife with a thinner blade will need to get it ready for me. I want the blade of that knife cleaned and then heated until it's extremely hot."

While that was going on, Anne used the short-bladed knife to finish cutting away Trent's shirt. The crowd pressing around her threw shadows over the table, making it difficult to see in the already dim barroom. Anne asked the miners and bartenders and saloon women to step back, and they did so grudgingly, all except Red Sally, who didn't appear to be budging from Trent's side.

"Is the other knife ready?" Anne asked when she had laid bare the ugly, red-rimmed hole in Trent's side.

"Here it is," Sally said, passing the knife over to her from the miner who had been heating the blade over a lantern flame.

"I need some whiskey," Anne said as she studied the wound, "preferably a full bottle."

If anybody thought that was an unusual request, no one said anything. A bottle of whiskey was produced and handed to Anne, who said, "Pull the cork out, please."

"Oh yeah," muttered the bartender who had fetched the liquor. He bit the cork and jerked it from the neck of the bottle with his teeth, then gave the whiskey back to Anne.

She dribbled a little of the stuff on the blade of the knife, just as an extra precaution, then poured it liberally on the wound in Trent's side. The gambler, who had slipped into a half-conscious state, twitched and pulled his lips back in a grimace of pain, but he didn't cry out. A brave man, if not an entirely honorable one, Anne thought.

Then she said, "Hold him down. This won't be pleasant."

It wasn't. Stoic though he might have been, Trent was unable to hold back a few groans as Anne used the thin-bladed knife to enlarge the bullet hole, making a cut on either side and pressing the flesh apart with the fingers of her other hand. She slid the knife blade into the gap, searching for the bullet. There was no resistance to the blade at first, and with every inch that she penetrated Trent's body, her spirits sank. If the bullet was too deep, she wouldn't be able to get it.

Then, when about four inches of the blade had disappeared into the wound, she touched something hard and unyielding. A rib? No, when she moved the blade slightly, the obstruction shifted, too. The thing she was touching could have been a piece of shattered rib, she supposed, but instinct told her it was the bullet.

"I think that's it," she breathed, and her voice was the only sound in the saloon except for Trent's labored breathing. Several men were holding his shoulders and legs to keep him still, and Sally had one of his hands in both of hers. Anne wondered if he had passed out; she hoped that was the case. It would make the rest of the operation easier.

Carefully, she tried to work the tip of the blade underneath the bullet so that she could lift it out that way, but the object kept slipping away from her. She was going to have to get a better grip on it. A pair of Thaddeus's forceps would be perfect, but his medical bag was back at the cabin and Anne wasn't sure there was time for someone to go fetch it. Trent might run out of luck before then.

She caught her lower lip between her teeth, hesitated for a moment, then brought the knife out of the wound and laid it aside. "Did you get it?" Sally asked eagerly.

"Not yet," Anne replied. "Hang on to him very tightly."

When she had received nods of confirmation from the men holding down Trent, she used the fingers of her left hand to spread the wound open as far as she could, then reached into the bloody aperture with her right hand. She willed her fingers to become longer, more slender, as she probed for the bullet again. Her fingers stayed the same as they were, of course, except that within seconds they were coated with warm, sticky blood.

She touched something, reached a little farther, felt two fingers slide around the flattened lump of lead that had been a bullet. Not daring to breathe, she tried to lift it and felt it come up a little. Quickly, she moved her fingers under it even more. The bullet, slick like her fingers with Trent's blood, threatened to slip away from her, but she managed to hang on to it as her pulse hammered feverishly in her head. She began withdrawing her hand, the bullet coming with it, cradled in her fingers like a precious bud of life, rather than the bringer of death. Up, up . . .

And out. Anne's hand emerged from the wound and her fingers closed tightly around the misshapen bullet. "I've got it!" she cried, throwing her head back and closing her eyes as a great tremor shook her.

She couldn't give in to the strain now; there was still work to do. "I need a needle and some strong thread," she said as she dropped the bullet on the table beside Trent and picked up the whiskey bottle. She poured the liquor into the wound until the ugly hole was overflowing. The whiskey that spilled back out onto the table was tinged with the red of the gambler's blood.

Anne had no idea where the needle and thread came from. One second she didn't have them, the next they had been thrust into her hands by one of the onlookers. Making an effort to control the trembling in her fingers, she began sewing up the wound.

Somehow it got done, and when Anne called for bandages, the saloon women fell all over themselves trying to be the first to rip off a piece of petticoat. That honor fell to Sally, and Anne folded the section of garment into a neat square that she pressed to the wound. Other strips of petticoat were handed to her, and as the men who had been holding down the gambler lifted him up, Anne bound the bandage tightly into place.

"That's all I can do for him," she said wearily. "Take him to his bed and keep clean bandages on that wound as much as possible. We'll just have to wait to see whether or not he makes it."

As the men were about to carefully lift Trent, he roused enough from his stupor to open his eyes. His gaze fixed blearily on Anne, and he asked, "Did you . . . get it?"

She nodded. "I got it."

"Wh-why? Why would you . . . save my life?"

"Because you and I have the matter of my husband's gold to settle, Mr. Trent," Anne told him. "I couldn't let you die until we'd done that."

"G-gold . . . ?" That was all Trent got out before his eyes rolled up in their sockets again and his head lolled to the side. He was out cold.

Anne watched as Trent was carried up the stairs and into one of the rooms on the second floor. Sally followed closely behind the men carrying the gambler, and Anne had a feeling the woman had appointed herself Trent's personal nurse. Anne was still trembling inside, but for the moment her rioting emotions and her tautly stretched nerves were still under control.

One of the other saloon women put a hand on her arm. "We can't thank you enough for what you did for the boss."

"Nonsense," Anne said. "I told Mr. Trent why I did it. No thanks are necessary."

But she would have tried to save his life even if she hadn't wanted to settle the problem of the gold with him, she realized suddenly. More of Thaddeus's personality had rubbed off on her than she had realized, she supposed. He never turned his back on anyone who needed his skills, even though in the end his dedication to his calling had very likely cost him his life.

"Say, ma'am," one of the bartenders spoke up, "did you ever think o' takin' up doctorin' yourself? I don't reckon I ever saw anybody do a better job than you just did."

Anne shook her head without thinking about it. "I'm not a doctor," she said. "I'm not trained for it."

One of the miners snorted. "Better trained than most of the sawbones we got out here west o' the Mississipp', far as I could tell. Even if you won't get hitched with any of us, Miz Palmer, you reckon you could stay around a while and patch us up when we need it?"

The question surprised Anne and forced her to consider the situation. She didn't plan to go anywhere until she either squared accounts with Patrick Trent or heard a reasonable explanation from him why she was suddenly a poor woman. Perhaps while she was waiting, she could start building up her "poke," as the miners called it.

"I don't know what I'm going to be doing in the future, but as long as I'm here, anyone who needs medical attention can come to my cabin," she heard herself saying. "I'll do the best I can."

"All right!" one of the miners whooped exuberantly. "Ophir's got itself a sawbones again!"

Anne looked down at her crimson-stained hands and found herself smiling. She said quietly, "I just hope that after I've treated a few more patients we won't have to change the name of the camp back to Bloody Gulch!"

Seventeen

The year 1849 rolled on toward 1850. As the months passed, San Francisco saw more than its share of trouble with the boom continuing unabated, goldseekers pouring into the city from the four corners of the earth. People stopped referring to them as Argonauts and adopted a new name for the hordes of would-be miners, one that would prove to be more popular and long lasting: forty-niners.

Not just goldseekers came to the city by the bay, however. Saloonkeepers, prostitutes, gamblers, thieves, cutthroats . . . all of them flocked to San Francisco until soon the respectable citizens were outnumbered. It was worth a man's life to venture alone into some areas after dark, and certain neighborhoods were dangerous even in the light of day. The Hounds, a group of toughs from New York who had originally come to California as a volunteer regiment during the war with Mexico, ran roughshod over the city, stealing whatever they wanted, beating anyone who got in their way, and wrecking the establishments of merchants who didn't cooperate with them. For some reason, the Hounds declared virtual war on the immigrants who had come to San Francisco from Chile, going so far as to burn to the ground the tent city where most of the *Chilenos* were staying. The city was up in arms about the Hounds, but there seemed to be nothing anyone could do to stop their reign of terror.

Late in the year, an even more dangerous problem cropped up. On the day before Christmas, a fire broke out that raced through the city, engulfing many of the buildings made of

wood and canvas. A warehouse full of explosives intended
for the gold fields was blown completely off the face of the
earth when its contents detonated, spreading the fire even
more. The bucket brigades that formed to battle the blaze
were no match for it, and much of the city was leveled.
Adding to the confusion and terror were gangs of looters,
including the Hounds, that roamed through the burning city.

The people of San Francisco were nothing if not resilient,
however, and the smoke had not even stopped rising from
the ashes and burned-out rubble before the rebuilding began.

It was going to take more than a fire to keep this city
down-and-out.

Nathan brought his wagon to a stop in the middle of what
passed for a street in Angel's Camp, a settlement on a tributary of the Calaveras River. This was farther south than the
camps he had worked the year before, but it was an area
teeming with miners, and that meant plenty of customers and
potential partners for Emily Woodward.

Emily had been lucky back during the winter. The big fire
had missed Woodward's Emporium, and the store had done
an incredible amount of business in the first few weeks after
the devastating blaze. With so much of the city in ruins,
those businesses that had survived and still had goods for
sale could have stayed open twenty-four hours a day, such
was the demand. Nathan had stayed in the store along with
several other men hired by Emily, all of them armed with
pistols and rifles in case of looters. There had been no trouble, however, and Nathan was thankful for that. As it was,
he was still waking up some nights drenched in sweat after
nightmares about having to shoot Brody. He wasn't sure if
he could ever kill anyone again.

Many of the abandoned ships had been cleared out of the
harbor by now, and sea traffic was steady again. Captains

and crews had realized there was money to be made simply by doing their jobs and making sure their cargoes were delivered safely. With a dependable flow of goods again, Emily invested heavily with the profits she made during the weeks after the fire. The upshot of the whole situation was that the emporium was bulging at the seams with merchandise and supplies, and now that it was spring and the snow in the foothills and mountains had begun to melt, Nathan was back at work carrying goods to the mining camps such as this one.

"Here we are, boy," Nathan said to the huge dog sitting on the wagon seat beside him. Hardrock was his constant companion, and Nathan had come to think of the animal as more of a friend than a pet. Not only that, but the dog was an added measure of protection. Most thieves would think twice before trying to rob a man with a dog like Hardrock.

Angel's Camp was a fairly new settlement, and Nathan didn't see any permanent buildings, only tents. Many of the miners had seen him driving in and were wandering toward the wagon now, curious to see what the newcomer was up to. Nathan unlashed the canvas cover on the back of the wagon and threw it back to reveal the supplies he was carrying. The routine was the same as the year before—up to a point.

This year, the goods Nathan carried were not for sale.

He gave a friendly nod to the first miners to reach him, a trio of men in woolen shirts, canvas pants, and worn boots. All of them sported beards and shapeless hats crammed down on tangled hair. One man pointed at Hardrock and asked, "What'n hell's that?"

"It's a dog," Nathan said. "His name is Hardrock."

"Biggest damn dog I ever seen," commented the second man. "Is he friendly?"

Hardrock lifted one side of his mouth in a silent snarl,

making the three miners step back quickly.

"Not particularly," Nathan replied, "but he won't bother you. He won't get down from the seat unless I give him permission . . . or unless he sees someone bothering me."

The third miner said hurriedly, "We ain't here to give you no trouble, mister. Don't sic 'im on us."

Nathan smiled. "I don't plan to."

"We just come to see what you got in the wagon."

"Take a look," Nathan offered, sweeping a hand toward the supplies in the wagon bed. "Hardrock won't mind."

The men came closer, craning their necks to peer over the sideboards of the wagon. When their eyes fell on the smoked hams and salt pork and slabs of bacon and sacks of flour and sugar and salt, Nathan could see how hungry they were. They looked with almost equal fervor on the picks and shovels and rolls of canvas, the tin washbowls and boots with no holes in the soles, the ready-made pants. One of the men reached out to touch a folded pair of trousers made of sturdy canvas dyed a dark blue and fastened together with tiny copper rivets at the seams for extra strength. "I never seen pants like this before," he said in an awed voice. "What'd you call 'em?"

"I don't know that they have a special name," Nathan said, "but they're made in San Francisco by a man called Levi Strauss."

"Look like mighty fine pants," muttered the man.

"And they're practically indestructible," Nathan pointed out. "Could you use a pair?"

The other miners laughed and indicated a wide gap in the seat of the first man's pants where his red woolen underwear showed through. "I hope to smile he could," one of the men said.

"You hush up," snapped the man with the hole in his pants. He turned back to Nathan and asked, "How much you want for a pair of Levi's pants?''

"They're not for sale, at least not yet," Nathan said.

More miners had gathered around by now, and the answer provoked some impatient questions from them. "How come you to bring this stuff out here if you don't figure to sell it?" one of the men demanded loudly.

Nathan held up his hands to forestall their protests. "My aunt is Mrs. Emily Woodward," he said. "You may have heard of her—she owns Woodward's Emporium back in San Francisco. I'm acting as her agent, and she wants you to know that she's willing to supply any man with a complete mining outfit and sufficient provisions in return for a share in whatever gold you find."

That announcement brought some more interested buzzing from the crowd of miners. Nathan could see at a glance that many of them were probably on their last legs as prospectors. Their clothes were ripped and threadbare, their boots run down at the heels and worn out on the soles. Some of the picks and shovels they carried over their shoulders had broken handles that were bound together clumsily with rope. Nathan had only been doing this for a short time, but he had already learned enough to judge that many of these men might be willing to take Emily's deal. If any goods were left over once he was through with the trades, then he could sell them outright.

"Say," one of the men spoke up suddenly, "would your name happen to be Jones, young fella?"

"That's right. My name is Nathan Jones."

"I heard of you!" the man exclaimed. "A fella from Rich Gulch told me about you. You're the one they call Grubstake Jones!"

Nathan nodded, feeling a flush creep over his features. Someone in one of the first camps he'd visited this spring had hung that nickname on him, and it had stuck. He wasn't particularly fond of it, but the miners seemed to enjoy it. "Grubstake" seemed an awfully silly thing to call a grown man. As long as the miners went along with Emily's deal, though, Nathan supposed they could call him anything they liked.

"That's right," Nathan went on, warming to his speech. "I'm Grubstake Jones, and I'm here to do some business with you, gentlemen. Now, who among you is interested in having the finest mining outfit money can buy?"

In less than an hour, he had worked out deals with a dozen men who were willing to part with a share of whatever gold they found in the future in return for a chance to keep searching for the precious yellow stuff. Nathan saw their eyes light up, he saw hope return to faces that had been almost overcome with despair, and he thought, not for the first time, that perhaps Emily was right. It was true that she demanded a hefty percentage of future strikes, but maybe that was a small price to pay for something like hope.

Once the papers were signed, with a wavering cross mark in the case of the many miners who couldn't write, Nathan began passing out the goods, and in no time the wagon was empty. "I'll be back in a week to check and see how you're doing," he told the men as he climbed onto the seat next to Hardrock and took up the reins. That was another part of his job, making sure none of Emily's "partners" tried to cheat her out of her rightful share of his findings.

Before the summer was over, he thought, he was going to wind up driving all over these foothills, from the Fresno and Mariposa Rivers in the south to the Feather and the Sacramento in the north. He'd probably get to know the Sierra Nevadas better than nearly anyone else in this part of the country. That was all right, he decided, as long as he didn't have to swing a pick or squat in an ice-cold stream while he was doing it.

"Let's go home," he said to the dog as he swung the wagon around and left Angel's Camp behind, pausing the vehicle for a second to let a big bullfrog make a prodigious jump across the trail in front of him. As he prodded the mules into motion again, he mused aloud, "Grubstake Jones . . . what a ridiculous name! Sort of like calling a dog Hardrock, don't you think?"

Beside him on the seat, Hardrock gave a loud bark, and Nathan laughed. With the mules going along at a brisk gait, Grubstake Jones and Hardrock rolled on down the trail.

"I'm glad you agree with me, Sam. Something has to be done about these gangs, or San Francisco is never going to be a safe place for decent citizens to live."

"I'll talk to a few of the other businessmen we can trust and see about putting together some sort of group," Sam Brannan said as he left Emily's office and entered the main room of the store. "A sort of vigilance committee, I suppose you could call it," he went on.

"Vigilance is what we need," Emily agreed, following him out of the office. "Otherwise the Hounds and the Sydney Ducks will take over the town and tear it apart, like two dogs fighting over a bone."

Cassandra stood at the other end of the counter listening to the discussion between her mother and Sam Brannan. Emily had asked Brannan to come to this meeting today at the emporium; as two of the leading business people in the city, it was in their best interests to try to break the gangs' stranglehold on San Francisco. They were not only civic leaders, but their profits were also at stake. If the law-abiding inhabitants of the city were run out, no one would be left to buy the merchandise in the stores owned by Emily and Brannan.

Not only was Brannan a merchant, but he had become something of a financier, too, lending money to other businessmen, individual miners, and some of the mining syndicates that were beginning to form. It was vitally important to him that San Francisco have at least the rudiments of law and order. Emily was equally troubled by the increasing lawlessness. The Sydney Ducks, a gang made up of Australian immigrants, had proven to be even more ruthless and dangerous than the Hounds. Their atrocities were too numerous to count, and so far the small, corrupt San Francisco police force had done nothing to rein them in.

Cassandra knew all about the problem with the gangs. She read the newspapers and kept up with what her mother said about the roving bands of criminals. She knew the situation was becoming desperate.

And she didn't care about it at all, not really.

She hoped the gang violence continued to bypass her mother's store, of course; she wouldn't wish anything bad to befall Emily. But Cassandra was tired of the city's problems, tired of the city itself. Sure, there was plenty of excitement in San Francisco, but it couldn't compare with the thrill of finding a fortune in gold. *That* was what she really wanted. She listened to the tales told by men who had been to the gold fields and who planned to return there, and she knew that was where her own destiny lay.

Emily had thwarted her at every turn, though, and Cassandra had decided she was going to give her mother only one more chance.

She waited until Sam Brannan had said his good-byes and left the store, then approached Emily. "I want to talk to you, Mother," Cassandra said.

"Is there a problem, dear?" Emily asked, meaning was there a problem with the store. Cassandra knew that quite well. It would never occur to Emily that her daughter was stifling here, spending her days clerking in the emporium and making pen scratches in a ledger.

"Yes, Mother," Cassandra said without hesitation. It wasn't a lie. There was a problem, all right, just not the sort that Emily expected.

Sounding slightly impatient, Emily said, "Well, tell me about it."

"Not out here. In the office."

Emily looked around. Several other clerks were working at the moment, and the store could be safely left in their hands for a short time. She nodded. "All right."

When they were in the office and Emily was settled behind the desk as usual, she looked up at Cassandra and said, "Sit down, dear."

Cassandra shook her head. "I'd rather not. This won't take long, Mother. Nathan should be back soon, and when he leaves for the gold fields the next time, I want to go with him."

An irritated expression passed across Emily's face. "We-'ve had this discussion before," she snapped. "The gold fields are no place—"

"For a young lady like me," Cassandra finished. "I know. But Mother, more women are going out there than ever before. There are quite a few good-sized settlements now. It's not like I'd be going off into some godforsaken wilderness!"

"There may be some settlements," Emily said grimly, "but those settlements are full of crude, dangerous men."

"Men whom you don't seem to mind grubstaking."

"That's different. That's business. I don't have to associate with them. Nathan handles that part of the arrangements for me."

"You trust Nathan to go out there."

"He's a man," Emily said. "He can look after himself."

Cassandra gave an unladylike snort. "If he's lucky. I like Nathan, but he's hardly the rugged frontier sort, Mother.

He's no more like the other forty-niners than, well, than I am.''

"You've proven my own point for me," Emily told her with a smug smile. "I'm willing to allow my nephew to take some chances: he's well paid and he knows the risks. I'll not allow my daughter to be exposed to that sort of thing.''

Cassandra's eyes narrowed dangerously. "Is that your last word on the subject?''

"Indeed it is," Emily said sternly. "And I would appreciate it if you would *not* bring up the subject again, young lady.''

With a sigh, Cassandra nodded. "All right, Mother. I can promise you that I'll never say anything to you about it again.''

"That's good. I'm glad to see that you're showing some common sense. There are times when I think you're seriously lacking in such a quality." Emily stood up. "One of us should go out into the store again. I don't like to leave the clerks on their own too much.''

That's because you don't trust them, Mother, Cassandra thought. *You don't trust anyone, especially your own daughter.*

But as she followed Emily out of the office, Cassandra renewed to herself the promise she had made to her mother. Never again would she ask Emily's permission to go to the gold fields.

After all, what she didn't ask about, her mother couldn't forbid . . .

Cassandra moved as quietly as she possibly could down the stairs, knowing from past observation which of the steps creaked and which ones didn't. Emily was a sound sleeper, but she seemed to have some sort of sixth sense when it came to things being amiss in the store.

And something was definitely amiss tonight, Cassandra thought with a tiny smile.

For one thing, she was totally nude as she slipped down the stairs from the living quarters above.

She had left her nightdress in her room, along with all of her other personal belongings. This was the start of a new period in her life, and she wanted it to be a fresh beginning. She would take only the things she needed from the store downstairs.

The big main room was dim, lit only by a lantern on the rear counter with its wick turned down as low as it would go and continue burning, plus the faint glow that filtered through the windows from the streetlamps outside, which were few and far between. Cassandra knew the layout of the room as well as or better than anyone else, however, and the lack of light did not bother her as she made her way around the store, picking out by feel the items she wanted.

Luckily, the emporium stocked a wide variety of sizes of ready-made clothes. Cassandra was able to find a pair of red woolen underwear that fit her fairly well. She picked out the smallest pair of pants that Emily bought from Mr. Levi Strauss, and she pulled them on to find that the waist fit, even though the legs were a few inches too long. She rolled them up around her ankles. That was followed by a linsey-woolsey shirt, then a pair of thick socks—and yet another pair of socks when the smallest boots she could find were still a trifle too big. With the extra socks the boots were a comfortable enough fit.

Cassandra moved to the counter containing sewing notions and supplies and found a pair of scissors. Knowing that her next task wasn't going to be easy, she took a deep breath, gathered a thick clump of hair in her free hand, and started cutting. It took her only a few minutes to hack at her blond hair until it was short all over her head. That made the hat she picked out fit just fine. She gathered up the hair she'd cut off and dumped it into a waste bin.

So far, she had carried everything out in utter silence, save for the soft whisper of the scissors. Now she was going to have to be even more careful as she began gathering the supplies she would need. Earlier in the day, she had made sure there were a couple of large canvas bags underneath the main counter, and she fetched them now and began to fill them with provisions for the journey facing her. She packed plenty of food, a tin washbowl for panning, a pick and a shovel with the handles temporarily removed for easier carrying. As she placed items in the bags, she periodically judged the weight carefully. She couldn't afford to make the bags heavier than she could carry, because she didn't plan to buy any mules until she was across the bay in Sausalito.

Emily would guess right away where she had gone, of course, even though it had been over a week since their last discussion of the matter and Cassandra's promise not to mention the gold fields again. Cassandra had the same stubborn streak her mother did, and Emily knew it. But Nathan had already returned to San Francisco and left again, bound for the northern part of the gold-field country this time; it would be a week or more before he got back from there. Emily would be less likely to send a stranger after her runaway daughter, although there was always the chance she might do it; Cassandra wouldn't venture a firm guess on that point. But she was confident that by the time Emily sent someone after her, she would be well on her way, beyond the reach of her mother at last.

She felt a pang of regret as that thought crossed her mind. Her goal in leaving was not to hurt Emily. Cassandra loved her mother and did not want to cause her pain. But there was her own pain to consider, the pain of being stuck here in San Francisco when the gold fields were out there beckoning to her with their riches and adventure. Perhaps there was something wrong with her, Cassandra considered. Most young women of quality were supposed to dream of husbands and children and servants and a fine home, not of tramping through the wilderness and finding a fortune in gold. Maybe this wanderlust she felt was a sickness.

But regardless of whether it was or it wasn't, Cassandra could no longer deny it. She had to strike out on her own, make her way in the world on the terms she and no one else set. Destiny was out there waiting for her, she sensed as she unlocked the back door of the store, hefted the bags of supplies, and carried them into the rear yard.

Destiny . . .

After she had relocked the door, she slung the bags over her shoulders and set off into the predawn darkness to find it.

Eighteen

"Come on, damn it!" growled the burly man with the thick blond beard as he tugged on the mule's lead rope. It was a good thing mules were so strong and tireless and could get by on bad graze and sparse water. Otherwise anybody stuck with one of the blasted beasts would probably shoot the blamed thing within a week just out of sheer frustration.

Boone Blakely gave up. He let go of the lead rope and stalked over to a large rock nearby. As he crossed his arms over his chest and sat down, he glowered at the pack animal. "All right, you win," he said. "Stand there in the hot sun as long as you want to. I hope your brains fry, what little you've got of 'em."

The mule regarded him stonily and stayed where it was.

Boone sighed and slid down the rock so that he was sitting beside it, rather than on it. That gave him a little shade. Over the past couple of years he had learned that springtime didn't last very long in the Sierra Nevadas. It seemed like one week there was ten feet of snow on the ground and a howling wind out of the east bringing more, and the next week the snow was all gone and the sun was beating down hard enough and hot enough to cook a man's brain to mush. The only place worse for changeable weather, as far as Boone knew, was Texas.

He was on a ridge overlooking the Middle Fork of the American River, not far as the crow flies from Coloma and Sutter's Mill, where the whole thing had started. The mill that Boone had helped to build had gone out of business, or so he'd heard. No one was interested in lumber or sawmills when there was gold to be found. In fact, old John Augustus Sutter himself had had nothing but trouble since the discovery James Marshall had made. Considering that Sutter owned so much land in the area, a man might have thought that he would wind up richer than anybody else, but it hadn't worked out that way. As usual, greedier folks had found ways of getting their hands on Sutter's land without ever paying him a cent for it or cutting him in for a share of the gold they found there. The way Boone heard it, Sutter spent most of his time these days in court, trying to get some of his land back. His settlement of New Helvetia, which he had envisioned ruling like some sort of little European kingdom, was nothing more than a fading dream now.

Dreams faded all the time, though, Boone thought as he leaned back against the rock and tipped his hat down to shade his eyes. Anybody who believed in dreams was a damned fool, because they were about as real as phantoms.

Boone closed his eyes and mulled over the surprising fact that he was this close to Coloma, which was a good-sized town now. He tended to avoid the bigger settlements and had ever since that Texas Ranger, Dan Logan, had unexpectedly let him go. Boone hadn't seen or heard anything of Logan in almost a year, and that was the way he liked it. Maybe that strike in the gully had been as rich as it looked and the ranger had gone back to Texas a wealthy man. There was even a chance that Logan was dead by now, considering how many ways there were for a man to get killed in the gold fields, and if that was the case it wouldn't have broken Boone's heart, although he'd felt like the ranger was a decent enough sort for a lawman.

He couldn't work up any sympathy, though, for somebody who'd wanted to take him back to Texas and watch him swing at the end of a rope.

Those dark thoughts were running through his head as he dozed off, and when something nudged him on the shoulder a little later, he jumped and yelled, "Goddamn it!" His hand went instinctively to the knife sheathed at his waist. He didn't have a gun, but the big knife would serve him just as well in a close fight.

Except that there was nobody threatening him. The mule stood over him, and he knew the animal's nose was what had nudged him. Looked like the mule was ready to get in the shade, too, and wait out the hottest part of the day. Boone caught hold of the lead rope and used it to help lift himself to his feet.

"Come on, jughead," he told the mule as he jerked it toward a stand of pines about a hundred yards farther along the ridge. They would rest there for a while and then move on toward Murderer's Bar, Boone decided.

Since he and Logan had parted company, so to speak, Boone had headed south, working his way past the Cosumnes, the Mokelumne, the Calaveras, and the Stanislaus Rivers, all the way down to the Mariposa, where large numbers of Mormons from over in Utah Territory had come to look for gold. Boone had wintered there and regretted the decision, since the Saints, as they called themselves, didn't hold with drinking. The cold months of winter were harder to tolerate without whiskey, which was in sparse supply in that part of California.

But he had survived, which he seemed to have a knack for doing, and when the snow began to melt, he started north again, stopping along the way to chip samples from every likely looking outcrop of rock. So far he had found only a little gold, just enough to keep him in supplies.

And those supplies were running low again now. He figured he had enough food to last another couple of days, and that was all. He didn't have any nuggets, and if he turned his poke upside down and shook it good and hard for a while, not enough dust would fall out to make one good pinch of the stuff. He was in sad shape, and that was the truth.

Well, maybe he could sell the mule when he got to Murderer's Bar, or trade the bad-tempered beast for some supplies. He could have gotten rid of the mule in Coloma for sure, but he'd skirted around that settlement, since it was in the center of the gold fields and served as the unofficial jumping-off spot for most of the miners who came out here. Too great a likelihood he might run into Dan Logan, Boone had decided, assuming the ranger was still alive.

Boone hobbled the mule and stretched out under the pines to wait until the sun was lower in the sky before resuming his journey to Murderer's Bar. As usual, his thoughts turned to what he was going to do after that. He had spent two years looking for gold, thinking that any day now he'd make his strike, and yet if he'd been able to put together all the nuggets and dust he had found since his initial run of good luck, he doubted if it would all add up to more than he had made in wages working as a carpenter on that damned sawmill. He had talked to all different sorts of people in the past two years, because the lure of gold drew every kind of man under the sun, some of them highly educated. One of them had referred to Lady Luck as Dame Fortune.

Damn Fortune was more like it, Boone reflected. And it sure hadn't treated him like a lady.

Maybe it was time to admit that not everybody looking for gold was going to strike it rich. Maybe it was time to put the gold fields behind him once and for all. Once he had dreamed of hiring a sailing ship to take him to some beautiful island in the South Seas. He might not be able to afford that, but he could sign on as a member of the crew and get there that way. He had never been on a ship in his life, but after a couple of years of mining, how hard could the work be? And when he got to where he wanted to go, there wouldn't be anything to stop him from jumping ship. Then, with the memories of Texas thousands of miles behind him, maybe he could finally forget.

It was a nice thought, and Boone dozed off again with it playing through his head.

"How long did you say she's been gone?" Nathan asked in disbelief.

"Almost two weeks," Emily Woodward replied. Her voice held a defensive tone, which was unusual for her. Nathan had seldom if ever heard her sound like she thought she might be in the wrong.

He grimaced and said, "She could be almost anywhere from the Calaveras to the Yuba by now. Did you send anyone after her?"

"Sam Brannan sent a man to look for her when I discovered she was gone. He couldn't find her. One of the men who works on the ferry remembered seeing someone who might have been Cassandra, but he had no idea where she went after she reached the other side of the harbor."

Nathan began to pace back and forth in front of the store's main counter. This was a fine homecoming, he thought bitterly. He'd had nothing but trouble on this trip, from heavy rains that had slowed him down to a cracked axle on the wagon. Now, when he finally made it back to San Francisco, he found that his cousin had evidently run off to the gold fields. Blast the girl!

And yet he could understand. Cassandra was a high-spirited girl, and the very education that Emily had insisted she receive had made her even less likely to accept the plans that Emily had laid out for her. Emily was content to devote her time and energy and, yes, her passion to the emporium, but Cassandra . . .

Cassandra wanted other things in her life, more exciting things. Like looking for gold.

"The man on the ferry wasn't sure it was Cassandra he saw?"

"All he remembered was a small man in clothes that matched the ones taken from here, carrying a couple of bags that could have been full of supplies. Cassandra appears to have outfitted herself as well as she could, considering she didn't have any mules to carry the bags."

"She could have gotten some mules in Sausalito," mused Nathan. "The ferryman thought the person he saw was a man, you said?"

Emily took a small bag from under the counter. "Cassandra cut off her hair before she left. I'm sure she intends to try to pass for a man. At least I hope so."

As she spoke, Emily upended the bag and let the thick clumps of blond hair spill out. Nathan blinked at them, reached out and touched them lightly. He was a little surprised that Emily had kept them. If anything happened to Cassandra, that hair might be all that Emily had left of her daughter, but Nathan wouldn't have expected such a thought to occur to her.

"You haven't sent anyone else after her since Brannan's man couldn't find her?"

"No, I waited for you to get back, since you know Cassandra and you know those foothills as well as anyone by now. I expected you to return sooner."

"I already explained what happened. I thought I'd be here before now myself. I wish I had been." Nathan sighed. "I wish I'd been here when she made up her mind to leave. Maybe I could have talked her out of it."

"I doubt that. Cassandra's as stubborn as a rock! She always has been."

And I wonder where she gets that from? Nathan thought, but he kept the comment to himself.

Emily crossed her arms and regarded him intently. "Well, what are you going to do?"

For a moment, Nathan felt like pointing out that Cassandra was *her* daughter, not his. She was Emily's responsibility. But she was also his own cousin, and he liked her. He wouldn't want to see her come to any harm out there on the edge of the Sierra Nevadas, and there was plenty of trouble she could get into if she wasn't careful—or even if she was.

"I'm going after her," he declared. "Like you said, I know the country, and more importantly, the miners have gotten to know me. Most of them have heard of Grubstake Jones by now, I reckon."

"Grubstake Jones?" repeated Emily. "What in the world is that?"

Nathan waved off her question. "Just a nickname. It doesn't matter. What's important is that while I'm looking for Cassandra myself, I can also put the word out that I'm looking for a little fella who matches her description. I wish I knew what name she's using."

"You're not going to tell people that she's a young lady?"

"If she's got folks fooled already, it'll be better not to announce what's really going on. Safer for her in the long run."

Emily frowned, and Nathan knew the thoughts that had to be going through her head. Her features were pale and drawn with genuine worry, another emotion that Nathan had hardly ever seen her reveal. It looked like Emily was human, after all, even though she kept it covered up most of the time.

He put a hand on his aunt's shoulder. "I'll find her if

anybody can," he promised. "If she's out there, I'll bring her back."

He hoped for Cassandra's sake that he could keep that promise.

Cassandra had never dreamed that a person's feet could hurt so much. The extra socks in the boots served as padding, but she still developed blisters. With each step, pain shot up her calves and into the aching muscles of her thighs. Her arms and shoulders were almost as sore from hauling on the mule. The man who had sold the animal to her back in Sausalito had sworn that the mule was gentle and tractable, but Cassandra had never seen any creature on God's earth as stubborn as this beast.

Except perhaps her mother, she thought with a smile, even though she was exhausted.

Two weeks had passed since she had left San Francisco in the early morning hours, catching the first ferry across the bay and buying the mule as soon as the livery stable near the ferry landing had opened for the day. The purchase had taken most of her money, because she hadn't brought much with her. She had a little extra for emergencies, but not enough to tempt robbers. She could have taken money from the till in the store, but that would have been stealing. Somehow, taking the clothes and the supplies didn't seem nearly as bad.

Without enough funds to purchase a ticket on one of the boats traveling up the Sacramento River, Cassandra had been forced to walk the whole way, leading the pack mule as she trudged along a trail that was by now well worn by the feet of thousands of forty-niners. The first few days had been utter misery. She had never before walked more than a mile or so at a time, and keeping up a decent pace from morning until evening meant being tortured by sore muscles and feet.

Even now, after a couple of weeks, she still hurt a great deal of the time. But she had the resilience of youth going for her, and each day, it seemed, she could feel her muscles hardening and growing stronger.

There were plenty of other travelers. The incredible flow of would-be miners during the last half of 1848 and all of 1849 had slowed somewhat, but the roads were still busy. Cassandra shared campfires with some of the men, contributing some of her supplies to the cookpot. She kept the wide, drooping brim of the brown hat pulled down in front of her face, and when she had to speak she used a hoarse, throaty voice and kept her responses as short as possible. The other miners pegged her as a young man, maybe even a boy, but that wasn't so unusual. Children as young as ten had gone to the gold fields, many of them runaways or orphans. They weren't any more immune to the lure of riches than their elders were.

Still, it was frightening when Cassandra had to spend too much time around other people. She was afraid someone would stumble on her secret. She didn't know what would happen if that occurred. That would depend on who discovered her real identity. She might be sent back to San Francisco . . . or she might be molested and murdered. She was glad that thought hadn't occurred to her before she left, otherwise she might still be behind the counter of the store.

But there was no reward without risk, no excitement and glory without the chance of danger. Cassandra tightened her grip on the mule's reins and muttered, ''Come on, you brute,'' as she led the animal along the trail.

She had passed Sacramento City, which was well on its way to becoming a large town by now, and Sutter's Fort, which still stood despite the misfortunes of its owner. Then she had started up the American River toward Coloma. That was the site of the original strike that had started the gold rush, she'd heard, and that was where she intended to begin her own search for the precious mineral. It stood to reason that all the gold in that vicinity would have been found by now, since the mad scramble had begun there and worked its way outward, but Nathan had told her that men were still making strikes in the hills along the American River. There seemed to be so much gold that the supply would never run out.

Cassandra didn't care about that. She just wanted to make a strike of her own, and what happened after that didn't matter. She would have known the thrill of the discovery.

Coloma turned out to be a bustling community sprawled out on both sides of the American River where it flowed through a broad valley before bending abruptly to the north. Rugged, wooded hills overlooked the settlement on one side; the heights on the other side were a bit more gentle, and it was from them that Cassandra had her first look at the place. She saw a large wooden building in the center of town, right beside the river, and wondered if it was the famous Sutter's Mill, where gold had been discovered in the millrace. What gold was in the river would be long gone by now, of course, but that was not true of the surrounding hills. There were thousands of nooks and crannies where the soft yellow metal could still lurk, not to mention the creeks running through those hills where the flecks of gold dust could be panned out.

Feeling the excitement growing in her, Cassandra tugged on the mule's reins and headed down the hill toward the settlement. She would have to be careful, she knew. The more people that were around, the more chance someone would tumble to the fact that she was a woman.

Coloma didn't really have any streets. The buildings were laid out in a haphazard pattern, a sure sign of a boom town that had sprung up without any real thoughts about its long-

term existence. Cassandra wandered among them, taking in
the sights and sounds and trying to contain her excitement.
This was it, the real thing, the center of the gold fields. This
was what she had left San Francisco to find.

"Watch out, shorty!"

At first she didn't realize the shout was directed at her.
Then, in the next instant, a figure came hurtling out of the
log building she was passing. With a wild yell, the man lost
his balance and fell into a large puddle of mud, almost at
Cassandra's feet. The sticky stuff splashed up, getting on her
boots and trousers even though she leaped back and tried to
avoid it.

She stifled the startled, high-pitched exclamation that tried
to burst out of her mouth. Taken by surprise as she had been,
she had almost given away her true sex. Instead she lowered
her voice and grunted, "Damn! Watch where you're goin',
mister!"

The man rolled over, spitting mud out of his mouth and
grimacing. He shook his head and then grinned up at Cassandra, his teeth startlingly white in a face coated with dark
brown mud. "Sorry, old boy," he said. "I didn't really have
any choice in the matter, however. You see, I was, ah, asked
rather strenuously to leave that establishment."

Cassandra glanced at the log building, which had a crude
but effective sign over its door reading *SALOON*. A burly
man in an apron that long, long ago had been white stood
in the doorway with his brawny arms crossed, a glare on his
florid face. He called out to Cassandra, "That Englisher son
of a bitch means I throwed him out o' here! And he damn
well deserved it for bein' stupid enough to try to pass off
fool's gold for the real thing."

The man sitting in the mud puddle spread his hands in-
nocently. "How was I to know?" he asked. "I took the

nugget on good faith from the man who gave it to me. He said it was the real thing.''

The saloonkeeper snorted contemptuously at that claim, shook his head, and pointed a blunt finger at the Englishman. ''Don't come back in my place again, you hear?''

''Of course, my good man, of course.'' The Englishman pushed himself to his feet, lifted his chin, and managed to look haughty despite being covered with mud. ''You can rest assured that I shall take my trade elsewhere in the future, after the welcome I received in your establishment, sir!''

With that, he turned and started to stalk off, pausing only long enough to look back at Cassandra and motion for her to follow. ''Come along, come along,'' he said briskly.

''What for?'' Cassandra asked.

''Well, old boy, after the splashing your boots and trousers took due to my misfortune, the least I can do is buy you a drink.''

Cassandra shook her head and said, ''Not with fool's gold. I don't want to get tossed out of no saloon.'' She kept her tone deliberately rough and harsh.

''No, no, no more fool's gold. I have dust, too. The genuine article.''

Cassandra hesitated. She didn't particularly want to have a drink with the Englishman, but maybe he knew his way around this part of the country and could give her some idea where to start looking for gold. *If* he could be trusted, that is, and that seemed to be a big if.

But things like this were all part of the adventure, she supposed, so she nodded and hurried to catch up with the Englishman. She had to maintain a brisk pace to keep up with his longer legs. He was tall and lean, and he had wiped away enough of the mud to reveal an interesting but definitely not handsome face. His nose was much too large, his chin was a bit weak, and his eyes bulged enough to remind

Cassandra of a frog. Still, she couldn't help but find him intriguing. He was the first Englishman she had ever talked to except for a few customers in the store who weren't really interested in conversation.

That wasn't this man's problem. "Peregrine Forsythe," he said, then had to repeat it before Cassandra realized he was telling her his name. "Remittance man extraordinaire," he went on. "Do you know what that is, my good fellow?"

Cassandra shook her head.

"I shall have to explain it to you, then," Peregrine said, grinning in anticipation.

The explanation took a while, which came as no surprise to Cassandra. She had already figured out that Peregrine Forsythe enjoyed the sound of his own voice. Over the next few minutes, she learned from his rambling discourse that he was the youngest son of a wealthy, aristocratic family in England. He was also something of an embarrassment, having been expelled from every school to which he had been sent. A washout as a soldier, there was nothing left for the family to do except send him to America, Peregrine admitted without the least trace of shame. He received a yearly allowance from his family—a remittance, hence the name—as long as he remained in America and didn't come home to dishonor his more successful relatives.

"It's all right with me," Peregrine went on. "They're a bloody stuffy lot, actually, and I've no real reason to go back. Much more exciting here in the colonies, don't you think?"

"This country ain't been colonies for nearly seventy years," Cassandra pointed out.

"Well, yes, but I'm old-fashioned, you see. It's always been my belief that you Americans will someday come to your senses and embrace the empire once more."

"Don't count on it," she told him gruffly.

They had reached another saloon, and Peregrine said, "Ah, perhaps the proprietor of this dram shop will be more reasonable and less quick to anger. Let's go in."

Cassandra shook her head to the offer of whiskey and asked for beer instead. She had never tasted whiskey, but she had sipped beer before and knew she could control her reaction to it, even though she hated the taste. Peregrine asked for a glass of sherry and then settled for beer himself when his request drew nothing but a puzzled, potentially hostile stare from the barkeep.

"So, my friend," Peregrine said after they had both sampled the warm, bitter brew, "you haven't yet told me your name."

Cassandra hesitated, then said, "It's Cass."

"Cass? That's all?"

She nodded curtly.

"Well, then, Cass, I take it you've come to California to make your fortune, like all these other seekers of wealth?"

Cassandra nodded again, determined to talk as little as possible. And apparently as long as she was with Peregrine, that wouldn't be too much of a problem.

"I had the same goal when I came here, having heard stories of the fabulous riches that were here for the taking. Now I've come to realize that only a few of the many ever experience that elusive wealth." He smiled broadly. "But I intend to persevere. After all, there's no law that says I mightn't be one of those privileged few, eh?"

"Right," Cassandra muttered into her cup of beer.

Peregrine looked at her shrewdly. "Would you perchance be interested in forming a partnership of sorts, Cass, old friend? I've a simply wonderful place picked out, but it's going to take two people to work it properly. This could be the chance of a lifetime, you know."

Cassandra shook her head. "I work alone," she said

curtly, not wanting to be rude to Peregrine but not wanting to encourage him, either.

He sighed. "Well, don't say I didn't warn you. When I'm a rich man with the biggest and best house in all of San Francisco, you mustn't be jealous of me. You won't be, will you?"

Once again, Cassandra shook her head. This Englishman was becoming tiresome, and she wished he would finish his beer and go away.

Instead, he leaned closer to her and lowered his voice to say, "I've grown fond of you, Cass. You're a right lad. I'm going to tell you where to go to find gold, even if you don't want to be my partner. A gesture of friendship, eh?"

Cassandra didn't say anything. She didn't trust the man, and she didn't want him getting too close to her. Even though her skin had been roughened by the elements these past two weeks, he might notice it was still not the skin of a man.

"Go up toward Murderer's Bar," he told her in a loud whisper. "You'll find a brook, the prettiest little stream you've ever seen, but it has the decidedly unlovely name of Stink Creek. There's gold on Stink Creek, gold, I tell you! I'll be up there as soon as I, ah, acquire the funds to outfit myself properly again. Are you sure you won't reconsider my offer?"

So that was what he wanted, Cassandra thought. He was broke and wanted to team up with someone else so that he could take advantage of their supplies. She shook her head firmly at his question.

He sighed. "Ah, well, more's the pity. But I have a feeling I'll see you up there, Cass. And before we're done, we'll both be bloody rich, eh?" A faraway look appeared in his eyes. "As bloody rich as anyone in England."

Cassandra doubted that quite strongly, but maybe he was

right about one thing. There could be gold on Stink Creek.

And she had just learned a lesson that had been driven home to every other forty-niner who had come to these foothills.

The only way to find out if there was really any gold where it was rumored to be was to go out there and look. She would stay here in Coloma tonight and rest up a little, but tomorrow she would be bound for Stink Creek.

Nineteen

If Cassandra thought getting to the gold fields had been a rugged task, trying to find the precious metal once she got there was even worse. Until she had spent a couple of days swinging a heavy pick and wielding a shovel from dawn until dusk she had never dreamed that a person's arms could hurt so much.

She had left Coloma and walked up to Stink Creek, several miles north of the settlement on the American River. The tip she'd received from Peregrin Forsythe obviously wasn't a secret, because the hills on both sides of the narrow valley formed by the creek were covered with miners. The air was full of a steady chinking noise as the blades of picks bit into the rocky soil and loosened it. Cassandra found a spot of her own and was soon adding to the noise.

The place she'd picked was a piece of flat land beside the creek where she could pitch her tent. The campsite was only about twenty feet wide. On the other side, the ground sloped up sharply in a stony bluff, and that was where Cassandra did her digging. She swung the pick steadily, amazed at how heavy it seemed to grow before the day was over.

But by the time the sun set on the first day, Forsythe's advice had proven to be good. Cassandra had found several nuggets among the gravel she chipped off the face of the bluff. She was no real judge of gold's worth, but she figured the nuggets would fetch a good price when she got back to civilization. As she uncovered each of them in turn, she felt a fresh thrill shoot through her at the sight of the dull yellow sheen they gave off.

This was just a minor strike, Cassandra thought, but it was a strike nonetheless. And that thought had her shivering with excitement. The discovery made all the hardship worthwhile, and she spent quite a few delicious moments thinking about what it would be like when she waltzed back into her mother's store with a fortune in gold in her poke. Then Mother would regret having been so stubborn.

Cassandra halfway expected Peregrine Forsythe to turn up around Stink Creek. She had left the Englishman passed out back in Coloma. He'd been dead drunk, to be honest about it. Cassandra felt a little bad about taking his advice and finding gold when he was broke and lacked the supplies to do some prospecting of his own, but those feelings passed rapidly. It wasn't her fault that Peregrine had had a run of bad luck, she told herself.

The first two days passed, then two days more, and Cassandra had to stop and rest for a day. Her muscles ached so badly that she could hardly climb out of her bedroll that morning. She needed to recover some of her strength—otherwise she might collapse and be unable to continue digging for gold.

She brewed a pot of coffee and fried some of the salt pork from her provisions, using the grease from the pork to soften up a couple of the hard biscuits she took from her pack. The sun was coming up as she prepared this breakfast, and already the air rang with the sound of men digging. The bank on the far side of the creek was choked with thick brush along this part of the stream, so there were no other miners close by in that direction. To the south on this side of the creek, Cassandra could see several men working their claims, the closest one about a hundred and fifty yards away. To the north was more brush, and in addition the slope dropped down steeply all the way to the water, so there were no camps in that direction for a good distance. Considering that there were men all up and down the valley, Cassandra was fairly isolated in this spot, for which she was thankful. Company wasn't something she wanted.

Suddenly, there was a rustling in the brush across the creek. Cassandra frowned as she set down her cup of coffee. It sounded like some sort of large creature pushing through the brush, breaking a path among the limbs and vines, and she felt a tingle of fear. There were still bears in these hills, she had been told. She wished she had brought a rifle or even a pistol with her, but she didn't have any weapons except for a small hand ax. As the crackling and popping in the undergrowth grew louder, she reached into her pack and closed her fingers around the handle of the ax. Her hat was pushed down tight on her head, the brim drooping in front of her face to conceal her features, and she wore the loose woolen shirt that made her smallish breasts even less noticeable. If the wanderer in the brush happened to be a man instead of a bear, he would probably think he was facing a youngster rather than a woman, once he broke out into the open.

Cassandra waited tensely. If the intruder was a bear, she could scream for help and some of the other miners nearby might come to her aid. That would give away the fact she was a woman, however, and she wasn't ready to do that just yet. Her breath rasped in her throat as she sat stock-still on the ground next to the small fire.

The noise was even louder now as whatever it was pushed branches out of its way. Suddenly Cassandra could not only hear the creature approaching, but she could see the limbs of the bushes swaying as well. Some of the undergrowth parted, and a huge furry shape loomed up on the other side

of the creek. Terror raced through Cassandra, and she felt
the scream welling up in her throat . . .

Boone Blakely stopped in his tracks and stared across the
little stream that had appeared in front of him. A man in a
battered brown hat and a woolen shirt sat on the other side
of the creek, next to the small fire that had drawn Boone's
attention. He'd smelled the woodsmoke and then the irresis-
tible aroma of hot grease and coffee, and he had turned toward the creek even though the brush was thick and difficult
to push through.

The stranger on the other side of the creek was a little
fella, not much bigger than a boy. He looked scared half to
death, too, with his mouth open, ready to scream. Boone
threw up an arm and called hurriedly, "Hold it, hold it! I
don't mean any harm!"

The other man's mouth dropped open even more, this time
in surprise. In a husky voice, he said, "You're not a bear."

"Not the last time I checked," Boone said with a grin as
he cuffed back his black hat. He supposed he might look a
little like some sort of wild animal, what with the bushy
beard he'd cultivated over the past year and the wolfskin
jacket he had won in a poker game up in Murderer's Bar a
couple of weeks earlier. The jacket was just about all he had
to show for his foray to Murderer's Bar. The prospecting
around there had been sorry as hell at the moment, and after
a few weeks of it, Boone had turned south again, intending
to circle around Coloma once more and strike out for some-
place he hadn't been before. The weather was getting too
warm to be wearing a wolfskin jacket, but at least the garment concealed the fact that his shirt had several large holes
worn in it.

The diminutive miner shook his head. "When I heard you

crashing through that brush, I thought you were a bear," he said. "Sorry."

"No apologies necessary," Boone said. He gestured at the creek. "Mind if I come across?"

The other man shrugged. "Suit yourself."

Boone splashed across the shallow stream, which was about ten feet wide at this point. "Haven't been up here long, have you?" he asked as he emerged from the creek.

"What makes you say that?" The miner sounded defensive.

Boone shrugged. "You don't go tramping onto another man's diggin's without permission, not unless it's by accident. And you'd better be damned careful about it then."

"Well, I don't mind." The man hadn't stood up yet, and he didn't seem to want to meet Boone's gaze squarely. Could be he was still a little scared, since he was small and this bushy-bearded newcomer was so big and brawny.

To put the gent's mind at rest, Boone said sincerely, "I'm not looking for any trouble. I just smelled your fire and that salt pork and coffee, and . . . well, it's been a while since I've eaten."

The little miner seemed to consider that for a moment, then nodded. "Sit yourself down and have something to eat," he invited. "You're welcome in this camp."

"Much obliged." Boone sank down cross-legged and tried to control his hunger while the other man filled a second cup with coffee and used a small knife to slice off a piece of salt pork. He tore a biscuit in half and handed that to Boone as well. Boone ate ravenously, saying around the food stuffed in his mouth, "This is mighty good. You don't know how I appreciate it, mister."

The miner nodded and ate his own food in silence for a few moments, then asked abruptly, "What's your name?"

Boone wiped the back of his hand across his mouth.

"Boone," he said. "Boone Blakely."

"I'm Cass, that's all."

"Well, Cass That's-All, I'm glad to meet you," Boone said with a grin.

There was more noise from across the creek, and Cass looked up sharply. "What's that?"

"Probably my old mule," Boone replied. "I left him tied up back there in the brush until I saw what sort of welcome I was going to get. I'll fetch him in a minute, soon as I finish this salt pork."

"I'll get him if you like," Cass offered.

Boone thought about it, then shook his head. "I don't reckon that'd be a good idea. He's pretty contrary, and it takes a strong man to get him to go anywhere he doesn't want to go."

Cass snorted. "Your mule can't be any more stubborn than mine, and I led *him* all the way out here from San Francisco."

"You did, did you? Well, go ahead if you want, but most gents wouldn't leave their camp and all their gear with a stranger while they went off looking for some mule that might not even be out there."

Cass frowned darkly under the wide, drooping brim of the hat. "Are you saying that you're a thief?" he finally demanded.

"Nope. Just reminding you that it pays to be careful out here. Reckon that must've slipped your mind."

"I suppose you're right. You can go get your own damned mule." Cass reached for the coffeepot again, a piece of leather wrapped around his hand to protect it.

Boone chuckled and said, "Right." From the looks of things, Cass was a little too thin-skinned and impulsive to last very long out here in the gold fields, but maybe the youngster would learn with time. *If* he lived long enough.

Boone found himself hoping that was the case. He felt an instinctive liking for Cass.

Too bad that when the time came, he was going to have to take everything the youngster had. But Boone was tired of struggling just to live day to day in the gold fields, and it was time to get out. To do that, he would need supplies, and Cass had supplies, plenty of 'em.

Yep, Boone thought as he sipped his coffee, it was a damned shame, all right.

So far, the big man called Boone Blakely didn't seem to have any idea that Cassandra was a woman. She offered up a silent prayer that that continued to be the case. Boone was friendly enough, at least on the surface, but Cassandra didn't trust him. He was big enough and probably strong enough to break her in half if he wanted to. Maybe he hadn't turned out to be a grizzly bear . . . but Cassandra hoped that he wouldn't prove to be just as dangerous.

When he was through eating, he went to fetch the mule he'd left in the brush; he returned grunting and cursing as he hauled the animal across the creek. He tied the mule to a sapling a good distance from Cassandra's mule, so that the two beasts wouldn't make each other nervous. As he came back to the campfire, he swept a big hand toward the bluff and asked, "Is this your claim?"

"That's right," Cassandra replied. "I don't allow any poaching on it, either."

Boone held up his hands, palms out. "Don't worry, Cass. I'm not after any gold you might've found. I'm just a little surprised that you're not working on it. Daylight's a-wasting."

Cassandra shook her head. "I'm not going to dig today."

"This a holiday or something?" Boone asked with a frown.

"Not that I know of. But I'm taking a day off anyway."
She didn't want to explain any more, didn't want to tell him
that her muscles weren't accustomed to such hard physical
labor. He already thought she was a rank amateur when it
came to digging for gold; she didn't see any need for him
to know just how much of a novice she really was.

"Suit yourself," he said with a shrug. "I'd be glad to
take a turn with your pick and shovel, though. I'd split whatever I find with you, fifty-fifty."

At first Cassandra thought that sounded fair enough. So
far she had found enough gold to make the effort worthwhile, but just barely. What if Boone uncovered a rich vein
though? He would have let himself in for half of it, and this
wasn't even his claim. Cassandra shook her head. "Thanks
for the offer," she told him, "but I reckon I'll do any digging that's done around here."

"Suit yourself," he said again. "Since that's the way you
feel about it, I think I'll get me a little snooze." He shifted
around so that he was half-reclining with his back and shoulders leaned up against a good-sized rock. He tilted his hat
down over his face.

Within minutes he was asleep, soft snores issuing from
him. Cassandra relaxed a little. For all of his size and rugged
appearance, Boone Blakely seemed not to be a threat. When
he woke up from his nap, he might want some more to eat,
but then he would probably move on. Cassandra sensed that
he wasn't the type to stay in one place for very long.

That was all right with her. She hadn't come out here
looking for a partner. Just the opposite, in fact. She wanted
to prove to her mother that she could make it on her own.
She wanted Emily to finally see her as something other than
a little girl, capable of keeping a ledger or clerking in the
store but nothing else. By the time this little adventure was
over, Emily was going to have to admit that Cassandra had

plenty of other skills and abilities.

After all, she had already found gold, hadn't she?

Cassandra stood up and stretched weary muscles. She rubbed a hand over her face. She felt dirty and grimy, and she realized suddenly that it had been weeks since her last bath. Back in San Francisco and in Boston before that, she had never gone so long without cleansing herself. She cast a glance at the stream. The water would be cold, but it would get some of the dirt off her. And it would be easy enough to wade upstream a short distance, around a bend so that she would be out of sight. Boone was still sleeping soundly. He would never know she was gone.

She would do it, she decided abruptly. Another reason she had come out here to the gold fields had been to learn to make decisions and act on them, not worry every little question to death like a dog with a bone. She knelt beside her gear and pulled a clean shirt out of one of the packs. Then, with a last glance at Boone's sleeping figure, she waded quietly into the creek and started upstream, her steps making tiny splashing noises.

Boone cracked one eye as Cass moved off up the creek. Even if Boone hadn't been only pretending to sleep, the noise Cass made stomping along the streambed would have roused him. The young fellow seemed to think he was being quiet, but actually he was making enough racket that some of the Comanches back in Texas could have heard him a mile away, Boone reflected with a little grin. The boy definitely had a lot to learn.

Boone had no idea where Cass was going and didn't particularly care. Once the youngster was out of sight, Boone could start gathering up the gear and loading it on his mule. He would leave Cass's mule, he decided. That would give the boy something to ride back down to Coloma, where he could make a fresh start. Maybe he could find work in the

settlement. Truth to tell, Boone thought he would be doing
Cass a favor by robbing him. Cass wasn't really cut out for
life in the gold fields.

A few more minutes passed, and then Boone slowly lifted
his head and opened his eyes all the way. Cass was nowhere
to be seen. With his grin widening, Boone pushed himself
to his feet and reached down to scoop up one of the packs
of supplies Cass had left behind. As he straightened again,
the sound of splashing came faintly to his ears.

Now that was curious, he thought. Cass was making a lot
of noise, almost like a drowning man thrashing around in
the water. Could the boy have stepped in a hole in the creek
and unexpectedly found himself over his head? Boone had
no way of knowing if Cass could swim or not.

The grin turned into a frown. There hadn't been any cries
for help, but maybe Cass wasn't able to call out. Boone
grimaced. Here he was trying to rob the kid, and he was
wasting time by worrying that something had happened to
Cass. That didn't make any sense.

But the things a man felt didn't always make sense, Boone
reminded himself. There had been plenty of proof of that in
his own life.

"Well, hell," he said aloud, then dropped the pack where
he had picked it up. It wouldn't take him but a minute to
check on Cass, and then he could slip back here and get on
with his business, which was to replenish his own supplies
so that he could get the hell out of the gold fields, once and
for all. He started along the creek bank, taking to the water
itself when the ground became too steep and choked with
brush alongside the stream.

Boone stayed close to the edge of the creek, so close that
some of the branches brushed his face as he walked. The
water was less than a foot deep, but with the holes in his
boots, his socks were soaked again in a matter of seconds.

He ignored the discomfort. Once he had gotten his hands on Cass's gear and put some distance between them, he could stop for a while, build a fire, and dry his feet in the warmth of the flames. He could almost feel it already.

The creek made a sharp bend, and the brush pushed out from the bank to obstruct the view upstream even more. Boone hesitated, then leaned forward, parting the branches so that he could peer through them. The splashing sounds were louder now, but he still hadn't heard any outcry from Cass.

Nor was he likely to, he realized as he spotted the youngster about twenty yards away, bending over with his back to Boone as he scooped up water from the creek and splashed it over his bare torso. Cass had taken off his shirt and hat and hung them on branches nearby, along with what appeared to be a clean shirt. The boy was taking a *bath*.

Boone grinned and shook his head. He had been worrying about nothing. Cass was just fine. He seemed to be enjoying washing in the cold creek water, so Boone knew he would have plenty of time to get back to camp and loot it. He was about to back off away from the bend and return to the clearing when Cass suddenly turned halfway around, putting his left side toward the watcher.

His eyes widening in shock, Boone muttered involuntarily, "Son of a bitch!" He stared at the small cone-shaped mounds of flesh on Cass's chest, each of them crowned by a large pink nipple that had hardened from the coldness of the water. They were smaller than most of the ones Boone had seen on the soiled doves that flocked to the gold fields along with the forty-niners, but they were definitely breasts.

Cass wasn't a boy after all. He—*she!*—was a woman.

She turned some more, so that she was facing Boone now. He stood stock-still, hoping that the brush along the bank of the creek would be enough to conceal him if he didn't move.

Her blond hair was hacked off short, and now that he could see the creamy skin of her breasts and belly, he could tell just how dark her face and hands had grown from the sun. She had obviously been out here in the foothills for a while, and the experience had toughened her up. Still, he should have tumbled to the fact that she was a woman, he chided himself. He hadn't been out in the wilderness for so long that he couldn't tell a gal when he saw one.

But he hadn't been expecting to run into a female out here, especially not one dressed as a miner and pretending to be a man. Boone supposed his mistake was understandable. But that still left him with a question.

What the hell was he going to do now?

He couldn't rob her, that was certain. Stealing a man's gear and leaving him to fend for himself was one thing, but Boone couldn't do that to a woman, not unless it was a matter of his own survival. And even then he wasn't sure if he could bring himself to do it.

Boone stayed there unmoving until Cass had turned her back again, then he carefully moved one foot and then the other until he had slipped downstream out of sight. He waded along the creek until he came to the campsite, then stepped out onto the ground and shook his head. She would be back in a few minutes, and he had to figure out what to do.

He looked down at his feet. His boots and the bottoms of his trousers were soaked, and if she was very observant, she might figure out what he had been doing in the water. He sat down cross-legged by the fire and began pulling the boots and socks off his feet.

By the time Cass came around the bend and down the creek, Boone had the legs of his trousers rolled up, and he was sitting with his bare feet held out toward the fire, which had started to die down. He grinned up at Cass and said,

"Howdy. I didn't know where you'd gotten off to, but I didn't figure you'd mind if I dried my boots and socks and warmed my feet a little. They got chilled when I waded across the creek a while ago."

"That's fine," Cass said stiffly, and now that Boone knew the truth about her, he could hear how she was trying to disguise her voice and sound more like a man. He wondered what her voice was really like. He would have wagered that it was soft and musical and could warm a man right down to his core.

What the hell was wrong with him? he asked himself as that thought crossed his mind. He had no business thinking such things.

"I just went upstream to look around a little," Cass went on. "Didn't figure you'd wake up so soon."

"Well, I'm a light sleeper," Boone said without looking at her. He didn't want to give anything away. He hesitated, then said, "I've been thinking, Cass. Maybe you and me should be partners."

Where in blazes had *that* come from? He hadn't meant to suggest such a thing, but the words had popped out of his mouth anyway. *Settle down, damn it,* he told himself. Since when did the sight of a pair of female breasts—and not overly impressive ones, at that—cause his brain to stop working?

Cass shook her head firmly. "I'm not looking for a partner," she said.

"Two men can dig twice as much as one," Boone pointed out.

"Maybe so, but I like being on my own." Cass stared at the dying embers of the fire for a moment, then added, "You can stay around today and tonight if you want, though. I've got plenty of food, and I don't mind sharing a couple more meals before you move on."

"Mighty kind of you," Boone said. "I'll take you up on the offer."

Inwardly he sighed. It looked like he was going to have to find somebody else to rob, damn the luck.

As the day passed, Cassandra's nervousness over Boone's presence eased somewhat. At first when she had returned to the claim and found him awake, she was afraid he might have seen her bathing and discovered her secret, but he gave no sign that such a thing had happened. He was friendly but not overly forward, and she had to admit he was good company. Originally from Texas, he had come out here to California before the gold rush even started, he told her, and in fact he had been working on Sutter's sawmill as a carpenter when James Marshall found the first nuggets in the bed of the American River. Since then he had been all up and down the gold fields, and she enjoyed his stories about his experiences.

His offer that morning to be her partner had taken her by surprise, and she had rejected the suggestion without really thinking about it, just as she had refused Peregrine Forsythe's earlier offer. She had come out here to be on her own, to prove what she was capable of. Besides, if Boone was around all the time, the odds that he would find out she was a woman would greatly increase. She couldn't risk that, no matter how much she found herself liking Boone.

Evening approached surprisingly quickly. They had made a midday meal on more of the hard biscuits, but Cassandra intended to fry up more of the salt pork for supper. Boone took that chore out of her hands, saying, "Let me take care of that."

She hesitated, then said, "Well, all right." She sat back and watched as he sliced off a slab of the pork, cut it into cubes, and dropped them into one of the iron pots he found in her gear. He added water from the stream, along with some plants he pulled up from the thick growth along the creekbank. He put the pot over the campfire that had been built up again, and a few minutes later a delicious aroma began to fill the clearing.

"I'm not sure what the name of those greens are, but they make a dandy stew," Boone said with a grin. "Too bad you don't have some potatoes to put in with 'em"

"Who says I don't?" Cassandra replied as she reached for one of the other packs. She pulled out a couple of small potatoes.

Boone took them, peeled them, and cut them up, dropping the pieces into the simmering mixture. When the stew was ready, he dished it out into wooden bowls, and Cassandra ate hers eagerly. The stuff tasted as good as it smelled.

"This is wonderful," she said enthusiastically. "The best meal I've had since I came up here."

"You learn to make do with what you have," Boone said with a smile and a shrug.

"Food like this is almost enough to make me think twice about that offer you made," Cassandra blurted out impulsively.

Boone lifted his eyebrows, his smile widening. "Is that a fact?"

Cassandra felt her face growing warm. She ducked her head so that Boone wouldn't see the flush creeping over her features. "Almost, I said," she told him, making her voice gruff.

He leaned back against the same rock where he had fallen asleep earlier. "Sure, I understand. Maybe you should sleep on it, Cass."

"Yeah. We'll do that."

She didn't have much to say to him after that, and she was grateful that he didn't press her on the issue. After they had finished off the stew, he got a moth-eaten blanket from the gear he had unloaded from his gaunt, rawboned mule and spread it on the ground. "You're going to sleep on that?" Cassandra asked.

"Sure, it'll do for me. Trust me, I've slept on worse."

She believed him. Even though he hadn't complained, she had a feeling he had experienced more than his share of hardships in his life. He was big and strong and probably a hard worker, and he would most likely be grateful for the opportunity to continue prospecting for gold if the two of them teamed up. After all, the men Nathan approached with his offer of a grubstake usually leaped at the chance. A partnership with Boone would be something like that, Cassandra reflected as she rolled up in her own blankets. If there was just some way of making sure that he didn't discover she was a woman . . .

Those thoughts were still running through her head as she dozed off.

She didn't know how long she had been asleep. All she knew as she was jolted awake was that something had just slammed into her side, sending a wave of pain through her and making her curl up and gasp for breath.

"Sorry, old boy," said a voice that was somehow familiar. "Just wanted to make certain you were fully awake before we continued."

"Stop jabberin', Forsythe," another voice put in harshly. "Let's shoot 'em and be done with it."

Forsythe, Forsythe . . . Cassandra was too stunned from the kick in her side to recall the name for a moment, but then she put it together with the voice and remembered the Englishman she had met in Coloma, the man who had given her the tip that sent her up here to Stink Creek.

"You're a very crude man, Albert," Peregrine Forsythe

said as he nudged Cassandra with a toe. She heard a brief metallic clatter and identified it as the sound of a pistol's hammer being drawn back and locked into firing position. Forsythe went on, "This young lad and I were almost friends once. I can't just kill him in cold blood with no word of explanation."

Cassandra blinked her eyes open, and in the dim light of the campfire's embers, she saw the tall, lean shape looming over her. The glow from the fire reflected dully on the barrel of the pistol he was pointing at her.

Where was Boone? she wondered wildly. Had the thieves already killed him? No, she realized, the one called Albert had mentioned shooting more than one victim. Boone had to still be alive.

As if to confirm that supposition, he growled, "You'd better hope that hogleg doesn't misfire, you bastard, or I'm going to be all over you."

"Shut up," snapped Albert. "Nobody told you to talk. All you got to do is die."

The pain in Cassandra's side was fading somewhat, becoming more bearable. She looked up at the Englishman and asked in a choked voice, "Peregrine . . . why . . . why are you doing this?"

Forsythe shrugged his narrow shoulders. "A man has to survive somehow, my young friend. Albert and I are broke, as you Americans put it, and it will be a long time before my next remittance draft arrives from England. If we are to continue with our search for gold, we have no choice but to provision ourselves somehow. You have plenty of supplies."

"We . . . we'll share them with you," Cassandra offered, knowing that she had to try to talk Forsythe out of this somehow. She and Boone couldn't just lie there and let themselves be murdered in their bedrolls.

Forsythe chuckled. "That's quite generous of you, but no

thanks. The supplies will last even longer if we take all of them, and you and your friend will no longer have any need of them in a moment.'' The barrel of the gun pointed unwaveringly at Cassandra's face as the Englishman went on, ''I offered to be your partner, lad, and you should have taken me up on it. I don't like being turned down only to have you associate with this ruffian.''

Cassandra thought about trying to explain that Boone wasn't really her partner, but she sensed it wouldn't do any good. Forsythe and Albert wanted to kill them, and nothing was going to dissuade them.

She was going to die here, she thought in despair, miles and miles away from home in the middle of a wilderness. Her mother would never know what had happened to her, would never know how close she had come to being a success on her own.

''Goodbye, Cass,'' Forsythe whispered, and he lifted his thumb from the hammer of the pistol.

''No!'' Boone bellowed. ''Leave her alone!''

He rolled and kicked up and out at the same time, the heel of his boot smashing into the groin of the man standing over him. Albert screeched in agony as his finger involuntarily jerked on the trigger of the gun he held. The weapon went off with a deafening blast. Cassandra screamed. She couldn't tell if Boone had been hit or not. One thing was certain, however: Forsythe had been shocked into momentarily freezing, but unless Cassandra took advantage of that opportunity, she would be a dead woman in a matter of seconds.

She levered herself into a sitting position and lowered her head as she drove herself upward toward Forsythe. The top of her head slammed into the Englishman's belly and sent him staggering backward. The gun in his hand went off, but Cassandra was too close to him. She felt a fiery finger draw a line of pain down her back, but after burning her the bullet thudded harmlessly into the ground where she had been a second earlier. While Forsythe was off-balance, she wrapped her arms around his thighs and kept pushing, driving him back off his feet.

Someone was yelling. She couldn't tell if it was Boone or Albert or both of them. Forsythe fell heavily, and Cassandra heard a sharp crack as he landed. He groaned and tried to twist the barrel of the gun toward her. She saw the weapon's muzzle swinging around in the dim firelight and reached out to grab the barrel. With all her strength, she held it away from her. Forsythe moaned again and went limp beneath her. The gun slipped out of his fingers, and startled by the unexpectedness of it, Cassandra fell to the side with the barrel still clutched in her hands.

She rolled off Forsythe and came up on her knees, still holding the gun. Quickly reversing it, she peered across the campfire at Boone and Albert, who were struggling on the ground. Breathing harshly through her mouth, she waited to see if she could get a clear shot at Albert. She looped both thumbs over the hammer of the gun just in case.

Boone didn't need her help. He had gotten his own hands on Albert's gun, and the revolver rose and fell suddenly, landing on Albert's head with a sound like eggs cracking open. Boone hit him again, just to make sure, Cassandra thought. Then he shoved himself away from the limp body and stood up. The gun was still in his hand, and he spun it around to cover Albert as he prodded the man in the side.

"Dead," Boone grunted. "What about yours, Cass?"

The question took her by surprise. She looked down at Peregrine Forsythe's face, which was contorted in painful lines. His eyes were open and staring glassily upward at the night sky.

"I . . . I think he's dead, too," she said. Holding the gun in one hand, which trembled because of the weapon's weight, she reached out with the other hand and felt the Englishman's chest. It was still, unmoving. He wasn't breathing.

She had killed him. The stunning thought went through her brain. She had no idea how it had happened, but he was dead and it was because of her. She began to shake all over.

Boone stepped around the fire with long-legged strides and knelt beside her. Gently, he took the gun out of her hand and then moved Forsythe's head a little. "Landed right on a sharp rock," he commented, as much to himself as to her. "Both of them wound up with busted skulls. Some coincidence, huh?"

Cassandra didn't want to think about coincidences, or about how close she and Boone had come to dying themselves. She lifted her hands to her face as the tears started to come, and it didn't even occur to her how . . . how feminine she was being.

Not that it mattered, she suddenly realized. She remembered what Boone had shouted as he made his move. *Leave her alone.*

Leave her *alone* . . .

He knew. He knew she was a woman.

That knowledge had barely sunk in on her when he folded her into his arms and pressed her tear-streaked face against his broad chest. "It's all right," he told her softly. "They can't hurt you now, Cass. They won't ever bother anybody again."

"It . . . it's Cassandra," she whispered.

He put his hand under her chin and tilted her head back so that he could look down into her eyes. "Cassandra," he repeated. "That's a mighty pretty name."

Then his lips came down on hers, and she knew that no matter what her plans had been when she came out here to the gold fields, after this night nothing would ever be the same.

Twenty

Patrick Trent studied the cards he held in long, slender, experienced fingers. He ticked them off in his mind as he slowly spread them out: king of hearts, king of diamonds, king of clubs, nine of diamonds, nine of spades. He couldn't have gotten a better hand, he thought, if he had dealt them himself.

As a matter of fact, though, this was a straight deal. Trent knew practically every trick of the trade that had ever been invented, but cheating wasn't necessary here in Ophir. Playing with the miners who came into the saloon, he won more than enough with an honest game.

And to tell the truth, that was a relief to him. He was getting too old to be walking that knife-edge of danger. Better to take the luck that came to him naturally.

"I'll raise you . . . twenty dollars," he said as he pushed a couple of chips into the pile in the center of the table.

A miner called Bedloe was his main competition in this game. The others were content to play for small stakes but usually dropped out when the pot began to grow. Bedloe was a plunger, though, and an arrogant poker player, a combination that was like manna from heaven to a man like Trent. Now the miner glared at Trent's chips for a moment, then tossed a small pouch of dust into the center of the table. "There's a couple hundred dollars worth o' dust in that poke," he growled. "Match that if you can, gambler."

"Oh, I can," Trent said, trying not to grin. He had drawn Bedloe in just as he'd planned, but it never paid to gloat. As he shoved chips forward to match the bet, he said, "I'll just take a look at those cards."

"You paid for it," Bedloe replied with a smirk. He placed his cards faceup on the table. "All full up, jacks and sevens."

Trent smiled, then said simply, "Not good enough." He put down his cards so that Bedloe could see the better hand for himself.

The miner scowled darkly, and for an instant, Trent read the accusation in his eyes. Bedloe was thinking about accusing him of cheating, but Trent knew there was no way the man could prove it. For one thing, it hadn't happened. Regardless, Trent couldn't let him get away with the accusation once it had been given voice. He would have to do something about it.

And that bullet wound in his side still pained him when the weather was right. He hoped Bedloe would have more sense than to start a fight.

At that moment, there was a slight commotion at the saloon's entrance. Trent shifted his cool gaze from Bedloe to the doorway and saw the woman who had just come into the saloon. A smile broke out across his face as the normal noises—the talking, the laughter, the scrape of a bow across the strings of a fiddle—resumed. While it was unusual to see a respectable woman in a saloon, Anne Palmer went where she pleased and was welcome anywhere in Ophir, including Trent's place.

Especially Trent's place, the gambler thought as he slipped an unlit cigar from his vest pocket and put it in his mouth.

Anne knew where he usually sat, and she came across the room toward the table. As she made her way across the room, Bedloe said uncertainly, "I don't know about this, Trent—"

"Oh, shut up," Trent said without looking at the miner as he rose to his feet. "The hand was honest, and I've got better things to do right now than kill you."

Bedloe flushed and started to get up, but one of the other men put a firm hand on his shoulder. "Let it alone," the man urged. "Trent's no cheater, and anyway, you don't want to cause no trouble while Miz Palmer's here."

Grudgingly, Bedloe subsided. Anyone who had been in Ophir for more than a few days knew that Anne was one of the most respected members of the community. In the months since the death of her husband, she had tended to the sick, patched up bullet wounds, and become as much of a physician as Thaddeus Palmer had been, despite her lack of formal training. In a frontier settlement like this, doctoring was usually as much a matter of common sense and experience as it was book learning.

Anne came up to Trent, who smiled a greeting at her. She looked lovely in a dark gray dress with a jacket of lighter gray over it. Her blond hair was tightly curled, and when she returned the gambler's smile, she looked younger than her years. "Hello, Mr. Trent," she said. "How are you feeling?"

"Just fine, Mrs. Palmer. What can I do for you?"

"I just wanted to come by and see if that bullet wound is giving you any pain. With the weather turning cooler like this, old injuries can sometimes be uncomfortable."

Just moments ago, Trent had been uncomfortably reminded that the healed-up bullet hole in his side did sometimes twinge a mite, especially on chilly mornings like the one today. But the sight of Anne was enough to make him forget all about it.

"I don't have any complaints," he told her with a grin, "unless it's the fact that you steadfastly refuse my invitations to dinner."

"That's not a medical matter," she pointed out, but he thought he saw a glimmer of amusement lurking in her blue eyes.

She liked him, he was certain of that. But her husband had passed away less than a year earlier, and Anne Palmer was a proper lady. She was not going to allow herself to become involved with another man until a sufficient mourning period had passed. Trent sensed that much without being told. At first it had thrown him for a loop, too. He wasn't accustomed to dealing with ladies like Anne. Propriety had never been much of a factor when it came to his friendships with saloon girls and prostitutes and female gamblers. Gals like that had healthy appetites, and they took what they wanted when they wanted it, much like Trent himself.

A woman like Anne was different, and in Trent's mind, she might well be worth waiting for. He knew he wasn't ready to give up on her.

"Have some coffee with me," he suggested, waving a hand toward the long hardwood bar on the other side of the room. He knew Anne didn't drink liquor, but she enjoyed a cup of hot coffee.

She hesitated only an instant, then nodded. "Thank you, I'd like that." She allowed Trent to put his hand lightly on her arm as he led her over to the bar.

In the mirror behind the bar, Trent saw Bedloe stand up and start toward the door. He was glad that the miner hadn't caused any trouble. It was bad enough that he and Anne had gotten to know each other because Trent had a bullet in his side at the time. He didn't want Anne to think that he was constantly getting into gunfights. Why, in the months since their first meeting, Trent had only been forced to kill two men, and there weren't many saloonkeepers in Ophir who could match that record for staying out of trouble.

Trent signaled for the bartender to bring them each a cup

of coffee. The man filled the cups from the coffeepot on the black cast-iron stove at the end of the bar. It was getting on toward the middle of the day, and the free-lunch trays had already been put out on the bar, but Anne didn't seem interested in food. She stood next to Trent, sipped her coffee, and said without preamble, "I've been thinking about leaving Ophir."

The words struck Trent like a fist in the belly, surprising him with their force. "Leaving?" he repeated. "Why in the world would you want to do that?"

"I never intended to stay permanently after Thaddeus passed on," Anne replied. "I was just trying to make up my mind what to do and save up some money while I was thinking about it. I have a sizable amount now."

Trent didn't doubt that. Most of the miners could be quite generous when Anne tended to them, paying her well for her medical services. She also collected some of her payments in food and supplies from the merchants in the settlement when she was called to care for them, which meant her living expenses were fairly small. Trent figured she had quite a poke built up by now. More than enough to take her back to San Francisco and from there to anywhere she wanted to go, in fact. The thought made his heart sink a little.

"You know that you've become an important member of the community," he told her. "Practically everyone in Ophir would be sorry to see you leave."

"Oh, I'm not sure that's true. The friends I made back when Thaddeus was still alive have never seemed to understand why I now associate with miners and gamblers."

Trent chuckled dryly. "The likes of me, you mean."

"Well, yes. The ladies don't understand that a doctor can't worry about the social status of his patients. And even though I'm not actually a doctor . . . well . . ."

"You're the best sawbones this place has ever seen, no

disrespect intended toward your late husband,'' Trent told her bluntly. ''And if those biddies from the quilting circle don't understand that or don't like what you do, I reckon you ought to tell them they can go and—''

He caught himself just in time, realizing that he was letting his anger get the best of him. It infuriated him that anyone could look down on Anne, especially those other women with their fancy airs. She didn't seem upset with him for almost losing his temper, however. In fact, there was a tiny smile hovering around her lips.

''Don't worry, Mr. Trent, those ladies aren't the real reason I'm thinking about leaving. I just wonder if it wouldn't be better for me to go back east and try to make a new life for myself. Get a fresh start. I can't stay here in this mining camp forever.''

''Why not?'' demanded Trent. ''Ophir's a pretty rough place sometimes, but it's getting better.''

She looked down at her cup. ''You forget, sir, I am a woman alone. This settlement on the edge of the frontier is no place for a woman to live by herself.''

What the hell was she really saying? he wondered suddenly. It sounded almost like she was warning him that if he was going to make a move, he ought to go ahead and do it. But surely that couldn't be right. A woman like Anne would never . . . why, she was so genteel that Trent just couldn't imagine her being so forward.

And yet that veiled smile of hers certainly looked familiar. He had seen it on the faces of plenty of women in the past, women who wanted him and made no secret of their desires.

Before Trent could say anything, there was another commotion at the entrance of the saloon. He glanced that way and saw that Bedloe hadn't left after all. The miner had paused at a table where some of his cronies were sitting, just inside the door. Bedloe had swung around now, and his knobby hands were clenched into fists. From the looks of the man sprawled at his feet, he had just used one of those fists.

"That'll teach you to bump into me, you goddamned heathen!" Bedloe shouted down at the man on the floor. "You're lucky I don't kick you all the way back to China!" As if he was trying to accomplish just that, he lashed out with a booted foot and slammed the toe into the fallen man's side.

"Dear Lord!" Anne exclaimed on the other side of the room. "Can't you do something to stop that, Patrick?"

Trent noticed that she used his first name in her dismay at the violence Bedloe was handing out. He also saw the hatred on Bedloe's face and knew the miner was taking out the anger he had felt earlier toward Trent on the luckless soul who had just jostled him.

The man cowering on the floor at Bedloe's feet was dressed in white pants and a loose-fitting white shirt, and his glossy raven hair seemed even darker by comparison with the clothes. That hair was braided into a long pigtail that dangled down his back. As Bedloe towered over him, the man held up his hands imploringly and babbled in a foreign tongue that was being heard more and more often in California these days. Trent didn't recognize any of the words but knew it by its singsong sound as Chinese.

The customers in the saloon had fallen silent as Bedloe continued to abuse the Chinese man, but no one made a move to go to the victim's aid. Bedloe had drawn back his foot to kick the man again. Trent glanced over at Anne, saw the outrage on her face, and knew he couldn't just stand by. He sighed and pushed away from the bar.

"Hold it, Bedloe!" he said, his voice not particularly loud but carrying across the room like the crack of a whip. "That's enough."

Bedloe looked up in surprise, the glare he had been directing at the Chinese man still etched on his face. "What the hell!" he exclaimed. "You takin' up for this heathen Chinee, Trent? I don't know why you even allow this kind o' trash in here!"

Trent strode across the room toward the entrance, his thumbs hooked in the pockets of his vest. "I don't encourage them to come in," he said, "but how am I going to stop them from begging? Most of them are starving, Bedloe, you know that."

"Let 'em starve," growled the miner. "A few less Chinamen around here'd be the best thing to happen to Ophir in a long time."

Trent paused. It was true that the Chinese were pouring into California and the gold fields in astonishing numbers these days. China had been ravaged by a series of droughts and famines over the past decade, or so Trent had heard. Thousands of Chinese men and women had fled the place, using the savings of lifetimes to purchase passage on ships bound for America. Those quarters were usually cramped and filthy, but the Chinese didn't care. They were on their way to what they hoped would be a better life. News of the gold strikes in California had reached all the way across the Pacific Ocean, and the promise of wealth drew the Chinese like moths to a flame.

But when they got here, they found there was no place for them. Chinese weren't allowed to own land or even dig for gold on someone else's claim as hired hands. With no money to buy passage back to their homeland, they were forced to struggle along in a hardscrabble existence. The women worked as prostitutes or laundresses, while the men, their fierce pride destroyed, either became beggars or retreated so far into their opium dreams that they never came out. Trent might have felt sorry for them—if he had ever really given them much thought.

Bedloe was going to force the issue. He laughed harshly and slipped a knife from its sheath on his belt. "I'm goin' to clip this bastard's tail. That'll teach him to try to come in where there's white folks."

Anne had come up behind Trent, and at Bedloe's threat she said sharply, "No, you can't do that! I've heard that it dishonors them to cut off their pigtail."

"This is none of your business, ma'am," Bedloe snapped. Clutching his knife tightly, he reached for the dangling pig-tail as the Chinese man tried to wriggle away from him.

Anne grabbed Trent's left arm, and the gambler sighed again. Like it or not, he was going to have to do something about this. His right hand moved toward the butt of the little pistol holstered under the long tail of his coat.

Nathan pulled the mules to a halt in the middle of the street. Soon the rains and snows would come, and the broad, dusty street would turn into a swamp. But the autumn rains had not yet begun in earnest, and after the heat of the summer just past, the mud in the street had dried to a hard crust that cracked under the hooves of the mules.

At the moment, Nathan wasn't thinking about mud, dried or swampy. His attention was fastened on the frantic young woman running toward him.

"Help!" she cried. "You must help me!"

Hardrock leaned forward on the seat beside Nathan and growled. "Easy, boy," Nathan told the massive dog as the young woman hurried up to the wagon and half collapsed against the nearest wheel, out of breath and obviously scared out of her wits. Nathan dropped to the street beside her and asked, "What's the matter?" as he put a hand on her shoulder.

She flinched away from him, twisting around and pressing

her back against the wheel. Her dark, almond-shaped eyes
were huge in her smooth, honey-colored face. Black hair
parted in the center of her head fell loosely past her shoulders. She wore the light-colored, loose-fitting clothes of the
Chinese laborers Nathan had recently seen more and more
often here in the gold fields, and the sleeve of her tunic fell
away from her forearm as she pointed a shaking finger at a
building nearby.

"My brother," she said. "They are going to kill him!"

Nathan felt a pang of pity. The Chinese had encountered
more trouble in the gold fields than they had ever expected
to find in America. If it had been up to him, he would have
grubstaked some of them with Emily Woodward's money
and supplies. But that would have caused more trouble than
it was worth, given the resentment the whites felt toward the
Orientals, and Emily had made it plain that Nathan was not
to give in to such impulses. Ever since Cassandra had disappeared, Emily had grown more and more concerned with
her profits. Nathan supposed they were all she had left.

But that didn't mean he was going to turn aside when a
scared girl was in trouble and needed help. She looked to
be no more than eighteen years old, and the fright on her
face made her appear even younger.

She understood at least some English; Nathan had already
discovered that much. So he said simply, "Show me."

She turned and ran toward the building she had pointed
out earlier, not looking back to see if he was following. His
long strides brought him to the rough plank boardwalk right
behind her. She hurried across the walk and through a door
that was already standing open.

With Hardrock at his side, Nathan stepped through the
door and stopped short, realizing that he had walked into a
dangerous situation. A Chinese man a few years older than
the girl was lying on the floor with a rugged-looking miner

standing over him. The miner had a knife in his hand and was crouching so that one good swipe with the blade would open up the Chinaman's throat. A few yards away, a well-dressed gent with brown hair and a moustache was holding a small pistol he obviously knew how to use. An attractive blond woman was standing behind him. The rest of the big room was filled with miners and gamblers and soiled doves—all of whom were staring at Nathan. Obviously, he had just interrupted a tense moment.

The Chinese girl went to her knees beside the young man, ignoring the threat of the miner with the knife. A torrent of words exploded from her. Nathan couldn't make any sense of what she was saying, but he figured the young man was the brother the girl had spoken of.

Everybody seemed to be waiting for him to say something, so he cleared his throat and asked, "What's going on here?"

"Who the hell are you?" growled the miner with the knife.

"Nathan Jones. I'd appreciate it if you'd put that knife up and step away from the young lady and her brother, mister."

The man with the pistol smiled coolly. "You're echoing my own sentiments, Mr. Jones," he said. "I just told Bedloe here to put up the knife and get out of my place."

Bedloe's glare switched back and forth between Nathan and the saloonkeeper, and it was a toss-up which man he hated most at the moment. When he made a slight move toward Nathan with the blade, a loud, menacing snarl came from Hardrock.

"What's that?" someone else in the room called. "A grizzly bear?"

"Almost," Nathan replied as several men laughed. He could sense that the tension in the saloon had just been broken, and he was grateful for that. He certainly hadn't meant to stumble into trouble. That was what acting on impulse got him, he told himself sternly.

Bedloe straightened and shoved his knife back in its sheath. "You're all a bunch of damned fools," he muttered as he started toward the door. He shouldered several men roughly out of his way as he swung wide around Hardrock in order to reach the entrance. He might be angry, but he wasn't foolish.

The saloonkeeper slipped his gun back into a holster under his coat and turned to raise his voice and say, "All right, boys, let's all get back to what we were doing." He stepped over to Nathan and extended a hand. "I'm Patrick Trent, the owner of this place," he introduced himself. "And I believe you said your name is Nathan Jones?"

"That's right," Nathan agreed as he shook hands with the man.

Trent glanced down at the huge dog, and an expression of recognition lit up his lean face. "You're the one they call Grubstake Jones," he said. "I've heard about this brute of yours."

"This is Hardrock, all right. Pleased to meet you, Mr. Trent."

Trent turned, put a hand on the arm of the woman with him, and said, "May I present Mrs. Anne Palmer?"

Nathan tugged off his hat and nodded to the woman, wishing he was a little more cleaned up. He had been on the trail for quite a while on this swing through the gold fields, though. Mrs. Palmer looked like a respectable lady, the kind you read about in the society columns of the newspapers back in San Francisco, and he wondered what she was doing in a saloon.

"It's an honor to meet you, ma'am," he said anyway.

Before Mrs. Palmer could reply, the young Chinese woman and her brother got to their feet and started shuffling toward the door. Trent said quickly, "I wouldn't go out there right now, you two. Bedloe could be waiting around to settle the score. He won't like being made to back down."

Nathan knew the saloonkeeper was correct about that. He caught the young woman's eye and nodded his agreement. "You'd better stay in here for a while," he said.

Trent shook his head. "They can't do that. But they can go out the back door. I'll send one of my men with them to make sure they get back to their shack all right."

"Thank you, Patrick," Mrs. Palmer said. Nathan wondered where her husband was, since she seemed mighty friendly with Trent. Maybe she was a widow woman, he thought.

"Hardrock and I will go along, too," Nathan said, thinking that the two Chinese might still be frightened and would feel better with more company.

"That's fine with me," Trent nodded. He caught the eye of one of the men behind the bar and said, "Clay, go with these folks and see that they get home all right."

The bartender frowned. "Aw, hell, boss," he protested. "I never signed on to nursemaid no Chinks."

Trent's features tightened, but Nathan said hurriedly, "That's all right, Mr. Trent. I'll tend to them. With Hardrock along, I don't think anybody will bother us."

Trent looked at the dog standing next to Nathan. The top of Hardrock's head came up almost to Nathan's waist. With a chuckle, Trent said, "I reckon that's true, Mr. Jones. I don't normally allow dogs in here, but I don't think I'd want to argue with that one of yours. Tell you what, when you're finished, come on back here and have a drink with me. I'd like to talk to you."

"Thanks. I'll do that." Nathan signalled to Hardrock. "Come on, boy."

Together, they went over to where the two Chinese waited

beside the saloon's rear door. Nathan opened it and indicated they should lead the way. He didn't speak any Chinese, and he hoped the girl spoke more English than she had demonstrated so far.

As it turned out, she did. As the three people and the dog walked down a narrow alley behind the saloon, Nathan introduced himself and asked the girl, "What's your name?"

"Wang Toy," she said without looking at him. "But I am called Lotus."

"Lotus," repeated Nathan. "Well, both of those are mighty pretty names. Which one do you prefer?"

The girl shrugged her shoulders and kept her eyes fixed on the ground in front of her. "I do not care."

"I'll call you Lotus, then."

The young man spoke up for the first time in Nathan's hearing. He said harshly, "That is what the Americans call her while they are rutting with her!"

Nathan blinked in surprise. Lotus turned toward her brother and let loose with another streak of that musical-sounding dialect. From what the young man had said, Lotus was a soiled dove, but Nathan thought he was pretty rude to point that out, considering how she had tried to help him when he was being threatened by that fella Bedloe.

Lotus's brother returned the argument, and after a moment he stalked ahead of them, his back stiff, and didn't look back as he followed the twisting alley toward an area of tents and crude shacks built of scrap lumber and oilcloth. Lotus crossed her arms over her chest and glared after him.

"My brother has lost the pride with which he was born," she said in a quietly angry voice. "This hurts him and makes him unforgivably rude."

Nathan shrugged. "Doesn't matter to me, Lotus. I never had a sister myself, but I reckon brothers and sisters have to wrangle some."

She looked over at him and smiled. "This . . . wrangle? It is like arguing?"

"That's what it is, all right. But don't worry about it, Lotus. Are you sure you want me to call you that?"

"It does not sound the same . . . coming from you. You said your name is . . . Na . . . Nathan?"

"Nathan Jones. Some folks call me Grubstake, just like they call you Lotus."

She smiled again. "I prefer Nathan."

"To tell you the truth, so do I."

She was a mighty pretty girl, he thought. And her smile was friendly. He reminded himself that it was her job to be pretty and friendly to the men she met, and he wondered if she would invite him into her shack when they got there.

And if she did, would he take her up on the invitation or not?

Nathan was just as glad that the question didn't come up. As they arrived at a shack so flimsy-looking that it seemed a good wind would blow it over, another girl pushed aside the piece of rotting canvas that served as a door and exclaimed, "Wang Toy?" She followed the name with a spate of Chinese.

Lotus listened patiently and then nodded. She turned to Nathan and said, "This is my friend Chao-Xing. Her name in your tongue means Morning Star."

Nathan took his hat off and nodded to Chao-Xing, who was a couple of years younger than Lotus. She wore her dark hair pulled back in a bun, and Nathan noticed right away that the skin of her hands was red and cracked. She was a laundress, he realized, although she was pretty enough to have followed the same profession as her friend.

"Nathan Jones," he said to her. "And this is Hardrock."

He indicated the dog with a sweeping motion of his hat, and the younger girl leaped back, her hands going to her mouth in fear. Hardrock just lowered his rear end to the dust of the alley and regarded the girl impassively. Lotus and Chao-Xing chattered between themselves for a few seconds, and Nathan remembered stories he'd heard about how the Chinese immigrants ate dog meat, just like the Indians on the Great American Desert. He hoped none of these people got any ideas about how well Hardrock would fill a cooking pot, because he figured they'd regret it if they tried to boil up this particular dog.

Even though he didn't speak their lingo, he gathered that Lotus's brother had reached the shack safely and was probably inside even as they spoke. He waited until there was a momentary lull in the talk, then nodded to the young women again and said, "I'll be going now. I hope I see you again before I leave Ophir."

"Thank you," Lotus told him. "You are . . . a good man, Nathan Jones."

"Glad somebody thinks so," he said with a grin. "Good day, ladies."

He put his hat on and started back down the alley, aware of the yellow faces watching him from the doorways of the other shacks. He hoped he could find his way out of here and get back to Trent's saloon all right. This part of the camp put him in mind of rat's nests he'd seen, the way the paths twisted around on themselves. He was glad for Hardrock's presence as the big dog padded along beside him.

Despite the rounds he had been making through the camps of the gold fields for the past couple of years, this was his first trip to Ophir. Already it had been a more eventful stopover than most. Nathan hoped that trend didn't continue. All he wanted was to do a little business and be on his way peacefully.

And of course, before he left, he would have a few questions to ask—questions about Cassandra . . .

Twenty-one

"This woman you're looking for, Mr. Jones," Anne Palmer said as she sat at a table in the rear of the saloon with Trent and Nathan, "you say she's your cousin?"

Nathan nodded. "That's right. Her name is Cassandra Woodward, and her mother Emily Woodward—my aunt—is the lady I work for. She owns a store in San Francisco. Aunt Emily, I mean, not Cassandra."

"Woodward's Emporium," Trent mused. "I recall seeing the place when I passed through San Francisco before coming out here to the gold camps. Your aunt must be a wealthy woman."

With a shrug, Nathan said, "She does all right, I suppose. She's in the business of backing miners who want to continue searching for gold but who lack the money to buy more supplies."

"And since you're her agent in these matters, that's why you're called Grubstake Jones."

"The name seems to have stuck," Nathan ruefully told the gambler. "It wasn't my idea, though."

Anne smiled. "It seems to fit you, in an odd sort of way, Mr. Jones." Her expression became more solemn. "I'm sure your aunt is very worried about her daughter."

"I think Aunt Emily has almost given up hope of ever seeing her again," Nathan said with a sigh. "It's been over six months since Cassandra disappeared, and I haven't found any sign of her. I've been all up and down the gold fields and put out the word I was looking for her every place I stopped." He shook his head. "There are so many things that could have happened to her . . . Still, I feel like I've really let Aunt Emily down by not finding her."

"It's possible that she doesn't *want* to be found," Trent pointed out. "I'm sure you've considered that, Nathan."

"Of course. She might've heard that I was looking for her and started deliberately avoiding me. But I think it's even more likely that something bad happened to her. That she's . . . well, dead."

Anne could tell that the word was very difficult for Nathan to say. Between his own fondness for his cousin and his feeling of responsibility to his aunt, he had to be suffering from a great deal of guilt due to his failure to locate Cassandra. Anne could understand that. She had felt plenty of guilt when Thaddeus died, even though his death was by no stretch of the imagination her fault. And she had experienced even more guilt when she realized how she was beginning to feel about Patrick Trent when her late husband had been gone less than a year.

"I wish I could help you," Trent told Nathan, "but I don't recall ever seeing a young woman such as the one you described come in here. I'll ask the boys who work for me, though, and I'll keep my eyes open."

"It's possible she's pretending to be a man," Nathan said. "She took some men's clothes from the store when she left, and she cut off her hair. She could still be keeping up the masquerade."

That would be incredibly difficult, Anne thought. She could not imagine denying her own femininity and pretending to be a man for months on end. The strain would be almost impossible to bear, and there were so many ways that her true sex could be discovered accidentally.

"I'll do everything I can to help," promised Trent. "The way you and that dog of yours pitched in earlier to help with

Bedloe, I owe you a debt of gratitude. I might've had to shoot that fool if you hadn't taken a hand, and I hate getting bloodstains on the floor.''

Nathan smiled. ''Glad we could be of help,'' he said dryly. ''Do you have much trouble with the Chinese here in Ophir?''

Trent shook his head and said, ''Not with the Chinese themselves. Most of them are so cowed they don't cause any problems. But some of the men who don't like them—men such as Bedloe—are usually looking for some way to stir things up. I'm afraid that if the Chinese keep coming here in such large numbers, sooner or later there's going to be a riot, sort of like the one I heard about in San Francisco where that gang called the Hounds tried to run out all the *Chilenos*.''

''I read about that in the papers, even though I was gone when it happened,'' Nathan said with a solemn nod. ''My aunt and a man called Sam Brannan and some of the other honest citizens are trying to get together a vigilance committee to put a stop to things like that.''

''Someone needs to,'' Anne put in. ''People should learn to get along.''

Trent leaned back and sipped from the little glass of whiskey in front of him. ''That's asking a great deal of human nature, my dear,'' he said, ''a great deal indeed.''

''People can learn if they want to,'' Anne insisted.

''I don't know,'' Nathan said. ''Lotus's brother seemed as angry and full of hate as Bedloe, he just wasn't brave enough to show it.''

''Lotus? That was the girl who brought you in here?'' asked Trent.

''Yes. I think she saw what was going on from the boardwalk and just ran out into the street looking for help from the first person she saw. That happened to be me.''

Trent tossed down the rest of his drink. "Well, watch your back while you're here in town. I don't know Bedloe well enough to say what he might do, but I reckon he wasn't happy about being forced to back down."

Anne felt a twinge of worry. She looked over at Trent and asked, "You mean he might try to even the score with you and Mr. Jones?"

The gambler shrugged unconcernedly. "Wouldn't be the first time somebody's been gunning for me. How about you, Grubstake?"

"Not really," Nathan replied. "Unfortunately, I might add. I don't like being a target."

"Nobody does." Trent looked meaningfully at the huge dog stretched out on the floor at Nathan's feet. "Luckily for you, you have an ally. I don't imagine Hardrock will allow anyone to slip up on you."

Nathan reached down and scratched the top of the massive head. "The old boy's good for something, all right."

Hardrock growled softly but didn't deign to open his eyes.

Nathan finished the beer he had been drinking, then he and Hardrock left the saloon. As he had explained to his new friends, he intended to camp on the edge of the settlement for a few days. Once word got around that Grubstake Jones was in town, any of the miners who wanted to accept Emily Woodward's standing offer of assistance in return for a share in any gold strikes could seek out Nathan and conduct their business.

"He seems like a nice young man," Anne commented when Nathan was gone.

Trent nodded in agreement. "Strikes me as the type who might be a little too hard on himself sometimes. I can't blame him for being disappointed at not being able to find his cousin, though. A young woman like that doesn't have any business being on her own in the gold fields."

"That's right. And you can see why I feel the same way."

Trent's gaze swung over to her and he regarded her intently for a moment. "It's not the same thing," he finally said. "Pardon me for being blunt, Anne, but you're no blushing maiden like Cassandra Woodward."

"Indeed I'm not," she said, returning his look squarely. "But I'm still a woman."

"I'm aware of that." Trent's hand moved slightly, his fingers coming to rest on top of hers as they lay on the table. "I'm well aware of that, Anne. I've just been waiting until the proper time—"

"Patrick." She drew a deep breath and tried to ignore the hammering of her pulse. Even though the saloon was crowded, it suddenly seemed as if they were the only two people in the place. She turned her hand over and linked her fingers with his, then spoke quickly before common sense could overwhelm the emotions she was feeling. She said, "To hell with being proper."

Trent began to grin and his fingers tightened on hers, and Anne discovered that he had been wrong about something. She might not be as young as Cassandra Woodward but she could still blush, she realized as the warmth spread over her face and Patrick Trent continued to hold her hand.

Nathan hoped he wasn't being foolish by coming back here to the Chinese quarter alone. Of course, he wasn't really alone; Hardrock was with him, and in a fight the big dog was worth at least two men.

He told himself that he just wanted to make sure Lotus and her brother were all right, since he had been in Ophir a couple of days now and hadn't seen them again. But he also knew that he wanted to see Chao-Xing once more. Lotus had said that the name meant "Morning Star" in English, and Nathan thought it was appropriate. He had taken one look at Chao-Xing and decided she was as beautiful as any morning star he had ever seen.

He was the recipient of quite a few curious looks from the inhabitants of this part of the settlement, but none of the Chinese seemed particularly hostile. All things being equal some of them probably wouldn't hesitate to slit his throat and take all the money in his pockets, but no one was likely to try that as long as Hardrock was at his side.

The route he had taken to the shack shared by Lotus and her brother a few days earlier was still fresh in his mind, and after a few minutes he saw that his memory hadn't played tricks on him. He recognized the crude little dwelling as he came up to it. The door stood halfway open, and Nathan paused outside it to call, "Lotus? Wang Toy? Are you in there?"

Footsteps sounded inside the hovel, but instead of the gracefully attractive young woman, her brother shambled into view. His clothes were filthy and rumpled, as if he had slept in them—or passed out in them, more likely, judging from the way his breath reeked of raw whiskey fumes. He gave Nathan a surly glare and rattled off a spate of Chinese.

Nathan shook his head. "Sorry," he said. "I don't understand the lingo. I'm looking for your sister. I'm looking for Wang Toy."

"You want Lotus," the young man said, and Nathan realized he didn't even know the boy's name. "You want whore."

Nathan frowned and said, "I wish you wouldn't talk like that. After all, she's your sister."

"Is true. Wang Toy is white man's whore." He was having more trouble with the language today, probably a result of his hangover.

"Look, I just want to make sure she's all right," Nathan said slowly, hanging on to his temper. He wanted to tell the man that if he hadn't been so weak and ineffective, Lotus might not have had to turn to prostitution for them to survive. But that was unfair, Nathan reminded himself. All the Chinese had come to this country not knowing how the deck was going to be stacked against them.

"Go 'way," the young man mumbled. "Lotus not here. She with white men. They pay her nuggets and dust and then they take her. You go 'way now. Come back with nuggets or dust. Then you can have Lotus, too."

Nathan's jaw tightened. "That's not why I'm here, damn it. I was just worried—"

The young man lurched out of the doorway, coming toward Nathan. He reached inside the folds of his stained shirt and produced a small but wicked-looking ax. "Go 'way I said!" he cried. "Go 'way!"

Hardrock growled and tensed, ready to leap, and Nathan caught hold of the loose skin at the dog's neck. "No, Hardrock!" he snapped. If the dog tore into Lotus's brother, it wouldn't be much of a contest. Hardrock would probably tear the young man's throat out with one snap of his massive jaws. Nathan didn't want that.

But he didn't want the young fool slashing at him with that ax, either. While he was hesitating, trying to decide what to do as the young man stumbled toward him, still brandishing the ax, a string of sharp words in Chinese crackled through the air. The young man came to a halt.

Chao-Xing hurried around the corner of the shack, carrying a basket of laundry. She continued to berate Lotus's brother, and as she came up to him, she balanced the basket on one hip and used her free hand to point angrily at him. He shouted back at her, obviously not pleased with her interference. For a second, he lifted the ax as if he intended to threaten her with it, and Nathan tensed, ready to release Hardrock if the young man made a move toward Chao-Xing.

He lowered the ax almost immediately, though, and tucked it away under his shirt as he continued to glower at the young woman. Turning on his heel, he stalked away with as much dignity as he could muster, which wasn't much under the circumstances.

"Thank you," Nathan said to Chao-Xing when Lotus's brother had disappeared down one of the alleys that twisted through this part of town. "I was afraid there was going to be trouble."

"Wang Loo is very angry," Chao-Xing said, and it took Nathan only a second to realize she was referring to the young man. Chao-Xing went on, "You should not have come here, Grubstake Jones."

He had to grin, both at her use of his nickname and the difficulty with which she wrapped her tongue around it. "I don't know where you heard that name," he told her, "but it's all right with me if you call me Nathan."

She nodded and repeated slowly, "Na-than."

"And would you rather I call you Chao-Xing or Morning Star?"

"My name is all I have left of my life in China."

Nathan hesitated when it became obvious that was all she was going to say on the subject. After a moment, he asked bluntly, "Is that good or bad?"

She shrugged. "There were many bad times there, but it was my home. Now those of us who came here have no homes. I do not know which is worse."

"You've got places to live and food to eat. I know it's a pretty rough life, but—"

"But it is all a Chinaman deserves. Is that what you were going to say, Na-than?" Her voice held a surprising amount of bitterness for someone who hadn't even reached the age of twenty yet.

"That's not what I was going to say at all," he told her.

"I don't have anything against you or your people."

"Then you will grubstake us, let us dig for gold like the others?"

"I can't do that," Nathan replied with a grimace. "It's my aunt's money, and she doesn't want any trouble."

Chao-Xing shrugged meaningfully and turned away, as if she hadn't really expected any other answer from him.

"Wait a minute!" Nathan said, reaching out to take hold of her arm. "I can't use Aunt Emily's money to grubstake any of you folks, but I've got money of my own. I could—"

He stopped as she shook her head. Her tautly drawn features softened a bit as she said, "No, that is not necessary. But I believe you would do this thing."

"I would," Nathan vowed.

"Perhaps in the future . . . I can speak for no one but myself. I have no family here in America. Wang Toy is like a sister to me, but she is the only one who cares. If you do this thing . . . if you help the Chinese, Na-than Jones . . . do it because it is the right thing, not because you feel sorry for me. I will be all right."

"I'm sure you will." Nathan realized he was still holding her arm. He felt the warmth of her flesh through the fabric of the tunic and abruptly let go of her, realizing he had been forward. Chao-Xing hadn't seemed to mind, though.

She looked down at the dirt surface of the alley. "I must go now," she said quietly. "I must deliver this laundry."

"I could help you," Nathan offered.

"No. This is my work. I will do it."

He nodded, not wanting to offend her sense of pride, which was evidently quite strong. As she started down the alley away from him, he said, "I hope I see you again."

She paused just for a second and looked back at him. In

a voice so soft he could barely hear it, she said, "I hope so, too."

Then she walked quickly down the alley and around a corner, her back held stiff and straight even with the weight of the laundry basket she was carrying.

"Come on, Hardrock," Nathan told the dog with a grin as he started back toward his camp on the edge of the settlement. He had left the Chinese section behind before he remembered that he hadn't seen Lotus. He hadn't even thought to ask Chao-Xing about her. But he was sure the young woman was all right. Otherwise somebody would have said something . . .

Lotus felt the sun on her face and the warm breeze and smelled the wildflowers that grew on the hill where she lay on her back with her eyes closed. She drifted lazily through the memories of her childhood and relived those days when life had been good, or at least tolerable . . .

She kept her eyes tightly shut and wished she could as easily close her ears to the animal grunts of the man who lay atop her, taking his pleasure with her. There was no warm sun, no smell of wildflowers. She was inside, and the canvas of the miner's tent blocked the rays of the sun, and the stench of the man's long-unwashed flesh overpowered any other smells. Lotus moved her hips unthinkingly and moaned from long practice so that he would think she was enjoying herself as well, instead of dwelling on memories of a time and place long gone from her life.

It did not matter what she did with this man or the other men in the settlement. None of it meant anything. All that was important was that they gave her the money she needed so she and Wang Loo could continue to live.

She wished they had never come to this country. But the famine had killed their parents and their other brothers and sisters; they alone had been left behind to make their way in life as best they could. Even then, however, Lotus had never dreamed that their path would lead them here to the place called Ophir.

The miner's body stiffened and shook as he reached his climax. He quickly rolled off of her and stood up, leaving her on the blanket he had spread on the ground. Lotus sat up and reached for the loose white trousers she had set aside earlier. She still wore the tunic.

"Not so fast, girlie," the miner said with a leering grin. He was buttoning his trousers. "You ain't finished yet."

Lotus was puzzled. "I do not understand," she said with a frown. "We have done what you wanted, and I have been paid—"

"Not just for me. You got somebody else to take care of."

Lotus started to object, but at that moment, the flap of canvas over the tent's entrance was thrust back, and a second burly miner stepped through. Lotus caught her breath at the sight of his face. She felt a shudder of fear and anger go through her as she recognized the man called Bedloe.

He smirked at her. "Howdy, little yella darlin'. You and me are goin' to have us a fine old time."

Lotus shook her head emphatically. "No," she said. "I will not do this with you."

"You been paid," growled the first miner. "You ain't got no right to get uppity now."

"You paid for yourself only—" she began.

"Who do you think's gonna believe that?" the man said with a bark of laughter. "The word of a Chinee whore agin that of a white man don't mean nothin'."

Lotus felt as if the blood in her body had turned to ice. She had never been so frightened in her entire life, not even when the ship bringing her and her brother from China had skirted the edges of a typhoon in the great ocean. She had been certain then that she was going to die.

But she had just discovered that there were terrors worse than death.

Without another word, she lunged for her pants, thinking that she could scoop them up and dart out of the tent before the two men could stop her. Both of them had obviously been drinking, and that would slow them down. Not enough, though, she found to her dismay seconds later as the one called Bedloe lashed out and slapped the back of his hand against the side of her head. She lost her balance from the blow and went to one knee.

Bedloe put a booted foot against her side and gave her a hard shove, sending her sprawling on the blanket. "No use in fightin', gal," he told her. "I'm goin' to get you anyway."

Again she tried to scramble up. This time the other man caught her and threw her down again with a brutal laugh. "I'll hang on to her, Bedloe," he said as he dropped to his knees beside her head. His fingers dug cruelly into her shoulders. "You do whatever you want to her."

"Hold her tight, Jasper," Bedloe told his friend. "She'll be squirmin' around something fierce before I get through with her."

Lotus saw him pushing down his trousers as he moved between her legs. She kicked at him, but he avoided the blow easily. Turning her head, she saw the arm of the one called Jasper only inches from her face as he held her for the assault. She darted her mouth toward his arm and sank her teeth into his flesh, which was bared by the rolled-up sleeve of his shirt.

Jasper howled in pain and jerked his arm away from her, skin tearing as he pulled away from her teeth. That caused him to release his grip, and Lotus sat up, looking around wildly for a way out.

All she saw was Bedloe's fist coming toward her face. She couldn't get out of the way in time. The punch smashed into her jaw and knocked her backward. Bedloe cursed her as he began to slap her, forehand and backhand, rocking her head first one way and then the other. Lotus tried to avoid the first few blows, but after that she was too stunned to do anything except lie there and endure the punishment.

She barely felt him grasping her thighs and wrenching them apart. She felt him penetrate her, though, felt the raw, rasping agony of his attack. Thankfully, it didn't last long. With a series of grunts, he finished, then slapped her again.

"For good measure," he said viciously.

Lotus was vaguely aware of being jerked to her feet and having her clothes thrust roughly into her arms. Then a shove sent her staggering out of the tent. She fell again, scraping her knees on the rocky ground outside.

"We're done with you," Bedloe told her from the tent's entrance. "Get the hell out of here and don't come back, you yella heathen. Not unless you want some more o' what we just gave you. That'll teach you people to think you're as good as white folks."

"How 'bout a drink, Bedloe?" asked Jasper, and laughing in satisfaction, both men disappeared inside the tent.

Lotus pushed herself to her feet. She knew she had to get dressed, had to get back to the shack she called home. But Wang Loo could not be told what had happened to her. If he found out, she thought, he would try to kill Bedloe and Jasper, and he would die instead. The miners would not hesitate to kill him. She had to prevent that.

It didn't matter, she tried to tell herself as she stumbled away from the tent. Her bruises would heal, and so would the abrasions where Bedloe had hurt her so badly. They had not taken her money, and that was all that was important, she told herself again.

But this time she knew she was wrong. What had been done to her was terrible and beyond forgiveness. It had to be avenged.

And to save her brother, she would have to take that vengeance herself . . .

Twenty-two

Cassandra rolled over and felt the warmth of the man's body next to her. She snuggled closer to him, and Boone's arms went around her. He muttered something sleepily, but she couldn't make out the words. Not that it really mattered, she thought. All she really cared about was that they were here together, the way they were meant to be.

She was lying with her back to Boone. His hand roamed under the blankets in which the two of them were curled up. He stroked her thigh and then moved his fingers up her flank and finally to her breast. Cassandra sighed in contentment as his warm palm closed gently around the mound of soft flesh.

Had there ever been a time, she wondered, when she wasn't in love with Boone Blakely? It seemed impossible now.

Long months had passed since that day when he had discovered she was a woman. The day he had kissed her for the first time. But not the last time, thankfully. They had been together ever since, working their way along the forks of the American River and up along the Yuba, until they had finally settled down here on Canyon Creek. The claim they had been working for the past month was a good one, a steady though not spectacular producer of gold. That was all right with Cassandra. She didn't particularly care anymore how much gold they found. As long as she and Boone were together, she considered herself rich.

The only problem looming over their heads was the fact that her cousin Nathan was still looking for her. They had heard stories throughout the gold fields about his quest. The last thing Cassandra wanted right now was to be found, but it was growing harder and harder for her to lie low. She had stopped going into the settlements completely, for fear that someone would spot her and recognize her and get word to Nathan of her whereabouts. If Nathan showed up and tried to drag her back to San Francisco . . . well, Boone was liable to kill him, and Cassandra didn't want that. Boone had quite a temper sometimes.

Cassandra stretched and turned her head. "Time to get up, I reckon," she whispered.

"I reckon," Boone repeated mockingly. "What kind of a way is that for a high-toned Boston lady to talk? You sound like a miner."

"That's exactly what I'm supposed to be, remember?"

Boone kissed the back of her neck under the close-cropped blond hair. "Only miner I ever saw that I'd want to crawl in a bedroll with."

She laughed. "And the only one you're likely to. Now come on, we've got work to do."

"Damn slave driver." His grousing was good-natured.

Smiling, Cassandra pushed the blankets back and stood up. She reached for her pants, well aware that Boone was watching her. Sinful it might be, but it felt good to stand naked in front of her man. She had no doubt, though, that her mother and Nathan would have been shocked and scandalized by her behavior. Emily's only passion was money, and in Cassandra's opinion Nathan had always been a little bit of a prig.

In a few minutes, she was dressed. She pulled the battered hat down over her hair as she stepped out of the tent. Even with her hair cropped off as short as it was, she seldom went out without the hat, just as a precaution.

Boone had tried to convince her to give up the masquerade

as a man, saying that he would protect her if there was any trouble, but Cassandra had stubbornly hung on to the deception. For one thing, she didn't put as much faith in the miners' code of rough chivalry as Boone seemed to. He claimed that none of them would harm a decent woman, but Cassandra didn't want to risk her virtue—or her life—on that idea. And on a practical level, it was easier to dig for gold in the pants and shirt and boots of a typical forty-niner, and the broad-brimmed hat provided plenty of shade. Most of the time, Cassandra didn't mind the getup.

The only time she regretted the masquerade, in fact, was after she and Boone had made love. Then, in those soft, hazy moments, she allowed herself to dream of lace and silk and all the things her mother would have thought a young woman *should* dream about. She could see herself in a wedding dress . . .

Boone wasn't the marrying kind, though, or at least so he claimed. It had taken Cassandra a while to accept that fact, but she could live with it just fine now. A bunch of words from a preacher didn't mean that a man and a woman loved each other any more than they might have otherwise. When Boone said that, it certainly made sense.

It was a pretty morning, Cassandra saw as she looked around the clearing where their camp was located. The night had been a little chilly, but the sun was beginning to warm things up, even though it had risen only a short time earlier. Already she could hear the ringing of pick and shovel against rock coming from the other claims in the area. Down the canyon through which the creek ran, she could see a contraption called a Long Tom sitting in the water. It was a modified sluice box used for sifting gold dust from the silt on the bottom of the stream. Sand was shoveled up from the streambed and thrown into the boxlike shape of the Long Tom. The creek's own current carried the sand out the other end while the heavier flecks of gold dust sank and were caught by the riffles along the bottom of the box. Many of the miners who worked the streams were adopting this more efficient method and abandoning their washbowls. It cost money to build a Long Tom, though, so some of the forty-niners had gone into partnership and formed mining companies. These bigger operations were the wave of the future, some claimed.

Cassandra didn't know about that and didn't care. She was happy to stay where she was, chipping a future of her own out of the rocky bluffs on the side of the canyon, a future for her and Boone.

He came out of the tent behind her, buttoning his shirt and yawning. He bent to pick up a wooden bucket from the ground. "I'll get us some water while you fry up some bacon," he said.

"Let me get the water," Cassandra responded. "It's your turn to cook, remember?" Her voice held a teasing tone.

Boone grimaced, but he held out the bucket to her. "You've turned into a better cook than I am, but I suppose you've figured that out by now. If you can eat what I rustle up, though, I can, too."

Cassandra took the bucket and grinned at him. "I'll be back in a few minutes."

"I'll be here," he told her.

She started down toward the creek, which ran about fifty yards from their claim. The bucket swung lightly from her hand as she walked. She felt unaccountably good this morning. She wanted to wash her face in the cold water of the stream, because she knew a brisk scrubbing would make her feel even better. That thought sent her memory back to the first day she had spent with Boone. He had admitted to her later that he'd spied on her as she took her bath, and although she had been angry at first, she had quickly gotten over that feeling. If he hadn't discovered that she was a woman, he might not have risked as much to save her from Peregrine Forsythe and the other would-be robber, both of whom had ended up with a sandy bank collapsed on them for a crude grave.

Cassandra frowned at that memory. Since that day, she and Boone hadn't run into any trouble, but she would always remember the stain of violence there at the very beginning of their relationship.

Something good had come out that day, though, something very good. And she was sure she would never regret inviting Boone Blakely to share her camp.

She reached the stream and moved along the bank. Anywhere along here she could reach down and fill the bucket with the cold, clear water, but she wanted to find a slightly more secluded spot for her morning necessities. There was an outcropping of rock and brush not far along the creek, and if she went around on the other side of it, she would have sufficient privacy. Boone wouldn't care how long she was gone; he was busy with the frying pan and the bacon.

She pushed some of the bushes aside and moved around the outcropping, holding on to her hat with her free hand to make sure a branch didn't snag it and pull it off. A glance over her shoulder told her that the campsite was no longer in view. This would do. She lowered the bucket to the ground, took the hat off, and knelt beside the stream. She put the hat beside her, then scooped up some of the water and dashed it into her face. The cold bite of it brought a gasp from her lips.

"Don't move, son."

The unexpected voice came from behind her and made her spin around in defiance of the order. Cassandra turned so swiftly that she lost her balance and sat down hard on the creek bank. Her eyes widened as she saw the tall, grim-faced stranger standing in the brush only a few feet away from her. She stared even more as her gaze fell on the long-barreled pistol he held. With the man pointing it at her the muzzle of the revolver looked as big around as a mine shaft. She could barely tear her eyes away from it as he spoke again.

"I'm a lawman," he told her in his deep voice, "and you don't have to worry about a thing. I ain't after you."

Cassandra's heart was pounding painfully in her chest. She looked up at him and saw the badge pinned to his shirt. It was a silver star set inside a silver circle. She forced herself to say thickly, "Wha-what do you want?"

"Not what. Who. And the fella I'm after is your partner." His eyes searched her face intently. "My name's Dan Logan, and I'm here to arrest Boone Blakely for murder."

The smell of the bacon rose from the frying pan and stirred Boone's senses. He grinned. Nothing like that delicious aroma to wake a man up on a morning like this . . . unless it was the feel of a woman snuggled up against him. That was even better.

Stumbling across Cassandra Woodward was just about the luckiest thing that had ever happened to him, he reflected. If it hadn't been for her, there was no telling what might have happened to him. He would have robbed or even killed to get out of the Sierra Nevadas and leave California behind him. That would have been just one more stain on his past. He would have been running forever.

He'd had enough of running. He and Cassandra were building a life together, he told himself. One of these days, when they had enough gold, they would go to San Francisco and sail away from there with their riches, bound for who knows where. It was a damned pretty dream, Boone thought, and if he kept repeating it to himself often enough, maybe it would even come true someday.

But not today, because when he lifted his gaze from the frying pan and glanced toward the river, he saw Cassandra coming toward him, the water bucket forgotten. Walking behind her was a tall man with a drooping moustache and a high-crowned hat. Boone knew him immediately.

The Texas Ranger—Dan Logan!

Boone whirled and dove toward the tent. He had a pistol in there, and he cursed himself for not wearing it. As he moved, Logan shouted, "Hold it, Blakely!" and triggered off a shot, shoving Cassandra aside as he did so. The ranger must have fired high on purpose, because the bullet whipped past several feet above Boone's head.

He didn't see any more, because then he was plunging through the entrance of the tent. He heard Cassandra yelling something in a half-scream, but he couldn't make out the words. His fingers delved into the packs as he went to his knees beside the stack of gear. A moment later they closed around the walnut grips of the pistol.

He jerked the weapon free and checked to make sure it was loaded, then slapped the canvas flap aside and ran out of the tent. Twenty yards away, Cassandra and Logan were struggling. She had hold of the ranger's gun arm and wasn't letting go. Logan tried futilely to pry her loose. Neither of them seemed to notice Boone's reappearance.

Boone lifted the revolver, then hesitated with his thumb looped over the hammer and his finger taut on the trigger. If he blazed away at Logan from this distance, he would probably hit the lawman, but he stood a good chance of gunning down Cassandra, too. Was his freedom worth the risk? And what the hell was Logan doing here, anyway? The ranger had given up his duty to hunt for gold.

Obviously, things had changed. Logan gave in to his frustration and swung a loosely balled fist at Cassandra's jaw.

The blow clipped her and sent her stumbling back away from him. As she released his gun arm, he pivoted toward Boone again.

Cassandra's interference had swung the advantage to Boone's side. He fired first, unhesitatingly now that Cassandra was out of the line of fire. Logan flinched, and Boone saw him reach down with his left hand to his left thigh. At the same time, the ranger squeezed off a shot of his own. Boone heard the lead sing past his ear.

He was about to fire again when Cassandra leaped back into the fight. She threw herself at Logan and wrapped her arms around his waist in a flying tackle. His wounded leg wouldn't support both of them, and they tumbled to the ground. Boone raced forward toward them, trying to get close enough for a sure killing shot.

Before he could get there, Logan threw Cassandra aside and rolled away from her. Boone stopped in his tracks and snapped a shot toward the ranger. Dust and rock splinters kicked up from the ground where the bullet struck next to Logan's head. Logan's gun bloomed smoke and fire as he triggered it again.

Boone felt a horrible impact against his hand and the gun he held went spinning out of suddenly numb fingers. He cried out in pain and shock and looked down to see blood welling up from the web of flesh between his thumb and first finger. Logan's bullet had ripped across there before smashing into the revolver and knocking it out of Boone's hand. It had been purely a lucky shot, a detached portion of Boone's mind told him, but lucky or not, the result was still the same. He was disarmed and facing the ominous barrel of the ranger's gun.

"Don't move, Blakely," Logan grated. "I'd just as soon not kill you, but you know I'll do it if I have to."

A few feet away, Cassandra had pushed herself to her

hands and knees, crouching like a wild animal about to leap
at its prey, and Logan must have sensed that, because he
went on, "And tell the lady to settle down or I'll put a bullet
through your leg so's I won't have to worry about you while
I'm dealin' with her!"

"Take it easy, Cass," Boone choked out the words. "He
means it. He's a cold-blooded son of a bitch."

What might have been a faint, grim smile played around
the corners of Logan's mouth as he touched the stain on the
left leg of his trousers. "Feels warm to me," he said. Awkwardly, but with the gun trained on Boone the whole time,
he pushed himself to his feet. "Step well away from that
gun, Blakely. I don't want you gettin' any ideas. Don't figure
it'd work with the cylinder smashed that way, but there ain't
no use in takin' chances."

"What do you want, Logan?" Boone asked as he moved
away from the gun that had been shot out of his hand. He
cradled that injured member in his other hand. The numbness
was wearing off and the hurt was ebbing into him. The
wound wasn't a serious one, but it was going to be painful.

"You know good and well what I want," Logan replied.
"I've come to arrest you for the murder of those folks back
in Texas."

Cassandra stared at Boone and repeated incredulously,
"Murder?"

Boone shook his head. "He's all mixed up, Cass. I didn't
murder anybody."

"That ain't the way the law sees it," snapped Logan.

"We've had this discussion before," Boone said with a
heavy sigh. "I thought you had other things on your mind
now, Logan. Things like gold . . . What happened? That
strike play out quicker than you thought it would, so you
decided to go back to packing a badge?"

"Nope. Not that it's any of your business, but that strike

was a mighty rich one. Wasn't the only one I found, neither. I reckon I've got close to ten thousand dollars in dust in my saddlebags.''

Boone's eyes widened. "Ten thousand . . . ? Then what the hell are you doing coming after me again? That's enough money to live like a king, at least for a while!''

"Finally figured out that I ain't a king,'' Logan told him. "I'm a Texas Ranger. And I hope I ain't dishonored the badge so much that I don't deserve to wear it again.''

Boone had to suppress a groan. Logan had had an attack of conscience. His guilt at abandoning the job that had brought him to California had eaten away at him for so long that finally he'd had to do something about it. And as for Boone Blakely and his plans . . . well, that was just too damned bad.

It wasn't fair! Boone raged inside himself. He had been free. Logan had believed him about what happened in Texas and let him go. The ranger didn't have any right to go back on that decision.

But the big Walker Colt in Logan's hand gave him the right to do anything he wanted, Boone realized bleakly. Like it or not, he was Logan's prisoner again.

This time wasn't completely the same, however. Now Cassandra was with him, and she said hotly, "You can't do this! Boone's no killer. I know him too well to believe that. There must be some mistake!''

"No mistake, ma'am,'' Logan said. "He killed a fella named Jason Stoneham and a young lady named Samantha McCarter.''

"That's a lie,'' Boone insisted. He looked intently at Cassandra. "I killed Stoneham, it's true, but it was self-defense. And as for Samantha . . . you've got to believe me, Cass, I never laid a hand on her! I wouldn't have hurt her. I—''

"You loved her, didn't you?'' whispered Cassandra.

Boone grimaced and dropped his gaze to the ground, not saying anything in reply to the question. That was enough of an answer for Cassandra.

She turned to glare at Logan. "What do you intend to do with Boone?" she demanded.

"He's goin' back to Texas," the Ranger replied. "He'll stand trial, and after that, I can't say for sure. There's a good chance he'll hang."

His voice bitter, Boone said, "Oh, I'll hang, all right. Jason Stoneham's father is a judge."

"This isn't fair," Cassandra told Logan, echoing Boone's earlier thought. "You know he can't get an honest trial back there."

"That's not for me to say, ma'am. All I know is that he's got to go back, or I won't be able to sleep sound at night. I've got a job to do, you see."

"A job!" Cassandra spat. "Is that all our lives are to you? A job?"

For a moment, Logan didn't answer her. Then he said heavily, "I'm done wranglin' with you two. Blakely, you put your hands behind your back. Ma'am, you take these here cuffs and put 'em on him." With his free hand, he took a pair of handcuffs from his hip pocket and held them out toward Cassandra.

"You expect me to help you?" she asked in disbelief. "I won't do it!"

"I'd be obliged, ma'am. You see, this leg of mine is still bleedin' some, and I ain't sure how much longer I can stand here like this."

Boone felt a surge of hope. If Logan collapsed—

"So unless you put these cuffs on him right now, I won't have any choice but to shoot him in the knee so he can't give me no trouble. He'll never walk again, I reckon, but that can't be helped."

An icy shiver went through Boone. "The bastard'll do it, Cass," he told her. "You'd better do as he says."

She didn't move at first, just stood there looking from one man to the other, gnawing her bottom lip in dismay. Then, hesitantly, she stepped forward and took the handcuffs Logan was holding out to her. She came over to Boone, who reluctantly put his hands behind his back.

"His hand is bleeding where you shot him," Cassandra told Logan accusingly.

"You can wrap it up once you got him cuffed." The ranger wiggled the barrel of his Colt. "Get it done, ma'am."

Boone heard Cassandra take a deep breath, then the cold metal rings snapped shut around his wrists. His wounded hand throbbed from holding it behind him, and he could feel blood dripping from the bullet gash.

Logan seemed to relax a little, and Boone could see now how pale he was. The bloodstain on his pants leg was bigger than it had been. Boone still held out hope that the ranger would collapse and Cassandra would be able to get him out of this mess.

Logan was nothing if not stubborn, though. He said to the two of them, "Blakely, you go over yonder to that tree and sit down beside it. Ma'am, when you get through patching up his hand, I'll give you some rope and you can tie him to the tree. I don't want either one of you gettin' any fancy ideas."

Cassandra lifted her chin defiantly. "Are you going to threaten to shoot me, too?"

"No, ma'am. But I've hogtied a few calves in my time, and I reckon I can fix you up where you can't cause no trouble. It won't be comfortable, though."

"You're a despicable man!" Cassandra flared at him.

"Yes, ma'am. But I aim to get back to Texas alive."

Twenty-three

Lotus moved slowly down the alley. It was dark, but she knew these twisting lanes well enough to make her way easily through them. She wore the same loose pants and tunic she always did, but tonight her raven hair was unbound and fell loosely around her shoulders. She knew she would be beautiful . . . if not for the swollen bruises on her face.

All day she had avoided her brother, knowing that Wang Loo would be crazy with anger if he found out what the miners called Bedloe and Jasper had done to her. He would stoke his rage with the white man's whiskey and go after the miners to settle the score, as the Americans put it. Either that, or his spirit would break even more and he would retreat to the shack where the air was filled with the sweetish sick smell of opium. Lotus didn't want either of those things to happen. She loved her brother and knew that deep down Wang Loo was a good man. He, like all the other Chinese, had been betrayed by the promises of a better life in America. He had believed the lie of a shining land where anything was possible.

Maybe anything was possible here, but not if your skin was yellow, Lotus thought grimly.

She stopped, leaned against the back wall of a building, closed her eyes, and took a deep breath. Her body ached badly from the punishment she had received at the hands of Bedloe and Jasper. For a moment she rested, then pushed away from the wall and continued on down the alley.

She had left the Chinese community behind and reached

the main part of the settlement. One of the buildings she passed was the rear of Patrick Trent's saloon. Trent was a good man, she thought, and he would treat her decently if she went to work for him. Perhaps when she had done what she had to do, and after her bruises had healed, he would hire her to work in the saloon. She would be pretty in one of the bright, spangled dresses his girls wore. She knew she would be.

Lotus lifted a hand to her head and rubbed her temple. Pain throbbed there, had ever since the men had struck her. But she could live with the pain once she had taken her vengeance on them. Pain was nothing new to her.

The sun had set a short time earlier, and shadows of dusk gathered thickly in the alley. A figure loomed up in front of Lotus, startling her. It jabbered nonsense at her as she recoiled away. A second later, she recognized the gaunt, shambling shape of an elderly Chinese man. The opium scent clung to him, and she knew he had come from the den. His gnarled fingers reached out for her.

She pushed him away gently, not wanting to be disrespectful to an elder. "Go home, little grandfather," she said. "You need sleep."

He cackled and made one last futile grasp for her. She fended him off easily, and still laughing, he stumbled on down the alley. Lotus took a deep, shaky breath, feeling a mixture of pity for the old man and anger at what this land had made of him.

Chao-Xing often said that the Chinese should keep working, that acceptance would come with time. Every time Lotus made some comment about the other girl leaving her laundry chores and following the same path Lotus had chosen, Chao-Xing stubbornly refused. It was a shame; Chao-Xing was pretty enough so that she would have done very well, and she was young, which would have made her even more attractive to the whites. But Chao-Xing would have none of it, and secretly Lotus envied the other girl's resolve. She wished she could have nothing to do with the Americans, too.

Not that all of them were bad. The one called Nathan had seemed kind, and she knew that Trent and the yellow-haired woman called Anne were friendly to her people. Most of them were like Bedloe, though, eager for any opportunity to degrade and cheat the Chinese.

Lotus put her hand on the shape concealed in the folds of her tunic, felt the cold hardness of steel. Bedloe would pay for what he had done, she thought with a tiny smile, and he would pay soon. She knew the places he frequented. It was just a matter of looking until she found him . . .

Jasper tripped over a rock as he and Bedloe stepped out of the tent saloon, one of the few left in Ophir. Most of the fly-by-night operators had already left the settlement and moved on to other, less permanent mining camps. But this dive was still in business, and the two miners enjoyed it because nobody there expected anything like respectability. A man could get drunk and carry on like the very devil, and nobody would look twice at him. Ophir was mostly getting too damned civilized, Jasper thought.

Out of habit, he reached down and picked up the rock he had tripped over. It was a chunk of stone the size of two fists held together. Like everybody else in the gold fields, Jasper had heard the stories of men accidentally finding vast fortunes right under their feet. He held the rock close to his face and squinted at it, looking for any telltale glints in the light that slanted through the open entrance flap of the big tent.

Bedloe laughed harshly. "Might as well throw it down, Jasper. I've fallen over that rock myself and already looked at it ever' which way. Ain't no gold in it.''

"Can't fault a man for hopin'," Jasper muttered as he tossed the stone aside.

"No, but I can fault him for bein' a damn fool. Come on.''

"What's your hurry?'' Jasper wanted to know.

"I'm in the mood to find me a whore. That Chinee slut took the edge off for a while, but I'm gettin' the itch again.''

Jasper shook his head. Bedloe was just about the randiest bastard he had ever known. But Bedloe had plenty of dust, and he was generous. That was enough to make Jasper stumble along after him. Both of them had put away enough rotgut to make a mule tipsy, and they were unsteady on their feet. If Bedloe found a whore, maybe he'd just watch, Jasper thought. He wasn't sure if he was capable of anything else, drunk as he was.

A pale figure appeared in front of them, startling Bedloe and making him come to an abrupt stop. Jasper bumped into him and asked, "Wha' th' hell—''

"Little Chinee gal,'' Bedloe said, the smirking leer as plain to hear in his voice as it would have been to see on his face, had there been more light. "What you want, little Chinee gal?''

"I am sorry I displeased you earlier,'' came the reply in a voice Jasper recognized as belonging to Lotus. The words were a little thicker than normal, owing no doubt to her swollen lips. She went on, "Your displeasure has dishonored me.''

Bedloe gave an ugly laugh. "I ain't so sure I wasn't pleased. I like it when a gal fights a little. Gives it more of a kick, like whiskey that has a good jolt.''

"I wish to make it up to you,'' Lotus said. "There are special things I can do . . .''

"Damned if I don't like the sound of that,'' chuckled Bedloe. "What you got in mind, girl?"

"Come over here," Lotus said softly, gesturing in the moonlight, her fingers curling gracefully. She backed toward the dark mouth of an alley.

Bedloe followed her, but Jasper hung back. He didn't much like the looks of this. He was drunk, right enough, but he wasn't totally addled. What if that girl had some of her kinfolk waiting in that alley? What if there were a bunch of Chinamen with hatchets lurking in that darkness?

Before Jasper could voice those concerns, Bedloe glanced back at him as if reading his mind and growled in irritation, "Come on, damn it. There's nobody else in that alley. Is there, gal?"

"Only I await you," she murmured seductively.

"Don't be as yellow as this here Chinee, Jasper," Bedloe mocked.

Jasper took a deep breath and followed his friend. But if anything happened, he was going to cut and run. Bedloe wasn't *that* good of a friend.

The three of them did seem to be alone in the alley, though, as Jasper realized a moment later. He didn't hear or see anybody else moving. Lotus had taken Bedloe's hand, and she led him over to the wall of a darkened store that was closed for the night.

"Lean against the wall," she told him as she sank to her knees in front of him. It was too dark to see exactly what she was doing as she moved toward him.

Bedloe gave a grunt and then a long sigh. Jasper could see part of his body, a dark bulk against the wall of the building. The lower part of his body was concealed by a patch of lightness that would be the clothes Lotus was wearing. Bedloe's breath rasped in his throat as the Chinese girl kept doing whatever she was doing. Jasper could only imagine, but what he imagined caused him to gulp. Maybe he wasn't quite as drunk as he had thought.

"Damn, that's good," Bedloe said. "You do that better'n any whore I ever had. Glad you come to your senses, missy. You'll earn your dust tonight."

Jasper wanted to tell Bedloe to shut up. He wanted to listen to the little sounds the girl was making in her throat. A moment later, Lotus leaned back away from the burly miner, and Bedloe growled in irritation.

"Why'd you stop?" he demanded. "What the hell are you—"

Lotus's hand moved suddenly, and something flickered in the faint light of the alley. Bedloe gave a bleat of surprise, then screamed in pain, his voice thin like a baby's.

He lurched away from Lotus, hands clasped to his groin. As Bedloe stumbled down the alley, still shrieking, Lotus whirled around in a crouch and lashed out at the stunned Jasper. He saw the little knife coming at him at the last moment and flung himself backward. The blade sliced the air only inches in front of his throat.

He heard himself making a blubbering noise of fear as Lotus came after him, and it was instinct alone that made him fling up an arm as she swung back at him with the knife. Their arms came together with a jarring thud, and Lotus said, "Oh!"

Anger replaced some of the terror in Jasper's head as he took advantage of the opportunity to grab Lotus's wrist. He was a foot taller and weighed twice as much as the Chinese girl, and now that he had his hands on her, it was no trick to twist her arm back until the knife slipped from her fingers. Jasper started to shake her. "What'd you do?" he demanded. "What'd you do to Bedloe?"

"Made him so that he will never hurt another girl!" she gasped. "Let go of me!"

Jasper looked toward the mouth of the alley. He could see

Bedloe silhouetted against the street, weaving back and forth as he clutched at himself. His screams had died away to wretched whimpers. As Jasper watched, Bedloe collapsed, folding up around himself like a limp rag.

Stone cold sober now, his drunkenness driven out by first fear and then rage, Jasper said, "Come on. You got to answer to somebody for this."

Suddenly, Lotus kicked him, aiming for his groin but hitting his thigh instead. At the same time, she jerked hard against his grip in an effort to pull away from him. For an instant, Jasper's grasp loosened, but before Lotus could escape, he tightened his hold again, pressing down even more cruelly now. With his other hand he slapped her, rocking her head to the side.

"Bitch! You've likely done for Bedloe, and you tried to kill me! You'll hang for this!"

He started to drag her toward the street.

Nathan was in one of the stores lining Ophir's meandering main street when he heard the commotion. Men were shouting as they ran past the mercantile, but he couldn't make out the words. Obviously, whatever had happened had caught the attention of the entire community.

The store clerk craned his neck to look past Nathan. "Something's got folks stirred up," he said. He gestured toward the counter. "We done here?"

Nathan nodded. There were a few small bags of provisions there. He planned to take them to Chao-Xing and Lotus before he left the next morning. He had done all the business he could here in Ophir, grubstaking more than a dozen miners with his Aunt Emily's money and supplies; and now it was time to move on. He couldn't delay any longer just because of the growing affection he felt for Chao-Xing and his friendship for Lotus.

The clerk scooped up the coins Nathan placed on the counter and dropped them in the till. ''Reckon I'll go see what's goin' on,'' he said as he hurried out from behind the counter.

Nathan was curious, too. ''I'll leave these supplies here and go with you,'' he said. Hardrock trotted along behind as the two men went to the front door.

It was easy to tell where the problem lay. The men running down the street were all going one direction, to the left as Nathan and the clerk stepped out of the store. They turned that way, and Nathan saw that several men had lit makeshift torches to throw a garish, flickering red light over the scene. A mob was rapidly growing.

''Must've been something bad to get folks stirred up like that,'' the clerk commented. He and Nathan walked quickly toward the knot of men in the street. Angry shouts came from the group.

''Cut it right off, she did!'' one man yelled. ''The bitch tried to rob us, and when Bedloe called her on it, she cut him!''

Sounded like some sort of bloody, sordid fight, Nathan thought. He grimaced. The mining camps that had grown into permanent settlements like Ophir were not as violent as in the past, but there were still plenty of incidents like these. Men died frequently out here, often not in very pretty ways—as if there was any pretty way to die.

Nathan moved closer, his frown deepening as he tried to recall where he had heard the name Bedloe before. He remembered almost immediately; that had been the name of the man threatening to cut off Wang Loo's pigtail a few days earlier when Nathan had first arrived in Ophir. If this was the same man, it sounded like his brutal nature had caught up with him. He'd had something cut off, and Nathan was willing to bet it wasn't a pigtail.

"Miners' coúrt!" shouted a man. "I'm callin' for a miners' court!" Others took up the cry.

Nathan had witnessed such informal proceedings before. With the nearest real court and judge over a hundred miles away, the men who had come here to the gold fields tended to hand out their own justice, often in the form of makeshift trials. Nathan didn't mind that; even a rudimentary form of law and order was better than anarchy, to his way of thinking. But something about this situation was different. He heard the thirst for revenge, not justice, in the voice of the man who had started the uproar. This was the same man, Nathan realized, who had been yelling a couple of minutes earlier about what had happened to Bedloe.

The crowd parted a little, and Nathan suddenly caught sight of the huddled shape on the ground, just outside the mouth of an alley. There was a dark stain around the body where blood had puddled. A shiver went through Nathan at the sight. Nobody could lose that much blood and still be alive. Bedloe was dead, all right.

"See!" cried the man who was egging on the crowd. "See what that whore done to poor ol' Bedloe, who never hurt nobody in his life!"

Nathan knew that claim wasn't true, but he kept his mouth shut among the onlookers. Bedloe evidently had quite a few friends among this crowd, or at least men who would take his side over some soiled dove with robbery and murder on her mind. Not wanting to direct any of their anger toward him, Nathan edged toward the back of the crowd. He didn't know what they would do with the woman, but he wasn't sure he wanted to know.

That was when the mob parted a little more and a terrified, struggling young woman in light-colored tunic and trousers was pulled forward in the grip of two brawny miners. Nathan froze at the sight.

Lotus!

"Here she is, Jasper," one of her captors said to the man who was goading the crowd to action. "What'll we do with her?"

Jasper folded his arms and glared at Lotus, who refused to wilt under his gaze. "We'll let the miners' court decide that," he said harshly.

Nathan felt his heart pounding in his chest. When he had heard that some prostitute was in trouble, he had never expected it to be Lotus. It made sense, though. Lotus had had trouble with Bedloe before. Nathan was sure now that the dead miner was the same man he'd confronted in Trent's saloon.

But something else must have happened for Lotus to have killed Bedloe. Nathan could hardly bring himself to believe the charge.

Then the light from one of the torches spilled across Lotus's face, revealing the ugly bruises on her defiant features. Nathan bit back an angry exclamation. Someone had beaten her quite badly, and he was certain Bedloe had had something to do with it.

Jasper began pointing out men in the crowd, stopping when he had indicated a dozen of them. "You boys'll be our miners' court," he said. "You decide what to do with this murderin' yellow bitch."

"Reckon that's easy," one of the men answered with a leering grin. "String 'er up!" That brought shouts of agreement from his companions.

Nathan knew he couldn't stand by and watch this happen. In a low, warning voice, he said, "Hardrock." The dog pressed against his leg, lips drawn back in a snarl, the fur on its back standing up stiffly. Nathan moved forward, and Hardrock came with him.

"Wait a minute!" Nathan said, lifting his voice to be

heard over the noise of the crowd. "Wait just a damned minute!"

Some of the voices around him died away as curious stares were turned in his direction. Men moved back instinctively when they saw Hardrock. Nathan seized that momentary advantage and pressed forward, moving all the way up to the clearing in the center of the crowd where Jasper, Lotus, and the two men holding the Chinese girl were standing.

"Who're you?" Jasper demanded impatiently. "Hold on, I recognize you now. You're the gent they call Grubstake Jones, ain't you?"

"That's right," Nathan admitted. "But who I am doesn't matter. What you're trying to do here is wrong. You can't hang this girl."

"I reckon we can," snapped Jasper. "She was found guilty by a duly appointed miners' court—"

"Guilty of what?" Nathan cut in.

"Well, murder, for one." Jasper pointed to Bedloe's lifeless body. "She cut up that fella so bad he bled to death. And she was tryin' to rob us—"

"That is a lie," Lotus said. "I am not a thief."

Nathan turned to her. "Did you cut him?" he asked.

Lotus hesitated, then nodded. "Bedloe and this man—" She pointed to Jasper. "They raped me and beat me."

Several of the men laughed raucously. "Hell, you can't rape a whore!" one of them called. "It ain't possible!"

"And I never seen a woman yet who couldn't do with a good beatin' ever' now and then," another man said. "Let's string the bitch up!"

This was insane, Nathan thought. It couldn't be happening. These were normal, rational men. They couldn't intend to hang a young woman just because she had defended herself and her honor.

"These miners' courts aren't legal—" he began, knowing

that logic was unlikely to do any good but determined to at least try to make them see reason.

Lotus interrupted him. "Do not waste your time, Nathan," she said, her voice dull with despair. "They know what they want to do."

"Did you hear that?" Jasper shouted to the mob. "She called him Nathan! They know each other. He's prob'ly been doin' her, too!"

Nathan held up his hands to try to calm the angry outcries. "There's nothing between this woman and me!" he insisted. "I just don't think it's fair—"

"The miners' court decided! She's got to hang!"

There were too many of them, Nathan realized. Too many to persuade, and too many to fight. But maybe he could bluff them.

"Let her go and then step back," he said coldly to the men who were holding Lotus. "Otherwise I'll turn my dog loose on you."

The men darted nervous glances toward Hardrock, who was something of a legend in the gold fields. Nobody wanted to have his throat torn out by the beast, which was trembling with its desire to attack. But nobody wanted to see the mob denied of its vengeance, either. Jasper threw fuel on the flames by saying scornfully, "Hell, mister, nobody's going to back down from a *dog*. What kind of men do you think we are?"

"Fools," Nathan muttered.

That was a mistake. Jasper's face contorted in anger, and he swung a fist at Nathan's head. Nathan ducked the blow and threw one of his own, catching Jasper on the chin with the punch and rocking him back. The sudden exchange of blows ignited the crowd's tension and made men leap toward Nathan with curses and angry cries.

Hardrock tore into them, but someone swung a shovel and

bounced it off the dog's thick skull. The impact wasn't enough to knock Hardrock out, but it stunned him. At the same time, men pressed around Nathan, and he felt fists thudding into him. Lotus screamed over the shouts of the mob. Nathan flailed around him with both fists, feeling some of the men fall away from him. But others took their place instantly. The melee closed tighter and tighter around him until he felt himself being shoved off his feet. He struggled desperately to stay upright.

It was no use. He went down, and men began to kick him. He rolled from side to side, but with each turn more boots crashed into his body. He could no longer see or hear Hardrock, and he prayed the dog would be all right. Men who would lynch a young woman like Lotus would also kill a dog, Nathan thought frantically.

Of course, he had his own problems to worry about, like getting stomped to death . . .

In the end, he didn't even know when he passed out. One second he was still being jolted by the vicious kicks of the mob, and the next he was gliding deeper and deeper into a black pit that closed around him and held him like tar. His last conscious thought was that at least he couldn't feel the beating anymore.

In fact, he couldn't feel a damned thing.

Twenty-four

Nathan was drowning in that tar pit, and as that realization gradually came over him, he began trying to swim to the top of it, fighting desperately against the deadly, clinging, stygian stuff. For what seemed like an eternity, he struggled against its grip, then suddenly broke free.

Pain washed over him. The tar pit had not been real, he knew that now, but the jolts of agony shooting through his body and head certainly were. Blackness still surrounded him, but he realized that was because his eyes were closed. Something was crusted over them, holding them shut. He figured out after a moment that it was dried blood.

He was lying on his face, and the taste of dirt was in his mouth. He groaned softly as he tried to will his muscles to move. They didn't want to obey his brain's commands, but he insisted stubbornly. A series of twitches ran through his body. At least he could move a little. That was a relief.

Something rough and wet touched the side of his face, and he almost screamed at the abrasive swipe across his scraped and bruised skin. The pain drove him to move the arm on that side of his body. He touched coarse hair. The licking continued.

Hardrock was alive. That thought worked its way into Nathan's brain. Hardrock was alive and licking his face. He groaned again and slowly forced his head up.

With an effort that brought beads of sweat to his forehead, Nathan knuckled the dried blood away from his eyes and finally opened them. Hardrock let out a plaintive little whine beside him. Nathan swung his head toward the dog. There was matted blood in Hardrock's fur around the ears and along his muzzle, but the dog was on his feet and seemed to be all right.

"G-good fella," Nathan whispered. He wanted to pet Hardrock, but he was too tired. Instead he got his hands flat on the ground and pushed a little, gradually levering himself up so that he could look around better.

A second later, he wished he hadn't gone to the trouble.

It was still night, and Nathan guessed he hadn't been unconscious for all that long. The street was fairly well illuminated by the lanternlight that spilled out through the windows of the buildings lining it. In addition, the moon had risen, a round, silvery ball that cast its glow down over the settlement. All in all, there was plenty of light for Nathan to see the figure dangling limply at the end of a rope that had been flung over the branch of a nearby tree.

Lotus.

He could make out the white tunic and pants and the long black hair that spilled loosely down her back. There was a strong wind blowing tonight, and the body turned slowly at the end of the rope. Lotus's arms hung loosely at her sides. Her feet were perhaps a yard off the ground. This atrocity was not like the fast drop from a gallows, Nathan knew. There had been no clean snapping of the neck, no quick death. Lotus had been hauled up into the air to strangle and struggle frantically for breath and slowly kick her life away. The sight was the most hideous thing Nathan had ever seen.

Gradually, over the roaring of the blood in his head, he became aware of sobbing and looked over to see a figure kneeling at the base of the tree where Lotus had been lynched. From the size of the figure and the fact that it wore the same type of light-colored clothing, he figured out that it was Chao-Xing kneeling there, mourning the death of her friend. Nathan struggled to pull himself onto his hands and knees, then made another monumental effort to get to his feet. Keeping his gaze fixed on Chao-Xing, he staggered toward her.

When he reached the tree, he put out his hands and leaned gratefully against the rough bark of its trunk. He avoided lifting his eyes to the young woman's body hanging so near him. "Chao-Xing," he said, his voice sounding thick and rough to his ears.

For a long moment, she just kept crying and made no sign that she had heard him. He repeated her name, and this time she looked up. "N-Na-than?" she whispered.

"Are . . . are you all right?"

"They have killed Wang Toy." Her voice was flat and drawn with pain.

"I know. I . . . I tried to stop them . . ."

She stood up from her kneeling position, uncoiling from it with a natural grace even under these tragic circumstances. She put out a hand toward him, stopping before she actually touched him, and said, "You are hurt?"

"I'll be all right," he told her. He was breathing heavily and he still hurt all over, but he was feeling a little better already. His sorrow and rage at Lotus's death had made him forget about his own injuries. "Were . . . were you here . . . when it happened?"

Chao-Xing shook her head. "We heard talk that the miners were hanging a prostitute, and we were afraid. We came to see . . . but we got here too late."

"We?" Nathan repeated.

"Wang Loo was with me."

Nathan felt a shiver go through him. "Where is he now?"

"He went to find the one called Jasper, the one who lied about Wang Toy. There were men still here when we arrived, men who stood around laughing and talking about what had happened. This is how we know about Jasper and the one known as Bedloe.''

Nathan closed his eyes and leaned his head against the tree trunk. ''Oh, Lord,'' he said quietly. ''Wang Loo's going to get himself killed.''

''He must avenge his sister's death,'' Chao-Xing said stiffly. ''It is a matter of honor.''

''Yeah.'' Nathan nodded. ''I reckon I can understand that.'' He pushed himself away from the tree, wishing that he felt a little steadier. ''I'll see if I can catch up with him, keep this from getting any worse.''

This time Chao-Xing actually laid her hand on his arm. ''But you are hurt,'' she protested.

''I'll recover. Wang Loo won't, by the time Jasper and his friends get through with him.''

Before Nathan could stumble toward the saloons where Jasper would likely be found, he spotted two figures hurrying down the street toward the tree. They came out of the shadows, and he recognized them as Patrick Trent and Anne Palmer. Trent exclaimed, ''Good Lord, Jones, what happened?''

''A fella named Jasper and some of his friends had a miners' court,'' Nathan explained wearily. ''They lynched Lotus . . . Wang Toy.''

''Oh, no,'' Anne said, bringing her hands to her mouth as she looked up at the dangling body.

Trent let out a bitter curse. ''When Anne and I got back to the saloon, I heard from one of my bartenders that something had happened down at this end of the street. I never dreamed it would be as bad as this!''

''Bedloe's dead,'' Nathan continued. ''Lotus killed him. She admitted that. But he and his friend Jasper raped her and beat her. Bedloe deserved what he got. You know anything about Jasper?''

''He's cut from the same cloth as Bedloe,'' Trent replied

grimly. "I can believe damn near anything about him."

Anne took Nathan's arm. "Come with us, we'll take you back to the saloon and clean you up. You look like you've taken quite a beating yourself."

Without being rude about it, Nathan shook off her hand. "Can't do that," he answered. "Lotus's brother has gone after Jasper. I've got to catch up with them before he gets himself killed."

Anne began worriedly, "But you're in no shape to—"

Trent stopped her with a gentle touch on her arm. "I reckon Nathan knows what he's got to do, Anne. And so do I." He turned to face Nathan. "I'll go with you. Two of us'll likely be more able to talk sense and head off any more trouble."

"Thanks," Nathan said sincerely.

Anne wasn't so easily convinced. "Patrick, you can't," she said as she clutched his hands. "Nathan's already hurt, and you could be injured, too, if there's more fighting. Tonight of all nights—"

"I'm sorry, Anne. But this is just going to get worse if we don't do something about it now."

Nathan agreed with Trent. If Wang Loo went after Jasper, the young man would likely wind up dead. And Wang Loo's death, on top of Lotus's lynching, might be all it would take to goad the Chinese into rioting against what they saw as oppression by the miners. A lot of people could die, and Ophir might go up in flames before it was all over. He and Trent had to stop that if they could.

If it wasn't already too late.

"Go, then, if you have to," Anne said dully. "But don't count on me being here when you're through, Patrick. I've already buried one husband. I won't bury another."

With that, she turned to Chao-Xing, put her arm around the shoulders of the Chinese girl, and led her away. Trent watched stonily as they made their way down the street.

"Husband?" Nathan asked, trying to keep his mind off the way his head was throbbing.

"We took Anne's carriage over to Coloma and got married this evening," Trent replied. "She was a little worried that it hasn't been long enough since her first husband passed away for it to be proper, but she was convinced it was the right thing to do." He chuckled hollowly. "Now she's probably not so sure." Turning to Nathan, he put a hand under the younger man's elbow for support. "Come on. We've got to find Wang Loo and Jasper before things get worse."

Nathan nodded and started down the street with Trent, Hardrock trailing along behind. He hoped they would be in time.

But he had the feeling that on this night, things were indeed going to get worse before they got better.

The angry shouts led them straight to their destination, a crudely built log saloon on one of Ophir's side streets. There were several men standing around the open doorway of the saloon, and as Nathan and Trent approached, the onlookers stepped back quickly to avoid a figure that hurtled out. The man slammed into the ground, rolled over several times, and came to a stop facedown. He struggled feebly to get up, pained groans issuing from him as he did so.

Another man, this one dressed in the woolen shirt and canvas pants of a miner, strode out of the saloon and went over to the fallen figure. He drew back a foot and kicked the man on the ground, viciously driving his boot into the man's side. As the man on the ground curled up in agony, the miner reached down and grasped his pigtail, using it to jerk his head up. A knife appeared in the miner's hand.

"Can't decide whether to cut your throat or just slice your pigtail off and send you back to Chinee-town to tell all your heathen kin they can't get away with murderin' white men!"

Nathan could see the face of the man on the ground, and it came as no surprise when he recognized Wang Loo. The features of the young Chinese were battered and bloody. Obviously, Jasper had roughed him up before tossing him out into the street.

One of the bystanders yelled, "Cut off the Chinaman's pigtail and feed it to him, Jasper!"

"Teach the little yellow bastard a lesson!" chimed in another man.

Nathan and Trent had come to a halt a few yards away. No one had noticed them yet; the attention of the crowd was focused on Jasper and Wang Loo. Nathan looked over at the saloonkeeper, who nodded at him. The time had come to take a hand in this game.

Trent slipped a hand inside his coat and brought out his small pistol, which was accurate enough and packed enough stopping power to be effective at this range. He leveled the gun at the miner and said loudly, "Put down the knife and step away from that man, Jasper!"

Jasper's head jerked up in surprise. He peered through the shadows in the street and muttered, "Who the hell—"

Trent stepped forward. "You know me, Jasper," he said. "All you men do. You know I'll shoot if I have to."

"This ain't none of your business, you damned tinhorn," growled Jasper as he fixed Trent with a cold, hostile stare. "You're the one best be backin' off."

As he eared back the hammer of the pistol, Trent replied just as coldly, "I won't tell you again, Jasper."

Nathan moved up next to his friend. "You've had your revenge on Lotus," he said bitterly. "You hanged an innocent woman. What more do you want, Jasper?"

"Innocent?" the miner repeated angrily. "Innocent, hell! She was a whore and a killer. She cut off everything that made poor ol' Bedloe a man and watched him bleed to death, just 'cause we wouldn't let her get away with robbin' us.''

Wang Loo twisted his head to look up at Jasper and exclaimed wretchedly, ''Liar! My sister laid with the white men, but she was no thief!''

''Shut your filthy yella mouth—'' Jasper moved the blade closer to Wang Loo's throat.

''Jasper!'' Trent's voice was as sharp as the miner's knife. ''I won't tell you again, blast it. Let go of him and step back.''

Jasper glanced around, the first signs of nervousness appearing on his face. ''You boys goin' to let this dude get away with talkin' to me like that?'' he asked the bystanders, most of whom were his fellow forty-niners.

For a moment, there was no answer, then one of the men said hesitantly, ''Well, hell, Jasper, Trent's got a gun. 'Sides, he owns the best saloon in town, and I want to be able to get a drink in there when I've got enough dust.''

Mutters of agreement came from the other men, and Trent said coolly, ''Looks like you don't have as many friends here as you thought, Jasper. They're mighty brave when there's a whole mob of them against one Chinese girl, but they're not as quick to face real trouble.''

Jasper stayed where he was for a few more seconds, then with a grimace abruptly released Wang Loo's pigtail and stepped back. ''That was a proper miners' court that convicted the girl,'' he complained. ''Weren't nothin' illegal about that hangin'.''

''Except that you were lying about Lotus trying to rob you,'' Nathan said, making sure his voice was loud enough to carry to all the men.

Jasper glared at him. ''Mighty strong words, accusin' a man of lyin' that way. Especially a white man. What've you got to back it up, Jones?''

Nathan had been thinking furiously, and he thought he saw the answer. He said, "I'm curious about something, Jasper. If Lotus was trying to rob you, like you claim, then what was Bedloe doing with his, ah, manhood out where Lotus could do what she did?"

The miner's mouth opened, then closed, then opened again. "What? What the hell kind of question is that? That ain't got nothin' to do with—"

"It's got everything to do with it," Nathan snapped as he stepped closer to Jasper, being careful not to get between the man and Trent's gun. "I don't think Lotus tried to rob you at all. I think you and Bedloe attacked her again and she was just trying to defend herself. You beat her up so bad earlier, I'm sure she was afraid that you'd kill her this time."

"That's a damned lie!" Jasper burst out. "She tried to rob us, I tell you!"

He glanced around, and Nathan saw the nervousness growing in his eyes. There were mutters of confusion going through the crowd of forty-niners, as they thought about Nathan's question and saw that his theory made more sense than the story Jasper had been spreading. A thief wouldn't waste time making a robbery victim open his trousers.

"You're the liar," Nathan said quietly. "And you just goaded the rest of these men into hanging a woman who didn't deserve it, no matter what she'd done."

"Didn't deserve it? She killed Bedloe!"

"After the two of you raped her and nearly beat her to death."

"What if we did?" Jasper demanded hotly. "She was a whore, and a Chinee whore, at that! You sayin' she deserved anything like justice?"

Nathan looked Jasper in the eye. "I'm saying you're more of a murderer than Lotus ever was."

"Son of a bitch!" Jasper exploded. He lashed out, leaping

forward to swing the knife at Nathan's throat.

Nathan moved as quickly as he could, trying to get out of the way of the knife thrust and give Trent a shot at the miner. Jasper had just admitted that he and Bedloe had attacked Lotus first, and Nathan knew that Wang Loo would probably be safe now. The other miners already felt bad enough about the way they had taken Jasper's word and strung up Lotus. But none of that would do Nathan any good if he stood there and let Jasper cut his throat.

The knife whipped through the air a couple of inches in front of Nathan's face as he ducked back. Jasper didn't let up on the attack, though. He plunged after Nathan, using the younger man as a makeshift shield. Trent couldn't get a clear shot as long as the two of them were so close together. Jasper rammed his shoulder into Nathan's chest and knocked him back even more.

Nathan felt his feet go out from under him, and he fell heavily. The jolt as he landed on his rump sent pain smashing through his already aching head. His muscles were stiff and sore, slowed by the punishment he had taken earlier. As Jasper landed on him and drove the knife toward his body, Nathan barely got his hand on the miner's wrist in time to turn aside the thrust.

The point of the blade scraped along Nathan's left side, leaving a line of fiery pain behind it. As he held on to Jasper's wrist with his left hand, Nathan brought his right first around and clubbed it into the side of the miner's head just above the ear. The blow knocked Jasper halfway off Nathan, and with a heave of his back, Nathan threw the miner into the street.

He could have scrambled up and let Trent handle things from here; the saloonkeeper had the gun, after all. But Nathan's brain was on fire with anger, and he knew he couldn't walk away from this. He rolled onto hands and knees and dove after Jasper, reaching out to grab the miner's knife wrist again.

This time Nathan had the advantage, and he smashed the back of Jasper's hand against the hard-packed dirt of the street. Jasper's fingers loosened and the knife slipped away from him. Nathan slapped at it, knocking it away rather than trying to pick it up himself. He was vaguely aware that the onlookers were shouting raucously and yelling encouragement to Jasper. A few of them were even cheering Nathan on, although he barely heard the excited cries.

His own aches and pains were gone, consumed along with everything else by the rage that filled him. He got his left hand on Jasper's throat, the fingers digging brutally into flesh. With his right hand, he drove punch after punch into Jasper's face, ignoring the blows that the miner flung up at him. Jasper's struggles became weaker and weaker, but Nathan seemed to gain strength as he pounded the man underneath him. In the flickering light that came from the door of the saloon, Nathan saw Jasper's features become covered with blood and gradually change shape as the blows hammered into his face.

Finally, some of the onlookers grabbed Nathan by the shoulders and hauled him off, throwing him toward Trent so that he rolled to a stop at the saloonkeeper's feet. Nathan hardly knew where he was. His heart was thudding heavily and he drew great gasping breaths of air. Tears streaked the dust on his face. For a few moments there, he had been as close to insane as he ever wanted to be.

"Get Grubstake out o' here, Mr. Trent," one of the men said. "I reckon he's paid Jasper back for what happened."

"That girl's still dead," Trent said coldly.

"Yeah, and it looks like we were all in the wrong about that," the spokesman for the crowd replied. "But there's nothin' we can do about that now. I got a feelin' Jasper'll be movin' on after this. Let's just all go home and try to forget about it.''

Nathan looked up. ''Forget about it?'' he raged. ''Forget about Lotus—''

Trent leaned over and put a hand on his shoulder. ''You can't fight everybody in Ophir, Nathan. You saved Wang Loo and handed Jasper a beating he'll never forget. That's the best you can do. Like the man said, let's go home.''

Nathan shook his head groggily. Home was a long way from here . . . if he even had one anymore. He managed to pull himself into a sitting position and draped his hands over his drawn-up knees, letting his head droop on his chest. Hardrock came up and nuzzled his jaw.

''I'm surprised that dog of yours didn't jump into the fracas,'' Trent commented as he put a hand under Nathan's arm and helped him to his feet.

''Maybe he figured this was one fight I ought to handle on my own,'' Nathan said. Now that his anger was beginning to wear off, he was starting to hurt again. He would need a couple of days in bed and some good strong liniment before he'd be himself again.

He glanced around for Wang Loo. There was no sign of him. Probably crawled off during the fight, Nathan thought. Something lying in the street caught his eye as it shone in the lanternlight. The little Chinese ax that Wang Loo carried, that's what it was, Nathan realized. A few feet from the weapon, a couple of miners were helping Jasper to his feet. A moan came from Jasper's ruined lips. He made a bubbling sound when he breathed, and fresh blood welled from his nose and mouth.

Suddenly, as Nathan and Trent turned away, a roar of hatred came from Jasper, the shout sending droplets of blood spraying into the air in front of him. With the strength of a madman, he tore out of the grip of the men who had just hauled him to his feet. He bent and scooped up the ax Wang Loo had dropped, then flung himself toward Nathan's back.

Nathan twisted around and saw the horrifying vision of the blood-covered man leaping at him, the Chinese ax raised high in the air for a killing stroke. Jasper started the blade sweeping down, and in another second it would bury itself in Nathan's skull.

Before that could happen, the little pistol was in Trent's hand again, the gambler's dexterity making it seem like magic. The gun cracked wickedly, once and then again, and Jasper's head jerked back, two small black holes appearing just over his left eye. Jasper swayed for a moment, then folded up like a house of cards and collapsed in the street at Nathan's feet.

In the stunned silence that followed, Trent said quietly, "I suppose everyone here recognizes self-defense when they see it."

One of the miners nodded. "Reckon Jasper went crazy, all right. He'd've cut Jones's head off and come after you next, Mr. Trent. We'll bury 'im. You best go on back to your place and take Jones with you. This is over."

"Yes," Trent agreed. "It's over. Come on, Nathan."

Nathan was glad to have the saloonkeeper to lean on as they made their way down the street, Hardrock bringing up the rear. "You saved my life," he said shakily.

"You seem to need someone to look after you," Trent said with a chuckle. "No offense, Nathan, but you're really not the type to go around righting all the wrongs and avenging everything evil that happens. There's too much of it in the world, anyway."

"You're right," Nathan said, wincing not only with each step but with each word that passed his swollen lips. "But sometimes a man's got to try."

"Yes," Trent agreed quietly. "Sometimes a man's got to

try. I just hope my wife understands that.'' He paused, then repeated, ''My wife. I never really thought I'd be saying those words. I assumed I'd die a bachelor. I never thought I'd run into anyone like Anne, though. I hope she's waiting at the saloon.''

''So do I,'' Nathan said sincerely. He left unspoken the hope that Chao-Xing would be with Anne Palmer . . . Anne Trent, now. He wanted to see the young Chinese girl again, to tell her how sorry he was about everything that had happened, to try to explain to her that not all of the men here in America were like Jasper and Bedloe. They weren't all evil. Some of them were actually pretty decent, even if the things they tried to do didn't always work out right. He sensed somehow that it was important to make Chao-Xing realize those things about America . . . and about him.

But for now, he and Trent had to make it back to the saloon, and the walk seemed longer than usual. With Nathan leaning on the gambler and Hardrock ambling along behind, the two men limped on down the street and into the night.

Twenty-five

Cassandra stared into the flickering flames of the campfire, her face solemn and brooding. She wasn't wearing her hat, since Dan Logan already knew she was a woman. In fact, during the two days they had been traveling together, the ranger had seemed painfully aware of that fact. He'd gone out of his way to be overly polite to her, but without once letting down his guard.

What was he afraid of? she wondered. Did Logan really think that she would hit him on the head or try to take his gun so that she could rescue Boone?

Well, she might if she got the chance, Cassandra decided. A woman would do almost anything for the man she loved.

"Here," Logan said from beside her. "You got to eat."

She glanced up at him dully. He held a plate of beans and bacon and a cup of coffee. Cassandra hadn't eaten since breakfast that morning, and they had put a lot of miles behind them since then. The food smelled good.

But a part of her said that she would be betraying Boone by cooperating with this tall man from Texas. She said, "I'm not hungry."

"No offense, ma'am, but that's a lie. I'm old enough to know that nobody spends all day in the saddle without gettin' a mite hungry."

From the other side of the fire, Boone said, "Go ahead and eat, Cassandra. It won't help either of us for you to starve yourself."

That was true, she decided. If the opportunity ever did

arise for them to escape from Logan, they would be more likely to succeed in the attempt if she was at full strength.

With ill grace, she took the tin plate and cup from the Texan. "Don't expect me to say thank you," she snapped.

"I don't reckon I do," Logan replied. He went back around the fire to hunker on his heels and sip his own coffee. As she ate, Cassandra noticed that he never looked directly into the fire. He had explained on the first night that it was an old habit of his. Staring into a campfire ruined a man's night vision, which could prove fatal if somebody tried to sneak up on him out of the darkness. Being alert and ready for trouble seemed to be a way of life for Dan Logan.

Why couldn't he have kept on looking for gold and left them alone? He was rich already from the strikes he'd made. Why had he let his conscience bother him to the point that he had to assuage it by taking Boone back to a hangrope in Texas?

Cassandra couldn't answer those questions, but she was afraid that fate had turned against her and Boone. The happiness they had planned together was never going to come about now.

But she couldn't give up. They were still in the foothills of the Sierra Nevadas. Travelers couldn't make very good time in this rugged country, and it would probably take them a couple of weeks just to cross the mountains. The whole trip to Texas might take as long as two months. Surely during that time, there would be a chance for them to get away, Cassandra told herself.

After all, Logan had left her untied, even though Boone was trussed up tightly most of the time. The ranger's rough code of frontier chivalry wouldn't allow him to mistreat a woman, however.

And that was his mistake, Cassandra thought as she finished the beans. Logan would regret trusting her.

Logan drained the last of his coffee and stood up. "Think I'll take a turn around the camp," he said. "Miss Woodward, I'd be obliged if you'd stand up."

"What for?" Cassandra asked suspiciously. Maybe Logan wasn't as chivalrous as she'd thought.

"I want to make sure you don't get no ideas about turnin' Blakely loose while I'm takin' a look around. Stand up and hold out your hand."

Cassandra hesitated, not wanting to cooperate with Logan but knowing that the ranger was capable of standing there all night waiting for her to comply with his request. She sighed and got to her feet, then stuck her left hand out toward him.

He snapped one ring of a set of handcuffs around her wrist, then secured the other ring to a tree branch. The chain between the two rings of the irons was over a foot long, which gave her a little freedom of movement but not enough to reach Boone on the other side of the fire. And Boone couldn't come to her because Logan had his ankles lashed together and his hands tied behind his back. They could talk to each other, but that was all.

"Won't be gone long," Logan told them as he picked up his rifle. "Probably don't have any reason to scout around, but it's another of them old habits."

He moved off into the darkness, disappearing rapidly past the spot where the horses and Cassandra's mule were picketed. Even though the brush was thick around this clearing where they had made camp, Cassandra couldn't hear any crackling of branches to mark Logan's passage. The man moved like one of those Indians back in Texas.

"I'm sorry, Boone," Cassandra said after a moment. "I wish I could come over there and turn you loose."

"So do I," he replied dryly. "But don't worry, Cassandra. Our luck's bound to turn. It was luck that got me away from

Logan the first time. It'll happen again.''

"I hope so," she said fervently. She hesitated, chewing on her bottom lip for a second as she thought about what to say to him next. This was the first time they had really been alone since Logan had recaptured Boone, and she didn't want to ruin the moment. On the other hand, the moment was pretty well ruined already, what with handcuffs and all, and there were things she wanted to know. She took a deep breath and said, "Boone . . . I wish you'd tell me about what happened in Texas.''

For several seconds that seemed to stretch out into an eternity, Boone didn't say anything. Then, with a sigh, he told her, "I reckon you've got a right to know. You've gotten yourself into trouble on my account. But you've got to believe me, Cassandra, when I say that I've never murdered anybody." His voice hardened. "I killed Jason Stoneham, yes, but it wasn't murder.''

"I believe you," whispered Cassandra.

Boone took a deep breath and went on, "There was a girl . . . a beautiful girl named Samantha McCarter. I guess I was in love with her. I was so young I didn't really know what love is, but I knew I wanted Samantha.''

Cassandra nodded, even though the words Boone spoke about the girl called Samantha hurt her a little. "I understand," she said.

"But Jason Stoneham had his eye on Samantha, too. I guess you could say we were rivals, but Jason's pa was rich. The old man was a judge and owned the biggest ranch in the county, to boot. Jason never figured I was any real competition for Samantha. But after a while, she chose me over him.''

"Did the two of you . . . get married?''

Boone shook his head. "Never had the chance. Samantha told me she loved me and said she was going to tell Jason that it was all over between them. I wasn't there when Jason rode by the McCarter place and neither were Samantha's folks, but I came along a little while later.'' His voice shook slightly as he continued, ''I found Samantha there. Jason had gone crazy when she told him she'd picked me. I reckon he felt like if he couldn't have her, nobody could. So he beat her to death, right then and there.''

A horrified shudder ran through Cassandra. ''How awful! You must have been devastated.''

''I was plenty upset, maybe a little crazy myself right then. I rode out to the Stoneham ranch and found Jason in the barn. I told him I'd found Samantha. He didn't deny what he'd done. He just tried to gut me with a pitchfork. I shot him to save my own life . . . and to avenge Samantha.''

''Then why in God's name were you charged with murder?''

Boone laughed humorlessly. ''I told you, old man Stoneham is a judge. A rich, powerful man. He swore out the warrant against me. You see, the whole country knew that Jason and I both wanted Samantha, but nobody else except me and Jason knew that she'd picked me. Judge Stoneham made it sound like she had chosen Jason instead and that *I* was the one who killed Samantha when she told me about it. That was a damned lie, of course, but I had no family and precious few friends to stand up for me. The law came after me and I knew what would happen if they caught me. So I lit a shuck out of there. I hated to run, but there wasn't anything else I could do.'' He looked down at the ground and shook his head. ''Lord, I can still see Samantha . . . I still wake up sweating and calling her name sometimes. At least . . . I used to until I met you.''

''You poor man,'' Cassandra said, her voice full of pity. ''I'm so sorry, Boone. Does . . . does Mr. Logan know what really happened?''

"He knows," Boone said. "But I don't reckon he cares. He's so damned stubborn, he doesn't care if I'm innocent or not."

An idea occurred to Cassandra. "My mother has plenty of money. I'll get in touch with her. I'll send a letter back to her at the first settlement we come to and ask her to arrange to hire a lawyer for you back in Texas. We'll get help for you, Boone. We won't let that Judge Stoneham or anybody else take advantage of you. We'll force them to give you a fair trial, and then the truth will come out."

He looked at her across the fire and smiled faintly. "I appreciate the thought, Cass, but I don't know if it'll do any good. Stoneham's a mighty powerful man, and nobody wants to buck him."

"You'll see," she insisted. "It's going to be all right."

Her heart went out to him as she saw the depth of despair on his face, but before she could say anything else, a crackling in the brush told her that Logan was returning. The ranger stepped into the clearing a moment later and announced, "Nobody skulkin' around, far as I can tell. Didn't really think there would be, but it never hurts to check before turnin' in."

"You don't really expect me to sleep tied up like this again tonight, do you?" Boone asked.

Logan ran a thumbnail along his beard-stubbled jaw. "Well, I expect it don't make for a very good night's sleep. But I figure *I'll* rest a whole lot easier knowin' you can't get loose, Blakely. Sorry." He turned to Cassandra. "I'll let you loose from them cuffs now, ma'am."

He took the key from the pocket of his bib-front shirt and unlocked the irons, then stowed them away in his gear again. Cassandra rubbed her left wrist, hoping to make him feel at least a little guilty, but Logan didn't seem to notice the gesture. He moved off to the far side of the clearing, where there were quite a few pine needles scattered on the ground, to spread his bedroll.

"I've told you before, Miss Woodward, that I'm a pretty light sleeper, so I wouldn't go to movin' around much during the night. I'd be liable to think you were tryin' to get Blakely loose. Any trouble of that sort and I wouldn't have no choice but to shoot him in the knee, just to make sure he couldn't run off."

"I won't try anything," Cassandra snapped.

"Good. I'll take your word for it."

That was fine, Cassandra thought. Logan could keep on taking her word, and eventually it would backfire on him. She would have no trouble breaking her promise when the time came.

She wondered, in fact, just how far she would go to save Boone Blakely . . .

The days started to run together as the three of them continued heading generally east through the Sierra Nevadas. Of course, crossing a mountain range meant a lot of twisting and turning of the trail, and they often found themselves riding north or south for several miles before the path swung east again.

Logan was still damnably alert, but that didn't stop him from talking. He talked about Texas and his life there as a ranger, and he talked about the months he had spent in California hunting for gold. Boone seemed to ignore him most of the time, and Cassandra tried to as well. But she found herself listening to Logan's yarns, especially his tales about Texas. The ranger made it sound like a magnificent place.

But it was the place where Boone had been unjustly charged with murder, Cassandra reminded herself, the place where he might be hanged for a crime he had not committed.

She could not allow her resolve to be lessened by Logan's homespun charm.

He seemed genuinely concerned about her, however, making sure that the pace wasn't too grueling, that she got plenty of rest and had plenty to eat. Logan was more solicitous, in fact, than Boone was, but that was understandable, Cassandra thought. Boone had retreated into a sullen silence that he preserved most of the time. She certainly couldn't blame him for that, under the circumstances. In fact it made her more determined than ever to see that he received justice once they reached Texas.

After a week on the trail, they camped in a high meadow with a stream meandering through it. Cassandra heard something that sounded like a faint roaring, but she couldn't locate its source until Logan pointed toward a high, rocky bluff at the east end of the meadow. Cassandra's breath caught in her throat as she saw the waterfall spilling over the edge of the bluff. In the red glow of the setting sun the stream sparkled brilliantly as it tumbled over the brink and plunged some fifty feet to a crystal clear pool at the base of the bluff.

"It's beautiful," Cassandra said softly. "Don't you think so, Boone?"

Boone just grunted, and Cassandra bit her lip. Of course he wasn't going to be impressed by scenery, no matter how pretty it was.

Logan crossed his hands on his saddle horn and leaned forward, grinning at the waterfall. "Reminds me of a few places back in the hill country. I've seen the Medina and the Guadalupe form waterfalls like that, up around Bandera Pass. Mighty pretty country. But I reckon this here California's just as pretty."

"That's quite an admission, coming from you," Cassandra said tartly. "I didn't think you'd ever admit that some other place could be as good as Texas."

"Well, ma'am, as a Texan born-bred-and-forever, you won't hear many such comments comin' out of this ol' boy's mouth. But I ain't blind, neither, and pretty's pretty, no gettin' around it."

His gaze stayed on her face for a few seconds after he spoke the words, just long enough for Cassandra to feel a flush creeping across her features. He couldn't have been trying to compliment her, could he? Surely not even a crude frontiersman like him would be so . . . so . . .

She pushed the thought away and said, "In the morning I'm going to ride over to that pool and take a bath. I hope that's all right with you, Mr. Logan." Her tone suggested that she planned to go ahead with it whether it was all right with him or not.

"I reckon that'll be fine. Blakely and me'll stay here and keep each other company. Just don't go runnin' off on us. This is pretty wild country, and a gal alone could get lost and maybe hurt."

"Don't worry about that. I intend to accompany you all the way to Texas. I'm going to see to it that Boone gets a fair trial." She hadn't said anything to Logan about her plans, and as he gave her a sharp look, she wished she had kept her mouth shut now. It was too late for that, though.

"I hope you do, ma'am," he said, and she thought he sounded sincere. "I never figured on anything else."

"Then you're a blind fool, Logan," Boone said, speaking up for the first time in long minutes.

His lean features hardening, Logan pulled his horse around and pointed to a broad grassy spot not far away. "We'll make camp over there," he said. "Come on."

There wasn't much talk between them that night around the campfire. Boone was more closemouthed than ever. His face was becoming drawn and lined, and Cassandra knew that he was feeling the strain of his captivity. As for her, she was growing more and more confused. She knew she ought to hate Dan Logan for what he was doing, but the more she got to know him, the less evil he seemed. He was just a man caught in less than perfect circumstances, trying to do the right thing without really being sure what it was.

And Logan liked her; she was sure of that. Perhaps she could turn that to her advantage and use it somehow to help Boone . . .

Morning dawned clear and cool, and Logan knew the water in the pool was going to be downright cold. Cassandra was determined to go through with her bath anyway. He watched as she rode her mule toward the waterfall and behind a screen of trees and brush that ran part of the way around the pool at the base of the bluff. That would give her all the privacy she needed.

"Looks like we get to linger over our coffee this mornin', Blakely," Logan commented to the prisoner as he walked back to the low-burning fire. "How 'bout another cup?"

Boone shook his head. "Can't enjoy it with my hands tied behind my back. You ever have anybody give you drinks of hot coffee, Logan? You wind up with a burned mouth."

"Sorry," Logan said with a shrug. "But I ain't untyin' you, if that's what you're gettin' at."

"All right." Boone sighed heavily. "I guess I'll have another cup."

"Sure." Logan wrapped a piece of leather around his hand, reached out, and snagged the handle of the coffeepot. He lifted it from the embers at the edge of the fire and carried it over toward Boone. The tin cup Boone had drunk from earlier was still beside him.

Logan leaned over to pick up the cup, and suddenly Boone twisted around and lashed out at him with his feet, which were still bound together at the ankles. Logan grimaced and tried to jump back, but he wasn't quite quick enough. Boone's feet hit the coffeepot and knocked it back against Logan. The lid came off and the scalding liquid splashed over the front of the ranger's shirt.

The searing pain was enough to make Logan gasp and stagger back another step, slowing down his reactions so that he couldn't draw his gun fast enough as he saw Boone uncoiling from the ground. Somehow Boone's hands had gotten free. He slammed into Logan as the ranger tried to pull the Colt from its holster. Boone's fingers closed over the cylinder of the revolver.

With his other hand, Boone drove a punch into Logan's midsection. All the pent-up anger and desperation in the man went into the blow. To Logan it felt like the fist was going to go clear through his body and burst out his back. All the air was knocked from his lungs, leaving him gasping for breath as his head spun crazily.

He fell and Boone landed on top of him, driving his knees into the ranger's belly. Boone clubbed his hands together and smashed them back and forth across Logan's face. The Texan saw a red haze sliding down over his eyes and didn't know if it was blood or unconsciousness. He tried to shove Boone off of him, and suddenly the weight was gone. But so was the heavy Colt that had been on his hip.

Boone had plucked more than the revolver away from Logan. He had the ranger's bowie knife, too, as Logan saw a moment later after he wiped a shaky hand across his face and cleared away the blood from the gash on his forehead. Boone had opened up the cut with one of those sledging blows. Logan lifted himself on an elbow and saw the former prisoner sitting about ten feet away, sawing at the bonds around his ankles with the bowie. With the other hand, Boone trained the Colt steadily at Logan.

The ropes parted quickly under the razor-sharp blade of

the knife and fell away from Boone's legs. "Son of a bitch, that feels good!" Boone exclaimed. "At least it will once I get some feeling back. You're a vicious bastard, Logan, you know that?"

Logan dabbed at the blood on his head and grated, "You're a hell of a one to talk, Blakely. How'd you get your hands loose, anyway? That girl help you?"

"Cassandra doesn't know anything about it. I worked on those ropes all night. Tore off every fingernail I had and half the skin on my wrists. But it was worth it to see the look on your face when I jumped you, you stupid star packer."

"Reckon I must've got to trustin' you too much," Logan told him bitterly. "Hell, I almost liked you, Blakely. Got to where I felt real bad again about takin' you back to Texas."

"But you'd have done it anyway. I know you by now, Logan. All you care about in the long run is your damned duty." Boone eared back the hammer of the Colt. "Well, that duty's going to cost you your life, mister. I'm not making the mistake of letting you live again."

"Won't be the first ranger to die at the hands of some owlhoot," Logan said, hoping he was keeping the strain he felt out of his voice. "Reckon I won't be the last, either. You'd better shoot me 'fore that gal gets back, though. I wouldn't want Miss Cassandra to have to see such a thing."

"If you're so damned concerned about Cassandra, you could have left us alone in the first place. You just couldn't do that, though, could you?"

Slowly, Logan shook his head.

Some of the feeling had returned to Boone's feet by now, and he was able to stand up. He tossed the bowie knife aside, then motioned with the barrel of the Colt. "Get up, Logan. I want you on your feet, too."

Logan studied Boone's face, saw the cold set to the features and the dark soullessness of the eyes. He climbed awkwardly to his feet, his head still spinning a little from the blows, and said, "I heard what you told Miss Cassandra a few nights back about what happened with Jason Stoneham and the McCarter girl. I wasn't really scoutin' around the camp, I just wanted to hear what the two of you had to say to each other. You told me pretty much the same story a long time ago. And I just want to know one thing before you pull that trigger, Blakely—was there a word of truth in it?"

Some ten yards behind Boone, Cassandra waited for an answer to the same question. She knew Logan had seen her, but she'd left the mule back at the bottom of the waterfull and approached the camp on foot, quietly. When she'd seen the two men struggling, she had started to run forward to help Boone, but then she had seen him get the upper hand. After that, something—some instinct—held her back, made her approach silently. Boone had no idea she had returned to the camp, and she found herself just as anxious to hear how he replied to Logan's question as the ranger was himself.

And then Boone Blakely laughed harshly and said, "Not much."

The words hit Cassandra like a physical blow. He had lied to her about what happened in Texas, and now he was admitting it. What else had he lied about?

"Jason Stoneham and I both wanted Samantha," Boone went on, still breathing a little heavily from his exertions. "She picked him, though, instead of me. Hell, he had money and an influential family, and I was nothing and nobody. Samantha wasn't crazy. But she picked the wrong time to tell me about it, when nobody was home but her."

"So you beat her to death," Logan accused. He still

wasn't looking at Cassandra, but she sensed that he knew she was there.

"I lost my head," Boone said with a shrug. "I was sorry when it was over and I saw what I'd done. But it wasn't my fault, Logan. It was that damned Jason's doing. If he hadn't come between me and Samantha, none of it would have happened."

The cold words, the easy shifting of blame, the utter callousness of it made Cassandra sick. She stood there shaking from the emotions running riot through her, her hands clenched into fists.

"I figured Jason ought to pay for what he did," Boone concluded. "So I went to his daddy's ranch and got lucky, found Jason by himself in the barn. He looked shocked as hell when I told him Samantha was dead and then I planted a pistol ball right in his belly."

"And I was loco enough to believe it might've been self-defense, like you said." Logan shook his head in disgust. "You're mighty convincin' when you want to be, Blakely."

"I've been telling that story for so long it almost seems like the truth now. Cassandra sure believed it."

She started to say something to let him know she was there, then held her tongue instead. She wanted to see what else he had to say.

"What's it goin' to be now?" asked Logan. He blinked away a drop of blood that fell in his eye.

"I kill you and take your gold," Boone said bluntly. "Then Cassandra and I make a new start somewhere else. I'll just tell her that I had to kill you to save myself. She'll believe me, just like she believed me about what happened in Texas."

"No, Boone," Cassandra said from behind him. "I won't go with you."

He jerked around at the sound of her voice, his mouth

falling open in astonishment. Logan started to move toward him, but Boone recovered his wits almost instantly. He took a couple of quick steps to the side and swung the gun back to cover the ranger. "Cassandra!" he exclaimed. "What are you doing here?"

"I forgot to take a clean shirt with me," she said, not bothering to disguise the bitterness in her voice. "Think of that, Boone. It took a *shirt* for me to learn the truth about you."

"Listen, I don't know what you heard, Cass," he said quickly, "but you're getting all mixed up. I just want us to get away and start a new life somewhere. We can do that with Logan's gold."

"Only if you kill him."

Boone nodded. "It's got to be done. I won't leave Logan alive behind me again. With you or without you, I'm getting rid of him and taking that gold."

Cassandra started walking forward. "No, Boone. Mr. Logan's a good man. I won't let you hurt him anymore."

"Damn it, Cass, I told you I love you!"

Tears rolled down her cheeks, but the resolve on her face didn't waver. "And that was probably a lie, too, just like everything else." She was almost between Boone and Logan now. If she could shield the ranger with her body, she was sure Boone wouldn't shoot . . .

"Get back, blast it!" Boone shouted. "I won't go back to Texas—"

The gun in his hand roared.

For an instant, Cassandra couldn't believe that he had actually fired. But the deafening explosion of the gun had slammed into her ears like fists, and something else had struck her in the right side, spinning her halfway around. She was numb, unwilling or unable for a few seconds to admit that she had been shot. Then she caught her balance before she actually fell, righting herself and throwing her body at Boone.

Another gunshot crashed, but Cassandra couldn't tell if she was hit again or not. All she knew was that her hands were on the Colt now and she was holding on for dear life as Boone tried to throw her aside. He swung his other arm and backhanded her savagely, knocking her grip loose on the gun. She staggered back.

Logan flashed past her and tackled Boone, both men going down in the thick grass. A few feet away, Cassandra went to one knee, her strength deserting her in a warm red flood that soaked her shirt. She saw Logan swinging blow after blow at Boone's head, trying to ward off the gun at the same time. The morning sun shone dully on the polished barrel of the Colt as Boone swung it at Logan's head. Cassandra heard a thud, and her eyes widened in fear as Logan rolled to the side, perhaps knocked unconscious by the brutal blow.

The Texas Ranger was still moving, though. He kept rolling and came up on his knees as Boone tried to level the revolver at him. Cassandra spotted another glint of sunlight on metal as Logan's hand swept up with the knife Boone had cast aside earlier. The heavy, perfectly balanced blade flickered through the air as Boone fired again. Drops of red sprayed from Logan's shoulder as the ball knocked him backward.

Boone was on his knees, too, swaying slightly, his eyes bulging from their sockets as he stared down at the hilt of the bowie knife protruding from his chest. Logan pushed himself up again. Boone got his thumb around the Colt's hammer and began pulling it back for another shot.

Then his muscles went limp in death, and the gun slipped from nerveless fingers. Boone Blakely pitched forward to lie motionless, face down on the ground.

Cassandra saw that much and then fell sideways, landing in a black sea that sucked her under the surface.

She didn't know how long she had been unconscious or how badly she was hurt. All she knew was that she was on the back of Dan Logan's golden sorrel, roped upright into the saddle, and it was hard to breathe because of something bound tightly around her middle. She opened her eyes and saw Logan walking along in front of the horse, holding its reins and leading it. The left shoulder of his shirt was bloody, and he was staggering more than walking, but each step, unsteady though it might have been, held a strength and determination that would not be denied.

Cassandra found her voice and croaked weakly, "M-Mr. Logan . . ."

He didn't stop, but he turned and looked at her and said, "You hang on, Miss Cassandra, you just hang on tight. You're goin' to be fine. I patched you up as best I could, and if I remember right there's a settlement called Ophir not too far from here that's got a doctor. I'll take care of you, Miss Cassandra. I'll see that you're safe. You got my word on that."

And despite the pain washing through her, Cassandra found herself smiling, because she knew that unlike Boone, she could believe Dan Logan. She closed her eyes again and let that faith carry her on toward Ophir.

Twenty-six

Nathan walked to the top of the hill with Hardrock, as he did almost every day about this time. It was late in the afternoon, when the sunlight had a peculiarly golden quality to it, appropriate since it was shining down on the Sierra Nevadas where so many millions of dollars' worth of gold had been taken out of the hills and the streams.

But it was 1854 now, and the times were changing. Nathan knew it and could not bring himself to be sorry. The day of the individual miner—the Argonaut and forty-niner—who had come west to make his fortune through luck and pluck and hard work was drawing to a close. Most of the easily found placer gold had been harvested already, and to separate the remaining gold embedded in quartz required so many men and so much machinery that only the larger mining companies could afford to make the effort.

His Aunt Emily owned one of those companies, and it was quite successful. She had offered him the job of running it a couple of years earlier, but he had turned her down. Cousin Cassandra was doing a much better job of managing things than he ever would have, Nathan knew. Cassandra had a real head for business, just like her mother. In fact, Emily had been talking about retiring and settling down to just being a grandmother. Nathan didn't expect that to ever happen, though. Emily would never be content unless she was running *something*.

Maybe she ought to run for mayor of San Francisco, Nathan mused as he sat on the hilltop and looked out over the

green valleys and scratched behind the ears of the massive
dog sitting next to him. After all, her son-in-law Dan Logan
was already the county sheriff and doing a fine job at that.

Nathan figured he would never forget the night Cassandra
and Dan had come into Ophir, both of them covered with
blood and half-dead. Anne Trent had pulled them through,
of course; she might not have been an official doctor, but
there was nobody better at taking care of folks.

Never in his life had Nathan been more shocked to see
anybody than he was the night he'd found Cassandra. Or
rather, Cassandra had found him, since he'd been on the
boardwalk in front of Trent's place when Dan came staggering down the street leading the horse that was carrying
Cassandra. Once Anne had patched them up and Cassandra
could talk, she'd told Nathan some wild story about an outlaw from Texas. Nathan had never quite gotten the straight
of it, but that didn't matter. Cassandra didn't talk about those
days much anymore, and neither did Dan.

As for the Trents, Anne and Patrick had moved to Sacramento when Ophir went bust a couple of years ago, and
Nathan ran into them from time to time. They were doing
fine, even had a little one. Patrick had given up saloonkeep-
ing and was running a hotel instead, although Nathan understood that he still sat in on a high-stakes poker game
every now and then.

The sun was lower on the horizon now. The countryside
that spread out in front of Nathan was mighty pretty, and
looking at it like this, a man couldn't see all the ugly things
that had gone on in these foothills. No, instead he saw the
pines reaching toward the deep blue sky and the streams full
of clear laughing water and the birds soaring through the
crisp mountain air. It wasn't all wilderness, though. There
were towns scattered all through the foothills, thriving little
communities where people had made their homes. California

wasn't just a place to get rich anymore. It was a place to *live*.

Nathan liked to think he'd had a part in that. Along the way he had helped hundreds of miners through his job as his aunt's agent, and some of those men had founded the towns that would last. Some of them had never gotten rich, of course. Most of them hadn't gotten rich. But it didn't matter. Sometimes a man could stumble over a fortune that didn't have anything to do with nuggets or gold dust.

He stood up and brushed off the seat of his pants. He came up here because he felt proud when he looked over this land and knew that he'd had a part in building it. A small part, maybe, but it was something uniquely his. Grub-stake Jones hadn't been such a failure after all, he thought with a smile.

Then he turned and looked the other way down the hill at the sturdy log cabin, built with his own hands. He saw Chao-Xing moving around down there, with little Nathan toddling along after her. Chao-Xing was holding the baby they had named Lotus, and soon she would be going inside to prepare dinner. *Morning Star*, Nathan thought, and he looked up at the darkening sky and saw a faint glimmer of light there. Morning star and evening star, and he had both of them, and what man could want for more?

Suddenly, Hardrock gave a little bark and bounded off down the far side of the hill. Nathan turned to look and saw the dog chasing a rabbit. Hardrock was fast, but the rabbit was faster and reached the safety of its hole a few yards ahead of the dog. Hardrock gave a frustrated snarl and started digging at the hole in an effort to root out his quarry, dirt flying wildly as his heavy paws flashed back and forth.

Nathan chuckled and walked down the hill. "Come on, Hardrock," he said. "That rabbit got away fair and square. Leave him alone."

Hardrock ignored him, and Nathan knew he might have to hold the dog by the scruff of the neck and drag him away. Hardrock was a stubborn old cuss. Nathan bent and said a little more sharply, ''That's enough, Hardrock.''

That was when he spotted something glittering in the growing mound of dirt and gravel thrown up by the dog's paws.

Nathan's heart began to pound faster and harder. He felt a surge of the old excitement as he reached toward the mound. The setting sun was definitely shining on *something* there . . .

He brushed some of the dirt aside and picked up a rock. A small, gleaming nugget. His eyes widened as he stared at it.

A broad grin spread across his face as he realized what he was holding. He tossed the nugget aside, laughed, and said, ''Fool's gold.'' He reached down and took hold of the dog. ''Come on, Hardrock. We've got better things to do than chase after something we're not going to catch.''

Then, tugging the dog along at his side, Nathan Jones went down the hill toward home.

About the Authors

J.L. Reasoner is the pseudonym of bestselling authors James and Livia Reasoner. Writing both together and apart, they have produced many novels ranging from sagas of the American West to mysteries. Livia Reasoner is best-known as L.J. Washburn, author of the award-winning Lucas Hallam mystery novels. The Reasoners live in a small town in Texas with their two daughters.

As the Civil War raged in the South, the urgent call for doctors resounded in every corner of the nation. One family had the courage to answer the call.

THE HEALER'S ROAD

J.L. REASONER

• author of <u>Rivers of Gold</u> •

Doctor Thomas Black had no intention of leaving his family behind for the battlefield, but destiny brought the war to his family. His oldest child, Sara, ignores society's scorn for female doctors to follow in her father's footsteps. And after experiencing the pains of battle, John Black decides to study medicine, dedicating his strength and honor to healing instead of fighting. Together, the Black family will embody the true nobility of the American spirit during the savage conflict of the Civil War.

A Jove novel coming in October